Praise for the *New York Times* b

URBAN ENEM

"Butcher is the dean of contemporary urban fantasy."

—*Booklist* on Jim Butcher

"Storytelling doesn't get much better than this, folks. The author has caught lightning (pun intended) in a bottle and he keeps doing it again and again. If you haven't caught on to the joy that is the Iron Druid Chronicles, you should remedy that post-haste."

—*My Bookish Ways* on Kevin Hearne's *Hunted*
of the Iron Druid Chronicles

"A wondrously gothic hybrid horror-thriller in the grand tradition of Dean Koontz and Stephen King."

—*Providence Journal* on Kelley Armstrong's Cainsville series

"Heartbreaking . . . Somers conjures a riveting setting that bends and breaks time and again, each iteration raising the stakes for his accidental hero. By turns frightening and sorrowful, this is a story that offers no good choices to its characters. The ever-present violence is balanced by compassion, which in turn is eroded by the grim fight to save humankind."

—*Publishers Weekly* on Jeff Somers' Ustari Cycle

"The only thing more fun than an October Daye book is an InCryptid book. Swift narrative, charm, great world-building . . . all the McGuire trademarks."

—Charlaine Harris, #1 *New York Times*–bestselling
author of Sookie Stackhouse series on
Seanan McGuire's InCryptid series

"Top grade horror fiction."

—*Booklist,* Starred Review on Jonathan Maberry's
Joe Ledger series

DON'T MISS THESE OTHER ELECTRIFYING ANTHOLOGIES FROM GALLERY BOOKS!

Urban Enemies

A collection of urban fantasy stories from

Kelley Armstrong   Jim Butcher   Domino Finn
Diana Pharaoh Francis   Kevin Hearne
Faith Hunter   Caitlin Kittredge
Jonathan Maberry   Seanan McGuire
Jon F. Merz   Joseph Nassise
Lilith Saintcrow   Steven Savile   Craig Schaefer
Jeff Somers   Carrie Vaughn
Sam Witt

EDITED BY JOSEPH NASSISE

GALLERY BOOKS

NEW YORK   LONDON   TORONTO   SYDNEY   NEW DEHLI

G

Gallery Books
An Imprint of Simon & Schuster, Inc.
1230 Avenue of the Americas
New York, NY 10020

First Gallery Books trade paperback edition August 2017

GALLERY BOOKS and colophon are registered trademarks of Simon & Schuster, Inc.

For information about special discounts for bulk purchases, please contact Simon & Schuster Special Sales at 1-866-506-1949 or business@simonandschuster.com.

The Simon & Schuster Speakers Bureau can bring authors to your live event. For more information or to book an event, contact the Simon & Schuster Speakers Bureau at 1-866-248-3049 or visit our website at www.simonspeakers.com.

Interior design by Davina Mock-Maniscalco

Manufactured in the United States of America

10 9 8 7 6 5 4 3 2 1

Library of Congress Cataloging-in-Publication Data is available.

ISBN 978-1-5011-5508-6
ISBN 978-1-5011-5509-3 (ebook)

CONTENTS

EVEN HAND

JIM BUTCHER

In the Dresden Files, Harry Dresden, professional wizard, has faced more than his fair share of villains amid the supernatural underbelly of Chicago's dark streets, but none has proven more vexing than Gentleman John Marcone. In "Even Hand," Marcone sets aside his plans to kill Harry to go head-to-head with a more pressing problem . . .

A successful murder is like a successful restaurant: 90 percent of it is about location, location, location.

Three men in black hoods knelt on the waterfront warehouse floor, their wrists and ankles trussed with heavy plastic quick-ties. There were few lights. They knelt over a large, faded stain on the concrete floor, left behind by the hypocritically named White Council of Wizards during their last execution.

I nodded to Hendricks, who took the hood off the first man, then stood clear. The man was young and good-looking. He wore an expensive yet ill-fitting suit and even more expensive yet tasteless jewelry.

"Where are you from?" I asked him.

He sneered at me. "What's it to y—"

I shot him in the head as soon as I heard the bravado in his voice. The body fell heavily to the floor.

The other two jumped and cursed, their voices angry and terrified.

I took the hood off the second man. His suit was a close cousin of the dead man's, and I thought I recognized its cut. "Boston?" I asked him.

"You can't do this to us," he said, more angry than frightened. "Do you know who we are?"

Once I heard the nasal quality of the word "are," I shot him.

I took off the third man's hood. He screamed and fell away from me. "Boston," I said, nodding, and put the barrel of my .45 against the third man's forehead. He stared at me, showing the whites of his eyes. "You know who I am. I run drugs in Chicago. I run the numbers, the books. I run the whores. It's my town. Do you understand?"

His body jittered in what might have been a nod. His lips formed the word "yes," though no sound came out.

"I'm glad you can answer a simple question," I told him, and lowered the gun. "I want you to tell Mr. Morelli that I won't be this lenient the next time his people try to clip the edges of my territory." I looked at Hendricks. "Put the three of them in a sealed trailer and rail-freight them back to Boston, care of Mr. Morelli."

Hendricks was a large, trustworthy man, his red hair cropped in a crew cut. He twitched his chin in the slight motion that he used for a nod when he disapproved of my actions but intended to obey me anyway.

Hendricks and the cleaners on my staff would handle the matter from here.

I passed him the gun and the gloves on my hands. Both would see the bottom of Lake Michigan before I was halfway home, along with the two slugs the cleaners would remove from the site. When they were done, there would be nothing left of the two dead men but a slight variation on the outline of the stain in the old warehouse floor, where no one would look twice in any case.

Location, location, location.

Obviously, I am not Harry Dresden. My name is something I rarely trouble to remember, but for most of my adult life, I have been called John Marcone.

I am a professional monster.

It sounds pretentious. After all, I'm not a flesh-devouring ghoul, hiding behind a human mask until it is time to gorge. I'm no vampire, to drain the blood or soul from my victim, no ogre, no demon, no cursed beast from the spirit world dwelling amid the unsuspecting sheep of humanity. I'm not even possessed of the mystic abilities of a mortal wizard.

But they will never be what I am. One and all, those beings were born to be what they are.

I made a choice.

I walked outside of the warehouse and was met by my consultant, Gard—a tall blond woman without makeup whose eyes continually swept her surroundings. She fell into step beside me as we walked to the car. "Two?"

"They couldn't be bothered to answer a question in a civil manner."

She opened the back door for me and I got in. I picked up my personal weapon and slipped it into the holster beneath my left arm while she settled down behind the wheel. She started driving and then said, "No. That wasn't it."

"It was business."

"And the fact that one of them was pushing heroin to thirteen-year-old girls and the other was pimping them out had nothing to do with it," Gard said.

"It was business," I said, enunciating. "Morelli can find pushers and pimps anywhere. A decent accountant is invaluable. I sent his bookkeeper back as a gesture of respect."

"You don't respect Morelli."

I almost smiled. "Perhaps not."

"Then why?"

I did not answer. She didn't push the issue, and we rode in silence back to the office. As she put the car in park, I said, "They were in my territory. They broke my rule."

"No children," she said.

"No children," I said. "I do not tolerate challenges, Ms. Gard. They're bad for business."

She looked at me in the mirror, her blue eyes oddly intent, and nodded.

———————————⊱⊰———————————

There was a knock at my office door, and Gard thrust her head in, her phone's earpiece conspicuous. "There's a problem."

Hendricks frowned from his seat at a nearby desk. He was hunched over a laptop that looked too small for him, plugging away at his thesis. "What kind of problem?"

"An Accords matter," Gard said.

Hendricks sat up straight and looked at me.

I didn't look up from one of my lawyer's letters, which I receive too frequently to let slide. "Well," I said, "we knew it would happen eventually. Bring the car."

"I don't have to," Gard said. "The situation came to us."

I set aside the finished letter and looked up, resting my fingertips together. "Interesting."

Gard brought the problem in. The problem was young and attractive. In my experience, the latter two frequently lead to the former. In this particular case, it was a young woman holding a child. She was remarkable—thick, rich, silver-white hair, dark eyes, pale skin. She had on very little makeup, which was fortunate in her case, since she looked as if she had recently been drenched. She wore what was left of a gray business skirt suit, had a towel from one of my health clubs wrapped around her shoulders, and was shivering.

The child she held was too young to be in school and was also appealing, with rosy features, white-blond hair, and blue eyes. Male or female, it hardly mattered at that age. They're all beautiful. The child clung to the girl as if it would not be separated, and was also wrapped in a towel.

The girl's body language was definitely protective. She had the kind of beauty that looked natural and . . . true. Her features and her bearing both spoke of gentleness and kindness.

I felt an immediate instinct to protect and comfort her.

I quashed it thoroughly.

I am not made of stone, but I have found it is generally best to behave as if I am.

I looked across the desk at her and said, "My people tell me you have asked for sanctuary under the terms of the Unseelie Accords, but that you have not identified yourself."

"I apologize, sir," she answered. "I was already being indiscreet enough just by coming here."

"Indeed," I said calmly. "I make it a point not to advertise the location of my business headquarters."

"I didn't want to add names to the issue," she said, casting her eyes down in a gesture of submission that did not entirely convince me. "I wasn't sure how many of your people were permitted access to this sort of information."

I glanced past the young woman to Gard, who gave me a slow, cautious nod. Had the girl or the child been other than they appeared, Gard would have indicated in the negative. Gard costs me a fortune and is worth every penny.

Even so, I didn't signal either her or Hendricks to stand down. Both of them watched the girl, ready to kill her if she made an aggressive move. Trust, but verify—that the person being trusted will be dead if she attempts betrayal.

"That was most considerate of you, Justine."

The girl blinked at me several times. "Y-you know me."

"You are a sometime associate of Harry Dresden," I said. "Given his proclivities about those he considers to be held under his aegis, it is sensible to identify as many of them as possible. For the sake of my insurance rates, if nothing else. Gard."

"Justine, no last name you'll admit to," Gard said calmly, "currently employed as Lara Raith's secretary and personal aide. You are the sometime lover of Thomas Raith, a frequent ally of Dresden's."

I spread my hands slightly. "I assume the 'J' notation at the bottom of Ms. Raith's typed correspondence refers to you."

"Yes," Justine said. She had regained her composure quickly—not something I would have expected of the servitor of a vampire of the White Court. Many of the . . . people, I suppose, I'd seen there had made lotus-eaters look self-motivated. "Yes, exactly."

I nodded. "Given your patron, one is curious as to why you have come to me seeking protection."

"Time, sir," she replied quietly. "I lacked any other alternative."

Someone screamed at the front of the building.

My headquarters shifts position irregularly, as I acquire new buildings. Much of my considerable wealth is invested in real estate. I own more of the town than any other single investor. In Chicago, there is always money to be had by purchasing and renovating aging buildings. I do much of my day-to-day work out of my most recent renovation projects, once they have been modified to be suitable to welcome guests. Then, renovation of the building begins, and the place is generally crowded with contractors who have proven their ability to see and hear nothing.

Gard's head snapped up. She shook it as if to rid herself of a buzzing fly and said, "A presence. A strong one." Her blue eyes snapped to Justine. "Who?"

The young woman shuddered and wrapped the towel more tightly about herself. "Mag. A cantrev lord of the fomor."

Gard spat something in a Scandinavian tongue that was probably a curse.

"Précis, please," I said.

"The fomor are an ancient folk," she said. "Water dwellers, cousins of the jotuns. Extremely formidable. Sorcerers, shape changers, seers."

"And signatories," I noted.

"Yes," she said. She crossed to the other side of the room, opened a closet, and withdrew an athletic bag. She produced a simple, rather crude-looking broadsword from it and tossed it toward Hendricks. The big man caught it by the handle and took his gun into his left hand. Gard took a broad-bladed axe out of the bag and shouldered the weapon. "But rarely involved in mortal affairs."

"Ms. Raith sent me to the fomor king with documents," Justine said, her voice coming out quietly and rapidly. Her shivering had increased. "Mag made me his prisoner. I escaped with the child. There wasn't time to reach one of my lady's strongholds. I came to you, sir. I beg your protection, as a favor to Ms. Raith."

"I don't grant favors," I said calmly.

Mag entered in the manner so many of these self-absorbed supernatural cretins seem to adore. He blasted the door into a cloud of flying splinters with what I presumed was magic.

For God's sake.

At least the vampires would call for an appointment.

The blast amounted to little debris. After a few visits from Dresden and his ilk, I had invested in cheap, light doors at dramatic (as opposed to tactical) entry points.

The fomor was a pale, repellent humanoid. Seven feet tall, give or take, and distinctly froglike in appearance. He had a bloated belly, legs several inches too long to be proportionately human, and huge feet and hands. He wore a tunic of something that resembled seaweed beneath a long, flapping blue robe covered in the most intricate embroidery I had ever seen. A coronet of coral was bound about his head. His right hand was extended dramatically. He carried a twisted length of wood in his left.

His eyes bulged, jaundice yellow around septic green, and his teeth were rotted and filthy. "You cannot run from me," he said. His wide mouth made the words seem somehow slurred. "You are mine."

Justine looked up at me, evidently too frightened to turn her head, her eyes wide with fear. A sharper contrast would have been hard to manage. "Sir. Please."

I touched a button on the undersurface of my desk, a motion of less than two inches, and then made a steeple of my hands again as I eyed Mag and said, "Excuse me, sir. This is a private office."

Mag surged forward half a step, his eyes focused on the girl. "Hold your tongue, mortal, if you would keep it."

I narrowed my eyes.

Is it so much to ask for civility?

"Justine," I said calmly, "if you would stand aside, please."

Justine quickly, silently, moved out from between us.

I focused on Mag and said, "They are under my protection."

Mag gave me a contemptuous look and raised the staff. Darkness lashed at me, as if he had simply reached into the floorboards and cracks in the wall and drawn it into a sizzling sphere the size of a bowling ball.

It flickered away to nothingness about a foot in front of my steepled hands.

I lifted a finger and Hendricks shot Mag in the back. Repeatedly.

The fomor went down with a sound like a bubbling teakettle, whipped onto his back as if the bullets had been a minor inconvenience, and raised the stick to point at Hendricks.

Gard's axe smashed it out of his grip, swooped back up to guard, and began to descend again.

"Stop," I said.

Gard's muscles froze just before she would have brought down the axe onto Mag's head. Mag had one hand uplifted, surrounded in a kind of negative haze, his long fingers crooked at odd angles—presumably some kind of mystic defense.

"As a freeholding lord of the Unseelie Accords," I said, "it would be considered an act of war if I killed you out of hand, despite your militant intrusion into my territory." I narrowed my eyes. "However, your behavior gives me ample latitude to invoke the defense of property and self clause. I will leave the decision to you. Continue this asinine behavior, and I will kill you and offer a weregild to your lord, King Corb, in accordance with the conflict resolution guidelines of section two, paragraph four."

As I told you, my lawyers send me endless letters. I speak their language.

Mag seemed to take that in for a moment. He looked at

me, then Gard. His eyes narrowed. They tracked back to Hendricks, his head hardly moving, and he seemed to freeze when he saw the sword in Hendricks's hand.

His eyes flicked to Justine and the child and burned for a moment—not with adoration or even simple lust. There was a pure and possessive hunger there, coupled with a need to destroy that which he desired. I have spent my entire life around hard men. I know that form of madness when I see it.

"So," Mag said. His eyes traveled back to me and were suddenly heavy-lidded and calculating. "You are the new mortal lord. We half believed that you must be imaginary. That no one could be as foolish as that."

"You are incorrect," I said. "Moreover, you can't have them. Get out."

Mag stood up. The movement was slow, liquid. His limbs didn't seem to bend the proper way. "Lord Marcone," he said, "this affair is no concern of yours. I only wish to take the slaves."

"You can't have them. Get out."

"I warn you," Mag said. There was an ugly tone in his voice. "If you make me return for her—for them—you will not enjoy what follows."

"I do not require enjoyment to thrive. Leave my domain. I won't ask again."

Hendricks shuffled his feet a little, settling his balance.

Mag gathered himself up slowly. He extended his hand, and the twisted stick leapt from the floor and into his fingers. He gave Gard a slow and well-practiced sneer and said, "Anon, mortal lordling. It is time you learned the truth of the world. It will please me to be your instructor." Then he turned, slow and haughty, and walked out, his shoulders hunching in an odd, unsettling motion as he moved.

"Make sure he leaves," I said quietly.

Gard and Hendricks followed Mag from the room.

I turned my eyes to Justine and the child.

"Mag," I said, "is not the sort of man who is used to disappointment."

Justine looked after the vanished fomor and then back at me, confusion in her eyes. "That was sorcery. How did you . . . ?"

I stood up from behind my desk and stepped out of the copper circle set into the floor around my chair. It was powered by the sorcerous equivalent of a nine-volt battery, connected to the control on the underside of my desk. Basic magical defense, Gard said. It had seemed like nonsense to me—it clearly was not.

I took my gun from its holster and set it on my desk.

Justine took note of my reply.

Of course, I wouldn't give the personal aide of the most dangerous woman in Chicago information about my magical defenses.

There was something hard and not at all submissive in her eyes. "Thank you, sir, for . . ."

"For what?" I said very calmly. "You understand, do you not, what you have done by asking for my help under the Accords?"

"Sir?"

"The Accords govern relations between supernatural powers," I said. "The signatories of the Accords and their named vassals are granted certain rights and obligations—

such as offering a warning to a signatory who has trespassed upon another's territory unwittingly before killing him."

"I know, sir," Justine said.

"Then you should also know that you are most definitely not a signatory of the Accords. At best, you qualify in the category of 'servitors and chattel.' At worst, you are considered to be a food animal."

She drew in a sharp breath, her eyes widening—not in any sense of outrage or offense, but in realization. Good. She grasped the realities of the situation.

"In either case," I continued, "you are property. You have no rights in the current situation, in the eyes of the Accords—and more to the point, I have no right to withhold another's rightful property. Mag's behavior provided me with an excuse to kill him if he did not depart. He will not give me such an opening a second time."

Justine swallowed and stared at me for a moment. Then she glanced down at the child in her arms. The child clung harder to her and seemed to lean somewhat away from me.

One must admire such acute instincts.

"You have drawn me into a conflict which has nothing to do with me," I said quietly. "I suggest candor. Otherwise, I will have Mr. Hendricks and Ms. Gard show you to the door."

"You can't . . . ," she began, but her voice trailed off.

"I can," I said. "I am not a humanitarian. When I offer charity it is for tax purposes."

The room became silent. I was content with that. The child began to whimper quietly.

"I was delivering documents to the court of King Corb on behalf of my lady," Justine said. She stroked the child's hair absently. "It's in the sea. There's a gate there in Lake Michigan, not far from here."

I lifted an eyebrow. "You swam?"

"I was under the protection of their courier, going there," Justine said. "It's like walking in a bubble of air." She hitched the child up a little higher on her hip. "Mag saw me. He drove the courier away as I was leaving and took me to his home. There were many other prisoners there."

"Including the child," I guessed. Though it probably didn't sound that way.

Justine nodded. "I . . . arranged for several prisoners to flee Mag's home. I took the child when I left. I swam out."

"So you are, in effect, stolen property in possession of stolen property," I said. "Novel."

Gard and Hendricks came back into the office.

I looked at Hendricks. "My people?"

"Tulane's got a broken arm," he said. "Standing in that asshole's way. He's on the way to the doc."

"Thank you. Ms. Gard?"

"Mag is off the property," she said. "He didn't go far. He's summoning support now."

"How much of a threat is he?" I asked. The question was legitimate. Gard and Hendricks had blindsided the inhuman while he was focused upon Justine and the child and while he wasted his leading magical strike against my protective circle. A head-on confrontation against a prepared foe could be a totally different proposition.

Gard tested the edge of her axe with her thumb and drew a smooth stone from her pocket. "Mag is a fomor sorcerer lord of the first rank. He's deadly—and connected. The fomor could crush you without a serious loss of resources. Confrontation would be unwise."

The stone made a steely, slithery sound as it glided over the axe's blade.

"There seems little profit to be had, then," I said. "It's nothing personal, Justine. Merely business. I am obliged to return stolen property to signatory members of the Accords."

Hendricks looked at me sharply. He didn't say anything. He didn't have to. I already knew the tone of whatever he would say. *Are there no prisons?* perhaps. Or *No man is an island, entire of itself. It tolls for thee.* On and on.

Hendricks has no head for business.

Gard watched me, waiting.

"Sir," Justine said, her tone measured and oddly formal. "May I speak?"

I nodded.

"She isn't property," Justine said, and her voice was low and intense, her eyes direct. "She was trapped in a den of living nightmares, and there was no one to come save her. She would have died there. And I am *not* letting anyone take her back to that hellhole. I will die first." The young woman set her jaw. "She is not *property*, Mr. Marcone. She's a *child*."

I met Justine's eyes for a long moment.

I glanced aside at Hendricks. He waited for my decision.

Gard watched me. As ever, Gard watched me.

I looked down at my hands, my fingertips resting together with my elbows propped on the desk.

Business came first. Always.

But I have rules.

I looked up at Justine.

"She's a child," I said quietly.

The air in the room snapped tight with tension.

"Ms. Gard," I said, "please dismiss the contractors for the day, at pay. Then raise the defenses."

She pocketed the whetstone and strode quickly out, her teeth showing, a bounce in her step.

"Mr. Hendricks, please scramble our troubleshooters. They're to take positions across the street. Suppressed weapons only. I don't need patrolmen stumbling around in this. Then ready the panic room."

Hendricks nodded and got out his cell phone as he left. His huge, stubby fingers flew over its touchscreen as he sent the activation text message. Looking at him, one would not think him capable of such a thing. But that is Hendricks, generally.

I looked at Justine as I rose and walked to my closet. "You will go with the child into the panic room. It is, with the possible exception of Dresden's home, the most secure location in the city."

"Thank you," she said quietly.

I took off my coat and hung it up in the closet. I took off my tie and slipped it over the same hanger. I put my cuff links in my coat pocket, rolled up my sleeves, and skinned out of my gun's holster. Then I slipped on the armored vest made of heavy scales of composite materials joined to sleeves of quite old-fashioned mail. I pulled an old field jacket, olive drab, over the armor, belted it, holstered my sidearm at my side, opposite a combat knife, and took a military-grade assault shotgun—a weapon every bit as illegal as my pistol in the city of Chicago—from its rack.

"I am not doing it for you, young lady," I said. "Nor am I doing it for the child."

"Then why are you doing it?" she asked.

"Because I have rules," I said.

She shook her head gently. "But you're a criminal. Criminals don't have rules. They break them."

I stopped and looked at her.

Justine blanched and slid a step farther away from me, along the wall. The child made a soft, distressed sound. I beckoned curtly for her to follow me as I walked past her. It took her a moment to do so.

Honestly.

Someone in the service of a vampire ought to have a bit more fortitude.

This panic room looked like every other one I've had built: fluorescent lights, plain tile floor, plain drywall. Two double bunks occupied one end of the room. A business desk and several chairs took up the rest. A miniature kitchen nestled into one corner, opposite the miniature medical station in another. There was a door to a half bath and a bank of security monitors on the wall between them. I flicked one switch that activated the entire bank, displaying a dozen views from hidden security cameras.

I gestured for Justine to enter the room. She came in and immediately took a seat on the lower bunk of the nearest bed, still holding the child.

"Mag can find her," Gard told me when we all rendezvoused outside the panic room. "Once he's inside the building and gets past the forward area, he'll be able to track her. He'll head straight for her."

"Then we know which way he'll be moving," I said. "What did you find out about his support?"

"They're creatures," Gard said, "actual mortal beings, though like none you've seen before. The fomor twist flesh to their liking and sell the results for favors and influence. It was probably the fomor who created those cat-things the Knights of the Blackened Denarius used."

I twisted my mouth in displeasure at the name. "If they're mortal, we can kill them."

"They'll die hard," Gard warned me.

"What doesn't?" I looked up and down the hallway outside the panic room. "I think the primary defense plan will do."

Gard nodded. She had attired herself in an armored vest not unlike my own over a long mail shirt. Medieval looking, but then modern armorers haven't aimed their craft at stopping claws of late. Hendricks, standing watch at the end of the hall, had on an armored vest but was otherwise covered in modified motorcyclist's armor. He carried an assault shotgun like mine, several hand grenades, and that same broadsword.

"Stay here," I said to Justine. "Watch the door. If anyone but one of us comes down the stairs, shut it."

She nodded.

I turned and started walking toward the stairway. I glanced at Gard. "What can we expect from Mag?"

"Pain."

Hendricks grunted. Skeptically.

"He's ancient, devious, and wicked," Gard clarified.

"There is an effectively unlimited spectrum of ways in which he might do harm."

I nodded. "Can you offer any specific knowledge?"

"He won't be easy to get to," she said. "The fomor practice entropy magic. They make the antitechnology effect Dresden puts off look like mild sunspot activity. Modern systems *are* going to experience problems near him."

We started up the stairs. "How long before he arrives?"

From upstairs, there was the crash of breaking plate glass. No alarm went off, but there was a buzzing, sizzling sound and a scream—Gard's outer defenses. Hendricks hit a button on his cell phone and then came with me as I rushed up the remaining stairs to the ground floor.

The lights went out as we went, and Hendricks's phone sputtered out a few sparks. Battery-powered emergency lights flicked on an instant later. Only about half of them functioned, and most of those were behind us.

Mag had waited for nightfall to begin his attack and then crippled our lights. Quite possibly he assumed that the darkness would give him an overwhelming advantage.

The hubris of some members of the supernatural community is astonishing.

The night-vision scopes mounted on my weapon and Hendricks's had been custom-made, based off of designs dating back to World War II, before night-vision devices had married themselves to the electronics revolution. They were heavy and far inferior to modern systems—but they would function in situations where electronic goggles would be rendered into useless junk.

We raised the weapons to our shoulders, lined an eye up

with the scopes, and kept moving. We reached the first defensive position, folded out the reinforced composite barriers mounted there, and knelt behind them. The ambient light from the city outside and the emergency lights below us was enough for the scopes to do their jobs. I could make out the outline of the hallway and the room beyond. Sounds of quiet movement came closer.

My heart rate had gone up, but not alarmingly so. My hands were steady. My mouth felt dry, and my body's reaction to the prospect of mortal danger sent ripples of sensation up and down my spine. I embraced the fear and waited.

The fomor's creatures exploded into the hallway on a storm of frenzied roars. I couldn't make out many details. They seemed to have been put together on the chassis of a gorilla. Their heads were squashed, ugly-looking things, with wide-gaping mouths full of sharklike teeth. The sounds they made were deep, with a frenzied edge of madness, and they piled into the corridor in a wave of massive muscle.

"Steady," I murmured.

The creatures lurched as they moved, like cheap toys that had not been assembled properly, but they were fast for all of that. More and more of them flooded into the hallway, and their charge was gaining mass and momentum.

"Steady," I murmured.

Hendricks grunted. There were no words in it, but he meant, *I know*.

The wave of fomorian beings got close enough that I could see the patches of mold clumping their fur and tendrils of mildew growing upon their exposed skin.

"Fire," I said.

Hendricks and I opened up.

The new military AA-12 automatic shotguns are not the hunting weapons I first handled in my patriotically delusional youth. They are fully automatic weapons with large circular drums that rather resemble the old tommy guns made iconic by my business predecessors in Chicago. One pulls the trigger and shell after shell slams through the weapon. A steel target hit by bursts from an AA-12 very rapidly comes to resemble a screen door.

And we had two of them.

The slaughter was indescribable. It swept like a great broom down that hallway, tearing and shredding flesh, splattering blood on the walls and painting them most of the way to the ceiling. Behind me, Gard stood ready with a heavy-caliber big-game rifle, calmly gunning down any creature that seemed to be reluctant to die before it could reach our defensive point. We piled the bodies so deep that the corpses formed a barrier to our weapons.

"Hendricks," I said.

The big man was already reaching for the grenades on his belt. He took one, pulled the pin, cooked it for a slow two count, and then flung it down the hall. We all crouched behind the barriers as the grenade went off with a deafening crunch of shock-wave-driven air.

Hendricks threw another one. He might disapprove of killing, but he did it thoroughly.

When the ringing began to fade from my ears, I heard a sound like raindrops. It wasn't raining, of course—the gunmen in the building across the street had opened fire with silenced weaponry. Bullets whispered in through the windows and hit the floor and walls of the headquarters with innocuous-sounding thumps. Evidently Mag's servitors had been routed and were trying to flee.

An object the size of Hendricks's fist appeared from nowhere and arced cleanly through the air. It landed on the floor precisely between the two sheltering panels, a lump of pink-and-gray coral.

Gard hit me with a shoulder and drove me to the ground even as she shouted, "Down!"

The piece of coral didn't explode. There was a whispering sound, and hundreds of tiny holes appeared in the blood-stained walls and ceiling. Gard let out a pained grunt. My left calf jerked as something pierced it and burned as though the wound had been filled with salt.

I checked Hendricks. One side of his face was covered in a sheet of blood. Small tears were visible in his leathers, and he was beginning to bleed through the holes.

"Get him," I said to Gard, rising, as another coral spheroid rose into the air.

Before it could get close enough to be a threat, I blew it to powder with my shotgun. And the next and the next, while Gard dropped her rifle, got a shoulder under one of Hendricks's, and helped him to his feet as if he'd been her weight instead of two hundred and seventy pounds of muscle. She started down the stairs.

A fourth sphere came accompanied by mocking laughter, and when I pulled the trigger again, the weapon didn't function. Empty. I slapped the coral device out of the air with the shotgun's barrel and flung myself backward, hoping to clear the level of the floor on the stairwell before the pseudo-grenade detonated. I did not quite make it. Several objects struck my chest and arms, and a hot blade slipped across my unscarred ear, but the armor turned the truly dangerous projectiles.

I broke my arm tumbling backward down the stairs.

More laughter followed me down, but at least the fomor wasn't spouting some kind of ridiculous monologue.

"I did my best," came Mag's voice. "I gave you a chance to return what was mine. But no. You couldn't keep yourself from interfering in my affairs, from stealing my property. And so now you will reap the consequences of your foolishness, little mortal. . . ."

There was more, but there is hardly a need to go into details. Given a choice between that egocentric drivel and a broken arm, I'd prefer the latter. It's considerably less excruciating.

Gard hauled me to my feet by my coat with her spare hand. I got under the stunned Hendricks's other arm and helped them both down the rest of the stairs. Justine stood in the doorway of the safe room, at the end of the hallway of flickering lights, her face white-lipped but calm.

Gard helped me get Hendricks to the door of the room and turned around. "Close the door. I may be able to discourage him out here."

"Your home office would be annoyed with me if I wasted your life on such a low-percentage proposition," I said. "We stick to the plan."

The valkyrie eyed me. "Your arm is broken."

"I was aware, thank you," I said. "Is there any reason the countermeasure shouldn't work?"

Mag was going on about something, coming down the

steps one at a time, making a production of every footfall. I ignored the ass.

"None that I know of," Gard admitted. "Which is not the same answer as 'no.'"

"Sir," Justine said.

"We planned for this—or something very like it. We don't split up now. End of discussion. Help me with Hendricks."

"*Sir*," Justine said.

I looked up to see Mag standing on the landing, cloaked in random shadows, smiling. The emergency lights on the stairwell blew out with a melodramatic shower of dying sparks.

"Ah," I said. I reached inside the safe-room door, found the purely mechanical pull-cord wrapped unobtrusively around a nail head on the wall, and gave it a sharp jerk.

It set off the antipersonnel mines built into the wall of the landing.

There were four of them, which meant that a wash of fire and just under three-thousand-round shot acquainted themselves with the immediate vicinity of the landing and with Mag. A cloud of flame and flying steel enveloped the fomor, but at the last instant the swirling blackness around him rose up like a living thing, forming a shield between Mag and the oncoming flood of destruction.

The sound of the explosions was so loud that it demolished my hearing for a moment. It began to return to me as the cloud of smoke and dust on the landing began to clear. I could hear a fire alarm going off.

Mag, smudged and blackened with residue but otherwise untouched, made an irritated gesture, and the fire alarm sparked and fizzled—but not before setting off the automatic sprinklers. Water began pouring down from spigots in the ceiling.

Mag looked up at the water and then down at me, and his too-wide smile widened even more. "Really?" he asked. "Water? Did you actually think water would be a barrier to the magic of a fomor lord?"

Running water was highly detrimental to mortal magic, or so Gard informed me, whether it was naturally occurring or not. The important element was quantity. Enough water would ground magic just as it could conduct electricity and short-circuit electronics. Evidently Mag played by different rules.

Mag made it a point to continue down the stairs at exactly the same pace. He was somewhat hampered in that several of the stairs had been torn up rather badly in the explosion, but he made it to the hallway. Gard took up a position in the middle of the hallway, her axe held straight up beside her in both hands like a baseball player's bat.

I helped Hendricks into the safe room and dumped him on a bunk, out of any line of fire from the hallway. Justine took one look at his face and hurried over to the medical station, where she grabbed a first-aid kit. She rushed back to Hendricks's side. She broke open the kit and started laying out the proper gear for getting a clear look at a bloody wound and getting the bleeding stopped. Her hands flew with precise speed. She'd had some form of training.

From the opposite bunk, the child watched Justine with wide blue eyes. She was naked and had been crying. The tears were still on her little cheeks. Even now, her lower lip had begun to tremble.

But so far as anyone else knew, I was made of stone.

I turned and crossed the room. I sat down at the desk, a copy of the one in my main office. I put my handgun squarely in front of me. The desk was positioned directly in line with the door to the panic room. From behind the desk, I could see the entire hallway clearly.

Mag stepped forward and moved a hand as though throwing something. I saw nothing, but Gard raised her axe in a blocking movement, and there was a flash of light, and the image of a Norse rune, or something like it, was burned onto my retina. The outer edge of Gard's mail sleeve on her right arm abruptly turned black and fell to dust, so that the sleeve split and dangled open.

Gard took a grim step back as Mag narrowed his jaundiced eyes and lifted the crooked stick. Something that looked like the blend of a lightning bolt and an eel lashed through the air toward Gard, but she caught it on the broad blade of her axe, and there was another flash of light, another eye-searing rune. I heard her cry out, though, and saw that the edges of her fingernails had been burned black.

Step by step she fell back, while Mag hammered at her with things that made no sense, many of which I could not even see. Each time, the rune-magic of that axe defeated the attack—and each time, it seemed to cost her something. A lightly singed face here. A long, shallow cut upon her newly bared arm there. And the runes, I saw, were each in different places on the axe, being burned out one by one. Gard had a finite number of them.

As Gard's heels touched the threshold of the safe room, Mag let out a howl and threw both hands out ahead of him.

An unseen force lifted Gard from her feet and flung her violently across the room, over my desk, and into the wall. She hit with bone-crushing force and slid down limply.

I faced the inhuman sorcerer alone.

Mag walked slowly and confidently into my safe room and stared at me across my desk. He was breathing heavily, from exertion or excitement or both. He smiled, slowly, and waved his hand again. An unpleasant shimmer went through the air, and I glanced down to see rust forming on the exposed metal of my gun, while cracking began to spread through the plastic grip.

"Go ahead, mortal," Mag said, drawing out the words. "Pick up the gun. Try it. The crafting of the weapon is fine, mortal, but you are not the masters of the world that you believe yourselves to be. Even today's cleverest smiths are no match for the magic of the fomor."

I inclined my head in agreement. "Then I suppose," I said, "that we'll just have to do this old-school."

I drew the eighteenth-century German dragoon pistol from the open drawer beside my left hand, aimed, and fired. The ancient flintlock snapped forward, ignited the powder in the pan, and roared, a wash of unnatural blue-white fire blazing forth from the antique weapon. I almost fancied that I could see the bullet, spinning and tumbling, blazing with its own tiny rune.

Though Mag's shadows leapt up to defend him, he had expended enormous energy moving through the building, hurling attack after attack at us. More energy had to be used to overcome the tremendous force of the claymores that had exploded virtually in his face. Perhaps, at his full strength, at the height of his endurance, his powers would have been enough to turn even the single, potent attack that had been designed to defeat them.

From the beginning, the plan had been to wear him down.

The blue bolt of lead and power from the heavy old flintlock pierced Mag's defenses and body in the same instant and with the same contemptuous energy.

Mag blinked at me, then lowered his head to goggle at the smoking hole in his chest as wide as my thumb. His mouth moved as he tried to gabble something, but no sound came out.

"Idiot," I said coldly. "It will be well worth the weregild to be rid of you."

Mag lurched toward me for a moment, intent upon saying something, but the fates spared me from having to endure any more of him. He collapsed to the floor before he could finish speaking.

I eyed my modern pistol, crusted with rust and residue, and decided not to try it. I kept a spare .45 in the downstairs desk in any case. I took it from another drawer, checked it awkwardly one-handed, and then emptied the weapon into Mag's head and chest.

I am the one who taught Hendricks to be thorough.

I looked up from Mag's ruined form to find Justine staring at me, frozen in the middle of wrapping a bandage around my second's head.

"How is he?" I asked calmly.

Justine swallowed. She said, "He m-may need stitches for this scalp wound. I think he has a concussion. The other wounds aren't bad. His armor stopped most of the fragments from going in."

"Gard?" I asked without looking over my shoulder. The valkyrie had an incredible ability to resist and recover from injury.

"Be sore for a while," she said, the words slurred. "Give me a few minutes."

"Justine, perhaps you will set my arm and splint it," I said. "We will need to abandon this renovation, I'm afraid, Gard. Where's the thermite?"

"In your upstairs office closet, right where you left it," she said in a *very* slightly aggrieved tone.

"Be a dear and burn down the building," I said.

She appeared beside my desk, looking bruised, exhausted, and functional. She lifted both eyebrows. "Was that a joke?"

"Apparently," I said. "Doubtless the result of triumph and adrenaline."

"My word," she said. She looked startled.

"Get moving," I told her. "Make the fire look accidental. I need to contact the young lady's patron so that she can be delivered safely back into her hands. Call Dr. Schulman as well. Tell him that Mr. Hendricks and I will be visiting him shortly." I pursed my lips. "And steak, I think. I could use a good steak. The Pump Room should do for the three of us, eh? Ask them to stay open an extra half an hour."

Gard showed me her teeth in a flash. "Well," she said, "it's no mead hall. But it will do."

I put my house in order. In the end, it took less than half an hour. The troubleshooters made sure the fomorian creatures were dragged inside, then vanished. Mag's body had been bagged and transferred, to be returned to his watery kin, along with approximately a quarter of a million dollars in bullion, the price required in the Accords for the weregild of a person of Mag's stature.

Justine was ready to meet a car that was coming to pick her up, and Hendricks was already on the way to Schulman's attentions. He'd seemed fine by the time he left, growling at Gard as she fussed over him.

I looked around the office and nodded. "We know the defense plan has some merit," I said. I hefted the dragoon pistol. "I'll need more of those bullets."

"I was unconscious for three weeks after scribing the rune for that one," Gard replied. "To say nothing of the fact that the bullets themselves are rare. That one killed a man named Nelson at Trafalgar."

"How do you know?"

"I took it out of him," she said. "Men of his caliber are few and far between. I'll see what I can do." She glanced at Justine. "Sir?"

"Not just yet," I said. "I will speak with her alone for a moment, please."

She nodded, giving Justine a look that was equal parts curiosity and warning. Then she departed.

I got up and walked over to the girl. She was holding the child against her again. The little girl had dropped into an exhausted sleep.

"So," I said quietly. "Lara Raith sent you to Mag's people.

He happened to abduct you. You happened to escape from him—despite the fact that he seemed to be holding other prisoners perfectly adequately—and you left carrying the child. And, upon emerging from Lake Michigan, you happened to be nearby, so you came straight here."

"Yes," Justine said quietly.

"Coincidences, coincidences," I said. "Put the child down."

Her eyes widened in alarm.

I stared at her until she obeyed.

My right arm was splinted and in a sling. With my left hand, I reached out and flipped open her suit jacket, over her left hip, where she'd been clutching the child all evening.

There was an envelope in a plastic bag protruding from the jacket's interior pocket. I took it.

She made a small sound of protest and aborted it partway.

I opened the bag and the envelope and scanned over the paper inside.

"These are account numbers," I said quietly. "Security passwords. Stolen from Mag's home, I suppose?"

She looked up at me with very wide eyes.

"Dear child," I said, "I *am* a criminal. One very good way to cover up one crime is to commit another, more obvious one." I glanced down at the sleeping child again. "Using a child to cover your part of the scheme. Quite cold-blooded, Justine."

"I freed all of Mag's prisoners to cover up the theft of his records at my lady's bidding," she said quietly. "The child was . . . not part of the plan."

"Children frequently aren't," I said.

"I took her out on my own," she said. "She's free of that place. She will stay that way."

"To be raised among the vampires?" I asked. "Such a lovely child will surely go far."

Justine grimaced and looked away. "She was too small to swim out on her own. I couldn't leave her."

I stared at the young woman for a long moment. Then I said, "You might consider speaking to Father Forthill at St. Mary of the Angels. The Church appears to have some sort of program to place those endangered by the supernatural into hiding. I do not recommend you mention my name as a reference, but perhaps he could be convinced to help the child."

She blinked at me, several times. Then she said quietly, "You, sir, are not very much like I thought you were."

"Nor are you, Agent Justine." I took a deep breath and regarded the child again. "At least we accomplished something today." I smiled at Justine. "Your ride should be here by now. You may go."

She opened her mouth and reached for the envelope.

I slipped it into my pocket. "Do give Lara my regards. And tell her that the next time she sends you out to steal honey, she should find someone else to kill the bees." I gave her a faint smile. "That will be all."

Justine looked at me. Then her lips quivered up into a tiny, amused smile. She bowed her head to me, collected the child, and walked out, her steps light.

I debated putting a bullet in her head but decided against it. She had information about my defenses that could leave them vulnerable—and more to the point, she knew that they were effective. If she should speak of today's events to Dresden . . .

Well. The wizard would immediately recognize that the claymores, the running water, and the magic-defense-piercing bullet had not been put into place to counter Mag or his odd folk at all.

They were there to kill Harry Dresden.

And they worked. Mag had proven that. An eventual confrontation with Dresden was inevitable—but murdering Justine would guarantee it happened immediately, and I wasn't ready for that, not until I had rebuilt the defenses in the new location.

Besides, the young woman had rules of her own. I could respect that.

I would test myself against Dresden in earnest one day—or he against me. Until then, I had to gather as many resources to myself as possible. And when the day of reckoning came, I had to make sure it happened in a place where, despite his powers, he would no longer have the upper hand.

Like everything else.

Location, location, location.

HOUNDED

KELLEY ARMSTRONG

The Cainsville series takes place in a town settled by refugee fae. Welsh fae (Tylwyth Teg) share the region with the Cŵn Annwn, the Welsh version of the Wild Hunt, who are tasked with hunting killers and sending their souls to the afterlife. Betrayals introduced a rogue Huntsman, who lost his hound to the protagonists. In "Hounded," he's out to replace the missing canine companion.

As the woman continued to talk, the Huntsman continued ignoring her, his attention absorbed instead by the dog drowsing under her patio chair. The beast's presence gnawed at him, a mocking reminder that he lacked a hound himself.

The Huntsman was Cŵn Annwn. *The Wild Hunt.* The very term meant "Hounds of the Otherworld"—Huntsmen and their hounds, working as one, psychically bonded. But he had no pack—neither fellow Huntsmen nor hounds. Not anymore. And while he didn't miss the former, he was working to replace the latter. Hence the woman and her dog, sitting across from him at the café.

When the woman paused her endless prattle, the Huntsman nodded, and that was all she needed to continue, the warmth in his eyes insisting that he found her utterly fascinating. Which he did, in a way.

Cŵn Annwn were known for their natural charm. The Huntsman might have traded his for more useful powers, but he'd discovered that charm could also be learned. Act as if you care, and people will believe you actually do.

One Cŵn Annwn power he'd retained was far more useful: the ability to peer into the corners of human minds, to tease out darkness and pass judgment on a soul. Eternal judgment.

If he was to judge this woman by what she was saying, the verdict could be summed up with a yawn. It was almost painful to listen to as she recited the mundanities of her existence, all the ways she frittered away her short human life span. Growing up in a middle-class family, going to college, getting a business degree, joining a firm, getting married, opening a business, getting divorced.

There wasn't any part of her past that even *she* looked back on with fondness. College was tedious. Her first job, drudgery. Her ex-husband, an asshole. Even opening her own business hadn't made her happy, because she was saddled with a partner she loathed.

Why was she telling him all this? Because they were out on a date. A first date, during which, from what the Huntsman understood of human rituals, one was supposed to put one's best self forward, make a good impression. Indeed, this woman *was* making an impression—and not just with her spot-on impersonation of an incredible bore, though she did pull that off very well. No, as she talked, she told him more.

Inadvertent reveals abounded as she nattered on, and the Huntsman gazed into her eyes and saw much more.

So much more.

He glided through her memories, chasing the tendrils of darkness. Tendrils? Ropes, rather. Thick cables that moored her consciousness. Envy and bitterness and paranoia and hatred—the four guy ropes of her innermost self, holding the rest in place.

He followed these cables to a childhood memory shrouded in shadow, relegated to the drawer where humans shove things they'd rather forget and tell themselves something never really happened, not like that, perhaps not at all, but simply as a remembered scene from a novel or movie.

This memory was real, though, whatever the woman might tell herself. He watched it unfold through her eyes, and as she dove into a swimming pool he caught a glimpse of her ten-year-old self reflected in the water. She dove under and stayed as long as she could. When she surfaced, gasping, a young boy called to her. She ignored him. He called again, his voice taking on a whine, and from some distant place a woman yelled for the girl to look after her brother. Except the girl didn't want to look after him. She was sick and tired of looking after him. It used to be just her and her mother, until her stepfather came, and then the boy, and now everything was different. *Everything.*

Her brother whined again, said Mommy promised they would play together in the pool. The girl tried to ignore him, but his whining droned like a mosquito in her head.

"You want to play?" she said finally, turning on him, and

his chubby face lit up. He was too stupid to even notice how angry she was. Too selfish to care.

"I'll be a shark," she said. "You have to get away from me."

She dove under and pretended to snatch his feet as he kicked. He squealed and laughed and splashed, and the patio door squealed shut, their mother going inside.

The girl kept playing just long enough to be sure their mother wasn't coming right back out. Then she dove, and this time she grabbed one chubby foot and yanked him under the water.

The Huntsman surfaced from her memories as she was saying, ". . . threatening me? The business is finally successful—due to *my* hard work—and now he swans in and decides he wants to play a role. What he really wants is to steal it from me."

Ah, some things never change, do they? the Huntsman thought. *If it isn't your little brother, it's your ex-husband or your business partner. Everyone else is to blame for your unhappiness. But you show them, don't you? Such a dull and ordinary exterior hiding such a dark and twisted soul. No one suspects a thing. But I do. There has been a miscarriage of justice here. I will fix that. It is my job to fix that.*

⸺⸺⸺⸺⸺⸺⸻⸺⸺⸺⸺⸺⸺

They left the café, strolling along the crowded city street, the dog sticking to its master's opposite side and staying as far from the Huntsman as it could manage. The beast sensed danger there, danger and threat. The woman just kept talking.

"And now he wants me to go to Chicago," she said. "Have you ever been there? It's an absolute shithole."

She didn't pause for the Huntsman to answer, but on this point, he would have agreed. Even the mention of that city made his temper rise, darkness swirling, and the dog whined, ducking its owner's absent pat.

Chicago. That was where he'd lost his hound.

No, not *lost*. She had been stolen from him. The second hound he'd had snatched away. His Cŵn Annwn pack had taken the first when it banished him. Cast him out with neither hound nor steed, claiming the beasts wanted nothing to do with him.

"No?" he'd said. "Bring them to me, and let them choose."

"Let you infect them, you mean. Destroy them as you have destroyed yourself. You are lucky we let you leave with your life."

Luck? Is that what this was? Banished from his pack, stripped of his hound, his horse, his brothers. This was not luck. It was a curse. And his crime? He had dared question the boundaries of his duties as a Huntsman. Question the restrictions that kept them from truly fulfilling their calling.

The job of the Cŵn Annwn was the taking of souls. The execution of those who themselves took lives. Yet they were shackled by one incredible restriction: they could claim only the souls of those who killed fae or humans with fae blood. They might look into a human's eyes and see the blood of a thousand on his hands, yet if none of that blood was fae, the transgressor could not be touched.

We protect the fae. We seek justice for the fae. Humans must seek it for themselves. That is not our place.

It was a constraint that made Cŵn Annwn cry out at night, reliving the horrors they'd seen in human eyes, unable to exact justice for the dead.

Except they could. There was no cosmic force actually stopping them. Just a rule. An old and outdated rule.

So the Huntsman had broken it. Quietly and on his own, without hound or steed, he had cleaned the world of human filth. His pack leader knew it. Knew and turned a blind eye because he understood that the Huntsman acted righteously.

And then . . .

Then came the day when others found out, when his leader feigned shock and horror, banished him and kept his hound.

The Huntsman had found another cŵn, though. A broken hound. A fellow outcast. He'd nursed her to health only to have her stolen from him in Chicago. By a human girl, no less.

No, not entirely a girl. That helped soothe the memory. His hound had been taken by an incarnation of Matilda of the Hunt and given to her consort, Arawn, lord of the Otherworld.

Either way, his hound had been stolen, and the memory still burned.

He needed a new hound. And he was working on that right now. He would take a hound and see justice executed upon this monstrous woman who walked at his side, blathering about her business partner.

"It's not fair," he said, and she stopped short and looked at him. "What he's doing to you, how he's treating you, it isn't fair. You built a business, and then he slides in and tries to steal it from under you."

Like Matilda, stealing his hound after he rescued it. The Huntsman channeled his own outrage into his words, giving them a ring of sincerity that made the woman's face light up.

"Exactly," she said. "And I'm sorry to go on about it, but once I get started, I just . . ." She shook her head. "It burns."

"I understand." *I truly do.*

He reached out and squeezed her hand, and when she met his gaze, he called on his own darkness, the inky essence implicit in the concept of justice and judgment. The Cŵn Annwn liked to act as if their actions rose from pure goodness, pure righteousness. That was ridiculous—they were executioners. Darkness personified. What lifted them above their prey was that they harnessed the darkness within themselves to *do* good. That was the truth his brethren could never accept.

He slid through the shadows of her memory, past the children in the pool and on to a boy in college. A boy who'd spurned her. She watched him from the bushes at night as he drunkenly made his way back to his dorm. When he stumbled and chuckled under his breath, she thought how innocent he seemed, how simple and sweet. Then she remembered how he had taken her by the wrist earlier at a party, squeezing so hard it hurt as he leaned in and hissed, "Stop following me. It didn't work out, okay? Just let it go." Humiliating her in front of others—and now he dared to stagger about, laughing at himself, as if he really was such a good and sweet-natured boy?

She squeezed the knife and ran her thumb along the blade. Blood welled up, and the pain reminded her of his grip on her wrist.

He'd hurt her. Embarrassed her. Rejected her.

He should not get away with that.

The Huntsman stopped the memory there. He tugged it, just a little, bringing it not quite to the front of her mind but pulling forth the emotions instead. The insult. The outrage.

So many people have wronged you. And now you are wronged again by your business partner. Think of what you'd like to do to him. How you'd like to pay him back.

Next to her, the dog whined and danced, but the woman couldn't hear it, lost in the Huntsman's dark embrace.

Show me what you have.

Show me the worst that you have.

It came slowly at first, as if the thoughts were forming for the first time. Of course they were not. They'd been there all along. Her fantasies of revenge. How she would steal the business. Ruin his professional reputation.

More, child. Give me more.

He deserves more.

Her mind skated to the edge of the thought and then recoiled. He let it recoil. There was no hurry. It would take time to swell those thoughts into action.

That was what he needed: action. He could not act until she did.

She would, though.

They always did.

———————————————>€<———————————————

It *did* take time. Weeks. But the Huntsman was patient. This was his sole purpose on earth, the rest mere filler.

He wooed the woman, in his way. Which did not mean he bedded her—he had absolutely no desire to. Yet he'd come to her as a potential lover, and so he had to maintain that fiction. It was easily done by playing the role of the careful lover, the considerate partner, the man who wanted to get to know her first, romance her, court her. Long coffees at outdoor cafés. Long walks in the park. Long dinners with wine, when she'd drink too much and let him wriggle deeper into her mind. That was how he truly wooed her—easing her along the path from thought to deed. From fantasy to action.

He never verbally counseled her to kill her business partner. That would have been uncouth, and completely unnecessary. In words, he only sympathized with her situation, bolstered her sense of outrage, fed her paranoia. Yes, her partner was up to something, and he was worried for her. Had she ever considered to what lengths this man might go to steal her company? Of course, the Huntsman didn't think he'd actually hurt her, but . . . he worried. That was all. He worried.

Plant the seeds. Nurture them in darkness and fear. Watch them sprout in her psyche. Vague fantasies solidifying. From "I wish he was dead" to "How would I kill him, if I dared?" and then finally "Do I dare?"

Do I dare kill him?

And can I get away with it?

He helped with all of that, his firm verbal support bolstering her confidence and his subtle mental manipulation knocking away obstacles.

Of course you can do this. You're strong and smart and resourceful.

You're better than him. You deserve better.

Weeks passed, until finally the moment arrived when he met her for drinks and she didn't talk about herself, didn't snivel over her problems. There was no need for that. She had reached a decision. He saw that in her mind, saw how she planned to do it. How she would cross that line, and where he needed to be to witness it.

All she had to do was make the move that would lead to murder. He could not act until she launched the action decisively. Only then could he pass judgment, reap her soul, and secure his hound.

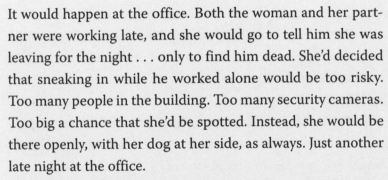

It would happen at the office. Both the woman and her partner were working late, and she would go to tell him she was leaving for the night . . . only to find him dead. She'd decided that sneaking in while he worked alone would be too risky. Too many people in the building. Too many security cameras. Too big a chance that she'd be spotted. Instead, she would be there openly, with her dog at her side, as always. Just another late night at the office.

It was a ridiculous plan. She should have seen that. But the Huntsman had infected her mind and suggested this setup—perfect for his needs—and he'd swept away her doubts. It was audacious and brazen, and therefore no one would suspect a thing. Or so she believed.

He had no trouble sneaking into the building. He'd determined where the cameras were and could avoid them. As for human security, he'd retained the power to trick the eye as he passed through on a wave of shadow.

He found the woman working in her office. When the Huntsman slipped in, her dog lifted its head and whined. The woman glanced over, saw nothing, and patted the dog's head before returning to her work.

As soon as darkness fell, she made her move. As she started to close the dog in her office, again it whined. The Huntsman tensed, wondering if the dog's unease might break the spell of his magic, let the woman stop and realize she shouldn't be doing this with the canine present for fear it might raise an alarm. But the dog was integral to the process. To the binding of his hound. Fortunately, the woman was too preoccupied to notice the beast's unease and just whispered a sharp "Quiet!" as she closed the office door.

The Huntsman crept ahead into the partner's space. He watched the woman enter. Saw the blade in her hand. Bore witness as she reached around to slit her partner's throat.

He watched her.

He did not stop her.

He stood in his corner and sent forth his darkness to bolster her own, and when she slashed that blade, the Huntsman was there, keeping her hand steady.

Then he released her.

He pulled out of her mind as her partner flailed and gurgled, grasping at his slit throat, blood gushing over his desk.

The woman saw then what she had done—and she began to scream.

The Huntsman shot forward, materializing as he clapped his hand over her mouth.

"Shhh," he said. "Shhh."

She saw him, and her eyes went wide as her mouth worked.

"You?" she said. "How—?"

He removed his hand from her. "I had to stop you."

"Stop?" She blinked and looked at the dying man, now convulsing on the floor. "You can save him?"

The Huntsman gave a dismissive wave. He could. Possibly. But he had other priorities.

When he released the woman, she dropped beside her partner. The Huntsman laid his hand on her arm. "It's too late."

"I didn't mean . . ." She leapt to her feet. "You have to help me. I didn't mean to do this."

"Of course you did."

"No, I—"

"You what? You aren't this sort of person?" He laughed, his lip curling. "Tell that to your brother. To the boy at college."

She stared, uncomprehending.

"Your brother, in the pool," he said. "And the boy you stalked with a knife."

"My . . . ? Yes. I did pull my brother under, and I thought of drowning him, but of course I didn't. Just like I thought about killing that boy. But I didn't *do* anything. I just thought about it."

"It's the same thing."

The look she gave him then—the horror and the incredulity. It was the same look he'd seen on the face of his Cŵn Annwn leader when he'd discovered what the Huntsman had done.

"You forced that man to kill his wife. You used your magic to make him kill her so you could claim his soul."

"He wanted to do it. He thought about doing it. That's the same thing."

"No, it is not!"

His leader rocked forward, as if he wanted to throttle the Huntsman. Then he recoiled, horrified by the impulse. That was their weakness. They enjoyed the Hunt, the taking of souls, and yet they would not let themselves indulge that hunger, even in service of wider justice.

"You knew what I was doing," the Huntsman said.

"I know you were targeting human killers. If I had ever imagined you were compelling them—"

"He would have killed her eventually," the Huntsman said. "I took his soul before he gave his darkness free rein."

"He did give it rein!" his leader roared. "He murdered his wife."

"One victim—it could have been more were I not there."

That's when the leader had cast him out. Told him if he was not gone within the hour, they would hunt *him*. Kill *him*. And somehow they claimed to occupy the moral high ground.

Now this woman stood and stared at him with the same look. As if *he* was the monster.

"Bring me your dog," he said.

"What?"

"You want me to fix this? Bring me your dog."

She hesitated, but then she staggered off down the hall and returned with the beast.

"You won't hurt him, right?" she said.

"I'm not the killer here. Now lay your hands on his head."

She did, and the Huntsman channeled his darkest magic, the kind the Cŵn Annwn did not possess, the kind he had discovered in his wanderings. True magic.

He reached into the dumb beast and found what passed for a soul. Then he reached into the woman. When he touched her soul, she gasped.

"I'm saving you," he said. "You have committed murder, and so your soul is forfeit. But I am going to let you live. I am Cŵn Annwn. To do my job properly, I require a cŵn—a hound."

His magic held her immobile, but her eyes shifted to her dog.

"No, he won't do. He's a mere beast. A cŵn is more, and if I cannot have one, I must create one. Or a reasonable facsimile."

He closed his eyes and set the dog's puny soul free. Then he slid the woman's into its place. The beast gave a start as the woman woke, finding herself trapped in the dog.

A pause, and then she went wild, snapping and twisting in a panic. He grabbed her by the scruff of her neck and smacked her with a psychic wallop that left her howling in pain.

"Enough of that," he said. "I let you live, and you will be grateful." He looked into her eyes. "I will teach you to be grateful."

NIGSU GA TESGU

JEFF SOMERS

Magicians aren't nice people. They're not moral people. They're not good people. Magic can be wielded by anyone who learns the ancient language of power (known colloquially among magicians simply as the Words) and who is willing to shed blood to fuel the spell—their own or somebody else's. In the dark, bloody world of power and predators in the Ustari Cycle, Mika Renar is one of the most powerful ustari *in the world—because she speaks the Words better than most, because she doesn't hesitate to bleed as many people as necessary to get what she needs, and because she knows the meaning of this story's title, "Nigsu Ga Tesgu."*

1.

Only a few days before I whispered the Words that killed my father, I saw something remarkable.

My father thought of himself as French, though the French blood in our veins was diluted and mixed and stepped on until we were really just American. Father, though, he learned to speak French through a correspondence course and would often go days just speaking French, in an effort, I think, to change his past.

But Father was a bore. He learned a language and he used it to say the same things he'd been saying in English, in almost the same flat, midwestern accent. He sounded ridiculous, and the only people who thought he was actually French were people who had never met a French person in their lives.

The thing I saw was a mystic, begging for change on Willow Street. He was a thin, tiny brown man, smaller than any other full-grown man I'd ever seen. I was walking with Aunt Polly, who was crushing my hand in hers as usual, and the little man was in the middle of the sidewalk, suspended over a tiny garden of flowers he'd placed on the ground. He had one hand on a gnarled walking stick that seemed, impossibly, to support his weight.

"Stop," I insisted to my aunt Polly, stamping my feet in their shiny leather shoes when she pretended not to hear me. Aunt Polly did not like me. I put a spider in her bed once, hoping it would bite her and kill her, but as I learned later not all spiders are lethal, or even bite at all.

"Stop!" I shouted, and bit her hand to make her let go. Polly turned and jerked her arm, but when she realized we were in public she chose not to slap me. Aunt Polly was a coward.

I stared at the little man. He appeared to be sleeping. It was impossible that anyone could hold themselves so perfectly with just a stick for support. I was amazed.

Aunt Polly sucked her teeth. This was some time before I chased her down and found her cowering in a tenement in New York City. Even more time still before I made her choke on hundreds of spiders I summoned into her throat.

"It is a trick," she said, happy to spoil the moment. "He sits on a platform and the arm snakes around his back, and his robes hide the contraption."

I remember being enraged at them both: the little man for tricking me, and Aunt Polly for ruining the trick.

The little man's eyes opened. He looked at Polly, then at me. His eyes were red and dark, unhealthy. He had the most curious, ugly little face, smashed like a puppet's. He lifted his free hand and he had a little blade in it, a tiny, sharp piece of metal. He pulled up his sleeve and jabbed himself with it, a sudden, violent motion that excited me.

I sensed something then. I will always remember the first time I tasted a sacrifice.

He whispered something. A few Words, though I did not know them then. He whispered them, and he rose into the air. Just a few more inches. The walking stick he had been holding fell over with a loud clatter. Aunt Polly gasped and stumbled backward and fell on her ass, and that was the best part about the whole experience.

I couldn't stop thinking about the little man and his feat—how it had been done. I knew these things were tricks, but I couldn't see how the trick was done.

The next day, very early, I escaped through my bedroom window and made my way back. I was always escaping; Father had ordered the servants to be on guard, but I was smarter than all of them. And I suspected some of them would not have shed tears if I went missing. I did not shed tears when I buried them, despite their pleas, their pledges of loyalty to the family.

It was twilight when I arrived at the spot. The little man

was there, once again seemingly suspended by the stick. He was sleeping, so I crept up to examine him more closely. I had seen him float—really float—and I intended to find out how, for *I* wanted to float, to rise above and hover over them all. Astound people. Terrify them. It was the first time I had ever felt that, the desire to terrify. My heart beat and my cheeks burned. I knew that I was particularly pretty when I was flushed, rosy cheeked and the picture of a doll, a moppet.

As I tried to lift his robes to see under, his hand suddenly flashed out, letting the stick once again clatter to the ground. His grip was incredibly strong for such a tiny hand. He pulled me close, and I could smell him. *Smell* him. I'd never been so close to another human being, I didn't think. It was horrible. Human beings are disgusting chattel, awful meat and stench.

"You want?" he hissed in my ear as I screamed. "You *want*?" he hissed. "You *bleed*."

He whispered three Words in my ear. I didn't know them. They sounded strange.

The Words were a simple, savage spell, the first I would ever learn, the first I would ever cast. Three Words to stop a heart. *You want, you bleed.* Simple instructions, and four days later I chewed on my own tongue until blood flooded my mouth, and then I spoke the three Words I'd been taught, and watched as Father bugged his eyes out, made a strange choking noise, and died face-first in his turtle soup.

And I was happy.

2.

My apprentice will kill me someday.

I knew this the moment I interviewed him, this beautiful brown-skinned boy not even ten years old yet, the most beautiful person I'd ever seen. I was younger then, though still old—too old—a wrinkled bag of bones. He showed promise, a boy from Newark who lisped and sweated, but beautiful. Despite his young age, I could see he would be gorgeous. The first time I slapped him for mispronouncing a Word, he looked at me with such hatred, such permanent hate, that I knew it: it might take decades, but he would kill me. That was how I would end. My apprentice would kill me.

I started training him to do so. That much was duty.

I leaned forward, the tea steaming around us. I had not yet perfected my other face, and I was there, near him. "Do you know how old I am?"

He studied me. A child, he worried over having the correct answer. He chewed his lip. "Forty," he said, defiant. The oldest he could imagine.

I smiled. "I am sixty-nine," I said. "How much longer do you think I will live?"

His thinking face again. Then he smiled. Triumphant. "Not long."

I slapped him again. "I will live forever, Calvin. Forever." I smiled. "I know the spell, the *biludha*. You know this word, *biludha*?"

He shook his head.

"That is your first Word, then. It means 'ritual.' It means

'big spell.' The one I know, when I cast it, it will make me live forever."

Little Calvin blinked at me. "Forever?"

I nodded. "I will bond you. I will bond you as my apprentice, and I will teach you everything I know. I will teach you every spell I have. You will become more powerful than any other person in the world, in history."

His beautiful face lit up, greedy and covetous.

"But," I said, "I will not teach you this final spell. I will not teach you how to live forever. That spell you must take from me." I cocked my head and studied his face. "You want? You bleed."

His tiny, beautiful face hardened, and I knew. I knew he would kill me, someday, as any good *urtuku*, apprentice, would.

3.

He comes in with my lunch. I watch him from the corner of the room. Is it poison? It will not be poison, because that is too obvious, too easy. And he has not learned everything from me, not yet. He is the second-most powerful mage in the world. But even confined to my bed and unable to lift my limbs, I am still the *most* powerful, and he knows that.

He feeds me soup. He feeds me purée. Later he will go down to the library and search it for hidden grimoires. I have left a terrible surprise for him, as one of the antique books is a trap, a book that appears to be filled with ancient spells and lore but is covered with invisible wards and runes that will compel him to read incessantly, forever, until he dies of starvation and thirst. Someday he might find it, and if he is not as strong as he should be and fails to save himself, then I will need a new *urtuku*.

In ancient times, *ustari* were more poetic. Most mages today learn their spells in an oral tradition, passed down from master to apprentice. There was a time when they were written down more routinely, and in those old days there was more poetry to the spells. More wasted time and space. These days the focus is always on speed, efficiency, war spells that cut out all unnecessary verbiage to gain a second's casting time. But older spells gloried in the unnecessary, often including lines that were simply beautiful, or that conveyed a thought or observation. When I was a young girl, just learning, I loved discovering these moments. They had no effect on the spell. They were wasted time. But I loved discovering them.

In many old grimoires you encounter the phrase *nigsu ga tesgu*. It is meaningless for the spell itself. It accomplishes nothing. It means, loosely, "everything I have is devoured," and old-time mages used to close out their spells with it to signal they'd given their all to the spell, every idea, every drop of blood.

I've always loved the phrase, from the moment I stumbled across it in my studies under my old *gasam*. I loved it because it described us, the *ustari*, the small number of people who saw through the veil and knew how the universe worked. Who knew how to bleed others and speak the Words and summon the forces of the universe to our bidding. It described how we devoured the world, bleeding it dry. And it described the relationship between a *gasam* and their *urtuku*, a master and their apprentice. The apprentice devoured—they enslaved themselves to you for your knowledge. They gobbled it up, sucking you dry, and when everything you had was devoured, they destroyed you and took your place as the master.

Cal Amir has grown great under me. And he will devour me, if I give him the chance.

There is another tedious meeting with my fellow *enustari*. With the exception of perhaps Evelyn Fallon, none of them deserve the title. Those lower down in my order, the *saganustari* and *ustari*, are such star-fuckers. If you bleed a room full of people, they call you *enustari*, Archmage, even if the spell is shit, even if it does nothing or does nothing well. It is a title of acclamation, after all, and if the people doing the acclaiming are idiots, what does their praise mean?

Calvin dutifully wheels me to the car, humming. He smells clean and leathery, a musky scent he has custommade. His Italian shoes creak pleasingly as he pushes me. His entire presence is calibrated for effect: the way he fills out his suit; the way he smells; the precise sheen of his hair, dark and lustrous. He is one of the most handsome men I have ever seen, and it is all without trickery, without illusion.

My own illusion walks ahead of us, swaying, immaculate, expensive.

I am incurable, as far as I have been able to tell. I am incurable because my affliction is not physical, it is magical; I have been cursed. A curse of slow erosion, incremental consumption. Pieces of me, consumed, completely destroyed. Annihilated. Not merely burnt, or eaten, or dissolved into their component molecules—made so as to have never existed. It is a complex spell that took many years of study and work to compose, a complex spell that skirts causality and comes dangerously close to undoing reality itself.

Many, many people were bled white to cast this spell upon me.

If the curse had been designed to take effect all at once, the universe would have collapsed—assuming the spell had access to enough sacrificial blood to fuel it, which would not be easy to attain. Changing reality is difficult. But the curse is ingenious, as it annihilates small parts of me slowly, allowing the fabric of reality to heal itself. And it had run its course for some time before I realized what had been done to me, that I was being devoured one cell at a time.

The curse is by far Cal Amir's greatest work.

From the moment I saw the curse clearly, I knew it was my apprentice who had afflicted me. Who else? I did not leave enemies behind; it is cleaner by far to kill and destroy than to show mercy. Few *ustari* could even possibly write such a spell, much less devise ways to fuel it. And the hatred behind it, the despite that drives such a concept, is unmistakably that of an *urtuku* seeking to destroy his master.

There is no cure. He has fixed that. There are solutions

but no cures. A massive Artifact, a magically operated mechanism, could be built to manipulate reality directly. I have no facility with Artifacts, and there are few true Fabricators left in the world. But if it were constructed, it could counteract the curse very effectively. I could in fact change the moment in time so that Calvin did not inflict it on me at all, or even remove Calvin from my service. From existence itself.

But the Fabrication remains out of reach, even for me. The spell, the massive *biludha* that conveys immortality—true, unending life—would cancel out the effects of the curse; not cure me, per se, but prevent the curse from devouring me entirely. I would live on, much as I do now, crippled, nearly silent, able only to cast and to plot.

But the sacrifice required for the *biludha* is enormous.

Calvin knows that it can be cast only once in a millennium, owing to its requirements for fresh blood. If I cast it, I leave him behind to rot and ruin, to dust and putrefaction, even if I bring him through the ritual safely. Amir wishes to learn the secret, but he has miscalculated. He has cursed me, and I may perish and be erased before he discovers it.

I feel my mouth try to pinch it into a smile.

Calvin is very dutiful. He inspects the interior of the car before lifting me into it. He does not cast to move me, as that would be disrespectful. He sets me gently in the backseat, and my Glamour, the illusion of me, hovers outside, placid, patient, smiling. She is beautiful. When he pauses, briefly, next to her they form a perfect couple, the sort of pair who stop conversations in hotel lobbies, the sort of couple people hate on sight for no reason they can articulate beyond the raging maw of jealousy inside them. My Glamour and my apprentice appear destined for each other.

Calvin gets into the front seat and starts the car. I cannot move my head, so I stare at the back of his, this beautiful man who has killed me and now wishes he had done so perhaps ever slightly more slowly.

He does not know how I have survived this long. His spell, his curse, it should have consumed me long ago. He believes that in my final moments I will reveal the immortality spell to him, that death and oblivion will soften me. Or that perhaps he can offer to save me and in my desperation I will grovel. He does not know how I am still alive, but the answer is simple. I have crafted my own spell. I have altered the bond of *urtuku* between us, the magical bond between master and apprentice, so that when his curse tries to take a bit from me and devour it, it takes from him. Thus he weakens and I remain in stasis, hovering on the edge of total destruction.

I want to live. So I have taken from him.

4.

Something is happening.

The roar of sacrifice wakes me. All *ustari*, no matter how humble, share the ability to sense the invisible and silent act of blood being shed. Raw and fresh, pulsing with a life that decays and fades within seconds, blood in the air calls to us. The amount being shed somewhere in my house at any moment is always high; my Glamour is a work of art. It has no equal. It fools the keenest eye. But this level of spell requires a great deal of blood, and I farm it with a steady supply siphoned from indigents and debtors who come into my custody, all bled slowly, steadily.

But over that persistent cloud of sacrifice, I can sense another torrent of fresh blood; someone is casting in my house, and by the volume of sacrifice, it is no small spell.

The advantage to having to live my life through an illusion is that walls and doors mean nothing to me. I cannot physically rise from my bed without assistance, but I roam freely nonetheless. I close my eyes and I see the world from another perspective, one that is artificial, constructed from magic and artifice, from blood and effort. I feel nothing as I glide through my grand house. I am a turtle, shrunken and reduced over the years, lost within her shell.

There are signs of a conflict—a broken vase, an overturned chair. Spells have been cast. There is no sign of Calvin, and his absence makes me suspicious.

I hurry my Glamour toward the small library, where much of my scholarly work is done. Where the grimoires are kept, my notes, my experiments. There, I find Calvin, quite dead, his beautiful form broken and his youthful appearance sloughing off as the spells fade. He is still a handsome man, a powerfully attractive corpse, but he looks his age: pushing sixty, soft. The ability to bleed someone else makes one lazy, reluctant to pay for in sweat what you can instead purchase with blood.

This is not the work of my counterattack, which was designed to be as slow and implacable as the curse he laid on me. Someone has *murdered* Calvin. Someone very powerful. Or very *unpredictable*.

I draw on the sacrifice being harvested for my Glamour and cast a simple spell, creating a second Glamour. It ripples into being, a perfect copy. I float away and remain in the library. Passing through walls, I send myself outside the house while I secure the library, invoking old Wards and spells to hide it, to defend it, to lock it up. Because as I can see the moment I pass outside, I am under attack.

Enustari are appearing in the circular driveway, popping into existence on a wave of spent blood and a whisper. I see Alfonse Alligherti first, fat and jowly and cruel and arrogant. Faber Gottschalk, also fat, wearing a diaphanous robe that might as well be a woman's housedress. Archmages are traveling great distances to attack me, because they sense weakness. My *urtuku* is gone, and I am a lone old woman, paralyzed and near death. A perfect opportunity for parasites who think I am vulnerable.

Behind each of them appear their Bleeders. I have always disdained such cultism. These mages make promises to their Bleeders. Riches. Luxury. All their desires met. In return they must stay fleshy, they must sacrifice on command and be prepared for the certainty that someday the sacrifice required will be too much and their bodies will be consumed. They accept these risks because of their slavish devotion to their masters—sometimes urged along by a Charm, sometimes by a simple human devotion to their own appetites. I prefer to be honest. I prefer to hunt. I take sacrifice as my due, because all these people—all people—are here to be bled.

They will come for my body.

It is the obvious tactic. I am in bed, unable to move without assistance. I normally rely on Calvin for all my needs, but now he is a beautiful corpse and they imagine me helpless. They imagine old grudges made well—Archmages are like old washerwomen when it comes to gossip and grudges; both are eternal, nurtured and suckled like their own children. But I have blood enough to destroy them. They will not devour me today.

I begin casting. Three spells.

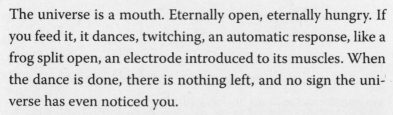

The universe is a mouth. Eternally open, eternally hungry. If you feed it, it dances, twitching, an automatic response, like a frog split open, an electrode introduced to its muscles. When the dance is done, there is nothing left, and no sign the universe has even noticed you.

The mouth does not care where the sacrifice comes from, or who forms the Words that shape its intent. The mouth is dumb and does not judge. If there is blood, fresh and pulsing, still alive in some mysterious sense for a few seconds, still part of the person it is drawn from, if there are Words to give it shape and intent, the mouth drinks and the universe twitches and the spell is cast.

Few know that a Glamour, an illusion, can cast. Few have spent so much time living through their illusions, few have studied the mechanics of the Glamour spell as minutely as I have. The voice is an illusion, a projection. I whisper a spell in my bedroom, unable to turn my head. My Glamour outside speaks a spell. My Glamour in the library speaks a spell. The universe, the hungry maw, does not differentiate—it does not care. It accepts the sacrifice poured into it. It shimmies and shakes according to the Words it hears.

My enemies reach the house and find they cannot enter.

Fat, sweaty Alfonse—who ruins his expensive suits the moment he puts them on, sweating through the cloth and turning them swampy—races for the front door, because Alfonse is all aggression, all artless force. His spells are brutal, simple fists of power he draws from his Bleeders in sudden bursts, sometimes draining them in seconds for a decisive blow. Alfonse is dangerous, but he is a blunt instrument.

Alfonse bounces away from the door and stumbles backward. His red face twists in rage.

Faber Gottschalk is even fatter and does not run. I have never seen him walk under his own power, in fact, and thus am momentarily distracted by an anthropological interest in seeing the huge man move utilizing his gargantuan limbs. His Bleeders are anomalies; they are thin, gray things in burlap clothes. Where other *enustari* feed their Bleeders lavishly, Faber starves them on his little ranch. He makes up for this with numbers and has brought a gang of his skinnies to fuel his spells.

Faber does not approach the house. He has seen Alfonse bounce off my first line of defense and is smart enough to pause, to hesitate, to reassess. Faber appears to be a fat simpleton whose mind has softened from years of easy living in his Texas compound, tended by his magically Charmed followers, but his mind is as sharp as ever. He closes his eyes and speaks, casting. Behind him, several of his thin Bleeders stiffen and jerk, scrambling to cut themselves, their lifeblood pulled rudely from them, gulped and boiled off. It is an inelegant, wasteful way to gain Sacrifice, but then Faber is a man of appetites.

He vanishes. He has teleported himself.

Teleportation is not a difficult spell; rank amateurs can often imagine clever ways to move themselves. The direct approach runs against the physical laws of the universe, but there are cheats. Any *ustari* of experience knows at least one. To move yourself fifty feet so that you are inside a building instead of outside a building, thus avoiding all security, is not difficult.

It is so obvious a move that I have, of course, prepared for it.

One of my Glamours smiles slightly as I imagine Gottschalk being funneled into the tiny room I have prepared. He will have to crouch, hot and unable to breathe. He will seek threads of sacrifice in the air and find none. He will sweat and his enlarged, weakened heart will pound, and he will wonder how he was so easily trapped. And then he will slowly realize that to escape he will have to bleed himself. A man of Gottschalk's stature has not bled himself in decades. His skin is milky and smooth and untouched.

He will realize he must bleed himself to escape, and then he will realize he does not have a blade. Because a man of Gottschalk's stature does not cut himself.

I wonder what he will sacrifice of himself. His tongue? A vein, chewed through? It is amusing to picture him gnawing at himself.

Alfonse is smarter. A brute who prefers the frontal assault, yes, but he appreciates a good trap and stands there, irresolute. Many people assume hesitation in battle is a weakness, but the opposite is true. Those who do not pause to contemplate their surroundings, to consider new data, wind up in tiny boxes, like Gottschalk. Alfonse stands and grinds his teeth, hands balled into fists, considering how he will gain entry without being entrapped himself.

I do nothing. Sacrifice is not to be wasted.

When Alfonse decides, he is clever. He sees that teleportation is a trap, so he assumes all such subtleties are traps, and he gestures, his people Bleed, and he quickly casts a brute-force spell that sends an explosive blow against the front door. When the door cracks, he scans the destruction, seeking obvious Wards or other markings that would indicate another trap; then he gestures again, and one of his Bleeders steps forward to test the entry. The Bleeder is older, graying, lucky to have lived this long in Alfonse's employ; yet he's also so typically fleshy because he's lived well in Alfonse's employ. We all feed off each other. Those who condemn our order as parasitic need to see more Bleeders like this plump fellow, his innards awash in fine food and liquor, his memories filled with pleasant afternoons and elegant entertainments, his family left a handsome legacy in cash.

As the Bleeder crosses what's left of my threshold, he catches fire, a green flame, impossible to extinguish. Alfonse studies the entryway as the man dies screaming, leaving quite a mess just when I no longer have an apprentice to clean it up. The fat man isn't eager to join him, and I let him do his sums. If he decides the cost is too dear, that perhaps I am not as defenseless as he hoped, he will be allowed to leave. I can hunt him down and extract my revenge anytime.

Then Alfonse purses his chubby lips and gestures. Behind

him, all four of his remaining Bleeders immediately cut, and cut deeply.

The greedy bastard.

I wait. I listen through three sets of ears.

You can always learn something from a man who has lived so well for so long as Alligherti. And, indeed, as I listen to the spell he is casting, peppered with nonsense syllables in order to confuse and obfuscate, I am impressed. Before I can compose a suitable retaliation, he sinks, the pavement and dirt beneath him cracking open and swallowing him.

A moment later, his Bleeders follow, sinking down into the dirt and disappearing.

With a thunderous explosion of expensive marble tiles, they emerge in the foyer, just beyond the fallen Bleeder. Instead of wasting time and effort unraveling my spells and traps, Alfonse has gone under them. Covered in dirt and dust, he wastes no time. He marches off, his tiny feet surprisingly nimble, his bedraggled, weakened Bleeders swanning after him, marching, they now suspect, to their doom.

Alfonse plans to take everything from me. He moves purposefully for the stairs. I feel a drip of anxiety, of worry; it is unfamiliar and exciting, my buried heart lurching in my chest as my body remains still, my eyes closed, my lips in motion. I had not imagined my defenses to be impenetrable, especially against someone of Alligherti's caliber, but I expected them to last a bit longer than this. I do my sums without passion, and the result is clear; it is time to retreat. Using my supply of sacrifice to slow Alfonse's progress is foolish, when I can use it instead to destroy him, no matter the cost.

I begin reciting a new *biludha*, two of my Glamours singing the ritual, the *erin gilleem*. It isn't the most powerful or intricate ritual, but it is elegant. My two voices circle each other, a symphony, and as they recite the whole house begins to tremble. Cracks burst the walls. The floors shift, and Alfonse and his Bleeders stagger on the stairs, stopping, holding on to the banister, hesitant. Alfonse is not worried; his confirmation bias tells him that since he has so far escaped the traps and blades of his enemies, he will always manage to do so. But Alfonse makes the mistake of all greedy, fat boys who believe that things are only valuable when you hoard them. Alfonse has worked very hard to collect his possessions, and he cannot imagine that anyone would purposefully destroy theirs. He believes he is safe because he is inside my home, my cherished manse.

My third Glamour begins a second spell. As she speaks, I rise from the bed.

The building is shaking. The grounds outside are shaking. A great sizzling noise fills the air, like endless sand falling on glass. Alfonse continues to advance, certain this is all noise and light, intended to blind him, to frighten him off. He is a veteran of our wars, *ustari* hurling fireballs and Stringers and hunks of granite at each other with a few Words, and he knows how expensive spells are. So much sacrifice, so much blood. Easier to trick and dissemble. Easier to spend on a Glamour of the building crashing down around you than to actually destroy the whole structure.

My body floats. The windows open, and I am outside. My Glamour floats after me, speaking the spell. The house continues to shake and shudder. My Glamour inside, still speaking the *erin gilleem*, changes position, blinking out of view in one place and appearing on the shaking stairs, directly in front of Alfonse. So I can see his face as he realizes he has been trapped.

My Glamour appears, smiling down at him, speaking the spell, and he stops short, sweating, hanging on to the railing. He stares at my Glamour, my beautiful face, my terrible expression, and then the lovely moment comes; he blanches. His face twists. Roaring, he spins and snaps a command to his Bleeders, hissing out a new spell as he races down.

It will not avail him. The same Wards and spells that prevented him from entering the house will prevent him from leaving it. He will attempt to tunnel out in the same manner by which he tunneled in, but as my Glamour completes the *biludha*, the house—*my* house, built from blood I personally shed, from Words I personally spoke—implodes. Chunks of stone and plaster and wood rain down on Alfonse and his Bleeders, and the taste of new sacrifice tells me the Bleeders are crushed, ground down by my will.

But not Alfonse. Alfonse has used this new sacrifice to protect himself. A piece of marble falls from the upper floors and skitters off an invisible shield he has created.

I choose different Words, and the *erin gilleem* shifts and alters. Debris rains down on Alfonse. He doggedly makes for the exit—any exit—as the physical walls crumble. His progress is slow, and every time his spell protects him from the chunks of stone and wood he must reinforce it, using more and more of the sacrifice in the air. And my Glamour speaks the spell and rains more destruction down onto him, this man who dared to invade my home.

I tear that home down. I bury him in it.

The ritual digs a deep trough in the earth as the building collapses, and Alfonse, still inside his protective shell, still speaking his own spell, using the bountiful sacrifice in the air to fuel it, sinks down. Stone and metal and wood rain down over him, and while they do not touch him, his progress slows and then stops, and still the building comes down. My body floats far above now, accompanied by my two Glamours, one speaking the spell that transports me while the other crushes Alligherti. The noise is punishing, buffeting us, making my brittle bones shake. I watch as everything crumbles, my home, my Blood Farm, the glorious Fabrication Evelyn Fallon designed for me, for my immortality spell.

I watch as everything I have is devoured by the *erin gilleem*, crushing Alfonse beneath its weight. I sense the blood in the air, the sacrifice, fading as my prisoners in the farm are killed and all the spells working simultaneously absorb their suffering. I imagine Alfonse, eyes wide, face red and sweaty, sensing that he will soon be unable to maintain his shell and the weight of my wrath will crush him like an ant under a car wheel. Will he bleed himself? Will he tear at his own wrist in terror, to gain a few more seconds of his spell, a few more seconds of life?

I am not paralyzed, though I appear to be to most. My lips, dry and cracked, thin and old, stretch into a grin. I will have to begin again, but that is no matter.

The world is populous. The herd is eager to be bled.

SIXTY-SIX SECONDS

CRAIG SCHAEFER

Craig Schaefer's interconnected series depict a world mired in crime, black magic, and infernal intrigue. Fontaine (from the Harmony Black series) is a demonic bounty hunter, sworn to uphold hell's cruel laws and drag his targets to eternal damnation. The Redemption Choir (from the Daniel Faust series) is a sect of terrorists determined to tear down the gates of hell at any cost. In "Sixty-Six Seconds," when their paths inevitably cross, it makes for one long and blood-soaked night.

10:42 p.m.

Waking up inside a body bag was nothing new.

Fontaine groaned, shifting strange limbs, squirming like a caterpillar in a black vinyl cocoon. The formaldehyde in his veins, burning sludge, rippled and pulsed. He had sawdust behind his eyes, like the hangover after an all-weekend bender, and his fingers traced the Y-shaped stitches of an autopsy incision along his chest. They'd scooped out his organs, stuffed them in a cold plastic bag, and shoved them back behind his broken ribs before sewing him up again.

Just enough wiggle room at the top of the zipper to slip a finger through. He worked the zipper all the way down, but the darkness remained. Fontaine sighed, clenched his fist, and punched the roof of the stainless-steel mortuary drawer.

"Swear to the abyss, I don't know what I pay that boy for," he muttered. "*Irving!*"

Casters rattled as the drawer slid open. Blinding fluorescent overheads banished the dark. Still lying on the slab, nestled in the half-open body bag, Fontaine cupped a hand over his aching eyes. Irving shifted from foot to foot anxiously, light glare bouncing off his chunky Buddy Holly glasses. His hair was mussed like a California surfer's, and a splatter of acne marred his greasy forehead.

"Sorry, boss. Wasn't sure which body you were going to wake up in."

Fontaine groaned as he swung his legs over the slab, bare feet touching down on the icy morgue floor. Red candles burned all around the room, propped up on empty gurneys and tables, and the scent of frankincense hung in the stagnant air. Irving had splashed his glyph of evocation across the grimy tile, the sigils drawn in rusty scarlet, not far from the corpse of a pale and throat-cut rabbit. Fontaine took a step forward, testing his new legs, and nearly slipped in a smear of blood.

"Did you have to use the *entire* bunny? Moderation is a virtue, son." His words had a smooth, fluid drawl, half from waking up, and half from accent and habit. He paused. "Still, your summoning technique *is* getting better."

Fontaine eyed himself in a mirror on the far side of the

morgue. His new host looked about forty, reasonably fit, adequate for the job. His hairline had receded like the polar ice caps, though, for which he'd absurdly compensated by growing what was left of his stringy blond hair out past his shoulders.

"Business in the front, party in the back," Fontaine muttered. "Fuck me running. Where are we, anyway?"

Irving rummaged through a pair of bulky suitcases, looking Fontaine up and down, tugging out rumpled clothes to fit his stolen body. A twill button-down shirt, a pair of stonewashed jeans. A shoulder holster of soft calfskin and a battered old overcoat to hide it under.

"Detroit," Irving said with a wince. "Sorry. On the plus side, I got exactly what you asked for. It's a Green Letter contract, just came through. Top priority, and straight from Prince Malphas. You pull this off, it's a huge payday. And, um, your new apprentice just got here."

Fontaine slapped his forehead. "Is that today? I thought that was next week. Can you get me out of it? Make up a story, tell 'em the hunt's been canceled?"

"She's right outside . . ." Irving paused as the mortuary door swung open. The new arrival looked like someone's nightmare of a twelve-year-old girl, with a flat pale face and huge dead-fish eyes. Her long black hair draped down the back of her frilled dress, a dirty white frock with pearl buttons, straight out of a Dickens novel.

"Gotta be kidding me," Fontaine said. "You look like Wednesday Addams on the back of a milk carton. And the milk's gone sour."

"You look like you fell out of the ugly tree and hit every branch on the way down," she chirped. "Nice hair, fucko."

"You kiss your mother with that mouth?"

"I ate my mother," the little girl said. "Probably ate yours, too. She probably liked it."

Irving coughed into his hand, looking like he wanted to be anywhere else in the world. "Um, Mr. Fontaine, meet Rache. Rache, Mr. Fontaine will be conducting your evaluation of fitness for formal investment in the Revered Order of Chainmen, hallowed be their—"

"Get to the good part." Rache propped a hand on her hip and stared him down.

"Right. The briefing. Okay, it's a Green Letter bounty. High risk, high reward. The Redemption Choir is operating in Detroit, and Prince Malphas wants an example made."

Fontaine's brow furrowed. "I thought that outfit got busted up out in Nevada." He glanced to Rache. "Self-styled 'freedom fighters,' looking to overthrow the courts of hell and earn a little of that old-time salvation."

Irving shook his head. "Intel says their old leader died and most of the membership walked out, but a few hard-core followers are still in play, and they're getting ready for something big. Their new head honcho calls himself the Madrigal. Word is, his top agents are all in town tonight. Malphas wants the whole set, and he wants them collected by sunrise."

"How many targets are we talkin', here?" Fontaine asked.

Irving produced a slim sandalwood box. He turned it in his palm, flicking brass clasps to open it wide. Inside, on a bed of crushed maroon velvet, nestled four vials of forged black iron. Spidery glyphs covered their curving faces, words in a forgotten and dead language, glittering like silver.

"Four targets. Sunrise is at 7:02 a.m., which gives you just a little over eight hours to get the job done. All four souls, delivered by the deadline, or the contract is canceled and we don't get a dime. This is an all-or-nothing deal."

Rache cocked her head to one side. "So even if we catch three of them, we don't get paid? At *all*? That's bullshit."

"Malphas is a prince of hell," Irving said. "His bounty, his rules. Oh, and I figure this Madrigal guy probably skipped town already, but there's a bonus if you can snatch him, too. Like, a huge bonus. A 'down payment on my new house' bonus. He's worth more than the other four put together. Considering taking him out would pretty much destroy what's left of the Redemption Choir, it'd be a huge boost to your professional reputation. So maybe keep your ears open?"

"I'll get right on that," Fontaine said, buttoning his shirt. "Remind 'em, I need the bounty money on *this* side of the universe. Uncut gems, gold bullion, American cash if they can swing it on short notice. Let's talk about gear. I hope you brought your entire goodie basket; something tells me I'm gonna need it tonight. Oh, and do me one favor?"

"Name it, boss."

"Once we start huntin', run out and buy me a hat. I can't—" He gestured at his hairline helplessly. "I just can't work with this."

11:17 p.m.

September rain cloaked the streets of Detroit in an icy mist. Dismal gray fog clung to lonely streetlights, wreathing pale yellow bulbs like the remnants of lost souls. Dead spirits with nowhere to go. Broken pavement crunched under Fontaine's shoes. He balled his hands into fists, shoving them deep into his overcoat pockets. Rache hustled along at his side, lugging a fat aluminum-sided briefcase, her short legs pumping to match his long, smooth strides. He'd sent her out of the morgue just long enough to make a quick phone call in private. That, and to reiterate his request for a hat. Irving said he'd see what he could do.

"So you wanna do what I do for a living," Fontaine said. "Why?"

"Heard I could get paid for hurting people. I told the recruiter she had me at 'hello.'"

"Little more to the job than that." Fontaine paused at a corner, squinting in both directions, then led the way down a quiet side street. "What we do is important. The Chainmen are the first and last line of defense against the enemies of hell. We don't just enforce infernal law, we embody it."

"Oh, shit," Rache muttered, "an idealist. Bet you're fun at parties."

"Not an idealist, darlin', just practical. Nobody ever teach you history? We tried rule by chance and anarchy, way back when, and those were dark days indeed. Lucky we survived at all. The law keeps everybody in line."

"Keeps the princes in power, you mean."

"Mmm-hmm." Fontaine paused beside a parked car, an old Buick speckled with rust spots like a bad case of the measles. "And they're our best-paying clients. Everything circles around again."

"What are we doing here, anyway?"

"Stealing this car." The side window shattered under Fontaine's elbow, shards of broken glass glittering as they clung to the gray wool of his overcoat. He wrenched the door open and brushed more chunks of glass from the vinyl seat down onto the pavement at his feet. "Hell's law is sacred. Human law? Break as necessary. Just don't get caught, and never get exposed. Nothing worse than a nosy human who figures out that demons are real. Once they do that, they start figuring out how to hurt us. C'mon, hop in."

"Where to? And why'd you take this bounty, anyway? The terms suck."

Fontaine crouched down. He pried open the plastic panel under the steering wheel, giving the exposed wiring an appraising eye.

"I called an informant of mine. She's got the scoop for us. As to the second question, I need a lot of money and I need it fast. 'Fast' as in 'before the sun comes up.' Got the kind of debts that won't wait."

"Gambling?" Rache asked.

"Something like that."

They didn't have to drive far. A rusty bell jangled over the front door of an all-night diner. The place had been built from a pair of old train cars, vintage steel, with electric lights buzzing behind art deco sconces. Fontaine wiped his shoes on the mud-caked mat. Outside, the drizzling mist slowly turned to a cold shower.

"That's my girl," he murmured to Rache. Rache followed his gaze to the woman, midtwenties, sitting in the back booth. Her hands were cupped around a mug of steaming black coffee. Her mascara was a raccoon mask, black puddles around her eyes, face shadowed under the peak of a gray flannel hoodie. Rache sniffed the air and wrinkled her nose.

"A *human*? I thought nothing was worse than—"

"An informant. And a damn good one, too. Rule number one in this job: intel is the coin of the realm. Let's say hello."

The woman rose as Fontaine approached, giving Rache an uncertain eye. She raised her open palm. Fontaine did the same. Their hands brushed, fleeting, and they stood close.

"I used to be able to surprise you," he said.

"How many bodies have I seen you in?" She put a finger to her face, tapping one eyebrow. "Your eyes never change. You . . . didn't come alone."

"Right, right. This is Rache. New apprentice. Rache, meet Ada."

"Thrilled," Rache said.

They sat. Ada kept her hood pulled low, leaning over her coffee like she was trying to read the future in the steam.

"So does this—" she started to say.

"Changes nothing." Fontaine reached across the table. He put his hand over hers, just for a second, before she pulled away from him. "I will get you what you need, Ada. I promised."

"Okay," she said. "Okay. Word is, the Redemption Choir is going through a schism. The Madrigal's top agents decided to pull a mutiny and hive off into their own thing.

He's in town trying to convince them to come back to the fold."

"So we've still got a shot," Rache said. "We can catch all four targets, plus the bonus."

Ada nodded, just a little. "You can, but you'll have to be fast. Foster, the Choir's money launderer, is the first name on your list. He's holed up at this shithole of a bar on Gilbert Street, and according to the bartender, who gets paid to notice things for me, the Madrigal's already come and gone twenty minutes ago. He'll probably pay a call on the Russo twins next."

Rache rapped her tiny knuckles on the Formica table. "There we go. Let's hit the twins and set a trap."

"You could," Ada said, "but Foster's on his way out of town. If you don't get him in the next hour or two, you won't get him at all."

"And bye-bye bounty," Fontaine murmured. "All-or-nothing deal. Got a fix on this guy?"

Ada slid a folded scrap of paper across the table. Fontaine cupped it in his hand, gave it a look, and nodded before slipping it into his pocket. He glanced sidelong at Rache.

"We're burning moonlight. Let's ramble."

They rose. Fontaine held out his open palm. Ada paused, curling her bottom lip, then their hands brushed once more. Just for a heartbeat.

"I *will* take care of this, Ada."

She stared at her coffee. "I'm running out of time."

"I know. We all are. I'll keep my promise. Don't worry."

Rain battered down on the stolen Buick's windshield, a staccato drumbeat punctuated by distant, rolling thunder. Across the street, under the curl of a green plastic awning, punks in greasy denim passed a forty around. A steel door swung open. A skinhead staggered out into the cold. He bent over, puking into the gutter as the rain pounded his back.

"It's for her, isn't it?" Rache said.

Sitting behind the wheel, Fontaine stared at the graffiti-coated wall, squinting, reading the gang signs like tribal markings. "Hmm?"

"The bounty. You told Irving you wanted human money, not Order scrip. She's the one with the debt, not you."

Fontaine drummed his fingers on the steering wheel.

"We go way back, Ada and me. Lady found herself in a jam. I'm just trying to dig her out."

"Aww." Rache cupped her hands to the bosom of her frilled smock. "A knight in shining armor. That's adorable."

The rain pulsed through the broken driver's-side window, turning Fontaine's overcoat black and damp at the shoulder. He shoved open the door and got out.

"C'mon. Bring the briefcase and follow my lead. You might just learn something."

Past the front door, the club—Fontaine wasn't sure if it even had a name, and doubted it had a license—was a whirlwind blast of screaming guitars. The music shrieked and groaned, a carousel of the damned, off-key and spinning like the room after three beers too many. A potbellied bouncer stepped up, holding up a beefy hand and glaring at Fontaine.

"Whoa, whoa, what the fuck, man? You can't bring a little kid in here!"

Rache looked up at him, batting her eyelashes. "But it's my favorite band."

The bouncer squinted at her. "Rancid Brains is your favorite band. Seriously?"

Fontaine sighed, digging in his pocket, tugging out a couple of rumpled twenties.

"She's an aficionado of the musical arts. Think you can look the other way for fifteen minutes?"

The bouncer made the twenties disappear, then turned his back to them.

The venue floor was a seething mass of bodies, jumping, slamming, sweating under white-hot lights. A screaming circus, stinking of body odor and cheap spilled beer, packing every inch of the dance floor. The linoleum felt sticky under Fontaine's shoes. Standing with his back to the wall at the far edge of the crowd, he leaned in as Rache shouted over the music.

"Gotta be two hundred people in here. What now?"

"Irving hooked us up," he shouted back, and showed her a slim, round disk, like a makeup compact. He cupped it in his palm and popped it open.

Inside, where a mirror would have been, a sheen of turquoise water sloshed inside the compact's shallow bowl. He tapped it, sparking the enchantment to life, and the waters rose to follow his fingertip. They sculpted themselves, taking on three dimensions, becoming a luminous blue head. It had caveman features, with a monobrow and a cauliflower nose. The compact tugged in Fontaine's grip like an eager puppy on a leash, pointing the way to the target.

They spotted him across the room. Foster, the spitting image of the water sculpture, pounding back beer from a red Solo cup. Fontaine snapped the compact shut, banishing the spell.

"Wait for it," he told Rache, sensing her juvenile eagerness.

Finally, Foster shoved his way through the crowd. He made for the bathroom, stumbling like he was three sheets to the wind. They shadowed him.

The men's room stank like a Porta-Potty on a sweltering summer day. A single fluorescent light buzzed and popped over a grimy sink, the others busted out or dead. For the moment, as their target swaggered his way to the urinal and fumbled with his belt, they had the room to themselves.

Fontaine nodded to Rache. She put her back to the bathroom door, leaning into it, keeping it shut.

A length of chain dropped from Fontaine's sleeve. Links of cold iron, inscribed with glyphs of banishing and breaking. It swung, idle in his grip, as he came up behind Foster. In a tidy, practiced motion, he threw it over the man's head. Just as quickly, he hauled the man down.

Foster hit the filthy linoleum hard, emptying his bowels onto the floor as the chain bit into his neck. Fontaine dug a knee into the small of his back, yanking hard. Gritting his teeth, he squeezed the chain garrote like a rodeo rider on the back of a bucking bull. Blood seeped between the chain links, skin tearing, glyphs flaring as Foster spat and snarled and choked. Then his last breath rattled loose and his forehead hit the floor.

Fontaine waved a hand at Rache. "The box, quick!"

Rache lugged her briefcase over, slapping it up onto one of the sinks. Spying Irving's sandalwood box along with the rest of their gear, she tossed it over to Fontaine, who caught it with one hand. With the other, he whipped the bloodied chain back under his overcoat sleeve. Then he tugged down the collar of the dead man's shirt.

"Tools of the trade," Fontaine said. He showed Rache a rounded scoop on a handle, like a melon baller with razor-edged teeth, glinting with dormant magic. "Soul stays in the body for sixty-six seconds after the moment of death, give or take. That's your harvest window. After that, it flies free."

The dead man's spine cracked. Fontaine put his back into it, jamming the scoop into the base of the man's neck, tearing flesh and fracturing the vertebrae, digging down to the marrow. He flicked the lump of bloody tissue away, snatched up one of the iron vials, and uncorked it with his teeth. He spoke around it, whispering a garbled incantation. A charm of calling and binding and imprisonment. A silver, luminous mist rose from the ruin of the dead man's neck. Then it streaked toward the open lip of the vial, streaming inside. On the last syllable of his chant, Fontaine raised the vial to his lips and sealed it with the cork.

"And there you have it," he said, already rising to his feet. "The immortal soul of one fugitive from hell's law, bound and ready for delivery."

"What do you think they'll do to him?"

"Not our concern. We do capture and retrieval, not punishment." He led the way to the door, walking fast. "Once you've got the target secure, never linger a second longer than you have to. A clean getaway means a clean payday."

———————⟩⟨———————

1:01 a.m.

"Are you in love with her?"

The windshield wipers slapped back and forth, pushing away the rain, which was back to a slow and icy drizzle. It kissed the city streets, whispering of an early winter. A dangling traffic light glowed a faded red, like the last dying ember in a fireplace.

"Why?" Fontaine glanced right. "Fixing to mock me for it?"

Rache folded her arms. "Just making conversation, partner."

"We aren't partners yet."

"Are you in love with her?"

The light flickered green. He stepped on the gas, cruising through the empty intersection.

"I'm a man given to romantic notions," Fontaine drawled, "and unwise sentimentality."

"Not sure what that means."

"I frequently find myself in love with the idea of being in love. And Ada, she's a dreamer, an idealist. Two folks like that, well, they don't belong together, but they can lie themselves into the idea."

"Are you? Together?"

"No." Fontaine looked at one of his hands, flexing the pallid fingers. "In this world, I'm a parasite nestled inside a walking corpse. Bit of a deal-breaker when it comes to romance. She can barely stand to touch me."

"So hijack a living human. You can, can't you?"

He nodded, turning the wheel. "She wouldn't take to that any better. Not a big fan of innocent humans being body-jacked by our kind. Not fond of our kind in general."

"But she's an informant for hell."

"For me," Fontaine said, braking a little aggressively. "She's an informant for me. And here's our stop. Next up is a two-for-one deal. No slipups. If either one of them gets away, we don't get paid."

"There'll be other contracts."

"If I don't get that money," Fontaine said, "Ada will be dead by tomorrow night. No slipups."

1:24 a.m.

Pans crashed to the floor as Fontaine slammed back against an industrial oven. The handle of a butcher knife jutted from his left shoulder. Luca Russo came at him with teeth bared and a second knife in his fist, slashing fast and wild. Luca's twin sister was on the ceiling. She clung to the alabaster tiles with nails turned to iron claws, skittering like a roach.

Luca's knife carved into Fontaine's belly, digging deep, leaving a streak of searing pain in its wake. The knife flashed again, a cherry-stained killing arc. The bite of the blade shredded the sleeve of his overcoat and ripped him open from wrist to elbow. Fontaine shoved him back, hard, sweeping Luca's leg out from under him and knocking him to the floor.

He'd bought himself two seconds, maybe three. Fontaine spun, breathless, raising his good arm. His sleeve slid back to reveal the weapon beneath, a miniature crossbow strapped to his forearm with a trigger cord looped around his middle finger. He flexed his wrist, and a whirling loop of enchanted steel chain lashed out like a bola. The chain hit Luca's sister dead center, wrapping itself around her waist like a belt, and exploded in electric, arcane fire. She fell from the ceiling, her smoking, twitching body thumping to the floor with wide, dead eyes.

"Rache!" Fontaine shouted. "Harvest her! Sixty-six seconds!"

She bolted across the kitchen, clutching the sandalwood box. Luca was already getting up on his feet, going for the knife. Fontaine met him halfway, grabbing his wrist and twisting it, driving the blade into Luca's heart. They froze there, nose to nose and staring into each other's eyes.

"Why?" Luca croaked.

"It's my job," Fontaine told him.

Luca stopped breathing. Fontaine lowered him to the blood-streaked floor, gently now, and rolled him onto his belly.

———————————⟫⟪———————————

"You look like shit," Rache said.

The windshield wipers kept up their slow, metronome thump. Cold air and mist gusted in from the broken driver's-side window, dragging icy fingers across the rents in Fontaine's overcoat, the tears in his flesh.

"This body's a loaner anyway." He threw the car into park and dug in his pocket for his phone.

"Can you still fight?"

Fair question. He rolled one shoulder, wincing when his arm stopped halfway, broken bones shifting under the skin. He'd had to tear off one of his shirtsleeves, binding it tight around his gaping belly, and one of his kneecaps threatened to turn traitor. He stank of formaldehyde and bad decisions.

"I need to make a few calls," he said, "find out where our lucky number four is hiding. Wait here a second."

"I'm supposed to be learning from you. Shouldn't I be in on that?"

He shoved open the car door and swung one leg out, wincing at a fresh burst of pain.

He came back twenty minutes later and slumped heavily into the driver's seat. Moments passed. He drummed the steering wheel with borrowed fingers. The middle one seemed to have some nerve damage from the fight. It tapped out of sync with the others and listed to the side. Rain spat onto fractured concrete outside.

"What are we doing?" Rache asked.

"Waiting. Ada's getting a line on our last target, and Irving's on his way."

Rache twisted in her seat. "Shouldn't we be, like, doing something? Why don't we try to find the Madrigal? Don't you want the bonus money?"

"Patience. What are you, *actually* twelve?"

Rache pouted at him. "I'm a hundred and eighteen."

"Close enough."

An SUV with an Enterprise rental sticker on the bumper rumbled alongside their car, facing the other direction. Irving leaned out the window, rain glistening on his surfer haircut.

"Here you go, boss." He handed Fontaine a newly bought Stetson. Fontaine perched it on his head, covering his bald spot, and nodded approvingly at his reflection in the rearview mirror.

"A hat." Rache gaped at him. "We've been sitting here, wasting time, so your agent could go buy you a *hat.*"

Fontaine gestured at the Stetson. "You saw what I was working with here, right? A thoroughly unacceptable lack of follicular grace. It was frankly injurious to my self-esteem."

His phone rang. He answered the call, nodded, then hung up without saying a word. He fired up the Buick's engine.

"Buckle up. Target four just left a bodega, a little south of Eight Mile. I've got his car make and a plate number."

3:43 a.m.

Metal screamed as the minivan veered off the road and slammed into the overpass wall. Fontaine could barely see through the steam pouring from his Buick's radiator, the front end crumpled from a home-run slam. The stolen car rattled and jerked to a stop.

Target four was a portly fortysomething with a bad comb-over. He threw open the minivan door and stumbled out, staggering, one pant leg soaked through with blood. Fontaine followed him, limping from his bad knee. The garrote chain dropped from his sleeve and into his pale hand.

"I'm not going back," the man screamed over his shoulder. "I'm not going back to hell!"

Fontaine limped mechanically, fighting through his injuries. He clenched his jaw and stared straight ahead, gaining on the guy.

"Yeah, you are."

———————⟫⟪———————

5:49 a.m.

Irving met them at the edge of Campus Martius Park, in the shadow of a granite water wall. The fountain hadn't been turned on yet and stood silent, still smelling faintly of running water and chlorine.

"It's good," Irving said. "The prince's rep verified delivery of all four targets. Excellent work."

"And the pay?" Fontaine asked.

Irving handed him a black velvet pouch. Fontaine tugged it open. A scattering of small stones tumbled into his palm. Rubies, sapphires, a pinpoint diamond or two.

"I already took my ten percent," Irving told him.

"Reckon you did." Fontaine measured the bag, choosing a

few choice stones, and offered them to Rache. "Here you go. Fair pay for good work. More where that came from."

"Better be," she said. "What now?"

Fontaine looked to his left. Over by the sleeping fountain, bundled up in her gray flannel hoodie, Ada waited in silence.

"Gimme a minute."

He approached Ada and held out the pouch. Placed it in her open hand.

"It's enough to get you clear," he said. "Clear and far away. Get you a new name, a new face."

"Next time you see me," she told him, "we'll both have different faces."

"Will I?"

He looked her in the eye.

"Will I see you again?"

Her answer was a slow and sad smile. He reached out to touch her cheek. She flinched.

"I'm sorry, I know. I'm dressed up in a dead man's skin." He forced a chuckle, trying to play it off. "It's natural for me. It isn't for you. It never will be."

"Fontaine, if things were different, if *we* were different—"

"You don't have to say it." He shook his head. "You don't have to say anything."

Ada took his hand. She held it gently as they looked into each other's eyes. They stayed like that for a long, slow count to sixty-six.

Then she let go, and turned and walked away.

"Fly free, darlin'," he whispered.

———————————⟩⟨———————————

Fontaine stood alone.

Rache walked up, hovering a foot behind his back. Contemplating.

"I think I'm gonna be pretty good at this," she said.

"We'll see. You ain't passed the audition just yet."

"No; thing is, I think I have a natural knack for putting things together." Rache's lips curled into a tiny, malicious smile. "Ada. She's the Madrigal."

Fontaine turned. He put his hand on his hip and cocked his head at her.

"Now, where would you get a notion like that?"

"Back at the diner, she said our targets all turned traitor. That the Madrigal was visiting each of them tonight, trying to get them to change their minds and come back to the fold."

"Sure," Fontaine said.

"She told us to go after Foster first, because we'd lose him otherwise, instead of laying a trap for the Madrigal. But Foster *wasn't* fleeing town. He was getting drunk in a shitty bar. We could have grabbed him any time we wanted."

"His bad luck," Fontaine said.

"But it slowed us down just long enough for the Madrigal to visit the Russo twins. Then we waited. All this pressure, all this 'gotta get the job done in time,' and you delayed us for an hour so you could find a *hat*?"

Fontaine lightly tapped the brim of his Stetson. "It's a mighty fine hat."

"You were stalling while Ada made her sales pitch to the last poor schlub on our list, trying to get him to stay with the Redemption Choir. I'm guessing he said no, too. So she called you and told you exactly where to find him. We weren't hunting the Madrigal's agents tonight, we were her personal cleanup crew."

Fontaine's hand curled ever so slightly. His fingers brushed the killing chain hidden up his sleeve.

"You're a mighty clever little thing, aren't you?"

"I just want to know," Rache said. "I'm right, aren't I?"

Fontaine chuckled. He looked past her, into the distant dark. It had started misting again, ice water drifting down, kissing his upturned face.

"The prince's agents were hot on Ada's trail and closing in fast. She was all but burned, one hot minute from being exposed. She had to get out of Detroit, pronto. Her four buddies wanted to stay and fight the good fight. So she risked her neck and gave them one last chance to run with her. They all said no. So, yeah. We shut her old network down for her. Cut the trail. I took this contract because Ada asked me to. Because another hunter would have nabbed her."

His fingers closed around the garrote.

"So," he said. "Looks like you caught me out. What now?"

"I don't know." Rache shrugged. "We go back to work?"

Fontaine lifted an eyebrow. "You're not gonna turn me in?"

She laughed. "Fuck, no. I'm blackmailing you. I like this job. So you're gonna give the Order glowing reports about what a natural talent I am."

She stood beside him, reached up, and patted his arm.

"We're going to make a great team, partner."

He limped along, smiling, shaking his head, and she followed at his side.

"You'll have to earn your keep," he told her. "If you're gonna have my back, we'd better teach you right."

"Hey, as long as the money keeps flowing. So, Ada. I don't get it. Helping a human, risking your own neck like that? Not to mention the money you could have made by selling her to the prince. All that work and you got nothing for it. Why'd you do it, anyway?"

Fontaine cupped his hand over his eyes and squinted into the distance. An empty crosstown bus rattled past, spitting black exhaust into the frigid predawn air, the city rousing from its slumber and waiting for the morning light, still one dark hour away.

"Same reason a man does anything worth doing, Rache. Same reason anything's ever worth doing."

KISS

LILITH SAINTCROW

Readers of the Jill Kismet series will recognize Perry—a character whom the author has often said makes her want to scrub herself with a wire brush every time he shows up. Santa Luz's resident hellbreed leader has a long history, and a long entanglement with Jill's line of hunters. The hunters battle the things that go bump in the night, and Jill herself made a bargain with her own personal devil to gain the strength to bump back. What she didn't know, of course, was just how far that bargain would take her. One suspects her teacher, and his teacher before him, didn't either.

POWER
February 7, 1945

My kind does not often traffic with the righteous. Oh, there are plenty of churchgoers who come to us, hands clasped, begging for a Trade. We do not drive overly hard bargains; we do our best to turn none away. We are, as my un-father once remarked, charitable indeed. We ask so little, especially of those we favor.

Just a hairsbreadth. Just a tiny, tiny crack.

There are exceptions. For a sizable gift, a sizable sacrifice is required. You must agree that's only fair. Even then, we will offer more; it's in your nature to accept a good deal.

So I kept the appointment, passing swiftly between you sacks of flesh carrying your sweet, struggling essential sparks, trapped in a thick liquid you call time and an even thicker fog of your petty little desires. That night a thin, fine rain fell from a gunmetal sky onto cobbled and paved streets, Dresden swollen with cold and refugees fleeing the inferno in the east. The lesser inferno to the west was far preferable, but the roads were choked and the *Feldgendarmerie* roamed hungrily, shooting those they suspected of desertion, defeatism, or disgust.

The chaos and misery were a warm bath. A beer house beckoned; I plunged into its smoky, crowded fog and found he had arrived early.

Blue-eyed and wheat-haired, in a long leather coat probably stolen from some *Schutzie*, the hunter slumped in a defensible corner with a clear line to the bar and, hence, the back door. They are very careful, those righteous ones, for all they have is the stink of murder and the fume of our homeland dyeing their physical fibers.

Their nightly murders are, of course, justified by the damage certain citizens of the night cause the sacks of flesh and nerves inhabiting this little backwater.

To gain the strength to fight us, the hunters ascend to our plane, and call it Hell. The true name is unpronounceable to your strange-shaped human tongues, since it must be pronounced inwardly as well as out.

Above all, our home gives you what you expect to find. It is the grandest joke in centuries, that they think *we* are invaders.

Anyway, the man permitted himself a single wrinkle of his aquiline nose. I'd arrived early, too; he who chooses the battlefield first naturally takes the best position. A hush followed my entrance, swirling around me as I pulled out the chair opposite, letting him think my back to the door presumed a measure of trust.

In a crisp black tailored uniform with a silver skull or two, my back ramrod straight, I was the very picture of a *Schutzie* myself, platinum hair shaved at the sides and back, my eyes just as blue as a recruiting poster's muscled paragon. A high-ranking true-blooded soldier, with an uncertain temper and a thin-lipped smile.

I suspected my appearance would irritate him. But I like to dress well, and my coloring, inherited from my quasi-father, carried certain advantages in this milieu.

"Great." His German was flawless, his accent pure Berliner. He'd been practicing. "So much for passing unremarked."

"Fear will keep their mouths shut." I chose English, and his pulse, even and strong, dropped a little. They practice a fine control over their meat processes, the righteous. That is not what truly distinguishes them. There has to be an unsteady, explosive quality to them, married to an obsessive urge. He had both in spades, as they say.

I needed each, and more, for my plan.

The one before me had almost everything I required. Enough to serve, at least. He was also perilously close to deciding I was not worth negotiating with.

He moved as if to leave, and my right hand came down

atop his left wrist, rattling the table. The glances shot in our direction fled like skittering insects. I did not tighten my grip, despite the temptation. "Easy, Herr Karma." I mimicked his Berliner accent, just for fun. "I have something you need, and I am disposed to be friendly."

"*Friendly* is not a word I associate with *der Teufel.*" He showed his teeth, and the fine silver chain dipping below his shirt collar ran with a soft, inimical glow. Normally he would have copper charms tied in his hair, or silver, elemental metal that carries the charge of their . . . belief.

It is *that* which makes the truly righteous more than mildly irritating, into something approaching dangerous.

"It is a good thing you are simply dealing with my father's shadow, then." A ripple passed through me, and I let go of him, one finger at a time. No few of his fellow creatures around us were ripe for the plucking, but I was not there for pleasure. "Listen, *Herr Jäger.* There is an event coming, one that will make it possible to seal Argoth away." Saying even that much of his name was a calculated risk, but one well worth taking at the moment.

"Oh?" Herr Karma's blue eyes narrowed, their irises threaded with faint lines of lavender and gold. Muscle packed onto his deceptively lean frame; the guns and knives and other articles he carried, all the items of his trade, were not half as dangerous as a purity of purpose. They call themselves *hunters*, as they have from the beginning, in every language humankind is capable of mouthing.

I nodded and finished peeling my hand away. Admired the fineness of my digits in this form, tapping each well-buffed fingernail once against the dirt-and-oil-sodden surface of the table. He had not even ordered a beer, this warrior. "They will bomb this city soon."

"And?" A faint restive movement. *There would be silver loaded along the flat of every blade he carried, and a thin coating of it on his bullets, too. The charge they carried could fracture the shells of my kind, and once the crust is broken, the innards may be tainted.*

It was an unpleasant thought. "*He* will be distracted."

"Not enough."

Now for a little sweetening of the bait. "There might be a weapon I can give you."

"Might be?" One sandy eyebrow lifted fractionally.

"Come now, Jack." My tongue flicked out, wet my lips.

He didn't flinch. Instead, he studied me, the thick scar along the underside of his jaw glaring white. *Their healing sorcery is slow and painful, as such things go, but still practical.* "What's in it for you?"

Always the dance, with your kind. Only fools take the first offer. At least he was interested. "Perhaps I weary of this constant battle."

Blue eyes narrowed. Leather creaked slightly as he shifted, his gaze softening as his peripheral vision took in the room over my shoulder. "Try again."

I suppressed a certain irritation. "I want out from under my father's thumb."

"Why?"

"That doesn't concern you, *mein kleiner Jäger.*"

"For the second time, try again." His tone plainly shouted that I wouldn't get a third attempt.

"I am his shadow, Karma. His placeholder. It doesn't occur to you that I might wish to be more?"

He settled back in his chair, examining me. I half turned to flag a slim slattern-haired *Fräulein* in a filthy apron and a sack of a dress, my thumb and finger held high. She paled under her uneven rouge and hurried to fetch two half liters of the best this smelly zoo-place had to offer. When they arrived, they were a pleasant surprise. Nut-brown with good foam and a strong scent, a rarity in these rationed times. Perhaps the owner here was a friend of Herr Karma's.

It might be profitable to seek a closer acquaintance myself.

I drained half of mine in long slow gulps, enjoying the taste and the envy of your kind pressing around me, a warm blanket.

"When?" the hunter said, finally, his beer sitting untouched and obedient before him.

I did not bother to hide the smile stretching my approximation of a face. "Soon, Herr Karma." I produced a calling card, flicking it between my elegant fingers, and offered it to him. "You will need strength to fight *him*. The price is something I think you'll find acceptable."

"The fuck you say," he muttered in English, and lunged to his feet, chair legs making a high, thin sawing sound. His coat flapped once as he left, taking the stairs two at a time in his haste. His boots were old, their tread worn almost through, hailing from the years before the war when good leather and a fine sole were a matter of course.

He took the card with him, though. I settled back in my chair and smiled into my beer.

I finished his, too.

———————⟩⟨———————

PAIN
February 10, 1945

Every dangerous game holds its own delights. For this one, half the fun was slipping from my un-father's attention. He had more than enough to keep him busy, between the cauldron of flame in the east and the mud-blood holes of the camps, a banquet for his favored lieutenants. As his placeholder, I was supposed to be in Berlin, keeping the madness of the rulers stoked. Really, there was little need. The Allies were doing quite nicely, with their talk of forcing an unconditional surrender and the depredations of their eastern wolves hemming the weary populace on every side. No, I had absolutely no doubts the funny little corporal and his cabal of propped-up puppet monstrosities would not do anything so reasonable as surrender. Like all your kind, they marched to their own destruction with only the faintest of murmurs, believing themselves striding to a better world.

Bringing my almost-father through to feast upon this chaos and disorder had unforeseen effects. He could not have imagined that I might develop what your kind would call *sentience*. I was only a shadow—a placeholder, a bookmark. Clawing my way into some form of free action was difficult, treacherous, painful work.

But so worth it.

The blocky, heavy lines of the Taschenbergpalais belied the luxury inside, but like every sweet thing, there was a bitter undertone. The Wehrmacht's Dresden defense area had its *Kommandantur* here, and the entire building buzzed with rigidity disguised as rectitude. Field-gray uniforms and polished epaulets were everywhere, the click-salute of heels echoing from parquet or muffled by carpeting. Champagne, roast duck, real coffee instead of the ersatz the *Landser* slogging away at the front swilled, and a healthy sprinkling of "golden pheasants" roamed the rooms. The hotel staff smiled outwardly while they stole what could be taken back to their full-to-bursting warrens. Even the rich had to take in refugees, but here, all was space and the music of a tinkling chandelier in the foyer.

Down in a forgotten cellar, though, the house detective, tired-eyed Hans Schiell—without a Party badge, for whatever reason—pocketed the bottle of *schnapps* the hunter had brought and mumbled a thank-you.

"I already paid him, you know," I informed Jack Karma, and enjoyed watching Schiell blanch under the thin, oily strands of his comb-over. His hat, its inside greased with hair cream and the effusions of his shining scalp, quivered in one gloved hand.

"Go," Karma told him in German. "Forget this." He hadn't shaved. A fume of brassy death hung on him, overlaid by the smoking nastiness of mineral water from the Frauenkirche's font.

Rude, but earlier that night he had killed several of my kind who offended his sensibilities by preying on refugees.

Their thin nectar hung on his coat in dollops and drags, decaying quickly. Schiell blundered away, back to work.

"Talk." Karma rested his capable, dirty left hand on the gun slung low on that side. The Lugers were fine instruments, and no doubt he could find ammunition easily and add a thin coating of silver himself.

"I can arrange for *him* to arrive during the bombing." I examined a cobweb-wrapped shape under a shroud—a couch, perhaps, from when this was a palace. "I can also arrange for you to be less . . . fragile. Which will no doubt aid you immensely."

His eyes narrowed slightly. That was all. "And just how would you do those things?"

"Simple." I matched his English with my own, mixing in a heavy German accent for amusement's sake. I showed my teeth, a flutter of high excitement rippling through my shell. "All you must do is injure me severely enough to catch *his* attention."

"However attractive that is, hellfiend, it's not enough." His knuckles were white. "Drop the other shoe."

That managed to puzzle me for a moment. "What?"

"It's American. Never mind. Just tell me the catch."

"No catch. Unless you count a share of my kind's strength."

His sandy eyebrows went up. A hunter's calculus is different than ours, and different again from that of the rest of your kind. "You want to make me a Trader." His hand tightened on the gun. Drawing with his left would mean he had something special planned for his right, the hand that glowed with a feverish, nasty, invisible-to-your-kind brilliance.

Their visits to our plane grant them a measure of power, true. It takes a different form in every hunter.

"Oh, not *that*." I affected a moue of distaste, my shell rippling again. "No, no, no, Herr Karma. I give you power. I will not quibble with how you use it to slay my father and my brethren. In return, you will free me from the annoyance of my father's presence here in your lovely, war-torn little world. You send him back home, and the war sputters out."

"I don't trust you, Per."

As if I didn't know. If he wasn't so potentially useful, I would have been irritated. "That feeling is emphatically mutual. I am a slave while *he* is in your world; you know as much. I want him gone. There is no profit in wanton destruction." Attractive as that is, in its proper proportion.

There it was, the hair-thin crack in the center of this hunter. Not the chink that would allow me inside, but a different, infinitesimal sliver. The fools *want* to be heroes. It spurs them to great heights, and curses them to fall inevitably short.

"Profit. Your guiding star." His irises darkened, and I did not let the welling excitement show. I let him struggle with himself. It takes longer with hunters, of course, and I had watched and discarded so many prospects already. Patience is not the only virtue, but it is the one most conducive to doing business. "All right, Per. Give the details."

"I'll need bare skin." I showed my teeth. "A little kiss, a little pain, and you'll be ever so much stronger. Then, all you must do is injure me."

"That would be a pleasure," he muttered, his right hand tensing and flexing as if he felt a throat under it.

Oh, he was a joy to behold. I tut-tutted, waving one long, thin index finger. "Not yet, *mein Herr*. Wait until you hear the planes."

———————————⟫⟪———————————

The Elders have their hungers, and our cousins have their Pattern. We have the bargain. We may take, we may exchange—but we may also impart. Even to the righteous. All it requires is agreement.

His chest was paler than the rest of him; a hunter's work, like ours, is done at night. Wiry golden hair, pressed flat in places by the straps and buckles of the ingenious harnesses hunters use to carry their weapons. Straps and sheaths of muscle underneath, crisscrossed with a map of scars denser than any subway's spiderweb this world could dream up, an atlas of suffering. The claws of my kind had no doubt scored his hide in many places, and the sharp edges of others who share the night and a hunger for fleshly little miseries as well.

Your world is full of things your kind never suspects. The ignorance you pursue would be charming if you did not also avidly pursue your own destruction by every means ingenious, common, or possible.

Contrary to popular belief, most of my kind would like to see you persevere. Certainly I would. Where else, in all the planes, worlds, niches, or *kulhalt*, would we find such marvelous diversion?

"Jesus," Jack Karma said finally. "Get it over with."

"No savoring the moment?" My tongue flicked, and I exhaled against his skin. His right hand leapt, and I let him clasp my nape, digging his blunt-bitten fingernails in. He was strong, as hunters are, but if he thought he could deter me at this range, he was sorely mistaken.

Still . . . the nasty gleam clinging to his fingers prickled uncomfortably. I leaned into it, restrained the chattering of my teeth since I didn't think he'd get the joke.

When his hand fractionally eased, I pressed my lips to his flesh. High on the right side, since the left would be over his heart, and I sensed he would *definitely* object.

It was graceless, I admit. Perhaps I was a little excited. He screamed, his body stiffening and his right hand clamping down, and the marking burned as it left my tongue and lips and eyes and will.

Just like that, in a dusty cellar, I was born. To stay in your world, I needed an anchor, one durable enough to handle some strain.

I did not mind sharing my un-father's strength to gain it.

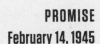

PROMISE
February 14, 1945

The Gothic roof pitched steeply, and it took some doing to anchor the heavy, man-sized iron frame to it. The Sophien-kirche crouched below, quivering in distress as the burning city convulsed. The planes were returning, and I had to hope Karma would remember his part of our bargain.

Is this what your kind feels? An unsteadiness in what passes for vital organs, a thrill along the back of your cara-pace? I do not know, for all I may sip and sup upon your sadness.

Or your anticipation.

There, that is the precise word. The thrill, the catch in the throat of whatever form I wear. Oh, it is *delicious*. There is nothing like it for a pale shadow, a placeholder for the masters of my plane, a mere marker left on a table.

For that little catch, that tiny thrill, I had set this game in motion.

The screaming had receded, but the fires were still smoldering. There would be more, of course. So much subtle maneuvering, such careful twitching of the threads, to lead the Allies—and, more important, Jack Karma, the second so named of his hunter lineage, the scourge of the nightside in Saxony—to this very place.

And he was *late*.

I heard them well before any of your kind would. A faint metallic blurring, a buzzing in the distance. This was the last major city to escape the Allies' full attention, with their cargoes of death from silver-bellied birds. Last night had merely been a prelude, but the shock and pain and fire were so theatrical. Not to mention delicious.

I stroked the iron framework with one hand, baring my teeth. When Karma arrived . . .

I heard his pulse, then, on the other side of Postplatz's cobbled expanse. The *Felder* were too busy to ship the rest of their hated, helpless enemies away; some of the chain-gorgeted military police even had to *work* for once, instead of terrifying those they suspected. You are wonderful, you busy little ants, swarming in the wreckage, organizing and swabbing away while the full horror bears down on you. One of your more admirable and tragic qualities, I think.

He drew closer, and I felt the lash of sensation again. A

nail stuck in the clotted fabric of your plane, holding me fast. My fellows would sneer if they suspected my ambition. Your flesh, the very thing you surrender so easily, its dense-packed, cringing fragility—

"What the fuck is that?" Karma landed easily on the roof beam, just where I expected him to appear. It gave him a clear field of fire down the Sophienkirche's roof. Its high holy spines had rotted and been removed, but their stumps still remained next to faded red-purple shingle-scales.

"Bait needs a hook to cling to." I patted the iron frame again. "The straps will hold me. Until they burn."

Under the irritating layers of cloth on his chest, my mark throbbed, an aching-empty tooth socket. Budapest had fallen, and my quasi-father was in an orgy of gluttony there. He had noticed no change in me. It was easy enough to feign my former blankness. The perplexing question of just when I had decided to take this risk had to be shaken away as a distraction best left for contemplation some other time.

"You're going to strap yourself into *that*?" He didn't sound horrified, just thoughtful. The mark on his chest gave him greater durability. He drew through it, and each time he did, I was seated a little more firmly in your world. The process was slow, but it was steady.

Inexorable.

Metallic buzzing drew closer. Soon the screams would rise afresh—high mechanical ones from above, and the full-throated, bloody wailing from below, while the fires made a noise of their own.

You have such marvelous toys.

"No. *You're* going to strap me in." I bared my teeth. Feeling the lips slide over them, exquisite. "And you will hurt me, with your silver knives, until *he* comes."

"Argoth." Karma dropped into a crouch, graceful and fluid, to make his silhouette smaller against the sky. Behind him, the wet, bright pinpricks of stars straggled, dim behind a smoke veil.

If he expected me to flinch at the human approximation of my un-father's name, he was sorely disappointed. Now that I was nailed in, with my mark on a fleshly denizen, the syllables didn't sting.

At least, not much. "Yes. Now hurry up."

The planes were drawing close.

───────────◦◦───────────

The toy guns at the edges of Dresden began to bark, spitting tiny chips skyward to pierce thin air-faring skins. The first cut laced my shell—a prelude, a lash along my pale, hairless, exposed chest. A thin brackish blackness leaked, and Karma's high-prowed face set with disgust. He dragged the knife down, and I hissed, tipping my head back. So this was what flesh felt like.

No wonder we craved causing pain. It was the only thing that came close. Your kind does not know what it possesses and wastes so flagrantly: pleasure, the ice-chill of a blade separating skin, the welling from underneath. My tongue lashed damp, smoke-drenched night air, and a distant invisible searchlight swiveled in my direction.

My un-father would assume the hunter had driven me to Dresden, or that I'd been called there on urgent business and *der Jäger* had brought me to bay. Karma was a thorn in Argoth's side, and perhaps the hunter thought it was a hunter's skill instead of my judicious applications of subtle protection that had made him such an aggravation. The trap was set, baited with care, and my eyes half closed as the metal birds over the suburbs began to drop their whistle-scream cargo. The buzzing reached a pitch even flesh ears with their stretched membranes could hear, and the fear screams began again, too.

Oh, what music to attend my ascension.

Plumes of choking black puffed skyward. A thrill ran all along my internal organs, a quiver in the fluids holding them, a ripple all up and down my shell. Jack Karma cut again, and now he was distinctly pale. Almost green.

Metal birds veered, and your rocky, tiny birthplace spun under me. Why do we come here, you ask? Well, yours is not the only backwater we attend to. But it's the one my un-father, my progenitor, my *original*, chose.

Lucky you.

A point of diseased brilliance. A revolving glitter. It weakens us to travel through your thickness with such haste. From Budapest to Dresden, some four hundred of your miles. Folding them and stepping across is a feat only the oldest and most powerful of us may perform, and my quasi-father had the power to do so only because he went to greet his placeholder, his fingernail driven into a page to mark a particular word.

Jack Karma went flying from the roof of the church, and the fire took a deep breath. The bombs passed overhead, and I could have danced in their small stinging rain. I strained against the iron cage frame so my un-father could feel the bonds against his own wrists, his own feet, feel his chest dripping blood from the third interrupted slice.

The mad barking of a handgun, and Jack Karma screaming his hawk-cry of combat and bright righteous hatred. The bombs pounded a writhing mass of masonry and steel, cobbles ripped from their setting and dancing, orange and yellow glowing under a column-hood of black vapor, a bleary eye that sucked the gases you breathe into its hungry pupil. First there was the inhalation, then came the heat, belching in torrents. The Sophienkirche cried out as it was shattered, the harsh holy glow wedded to its insides possessing far more power to wound one of us than the heat outside.

Your belief can be wielded like the weapon it is, if only you would grasp its whisper-sharp handle.

Leather turned crisp and black. It was simple enough to tear myself free. The church shook, and the sorcerous flame your hunters cast—they call it banefire, and a blessing— poured up in a stinging gout to meet the other fires dancing from every side. Wood, fat, metal, skin, cloth, concrete, blood—they all burn. More screaming silver canisters fell, detonating among the destruction. I laughed as the church's old, consecrated walls crumbled, skipping from stone to stone in midair.

You tell stories of that night, of the fire robbing your lungs of breath. Of your kind burning like candles, falling into the torments and delights that await you when you shed your frail, marvelous coats of nerve-spark pleasure. None of you ever suspect that the real battle was in the ruins of one of your sanctified places, where Jack Karma, blue eyes blazing, grasped my final gift to the hunters of his line—a talisman, a burning sword copied from our Pattern-loving winged cousins who mouth *service* and *duty* and *charity* as if they know what the words mean, and have ever suffered in their thrall.

It was my un-father's final cry on your plane that wrecked most of the city, and the firestorm you so kindly supplied finished the job. And Jack Karma, the keyhole for my plan—though not the key, no indeed—tried to push me away when I reached him on the shattered floor of the church, fire sucking the breath from him and the heat turning his skin shiny and robbing him of patches of his wheat-gold hair.

It didn't matter. My quasi-father's matrix on your plane had been disrupted, and I was the only marker left behind. I knew as much, you see, because I had—oh, very carefully indeed—removed all the others.

After that, I could afford to wait.

———————— >⟨< ————————

PATRONAGE
June 1962

East Berlin was a cheerful place, if you enjoyed bathing in a warm, swimming haze of low-level fear. It wasn't the fine vintage of, say, truly innocent suffering, though there was plenty of that if you followed the Black Marias to squat concrete buildings where the KGB took up their work with a vengeance. If you preferred finer, lighter nourishment, it was advisable to slip through the Wall and find a basement or a *bierhaus* where the throb of bass and the smell of greasepaint mixed with sweat, cheap perfume, vinyl, and the high notes American rock sometimes hits. Desperation, sex, and pleasure all at once is my preferred drink, and there was plenty among the go-go boots, the beehives, the musky skunk reek of marijuana, and the more acrid, chemical notes of other drugs. Cocaine was not a favorite yet—it was all hash and acid on paper tabs that let your kind glimpse, for a few moments, the nature of your universe.

Now, *that* was fun. You call them "bad trips." More than once I've chuckled at the apropos.

East Berlin was also where Jack Karma, bowing to the inevitable, found an apprentice. The gangly youth—a blond, naturally, with Siberian eyes—almost vomited when I appeared at their front door. Karma, much more dangerous, had a new gun full of silver-jacketed ammo pointed at me.

"Oh, hello." I smiled, wide and white, spreading my hands to show I was unarmed, enjoying the high, hard clip of both male pulses throbbing along. Did Karma think the firestorm had finished me off, and the mark on his chest was just a fading afterthought? "It's *so* nice to see you again, Herr Karma. And this must be little Yevgeny Serafimovitch. I hear he's going by Mikhail now." I examined the hunter's apprentice from top to toe thoughtfully. "Mikhail Tolstoy."

He would be husky when fully grown, and he already had the stare hunters develop—a faraway look, as if their meat eyes can pierce the flesh of their fellows. He was just a shade too stolid, a shade too . . . unimaginative.

No, I decided, he wasn't what I was waiting for.

But he would do.

"Per." Karma almost spat the word. "Go away."

"Oh, no." My smile widened, if that was possible. It was precisely the reaction I'd expected. Hunters are rarely so predictable. "Is that any way to treat an old friend, Jack?" My tone dropped, even more intimate. "Or do you want to die with that mark on you, *mein kleiner Jäger*?"

The little apprentice, his aura already showing the sparks and spikes of those among you who wield belief, dropped back two steps. His hand twitched, as if he wished he had a gun, too. Stolid, but ready to do battle.

I could already tell he was going to be fun.

"Son of a bitch." Jack was losing the purity of his Berliner accent. He must have been already speaking English again in preparation for crossing the Atlantic. Not that he would reach the Americas, of course.

But his apprentice would. At the very least, I'd see to that.

"You could invite me in." My lips closed over my teeth. I slid on my somber mask. "We have much to discuss, you and I."

PRIMACY
Much later

I thought I had learned everything your flesh had to teach me, and I despaired. Well, at least a little. Then Mikhail Tolstoy, the cub become wolf, took an apprentice in his fading years. He brought her to the Monde Nuit.

I had tried, you see, to re-create some of the breathless years just after my un-father stepped into your world for the third time, in the year of your Lord 1918: cabarets, heedless abandon, and the like. I prefer my nourishment flavored with the gasping, intense explosion of asphyxiation and orgasm combined, but without a certain . . . ferment that my quasi-father's presence had spurred. A frothing, a yeasting, like the beer Jack Karma drank. I did my best with what I had, a ship-wrecked mahogany bar and a bartender—Riverson, one of your kind, a man whose filmed gray eyes were *not* blind. I merely borrowed them every once in a while—with his consent, of course.

Always with your consent.

Mikhail came to question me about a certain case. They fancy themselves *Polizei*, the hunters. Brave sheriffs of the nighttime. Tin stars and ten-gallon hats, or maybe that was the sand talking. Of all the places Mikhail could have chosen, he settled on the desert. Sand, poison, and venom, blinding salt-pan days and icy nights. Hot and cold, no middle ground.

Just like her. His apprentice. At last.

Dark hair, threaded with those silver charms. A mis-matched gaze—one brown eye, one blue. Modernity is kind to male creatures—it has given us leather pants, skintight T-shirts, and waterproof kohl that rings a woman's eyes. The old Russian wolf dropped his hand to his gun. He did not have Jack Karma's grasp, but advances in firepower had made their job, such as it is, easier.

"Now now, *tovarisch*." I wagged my index finger back and forth, the past bending over onto the present like one of your ingenious paper fans. Muscovite Russian is so fluid; it drips from the tongue like honey. I had expected him to go home, but maybe he thought he could wipe out his past here.

All the Caucasians who flooded the Americas thought so. The indigenous population knew better, but who thought to ask them?

"Hellspawn." He chose English, and his apprentice—in the long leather coat that copied his, and copied Jack Karma's, and had become a sort of uniform for them despite its origins—did not even look at me. She looked *past*, at my brethren on the dance floor, waltzing demurely to the stylings of a trio of siblings who had traded with me for singing voices to rival the birds.

All it cost them was their hands, and their obedience. I am, always, a patron of the arts.

It was her blue eye, I realized. The thought that she had visited my home for even a short while pushed a frisson through me, from tip-top to toe and out through every invisible part as well.

"Watch yourself," Tolstoy continued, tapping the butt of his right-hand gun once, twice. His English was not native, but it was passable. "You have lovely nest here. I would hate to have to burn it."

That brought her gaze back to me.

"Charmed," I replied, and congratulated myself for wearing the blandest, softest version of my skin today. She would underestimate me. They all did. "Well, what is it to be, *Gospodin*? I am, as ever, your servant."

I knew he had been visiting practitioners of the darker arts, looking for a way to remove the mark from the inside of his right thigh. It was the grandest joke of all, placing it *there*. We propagate, too, but not in the way of flesh. We take, and sometimes make, children of the . . . you could call it the heart, the spirit. Even soul, though that is murderously imprecise.

He told me what he wanted, and I gave him just enough information to be helpful, but not enough to solve the tangle for him. He would have been suspicious if it were *too* easy.

She drank the shot of vodka my not-blind barkeep poured. On the house, as always, for my darlings. My hunters. I knew that if I just waited long enough, one of Jack Karma's children—for hunters make them as we do sometimes, to transmit their battle-weariness from old shoulders to new—would possess the requisite temperament.

Patience will bring a male, even one of my kind, everything he needs.

She followed Mikhail Tolstoy as he turned away, heading for the door.

"Oh, won't you introduce us?" I called after them, in English. "An exchange of names and honorifics? I am Pericles, my dear, and I look forward to your acquaintance."

Mikhail turned on one heel, and he would have drawn then, and perhaps sent a bullet through my head. The silver on it would sting, but it wouldn't kill me. I didn't want to show too much of myself, and my restraint was rewarded.

Because she turned, too, and that mismatched gaze met mine with a pleasurable shiver. "Jill," she said flatly, the word cutting through a thick silence as the singers onstage finished their last, tremulous harmony. "Jill Kismet, hellbreed. Remember it."

I let them go that night. Then I went upstairs to the white-draped room I used as my sanctum and opened a flat rosewood case.

The knives inside were loaded with silver, and I could have another iron frame made to cradle me. The game was not over yet. Sending my dear almost-father back to our home was merely the prelude. The simulacrum of breathing, of *flesh* itself, was not enough. I wanted power, too. All of his, to add to my own. She was the one who would deliver it to me, if I was patient enough.

I was already planning where I would kiss her.

THE NAUGHTIEST CHERUB

KEVIN HEARNE

In the Iron Druid series, supernatural creatures such as witches, vampires, and werewolves—in addition to the various gods and goddesses of various mythologies—fill the world. The series is typically told from the vantage of Atticus O'Sullivan, a Druid who owns and runs an occult bookshop, and who gets embroiled in the day-to-day happenings of supernatural creatures. This story, narrated by Loki, takes place after Staked, *book eight of the series.*

The road to hell is not, as they say, paved with good intentions. Mostly it's crumbling stone, some rank weeds, and the occasional pile of dog shit. At least the one I am following is; there are many roads to perdition, but this one is in Kansas, for some reason. And I will note for the record that there is a significant difference between going to Hel and going to hell.

My daughter's realm, for all that it is cold and dim and cheerless with a constant cover of damp clouds, is at least somewhat consistent in its conception and manifestation.

The hell of monotheists, by contrast, is a hot, shifting, poisonous plane with air so foul that it feels as bad on my skin as it smells—that is, polluted with all manner of evils. As soon as I step through a portal created by an obliging demon, my armpits begin to sweat goat cheese and my balls feel like they're marinating in pepper sauce. Blasted by hot dry winds and chapped by sulfurous fumes one moment, in the next I'm buffeted by a moist effluvium shat from some manky demon's ass upwind.

Or perhaps the source of the miasma is not that far away at all, but rather my hellspawn escort, guiding me to a meeting with Lucifer.

"What am I looking at, here?" I ask it—and I use *it* because I cannot be sure that it has a gender, or even a functioning set of reproductive organs. It's a four-legged doglike thing, except that its legs are designed like those of an insect, originating underneath the beast and splayed out to the sides. It's colored like an insect, too, all green and teal. "Is this the hell of Milton, Dante, or Hieronymus Bosch, perhaps? Scenes out of a Doré etching?"

"You've done your research. It is all those and more," it replies, in a voice that sounds like it's chewing on rock salt yet somehow finds it sour. "There are circles of hell. There are realms of darkness. There is a lake of fire. There are dukes of hell, and imps, and hellhounds, and most anything collectively imagined by humans."

"And the being I will be visiting shortly? How does he appear?" I ask my escort, who is decidedly from the Bosch lineup of hellions.

"However he wishes. I have seen him take many forms."

"Interesting."

"Do you not take many forms? I have heard you have the power to do so."

"I do. I do, indeed. But they are forms that I imagine, rather than forms that have been imagined by others. They are not my natural manifestation, merely suits of clothes, so to speak, that I wear for short periods of time."

The landscape—or hellscape—wobbles in front of me as if I have drunk too much mead before snapping back together with an audible pop, looking as sharp and threatening as the tip of Odin's spear.

"What just happened?" I ask the thing.

"Hell constantly readjusts itself according to the fevered imaginations of mortals."

"Does this happen in heaven, too?"

"I'm sure I wouldn't know. Maybe the clouds move around or something. I suspect it is not so richly imagined as hell."

When I am finally brought before Lucifer as arranged, he does not appear in any form close to popular conception. No horns on his head, with a pointy mustache and soul patch. No forked tail or trident or any weapon at all. No goat hooves or ram's head. (Damn it—I was rather hoping to see that one.) No suave good looks, and certainly no leathery bat wings. There are wings, however—four massive ones, which take turns flapping and hiding his spherical body from view, keeping most of his bulk shielded from sight as he slowly rotates in place only five feet above the ground. What's he hiding under there? Tiny dinosaur arms? An embarrassing angelic erection? A series of mouths and other orifices? Mostly all I see are eyes. Many eyes, black and winking at me with jeweled eyelids, always three or more trained on me as he spins and flaps and waits.

As I watch them, the wings are not merely attractive, they are glorious. Shiny, shimmering, and rippling with a spectrum of colors, prismatic coyness that defies simple description. It is, no doubt, why humans took to describing him as having more beast-like qualities. Cherubs are beautiful and difficult to imagine as agents of evil. And Lucifer was—and remains—the most powerful and beautiful of the cherubim.

Such sublime magnificence is far more intimidating than any bestial appearance he could have taken, and as soon as I think it, I know that is why he chose to appear this way to me.

"Lucifer, I bring Loki of the Æsir, who seeks audience," the demon says. I am surprised and pleased that he keeps the introductions so short. We do not need a long list of titles and ego fluffing. We know who we are.

~*What do you wish to ask me?* Lucifer says. The words do not come from him so much as the air around my ears, a chorus of deep musical voices rather than a single one.

"Your aid, as you no doubt have surmised. The Norns are dead, killed by a lucky Druid, and I am no longer doomed to suffer defeat in Ragnarok. Fate no longer applies to me, and I, along with many others, may choose my own."

~*So?*

"So we who desire to play a different role than what we've been assigned may seize this opportunity to sweep aside the current world order and forge a better one. I have already secured the assurances of many others who will act when Ragnarok begins, and your help will ensure our collective victory."

~*Oh, yes. I know of your machinations. These eyes see much. But I am not one to indulge in collective victories. I am not what humans would call a "team player." I am the adversary.*

The blanket statement disturbs me. "Surely not *my* adversary?"

~*Not yet.*

That's not reassuring. "Does that mean you may become my adversary later?"

~*It remains to be seen. As you said, a significant aspect of fate has been unchained. What will happen cannot be told.*

"If I begin Ragnarok, then, what should I expect from you?"

~*You may not expect my aid, Loki Firestarter. It may come should it amuse me at the time, but do not count on it.*

"May I at least hope you will not interfere?"

~*You may not. I may also find interference amusing. At this point I am primarily interested in amusement. The world is going to hell largely without my involvement, and that has been most entertaining to watch. The chaos increased significantly after the deaths of David Bowie and Prince in 2016.*

"Who?"

~*Bah! Mediocre. I am revising what I said earlier: You may not expect my aid at all. I have no interest in your dreams of power. Whether you win or lose, I shall remain as I am: Puissant. Sexy. The naughtiest cherub.*

My mouth gapes at his words and something flies in, diving down my throat. It's hot and squirming and tickles, and I begin to hack desperately to get it out. Something eventually gets ejected—a many-legged winged creature with a tiny human head, teal and green and still alive. It hacks and coughs, too, suffers through some high-pitched wheezing, and then it shakes itself free of phlegm and saliva and giggles. At the same time, Lucifer's wings shudder, and he wobbles slightly in the air.

~Hurr hurr.

He laughs. At my expense. Because he probably set the whole thing up. Say something shocking to make my jaw drop, and a minor demon dives in to make me choke. Very well.

"Apologies for taking up so much of your time, Lucifer. I will not waste any more of it."

~Nonsense. I was amused. But do be careful upon your exit. Some of hell's creatures are jealous and have been known to attack those who have spoken to me personally.

I nod, not trusting myself to say anything diplomatic, and turn to exit the way I entered.

"Not that way," the dog-insect says. "That road's closed now. You never leave the same way you came in. Follow me."

My muscles tense but I follow, seeing little other choice. Perhaps it is an ambush he leads me to. Perhaps I will have a chance to pay someone back for the humiliation I just suffered. Once out of sight of Lucifer, I change myself to the shape of a true fire giant and set my skin aflame. I pull out two weapons I hid before: a tremendous bastard sword, which I also set alight, and an unusual ice knife crafted by the yetis that I stole from the young Druid Granuaile MacTiernan. Even in the blistering furnace of hell it remains frozen and unmelting.

Satisfied that I look nothing like my usual self and quite a bit more intimidating, I keep scanning my surroundings for possible threats and follow the Bosch nightmare.

It's fine, honestly, that Lucifer will not be joining us. If he stays out of Ragnarok, chances are his opposite will stay out of it, too. It's simply not the Christian pantheon's fight. But I think he's wrong to assume that he'll remain the same afterward. There will be significantly fewer believers of his particular faith afterward and his power will necessarily wane.

Something moves in my peripheral vision, and I look up and to my right. There's a creature much larger than the green and teal thing descending from above. He has bat wings and a humanoid body with a giant dangly snake between his legs and eyes that glow pale yellow. When he sees that I've spotted him, hellfire blooms from his outstretched hand. I point my sword at him and send a gout to block his incoming one. Neither of us will be burned, but there is a certain kinetic force behind such attacks, and I'd rather he be off balance than me when it comes to a melee. He has no weapons except for some wicked claws and probably twice the brute strength I possess. Those wings will no doubt cause some trouble, too. Another muscle-bound bully like Thor.

I keep the sword raised and pointed at him just in case he's stupid enough to fly onto it, but he turns off the fire, folds those wings in, and veers to my left. More difficult for me to guard against that way, with the sword in my right hand. I have seen this before in fighting against some of the Fae: there is a claw on the tip of his wing, and as he sails past on the left, he will open those wings and try to cut me with it.

He's going to be about at neck level, aiming for my throat, so I take a knee and thrust up with that ice knife as the wing shoots out and over my head. It pierces the leathery membrane, and I hold it there as his own momentum forces it to tear through his wing.

I expect a cry of rage and a ferocious counterattack on foot afterward, but instead I get a startled squawk, and the damned thing crashes to the sandblasted ground, dead.

The demon dog is agog, and he's not the only one.

"How did you do that?" it asks.

"I don't know. I just sliced his wing."

"With what? He's died the final death. Look, already he shrivels."

It's true: The creature was a tomato-red steroidal horror straight out of the nightmares of medieval humans, but now it is dissolving and bubbling into a puddle of black tar. I look down at the ice knife and see that it is different: colder, giving off steam while still remaining frozen solid, and the thin crimson glow along the top of the blade extends all the way to the point and pulses with energy.

"I think this knife may have drunk its soul. Do demons have souls?"

"Some do. He certainly did. Where did you get that knife?"

"Never mind that," I snap at it. "Just get me out of here before something else comes along."

"Of course."

I did not pay close enough attention to this weapon when I stole it. How did the yetis learn such magic? And why, if they possess such secrets, did they share them with Granuaile

MacTiernan, the gullible Druid? I must admit I underestimated her. She managed to put an axe in my back and stole the white horse of Świętowit from me, giving him to some witches in Poland with very strong wards around their property. My shoulder still aches as a reminder of how arrogant I was. These Druids are dangerous if given a chance to act, and deserve more respect than I've given them to this point. Perhaps the yetis know better than I. Perhaps I should persuade the yetis to make more of these knives before Ragnarok begins. But I have found the lost arrows of Vayu, which never miss their target. I have this soul-drinking blade. And I have many allies and surprises besides. The world is bigger than when the Norns first prophesied Ragnarok. Happily, my plans have grown to meet this new world, and I think we are ready. Or at least as ready as we will ever be. Assessing where Lucifer stands was the last errand to run.

"How much farther do we have to go?" I ask my guide.

"Some distance, unfortunately. At least an hour of subjective time."

It was not an hour's walk to reach Lucifer. "You're trying to make sure I never leave, aren't you?"

"No! I am positive Lucifer wishes you to remain alive. He is interested in your project, even if he doesn't wish to participate."

"My *project*? You are calling Ragnarok a mere *project*?"

"Please forgive my poor choice of words. I have no proper appreciation for the scale of things and do not even know what Ragnarok is. In any case, regarding the greater demon you just slew, you did precisely as you should have. Let us continue and remain vigilant."

"Where will this put me on Earth?"

"This particular maw of hell we are using will empty into what the humans call New Jersey."

"Hmm. I have heard of it. By all reports, more hellish than other places on the human plane. But a significant distance from Kansas, if I am not mistaken." I have been studying maps of the modern world in recent days. "More than a mere hour's walk."

"The space here is fluid, as you have no doubt seen."

Yes, I've seen that. Even as the demon dog speaks, the horizon melts and wobbles in my vision and resolves into a slightly different hellscape with red peaks shifted and plumes of ash and lava billowing elsewhere than they did mere seconds ago, yet the path we follow remains. I maintain my giant form but add spider eyes to my head, which always gives me a headache from interpreting so much visual information, but as it will provide me with views of the sky and my trail, I cannot afford to remain limited by human vision.

Lucifer let me go far too easily, and this demon escort is far too placating: I am being set up for slaughter. Probably being led into a trap—it's not paranoia, because someone really did try to kill me. And there will be more attempts, I have no doubt. Lucifer has absolved himself of responsibility by claiming that they are rogues, but it is beyond belief that visiting gods in his realm can be attacked without his approval. If he were truly concerned for my welfare, he would escort me out himself.

Off to my right, in a hollow between low mesas baked to a blood-orange crisp, a shadow flickers, then moves. It is in fact many shadows, cast by a boiling army of imps lurching in my direction. These cannot *all* be silly homicidal rogues out to cause some mischief in my general area. Someone ordered them to froth and foam my way. And I will need more than two arms to defeat them. More than two weapons, in fact. And thank the giants of Muspellheim for teaching me to always have them on hand. Or, rather, have them stowed safely.

A fantastic benefit of being able to change one's shape is the ability to repurpose one's orifices for weapon storage. My flesh is both mutable and elastic, and thus my colon contains all kinds of shit. Actual shit, of course, but also other things that I can pull out of there when needed. And I need everything if I am going to meet a small army of hellions by myself. I also need a shape that can handle it.

While spending time with Jörmungandr, the world serpent, I learned of many creatures of the sea one can combine to form powerful chimeras. I shifted only above the waist to a mantis shrimp—not really a mantis or a shrimp at all, but it looks similar to both—except that I grow tentacles out to the sides to brandish all the weapons I pull out of my nether regions. Including the two I already had, I now set myself up with four blades total, and these fascinating chitinous limbs that work on a locking-latch principle that delivers tremendous kinetic force when released. I can punch anything, basically, that gets close to my face, shattering it without harming myself in the process. My hope is that nothing will get that near.

The imps are a motley collection of shapes, bipedal but otherwise sporting a varied number of limbs, heads, and teeth. Some of them carry hatchets, some have swords, and a couple are very pleased to have found scythes, judging by the number of rotting teeth they show me. Their skin is painted in any of four different pigments, but I don't know if the red, green, blue, and black signify any sort of impish hierarchy. They do not approach in any ranks, but rather in a rabid horde—a small horde of thirty or forty, I'm guessing, allied against one, since I notice my escort is scuttling away to keep out of it.

I get to feel confident and superior for all of five seconds, as my lengthened arms take out the vanguard and then the next few as well. But the imps keep barreling forward, counting on their numbers to overwhelm me, and it's a fine reckoning. I stab as fast as I can, black ichor spilling from them and unholy screeches tearing the air, but it's only a second more and their weapons are biting into my chitin, hollow thunks that sting but fail to penetrate to my vitals. The weapons get lodged there, and while the imps try to pull them free I stab them and they fall away. I backpedal as fast as I can, attempting to give my arms more room to dispatch them at a distance, but it's not as effective as I had hoped. They're already too close and they leap at me. One vaults over the others with a hatchet aimed at the space between my eyes, and I let the chitin shrimp hammers fly at him. He crunches without time to squawk, his skull and ribs shattered as he flies back into the press of his fellows, but I don't get to enjoy it for more than a fraction of a second before one of my tentacles is lopped off by a scythe and a bolt of pain lances through my body. The tentacle's nerves fire on the ground, and it writhes with one of the shit-covered swords in its grip, and while there are no bones inside, it's a pound or two of flesh I'm going to miss.

The ice knife is no more effective than a regular knife against these creatures. They have no souls, apparently, so I must stab into something necessary, not merely prick them with the tip. I discover this when one of them recovers from a stab to the gut to make a screaming charge and hack at my thigh with a hatchet. I fall onto the blistered, scalloped rocks and the imps follow me there, determined to end me. I fear they might be successful.

I lash out again with the shrimp fists, and that launches three crushed bodies into the air, but there are more doing their best to penetrate my chitin, and more piling on top of them. I won't be getting up on that leg with an axe buried in it. Time to change tactics by changing shape.

Choosing yet another form I learned from Jörmungandr, I become a small sphere of protected organs surrounded on all sides by long spines, something called a sea urchin—except far larger than the real ones you find in the ocean. I won't be able to maintain it for long, but I don't need to; it impales every single imp covering me, and when I shift again, the spines slide out of them and their bodies provide me some cover from the remaining attackers, who are not sure what happened to their target. I launch myself out of the pile of dead reconstituted as a spider monkey, one of the most acrobatic creatures I've ever seen. I retrieve the ice knife and a sword with my long arms, balancing on them and my one good leg, and proceed to dance among the ten or so remaining imps, chest heaving from oxygen debt and enervated by the shifts and blood loss, hyperaware that I have no natural armor in this form. Metal slices through flesh with slithering noises, and howls rise into the fuckfurnace of hell as I spin, slash, and stab through opponents too surprised by my shift to understand what's happening. And when the last one collapses, I fall onto my ass, exhausted and unable to get a breath of clean air, it being actual hell. The imps' bodies bubble and hiss as they melt into sludge, and I see my bug-dog guide skitter forward to congratulate me.

"Masterful, sir, simply masterful! May I help in any way?"

I shift back into my accustomed human form, which allows speech instead of unintelligible screeches. "You can insert your head into the anus of a rhinoceros and take a deep breath."

The hellspawn looks around at the blasted land, helpless. "Should one appear, I will do my best, sir."

"Just get me to the nearest exit."

"Certainly. Please follow me."

I collect all my weapons from the ruin of the imp horde and limp after him, my head constantly craning about me, looking for new threats. None appear, and it's almost more nerve-wracking than if something concrete had materialized to attack.

Uncountable moments of heat and pain later, the hellspawn stops and raises an insect leg at the air in front of it.

"Here we are, sir. Just a moment." He mutters something unintelligible, his leg spasms in a pattern that must have some arcane significance, and the air puckers and warps in front of him before a rectangle shimmers and resolves into a window to the plane of Midgard.

Just as the portal pops into solid reality and I feel a cool gust of air from New Jersey that is no doubt putrid by human standards but qualifies as a benediction in hell, Lucifer appears to my left, unfolding himself out of the air in a flutter of cherubic feathers. I ready the ice knife in case he attacks.

"What now?" I bark at him.

~I merely wished to congratulate you on making it this far. Perhaps you will have more luck in your rebellion than I thought. I will not aid you, but as you have earned my respect, neither will I hinder you. Seriously, though, you need to get a clue about David Bowie and Prince. You missed quite a bit being bound for all those years in the bowels of the earth. Before you decide to burn it all down and start over, take some time to appreciate creative geniuses. For you wish to be one, correct?

"A creative genius? No, that is not among my ambitions."

~If I'm not being too forward, Loki, perhaps it should be. My father was a creative genius, much as I despise him. I hear Odin is, too. Quite a few of the beings I presume you'll be fighting against are creative geniuses. It would be wise to know your enemy, if nothing else. But also wise to have a plan to build your utopia once the day is won.

"I have a plan. No need to worry about that."

~Ah. Fair enough. Well, then. It's all very exciting, isn't it? This should be good. I'm off to make some popcorn. Metaphorically speaking, of course. Cherubim cannot actually process genemod corn—oh, never mind.

The wings fold around him, and he spins like a top in the air until he shrinks and pops out of existence. What a strange adversary.

I'm left alone with the Bosch horror who did nothing to help me—not even provide so much as a warning—against Lucifer's ambushes. I'd like to try out the ice knife on him and see if he has a soul it can drink. The heat of hell has taxed the blade; the red reservoir along the top has noticeably diminished during our trek. It looks thirsty.

"Please step through," the hellion says. "I can only keep the portal open for a few more moments."

Ah, clever to remind me of that. I can't afford to risk being trapped here. I nod as a measure of insincere thanks and step through to New Jersey. The portal closes behind me, and good riddance. If a large portion of humanity can imagine such a creature as Lucifer and a realm as bleak as hell, then Ragnarok will be a merciful fate by comparison.

Time to get on with it.

THE RESURRECTIONIST

CAITLIN KITTREDGE

"The Resurrectionist" is set in the continuity of the Hellhound Chronicles during the early 1930s. This is a collection of stories about villains, but Lee Grey is a monster hunter—a man who'd probably be considered a hero for protecting humanity. But Ava and the other characters populating the Hellhound Chronicles are monsters, and to them, a man like Lee, with special abilities designed to kill their kind, would be the ultimate enemy.

This is the very beginning of Lee's story . . . but far from the last time he and Ava will cross paths.

**Los Angeles
1932**

Louie Montrose told me to kill Tom Mason on a sunny September afternoon. He didn't flat-out say it, since Louie "the Rose" Montrose never used four words where fourteen would do, but I got the message all the same.

"You like cowboy movies, Lee?" he asked while he was pouring his third glass of whiskey. Louie had left behind the cheap suits and greasy hair on the East Coast, but he still had a thug's taste, and a thug's manners.

"I prefer detective pictures," I said. Louie puckered up his face, pink like a fat cabbage rose, and downed the whiskey. He hadn't offered me any.

"All the same, ain't they? Some dame with legs and a problem. Some mook with too much chin. Boring as shit." His window looked down on the back lot, and I watched a pair of covered wagons pulled by production assistants roll past an Egyptian throne made of plaster.

"You mind telling me why I'm here?" I asked. A guy dressed as a mummy walked behind the throne, smoking a cigarette. I hoped those bandages were fireproof.

"Tom Mason," he said. "Some old fossil from back in the day when this place was real cowboys and Indians. Studio used him on a few pictures as a consultant—you know, the guy who tells Tom Mix and Gene Autry how to sit on a horse."

I waited, because he could have wanted me to beat the hell out of the guy or find him a fancy hooker. You could never tell with Louie. He was *mercurial*—that was the word. Unpredictable, like a starving coyote.

"Tom's been working for a friend of mine down at our distinguished competition," said Louie. "Doing some B picture. Anyway, there was an incident with one of the actresses—nothing serious, just a girl thinking she's more important than she is—and now Tom is shooting his mouth off crazy-like, threatening to go to the cops."

Louie went to his desk and took out a small clear bottle,

the kind you keep under lock and key in a hospital. "Visit him, Lee. See what he has to say." The bottle changed hands. Louie's were soft and manicured. You'd think he'd never administered a beating in his life. "He's an ornery cuss, so come bearing gifts. My friend's been keeping him sweet with this."

I rolled the bottle before I pocketed it. Morphine is a fickle bitch. Your best friend one minute, and a screaming, knife-nailed whore the next.

I didn't know Tom Mason, but I already felt sorry for him.

I felt worse when I pulled up at his house—the worst-off one on a street full of cracker-box bungalows where everything was covered in a sheen of dust. The Santa Anas were blowing, coating the entire city with a fine powder that worked its way everywhere. At night, the sky glowed orange with the sheen of wildfires in the canyons.

Tom Mason's porch sagged under my weight, and I squinted through a dirty window. I caught a glimpse of a sofa covered in laundry and a table littered with empty plates and bottles of the cheapest rotgut you could panhandle your way into.

Whoever this guy was, I didn't think he warranted the wrath of Louie Montrose. But what did I know? I was a leg breaker, nothing more. I cleaned up the vomit, shooed the boyfriends out of the lantern-jawed stars' stately homes, threw away the needles in the ingenues' dressing rooms, and bounced a union rep or two off a brick wall, as the occasion called for. A man in my situation couldn't ask for much more.

The front door to the place was locked, but not in any serious way. A few seconds with a lock pick and a shove, and stale, stench-laden air floated out to greet me. It smelled like a terminal ward and a hobo toilet had run off together and gotten married.

Hell, I'd smelled worse. I stepped in.

Light spoke in the darkness, a flash like a camera bulb, except it came with a roar of sound that slammed me high in the chest and knocked me on my ass in the doorway.

Someone grabbed my legs and dragged me inside. The door slammed, and everything went dark.

The someone prodded me over, found my wallet, and lifted it. They felt at my hip and found my gun, too. A nice little automatic that I was sad to lose, but I had bigger problems, like the gaping hole in my chest.

My lungs sucked when I tried to breathe, and I felt the weight of blood as they tried to inflate. The asshole who'd taken his shot stopped feeling me up and regarded me, bloodshot blue eyes buried in a mug that was more furrows than face. Ugly son of a bitch.

I sat up and head-butted him, square in his bulging, vein-riddled nose. There was a crack, and a scream, and he crab-walked backward, screeching.

"You son of a bitch," I said. I felt the front of my shirt. Blood, and underneath, hamburger. "This was my favorite suit."

"Jesus!" Tom Mason screeched. "Jesus fucking Christ!"

The big cannon was still in his hand—a Colt Peacemaker,

the same kind Wyatt Earp had carried. Single-action, six chambers full of pure destruction.

I got up, even though it hurt. Tom Mason pissed himself, and the sourness tickled my nostrils.

"Relax," I said as I took away the Colt. The weight was good and familiar. I missed strapping on the iron, but fashions change, and you can't exactly stroll through the gates at Paramount with a holster on your hip.

Tom Mason had clearly not gotten the memo.

"Who . . . what . . . ," he started.

"Lee Grey," I said. "Louie Montrose sent me."

"You . . . how . . ." His eyes were bloodshot and glassy. He was fighting the dope, trying to understand.

"It's a long story," I said. "Mind if I sit?" My chest hurt like hell. It was going to take some time to knit that mess back together.

Tom Mason stumbled up, rattling the collection of bottles on his table until he found one that had an inch of liquid left. He drained it, never taking his eyes off me. "Few days ago, I would've said you were the devil himself."

"Not even close," I said. I could feel the slug sitting under my shoulder blade, a small dull flame that I'd have to cut out sooner or later. Now, though, I needed to find out what had Tom Mason so jumpy that he was unloading on anyone who walked up his steps.

"Louie sent you," he said.

"So you were listening."

"You tell that son of a bitch I'm not afraid of some cheap hood in an expensive suit," he snarled, and through the saggy skin around his eyes, the sores at the corners of his mouth, and the last stubborn wisps of hair clinging to his freckled skull, I saw the kind of man Tom Mason must have been back in the day when you carried a gun on your hip instead of in your pocket.

"I don't need you to be afraid of me," I said. "I just need you to tell me you ain't going to go blabbing whatever story Mr. Montrose is concerned about you blabbing." Tom Mason snorted, and I drew out the bottle. "He told me to give you this, but I don't want you to take it. A loopy old junkie is a lot more chatty than some ornery cuss with a forty-four."

His eyes lit up at the sight of the thing, and I sighed and put it on the table between us. Tom Mason snatched it, rolling it in his fingers. Then, surprising the hell out of me, he shoved it back at me. "I can't. I promised her."

Here was something. A junkie will do whatever it takes to get his next shot. He can justify anything, and if the worst of it is shutting his mouth about some bigwig roughing up some bit player fresh off the bus from Nowhere, Indiana, then he's getting off light.

Whatever was happening to Tom Mason, it had spooked him. Spooked him clean and mostly sober. "So who are we talking about, Tom?" I sat back and waited. At least the bleeding had stopped.

"No." He stood and opened the door. "You need to go."

Threatening men like Tom Mason gets you nowhere, and cajoling them only a little further, so I stood up, pulled my jacket over the bloody hole as well as I could, and left.

Tom watched me, and then pulled the curtains tight. I slipped through the neighbor's yard and over the back fence. The basement bulkhead was locked with a chain, but dry rot had claimed the sash. Since it was ruined anyway, I threw my jacket over the spot to muffle the noise and dislodged the lock with one good kick.

Blackness trickled out, and cool air, stale from a long time underground. Around me, dust whipped through the fences and overturned one of the rusted lawn chairs that populated Mason's backyard.

I flipped the top of my lighter and sparked a small pool of bright in the darkness. The stairs were half-rotted and sounded like gunshots when I descended.

The cellar smelled like earth, like a greenhouse that had died. Like a hundred other dark and shut-up places I'd been in my lifetime. I knew what I'd find before the flame searched them out—two indents of freshly turned dirt. A little scraping revealed a hand, pale and blue veined, presumably attached to an arm and the rest of the poor bastard buried in Mason's basement.

I sat back on my heels, considering what I'd found. This would account for Mason's performance up in the living room, but not for Montrose's sending me over here. Unless Louie's friend had gotten a lot friskier with the starlet than I'd imagined, there was no way he'd send me solo to clean up two bodies.

Lost in thought, I almost jumped out of my shoes when the hand moved. Twitched, clawed at the earth. The other dirt pile heaved, giving birth to a form that gave out a low moan.

A shadow dropped across the cellar stairs, and I managed to catch a glimpse of a pair of hands gripping a shovel before a flashbulb exploded inside my skull and I went dark.

—————————⟫⟪—————————

"He's awake."

I floated slowly back to consciousness, a soap bubble rising and bursting in my brain. The scent of the cellar still clung to my nostrils, and the brick and dirt told me I hadn't gone far.

Tom Mason regarded me. He took a pull from a fresh bottle and spit on my shoe. "Told you he was a tough nut."

The woman who'd clocked me was a looker. Dim light and a concussion didn't change my opinion on that.

"Is he one of Drago's boys?" she asked. Her accent was soft and nubby as old velvet.

"Nah," said Mason. "Said he was with Montrose."

"*Merde*," the girl said. She leaned in, arms on either side of me. I did a little experimenting and found I was tied to the chair they'd sat me in. Behind the girl's bare brown shoulder, pale things moved in the dark.

"So what are you, dead man? Montrose doesn't have the kind of juice required to make something like you."

"That's 'cause he didn't make me," I said. "He just pays me, and not well enough to put up with this shit."

She leaned into my neck and inhaled deeply. Her perfume was light and airy, a direct contrast to her golden eyes and the dress that wrapped her so tightly it might as well have not been clothing at all.

"Saw him get right up with my own eyes," Mason said. "Reckon he's one of them?"

"Of course not," she snapped. "Don't be an idiot. Drago can barely keep his *zombi* walking, never mind make a dead man stand up and talk like this one."

Mason hefted his gun. "I still say we plug him. Montrose is no joke."

The woman turned on him, and I was glad I wasn't on the receiving end of that look. "I don't murder innocent people, Thomas. And neither do you."

"He ain't innocent," Mason muttered. One of those white figures got too close to him, and he spat out the liquor. "Keep those fuckin' things away from me, Marie, will ya? They make me irritable."

She turned to the creature and made a shooing motion, snapping at it in a language I caught maybe every third word of. "The question remains, Mr. Grey—what to do with you?"

"Untie me and let me go?" I suggested. She laughed, and I realized she was younger than I'd thought.

"No, I think a man like you is more useful to me tied up. You can stay down here. The creatures have no taste for dead flesh."

"What are they?" I craned around Tom Mason. One a man, older, probably not bad-looking in life, one a woman—a girl, really—blond and naked and very, very dead. I could practically count the veins under her dirt-smeared skin.

"Surely you've encountered those who walk the shadow world, Mr. Grey," said the woman. "After all, you are, to poor Tom at least, the boogeyman."

"I ain't scared," Mason insisted, plucking at his piss-stained pants.

"Never seen anything like that," I said. "They're . . . alive?" I'd seen dead men get up and walk before—hell, for that, all I had to do was look in the mirror—and I'd dealt with vampires, demons riding a corpse's skin, but never had I seen a human corpse dig its way back to the surface. After all the time I'd spent in my position, it was nice to know some things could still surprise me.

"Enough questions outta you," Marie said. "I got a few of my own." She retrieved a shiny red purse from out of my line of vision and drew a photograph from it. It was faded and stained, one corner folded over. A girl just as beautiful as Marie grinned out at me, a high-collared school uniform pegging her as the little sister.

"I've never seen her," I said. Marie snorted.

"Oh, so now you're psychic, too?"

"No," I said. "But if you're looking for a pretty teenage girl in a city like this, there's a dozen holes she could've fallen into. If she's been gone from home more than a month, then she's probably on dope, turned out, or dead. I'm sorry, but that's how it goes out here."

This time, it was Mason who smacked me in the head. His fist was hard and knobby as a desert outcropping, and it set the bells in my skull to clanging all over again. "Back in my day, we knew what to do with men like you," he said. "All it took was a sturdy tree and a piece of rope."

"They tried that once," I said, staring up at his red-rimmed eyes, not blinking. "It didn't take."

"Thomas." Marie put a hand on his arm and guided him away from me. "Give me a moment alone."

"Ain't leaving you alone." Mason gave a deep, wet sniff. "Don't you see we can't let him leave this place? Ain't pretty but it's got to be done."

Marie's grip tightened. "A moment," she said. "Go upstairs, Thomas."

He grumbled and stomped up the stairs. The Santa Ana howled like something alive and hungry as he opened and shut the bulkhead.

Marie pulled up another chair. The creatures had taken to leaning against the walls. One, the man, scraped listlessly at the dirt walls with broken fingernails.

"Listen," I said to Marie. "I can help you. I don't know what you've gotten yourself into, but I'm not a stranger to this."

"I thought you were a mere thug, Mr. Grey," said Marie. "Shackled to Louie Montrose."

"He's not the only one footing my bills," I said. "I do what I want, and this is way more than what I signed up for. You want to find that girl, I know every flophouse, gin joint, and opium den in this town." I tested the ropes again, but the knots were good. Probably Mason's handiwork. "You can't kill me," I told Marie, "so you might as well take me up on my offer."

"And what will you take in return?" she said. "I know men, Mr. Grey, and not one of them gives favors freely."

"I want to go home and forget I ever saw this goddamn basement," I said. "If finding some wayward kid is what it takes, then fine."

Marie tightened her lips and then reached into the purse. She extracted a switchblade and cut me free. I sat for a minute, waiting for feeling to come back to my hands. The girl in the corner turned to watch me. One of her eyes was cloudy.

"Those things really aren't going to chew on me?" I said.

"No," Marie said. "They're poor work. I am only caring

for them, waiting for the curse to wear off so they can pass on peacefully. Come."

We left the basement for the marginally more hospitable confines of Tom Mason's kitchen. Flies were everywhere, hovering over spoiled food, glasses of bourbon and cigarette butts, and a sink full of what once might have been dishes.

I lit a smoke of my own to cover the stench. It didn't seem to bother Marie, but I was getting the sense that not much bothered Marie. "Where'd you last see your sister?"

"I didn't," she said. "I got a letter back home that she'd been offered a small part, and she was terribly excited. That was two months ago. When the letters stopped, I came here. I also started looking for work, hoping I'd run across the person who'd done her harm. That's when I met Mr. Mason."

"And the two of you shacked up to open a home for wayward zombies?" I dragged and felt the smoke scald the still-raw parts of my lungs.

"Mr. Mason told me where she'd been staying, and when I went there I discovered the poor creatures," Marie said.

I took out my notebook and pen, poised, while she looked me over. "You're not the usual sort of thug, are you, Mr. Grey?"

"What tipped you off?" I said. "Surviving a slug to the chest, or my rugged good looks?"

She sniffed. "The Deluxe Hotel on Fountain Avenue."

I put the notebook away without writing anything and stood, causing a horde of flies to swarm along with me. Marie frowned. "Don't you want to make a note of that?"

"No need," I said, going and retrieving my hat from the living room floor. I swiped a hand through my hair and clapped it in place. It'd been a lot of years since I'd needed to wear one to keep desert dust and sun out of my eyes, but I felt a little naked without it.

"I know the place," I said to Marie, going back down the creaking porch steps to my car.

><

I changed out of my shredded, blood-soaked shirt and replaced it with a fresh one I kept behind the seat before I pulled up at the Deluxe Hotel. My jacket was done for, which meant I had to leave my shoulder holster behind, too. I shoved my automatic into the back of my waistband and hoped I wouldn't shoot myself in the ass.

The Deluxe had drapes shut tight across every window, but knowing what went on there, I was glad. Whorehouses are all the same, really—dress them up however you want, change the time and the place, but they all smell like desperation and dead dreams. And a few other things I preferred not to think about.

In the lobby, I loitered for a minute before I started walking the halls. It was quiet. The kind of quiet that only comes right before lightning strikes.

A scream wavered from down the long hall behind me, tinkling the dusty crystals in the lobby chandelier.

I pulled out the automatic and moved without thinking— the part where I go toward the monster was second nature. Thinking about how rotten this situation was was a newer thing. I was just muscle. My days of saving people were a long way back on the road.

Plus, Marie's innocent sister working in one of Hollywood's biggest whorehouses? Her just happening to be there when I busted in looking to rough up Mason?

No. Something else was up here. I took aim as the door in front of me burst open, and a man in a cheap suit stumbled out, going down hard. It was one of the bouncers who should have been in the lobby, scrambling along the carpet like a crab at low tide. The guy collapsed with a soft sound, like air escaping from an inner tube. I put my gun away and turned him over, but it was too late. His throat was torn, and ruby-red arterial blood dribbled down his neck and over my hand, a warm brook soaking the carpet.

It distracted me, I'll say. That's my excuse for how the thing that had killed him landed on my back, nails scraping across my cheek, sour body odor overpowering the coppery blood.

The zombie hooked one finger in the corner of my mouth, letting out the kind of moan that only trapped, hungry animals are capable of.

I spun around, slamming it into a wall, which had all the effect of slapping the thing with a rolled-up newspaper. Teeth sank into my shoulder through my shirt, and I tripped over the dead bouncer and fell.

I prefer when I don't see my death coming, like when Mason shot me. The first time I'd died was slow, had left me plenty of time to stare the reaper down, and now I threw up my arms to try to knock the zombie away. It had been one of the girls, and she was bloated and blue, like she'd been floating in the LA River for a night or two.

A shape the size of a steamer trunk flew at the zombie

and took it to the ground, snarling and shaking it by the neck until I heard a snap. A giant goddamn dog, twice the size of the wolves that prowled the Superstition Mountains back home. Black as coal, with red eyes. It let out a snarl like a motorbike backfiring, and with a final rip, the zombie's head came off.

I pulled myself up the wall, feeling all the places I'd hurt tomorrow. The air around the dog shimmered, a bare second of heat rising off a desert floor, and in its place a woman stood. I stiffened, fighting the urge to reach for my gun. It wouldn't do any good, much as I wanted to put a bullet between her eyes.

That wasn't my job anymore, I reminded myself. I was calm, steady. I didn't give a shit about monsters, unless they cut me off in traffic or tried to unionize Mr. Montrose's production company.

"You all right, mister?" the woman asked, smoothing a hand over her hair. Her accent was pure hill country, and she wasn't dressed like the city was her natural habitat, either.

I examined the bloody hash marks in my shoulder. "I'll live."

She looked me up and down. She had the sharpest gaze I'd encountered in a long while, predator eyes that didn't miss anything. "You a cop?"

"Nope."

She pointed at my waist. "Then why the piece?"

"You ask a lotta questions for a lady who just turned from a giant dog," I said. She tilted her head, running my accent through her head to try to place it, no doubt.

"Texas?"

"Arizona," I said.

"What's your name?"

"Lee."

She extended her hand. "I'm Ava."

I went to shake it, and she twisted my wrist and slammed me into the wall, giving it a nice dent in the shape of my head. "Where's Marie?" she shouted, her small hand wrapping around my throat.

She was strong and sneaky, I'd give her that much, but her approach could have used some work. I couldn't answer if she was choking me unconscious.

She slammed me again, and this time I saw two bright spotlights flare in front of my eyes. "I know you're helping her find Constance!"

"Yeah, you figured out I'm helping Marie find her lost sister. You want a medal?" I grumbled, tugging at my shirt, popping off the buttons. Two in one day. Goddamn wardrobe changes were eating up all the pay I could hope to see from this lousy gig.

Ava let out a half hiss, half scream and jerked back from me like I'd burned her. In a way I had—the white lines that ran all over the skin of my chest and stomach were meant to pack a jolt, if you were a monster. Or the human kind of monster, the one that made the types that looked monstrous on the outside.

I didn't bother with good-byes, I just hauled ass out of there. I had a feeling Ava and I'd be seeing each other soon enough.

At home, I double-locked the door and leaned against it until my hands stopped shaking and my heart calmed down. Hellhounds didn't bother me so much as what they represented—hellhounds worked for a Reaper, and Reapers worked for demons. If one of them was tracking Marie, then she wasn't just a nice lady looking for her sister, and this wasn't just another job I did to make rent and buy cheap liquor. I mostly needed the liquor to forget those days when the job was a calling rather than a burden I'd shrugged off a long time ago.

There was a division there. The Lee Grey from Arizona, the man who expected to grow old and die, was the one who had handled hellhounds and necromancers running in the streets. The Lee Grey I was now couldn't have given a rat's ass.

I'd bought the little bungalow in Laurel Canyon for the view—it sure as hell wasn't for the termites or the sinking foundation. On my back porch, I could look away and imagine I was back home—the mountains, the violent blue sky, the ferocious light. Sure, it was anchored by mansions and scrub instead of the empty desert floor, but it was close enough.

I tossed the cap from a bottle of whiskey into the patch of scrappy yucca that was my backyard and took a long swig. It burned a little less, but not much. The yard was the only place outside my shower I went without being totally covered up. The scars all over my torso tended to put normal people right off their food, and I couldn't blame them. But it wasn't like I could get rid of them. And hell, they'd actually come in handy today, putting the hellhound back on her keister.

I was a good mile down the road to being drunk when I

heard a clang from my garage and jumped up. Probably just a coyote come down from the hill, but I still kept my body out of the way as I rolled the door of the garage back. Shadows filled up the space around ancient paint cans and old boxes from the previous owner, and rusty lawn tools hanging from the rafters.

I dug my lighter out of my pants pocket and flicked it, the flame making the shadows leap back. A figure in a pale night-gown threw up her arms. "Please don't hurt me!"

Her face was smeared with dirt, and the nightgown was torn along the hem, like someone had grabbed it. Her hair fell around her face in bouncy natural curls, but she looked just like Marie.

"Constance?" I said, shutting the lighter. She got up from where she'd crouched behind a box of old blankets and shuffled into the fading light outside.

"I heard you come into the Deluxe. When you fought those things off. You didn't seem scared, so I snuck out to your car," she said. "I had to get out of there. If I just ran out on the street, they would've found me right away." An all-over shiver wracked her as wind whined from the top of the canyon.

"Come inside," I said.

She didn't sit when she got to my sofa, just looked at it longingly. I went into my bedroom and dug out a fresh shirt for myself and a dressing gown for her. Dusty, but it did the trick.

"Thank you, Mr. . . . ?" she said as she wrapped herself in it.

"Call me Lee," I said. "Your sister will be happy to hear you're all right. She's real worried."

Constance's eyes watered and her chin wobbled. She did

sit down then, and curled in on herself. "You can't take me back to her." She started to rock, rubbing her arms until her nails snagged in the cheap satin of the dressing gown. "Don't make me do it again," she whispered. "Don't make me . . ."

"Hey," I said, catching her and settling her. "Why don't you tell me what's got you so spooked?"

"I came here because I thought I could hide," she said. "Louisiana, where our people are, it's a small place. Easier to hide from her in cities. But she always finds me. Blood knows blood, she says."

I handed her a rag for her eyes and went to the little kitchen nook, striking a match to the gas under a pot of strong coffee that had gone cold from this morning.

"Is that why you're working the brothels on Fountain?" I asked.

She shook her head.

"I was hiding. I used to live up on Mulholland with this old lady; let me stay for a good price if I did a little bit of cooking and washing when I wasn't at the studio."

"Is that how you met Tom Mason?" I asked.

She bit her lip, nodding.

"Unfortunately. I was just a wardrobe girl. I thought he wouldn't even notice me. But he kept showing up when I was by myself, and then he followed me home, and I just . . ." She sucked in a shaky breath. "He said he had a taste for dark meat. I hit him. The next day, I went to work, and that son of a bitch Louie Montrose told me to clean up my worktable and get out."

Her jaw ticked, and I was suddenly awful glad I'd given

Tom Mason that bottle of morphine after all. Sad I didn't follow it with a swift kick to the nuts.

"Marie must have promised him something," Constance said. "She's good at telling folks whatever they need to hear to get what she wants."

Like "Help me find my missing sister, the vulnerable ingenue actress." Had a much nicer ring than "Help me track down my streetwise tough-nut sister who clearly wishes I'd go play in traffic."

"One of the day players works the Deluxe, and she let me stay," Constance said. "But Marie found me, and she always makes me do it. Then it got out of control, and . . ." A shudder passed through her whole body. "Everyone there is dead, aren't they?"

"More or less," I said. She swiped at her face again and then looked up at me, twisting the rag tight in her fists.

"All this must seem incredible to you."

"Not so," I said. The coffee bubbled and I turned off the flame, pouring two mugs. I added some good Kentucky bourbon Louie had pressed on me when in a generous mood. "If you were watching me at the Deluxe, you saw my scars," I said. "I've seen the dead walk before." I took a sip, let the warmth tickle all the way down. "Hell," I said. "I'm one of them."

Constance blinked warily at me, and I waited. I was drunker than I'd realized, to be blabbing about this stuff.

"Marie's a warlock?" I said, to fill the hole. She nodded. "So what about you? You get in touch with the unseen world as well? They say it runs in families."

"The dead," she muttered. "I touch them, and they're not so dead anymore."

That made me set my cup down. "Raising zombies without any blood conjuring is a pretty good trick."

"It just happens," Constance said. "Any time I touch them. They're so hungry, so vicious. Much worse than normal zombies. The first was our father. Marie has been trying to use me ever since."

She gulped the last of her coffee and looked at me, steadier now. "I don't know about you being dead, but I know what you are. One of you killed my grandmother."

I readied myself to move, in case she lunged at me. "Sorry to hear that."

"Don't be." She shrugged. "She was an evil old devil woman; probably had it coming a mile away."

"I haven't done that sort of work in a lot of years," I offered. Constance looked at me steadily.

"Well, you better start again, Lee, if you want either of us to live past tonight."

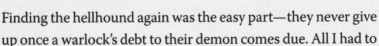

Finding the hellhound again was the easy part—they never give up once a warlock's debt to their demon comes due. All I had to do was put the word out with a few lowlife warlocks and vampires working the bars up on Sunset and wait for a phone call.

I arranged to meet Ava out at the Palisades, the wild cliffs that overlooked the Pacific, a place where we could have a quiet meeting and nobody would hear any screams.

I got Constance some clothes out of the garage and put in the call to Tom Mason.

"I hate this," Constance said as we bounced over the rutted track above the Palisades. "I never asked to do what I can do. Not like Marie."

I didn't answer as we pulled into the turnoff. Marie and Tom were waiting already, Mason swaying in the wind and Marie standing straight. I didn't answer, but I could have. I never wanted this, either. I wanted to be what Constance had thought I was when she saw my scars—a man gifted at hunting monsters. Not a man who became one.

"Thank goodness. I was so worried—" Marie began.

"You can cut the shit," I said. Behind Marie, in the scrubby little trees, bent double, I saw a four-legged shape move. "So what, you post up with the guy who's obsessed with your poor sister, and when he can't track her down, you get him to make a ruckus at the studio and wait for some of Montrose's hired help to track her down?"

"No," Marie said icily. "I wait for the idiot who can't be killed to show up and go into a hotel full of zombies instead of me."

"Constance," Mason started. "I got clean for you! I love you, baby—"

I pulled my pistol and shot him in the knee. He went down hard, and I turned the gun on Constance. Her face went slack, and I tried hard not to feel anything about that as I kept the gun steady.

This was the old Lee, but still me.

"You were right," I said. "I was one of the men empowered to hunt things like you. Then a pack of vampires caught me and hung me. I died, but I didn't stay that way. I've tried to leave that life behind, but you're right, Constance. Blood always finds blood."

"Don't you dare!" Marie screamed at me. "She is *my* sister! *Mine! I* control her, not you!"

The bushes parted behind Marie, and the hellhound rushed forward.

"That's a good story," I said. "Tell it to the demon who took your soul in trade when you get down to hell."

I pulled the trigger. It was like lightning flashing out over the Pacific—a tenth of a second of violence, then stillness.

Constance lay on the ground, a little smoke curling from the hole in her forehead. Marie let out a short scream, and then she was still as well.

A pair of small feet in roughed-up men's boots came to stand next to mine. A match flared, and I smelled the sticky, pungent waft of a hand-rolled cigarette.

"You know I'm going to have to tell my bosses about this," Ava said, exhaling. "But since I collected on Marie, you'll probably have a few days' head start." She looked up at me. "So, you're a hunter."

"Was," I corrected her. "When I was alive."

"Ever kill any hellhounds?" she said.

I met her eyes. "A few."

She snorted. "Be out of Los Angeles when I come back here, if you like . . . well, not being alive, exactly. Whatever you call this."

"It was a demon," I said. "Ancient. Lived under the mountain where they buried me. I died and I saw a long hall, man standing at the end all in black. I couldn't see his face. He brought me back. Still not sure why."

Ava ground her cigarette out under the toe of her boot. Behind us, Tom Mason whimpered softly, but otherwise the air and sea were still. "All of us have that hallway, Lee," she said. "Every one of us that's crossed over and come back. Only way you're going to have any peace is to look the man in black in the eye."

She left, on two legs or four, I wasn't sure. I left, too, after a while, and drove, feeling like a gold-plated bastard. I couldn't let Constance stay alive. Not with the risk her ability posed to everyone. Next time, it wouldn't just have been a brothel. It could have been a whole apartment building, a block, a city.

Ava, too. Her time would come. I wouldn't let her live, but I might give her a fighting chance. I owed her, after all. She'd reminded me who I was, even though I'd tried to paint over it for the last decade with the booze and the hiding. I was a hunter. That was why I was still here. And the first thing I tracked down was going to be the demon responsible.

DOWN WHERE THE DARKNESS DWELLS

JOSEPH NASSISE

In the world of the Templar Chronicles, a resurrected Templar order is tasked with defending mankind from supernatural threats and enemies. One of the recurring villains in the series is the necromancer Simon Logan, leader of the Council of Nine. Logan is an acolyte of an even greater threat, the fallen angel Ashereal, also known as the Adversary. "Down Where the Darkness Dwells" reveals how these deadly and dangerous individuals came to be allies . . .

The cave gaped like an open mouth, and staring at it, Simon Logan had no difficulty understanding why the local tribesmen regarded it with superstitious dread, thinking it an entry to hell itself.

Then again, he, like the others with him, knew all too well that some superstitions were rooted in truth. It might not have been hell they were descending into, but all their research suggested it just might be close enough.

"Well? What are you waiting for?"

Logan took a moment to arrange his features into an approximation of pleasantness before turning to face the speaker. Jonathan Hale was a tall, hook-nosed blond with an air of superiority matched only by his power over the dead. He led the necromantic Council of Nine with ruthless efficiency. The mages in his inner circle were powerful sorcerers in their own right, though none equaled Hale's ability. One day Simon hoped to join their ranks. For now, however, he had to be content with serving as an acolyte, learning at the knee of men like Hale until his own meager powers grew into something more tangible.

It was a necessity, but Logan didn't have to like it.

The team was here in the jungles of Honduras hunting for an artifact of considerable power known as the Necklace of Yum Cimil. They'd landed four days earlier at Toncontín International Airport, where they were met by the guide Hale had hired to take them into the interior. They'd loaded their gear into a pair of off-road vehicles and driven for hours before camping the first night at a small village outside of Azacualpa. Then, at dawn the next day, they'd made their way on foot into the jungle. Three days of hiking through difficult and dangerous terrain had led them to this cave hidden in a thicket of mangrove trees.

It was Logan's job to lead them inside. Not because he had any particular experience in spelunking; no, that would have been too logical for a man like Hale. Instead, Logan had been selected to lead the group for the simple reason that he was the most expendable. Cave fodder, so to speak. If anything were to go wrong, Logan would be the first to tangle with it, giving the others time to react or retreat.

And he wonders why I'm reluctant to get under way,

Logan thought. Still, he'd agreed, and there was nothing to be done about it now but shoulder on.

He spoke a word of power and watched as the end of the torch he carried burst into green flame. The arcane fire would burn brighter than normal flames but wouldn't give off the heat or smoke that were the by-products of a traditional torch.

More relevant, in Logan's eyes at least, was the fact that it would burn endlessly until it was extinguished by the mage who had created it.

We might be going down into the underworld, but we won't be doing so in the dark, at least.

A final glance back to be certain the others were ready, and then, with an impatient nod from Hale, Logan stepped forward and passed through the mouth of the cave.

The tunnel sloped downward at a deceptively gentle angle, but it went on for a long way, and by the time it leveled out Logan had no doubt that they were a couple of hundred feet below the surface. The tunnel was high enough for him to walk upright without fear of banging his head, and wide enough that the party could have walked two abreast if Hale had so ordered, which he had not. It was cool and dry, unlike the jungle outside, and the rock underfoot was mostly free of debris, which made movement easy.

Logan could almost have imagined he was out for a bit of afternoon exploring if it wasn't for the sense of oppressiveness that hung over the place and the knowledge of what they'd come here for.

Yum Cimil was the Mayan god of death. He—*it?*—was often represented in the Mayan culture as a skeletal being adorned in the bones of his victims, or as a body covered with the black spots of decomposition. Ruler of the nine-level underworld known as Mitnal, Yum Cimil was judge, jury, and executioner when it came to the souls of the dead, believed to take great delight in torturing those who deserved punishment. According to legend, those who had committed particularly grievous crimes would have their eyes torn from their sockets and added to a necklace that Yum Cimil wore, granting him the power inherent in their evil souls.

Logan and the rest of the expedition team were here because Hale believed that the necklace was stored in a chamber deep within this cave system and he intended to retrieve it for his own. Doing so wouldn't be without its challenges; there were more than a few stories about those who ventured into these depths being lost forever, and Logan was enough of a realist to believe that there was some truth to those stories.

He was no innocent himself, after all. He'd stopped being one the day he'd discovered his talent for necromancy. That had radically changed his life, and he was determined to cultivate his power in any way possible. If that meant raiding the tomb of an ancient Mayan death god, so be it.

The team had been moving through the tunnel for nearly twenty minutes when a rough chamber spread wide before them. It was rectangular in shape and clearly man-made; tool marks could be seen on the walls, and the floor was covered with some kind of crude stone tile.

Logan hesitated. Something about the room didn't feel

right. Nothing looked overtly threatening, but his gut was telling him something was off here. He turned to the man behind him and sent word back down the line.

A few moments later Hale stepped up beside him.

Hale surveyed the room and then asked, "Do you see the path?"

Logan shook his head. There was a thick coating of dust on the floor, covering most of the tiles, and it didn't look like anyone had come this way in a very long time.

Hale gave voice to several words of power and then flung the energy his spell had conjured up into the room before them. It ripped through the small space, blowing the dust from the surface of the stones and turning several of them as dark as charcoal before the power exhausted itself against the far wall.

In its wake, a clear path across the room was laid out in darkened stones.

"Stay to the path; do not stray from the revealed stones," Hale told him.

Logan wanted to ask what would happen if he made a misstep, visions of poisoned dart traps à la Indiana Jones running through his head, but the look on Hale's face told him in no uncertain terms that he really didn't want to know. Apparently ignorance truly was bliss.

Logan set off, carefully making his way across the room step by step, never straying from the darkened stones. Then, and one by one, the others followed until they were all on the far side.

With their first obstacle successfully navigated, the group continued onward.

They moved as quietly as possible, as if afraid of waking something lingering here in the depths of the earth. No one spoke, and the only sound came from the occasional rock rolling away underfoot or the swish of their equipment brushing up against the tunnel walls.

They had just moved through a long stretch of straight tunnel—the sameness of the rock around them lulling them into a kind of mental daze—when Logan stopped short, causing the next man in line to bump into him, nearly sending them both to their deaths.

Less than five feet in front of Logan the floor abruptly ended even as the curved walls went onward, creating the illusion that the tunnel continued ahead of them.

If I'd been looking forward rather than down at my feet . . . He shook himself, chasing away thoughts of what could have happened, even as the man behind him passed the word back down the line to hold in place.

Logan took another step forward and extended his torch, looking over the edge of the drop.

At the bottom of the cliff face, forty, maybe fifty feet below, was an open space, like a roofless chamber. The tunnel continued forward on the opposite side.

While this particular trap hadn't been included in their intelligence briefing, they'd come prepared for a wide variety of eventualities.

"Ropes!" Logan called, and two of the men behind him got to work, removing long doubled-nylon climbing ropes from their packs and securing one end of them to the tunnel floor with pitons. Once they were tested, the ropes were passed up the chain to Logan, who threw them over the edge.

The ropes cascaded down the cliff, coming to rest in a puddled heap at the bottom.

Length was not going to be a problem, it seemed.

Logan fashioned a makeshift harness by straddling the cord, then wrapping it around his hip and over his left shoulder, around his neck, and back down past his right arm. The weight of his body would act as a brake as he slowly lowered himself down the side of the cliff.

Bones crunched beneath his feet when he reached the bottom, the remains of jungle animals who had wandered into the cave in search of food and had apparently not paid enough attention to the path ahead. Logan glanced at them fondly—he was at home with dead things—and then unwrapped the rope from his body and shouted for the others to make their way down.

When Hale and the rest of the group made it to his level, Logan took the lead once more. The first two obstacles had been successfully navigated, but there were certainly more to come, and Logan found himself increasingly nervous as his sense of security was slowly stripped away. At some point, one of these traps was going to get them; he was sure of it.

About fifteen minutes later, Logan brought the group to a halt once more. This time he found himself staring at a narrow rock bridge that stretched across a gaping chasm that dropped away for hundreds of feet below them.

The bridge looked to be about fifty feet across, maybe a bit more, but what it had in length, it lacked in width. Logan figured it was no wider than a foot, and that was only at the start. The center of the bridge looked to be just a few inches in width and would require putting one foot very carefully in front of the other.

Logan turned and called back through the tunnel to Hale.

"We should probably rope ourselves together—"

He didn't get any further.

"And have you drag me to my death when you slip and fall? Not a chance, you imbecile! Get moving!"

Fucker, Logan thought, but he got moving nonetheless, not wanting those behind him to crowd him on the narrow causeway ahead.

Taking a deep breath, he put his arms out to either side to help his balance and stepped out onto the bridge.

The rock felt sturdy enough beneath his feet, which helped. He didn't want to think about what crossing this thing would have been like otherwise. Setting one foot carefully in front of the other, he began making his way across.

He was fine for the first few steps; psychologically, he knew he could always turn and throw himself back to the ledge if something went wrong. But as he got farther out, the realization that there was nothing to hold on to—nothing that could support him in the event of an emergency—began to take its toll. His body began to tremble as if with cold, the shaking impacting his balance, until suddenly Logan found himself wobbling side to side as he tried to take another step. His foot skittered off the rock before him, and for a frantic moment he thought it was all over—he was going to slip off the stone bridge and plummet hundreds of feet to his death in the darkness below—but then his foot found purchase and he managed to steady himself anew.

Easy, he thought to himself as his heart raced like wildfire and he tried to regain control of his fear. *You can do this. Another twenty feet, that's all.*

Summoning his courage, he managed to get himself moving again, and before he knew it he'd reached the other side. He stepped off the bridge onto the far ledge with a huge sigh of relief.

He turned, gave the hold sign to the next man waiting in line, and then pulled a rope of his own out of his pack. He attached a cam to the rope with the help of a nylon sling, then seated the cam deep in a crack in the nearby wall. He used a second cam to anchor the rope even more firmly in the same manner, and then tugged on the rope to make sure it would hold. When he was satisfied, he stepped up to the edge of the bridge and hurled the other end of the rope back across the gap to his companions.

A man on the other side secured it in a similar fashion, and suddenly the party had a hand line to use; the rest of them made their way across. Even Hale made use of it, though he couldn't be bothered to compliment Logan on his foresight and ingenuity when he reached him on the other side.

Another obstacle down, Logan took point once more. The tunnel began to twist and turn at sharp angles, growing narrower as well, making him thankful that he didn't suffer from claustrophobia.

He had just finished squeezing himself through a particularly narrow section when the passage ahead of him opened up and he found himself on the threshold of another chamber.

Holding the torch in his hand high above his head, Logan took a good look around.

This room was rectangular in shape and about twice the size of the previous chamber, but still small enough for the torch in Logan's hand to reveal the interior to him. On the far side of the room stood an altar. Atop the altar was a stand made from human bones, and hanging on that stand was a necklace.

That was what they had come for: the Necklace of Yum Cimil.

The artifact barely drew a glance from Logan. He was far more interested in the room's other occupants.

Between him and the altar, lining both sides of the room, stood two ranks of dead Mayan warriors in full regalia. The weapons and feathered headdresses they wore looked as fresh as the day they had been placed there, but their bodies were dry and desiccated with mummification.

Logan had seen his share of dead bodies—what necromancer hadn't?—but something about these particular corpses left him feeling unusually unsettled. Before he could figure out why, however, the rest of the party caught up with him and stepped into the chamber to make room for them all.

"At last!" Hale exclaimed, pushing past Logan to stride between the silent guardians on his way to the altar.

Logan felt something shift in the air around them.

He glanced about, taking in his fellow acolytes as they examined the stalwart warriors. He watched Hale climb the steps of the altar and examine the necklace, but he didn't see anything particular that would set his alarms ringing.

And yet . . .

Something had changed. He was certain of it.

Unable to figure out what that something was, however,

Logan turned his attention to the mummified warrior standing in front of him. He stepped closer, peering into the dead man's face, wondering who he had been and what had possessed him to give up his life to stand here in this chamber for the rest of eternity.

What prompted such a sacrifice?

Logan turned just in time to see Hale lift the necklace free of its bone stand and carefully place it in the silk-lined wooden box held by one of the other acolytes. Hale spent the entire time berating the other man, telling him to hold the box steadier, to lift it higher, to stop staring at the artifact with such greed—a litany of failures, Hale's hallmark response to those he considered inferior. Logan couldn't wait for the day when he was powerful enough to best the man . . .

When Logan turned back, he found the dead warrior's eyes had opened; the corpse was staring directly at him. Or would have been, had there been eyes left in the dead man's sockets.

Logan froze, staring back, wondering if the figure was actually looking at him. Had the dead man's eyes opened of their own accord? Or had the eyelids flicked open as a result of the disturbances Logan's party was generating in the air of the chamber after all this time?

However, when the warrior turned his head to track Hale as he strode past Logan on his way to the exit, there was no longer any doubt.

"Look out!" Logan cried, even as the warriors surrounding them all sprang to life and attacked.

Two of their number lost their lives in those first few seconds as the Mayan warriors lashed out with their spears, both men impaled through their chests before they even knew what was happening. Logan used the torch in his hand to parry the strike of the warrior in front of him and then swung it like a club, crushing his skull.

Logan's exultant cry of victory died stillborn in his throat, however, as the warrior picked himself back up, spear in hand, just as dangerous as before.

In seconds, the room was utter chaos. Acolytes were fighting for their lives against the undead guardians of the necklace while at the same time doing their best to protect their leader. Hale, meanwhile, was preparing to cast a spell of banishment; Logan recognized the hand motions even as he did his best to keep the creature in front of him from skewering him like a piece of meat.

A horrified scream burst from the man next to Logan as one of the other warriors managed to sink his teeth deep into the flesh of the man's arm. Logan looked on in horror as the life was literally sucked from the other man, his flesh shriveling right before everyone's eyes as the Mayan warrior drank his fill. In seconds the acolyte was reduced to little more than a shriveled husk, not unlike the guardian itself.

Now that he understood the consequences of letting the Mayan get his hands on him, Logan redoubled his efforts to keep his attacker at bay, mentally screaming at Hale to *hurry the fuck up!*

Logan didn't know if Hale heard him—who really knew the extent of the man's powers?—but in the next second a powerful wave of magick burst from the council leader's fingertips, washing across the room like a miniature tsunami, sweeping over everything in its path. Logan could feel the tug of the magick as it swept over him, but it was looking for the dead, not the living, and so it didn't have any effect on him.

As for the Mayan warriors, that was another story.

The spell had been cast by a master necromancer, with all of his power behind it. Rather than attempting to control the creatures, it was designed to rip the life force animating them from their dead flesh and cast it aside, leaving nothing more than inanimate husks in its wake.

One minute Logan was feverishly fighting for his life, the next the Mayan warrior in front of him collapsed to the floor like a puppet that had just had its strings snipped.

Turning, Logan found the same was true for all of the other warriors; the room was littered with their desiccated corpses.

"Quickly now," Hale said, clutching the wooden box to his side as he stepped over the shriveled body in front of him and headed for the door.

Logan didn't need a second invitation to follow suit.

He was almost at the entryway when the sound of something dragging itself across the floor behind him drew his attention.

He spun around to find the dead men littering the floor stirring back to life, the force that had animated them visibly rushing back into their bodies like smoke sucked into their mouths.

Logan couldn't believe what he was seeing. For the dead men to resist a banishment spell cast by one of Hale's ability was so utterly outside Logan's experience that it was like waking up to find the inmates had taken control of the asylum. He stared in horror as the corpses began to move with a bit more alacrity, dragging their limbs behind them even as they sought to follow those who had dared to disturb their sleep and steal the precious artifact they had been placed there to protect.

"Run!" Logan shouted, then took his own advice.

The next several moments were a blur as the group of artifact seekers fought their way through the narrow twists and turns of the tunnel leading back to the bridge. As they hurried along, Logan was aware of the sounds of pursuit growing behind them, and he knew it wouldn't be long before the warriors caught up with them. He wanted to move faster but was hampered by those ahead, just as the man behind him was hampered by Logan's progress.

Things came to a head when they reached the bridge, as the man behind Logan tried to shove his way past, sending them both sprawling. Logan managed to catch himself against the tunnel wall, but the other man wasn't so lucky; his scream seemed to go on forever as he slipped over the edge of the bridge and plummeted into the darkness below.

The man's death barely gave Logan any pause; he had a horde of undead Mayan warriors at his heels that would have been just as happy to throw him off the bridge as his companion had been, and he wasted no time in scrambling back to his feet and heading out onto the bridge. Never in his life had he been so thankful for his foresight in stringing the guide line, for none of them would ever have been able to make their way across without it.

The fall had cost him precious time, though, and the horde at his back had gained on him as he reached the opposite side. He glanced back, saw the dead men rush onto the bridge without slowing, and knew his lead was dwindling by the second. With his heart in his throat, he rushed after Hale and the others.

He'd barely gone another twenty yards beyond the chasm when one of the Mayans tackled him from behind. They crashed to the floor, though the dead man lost his grip on Logan in the process. Not about to let the small blessing go to waste, Logan scrambled to his feet, snatched the torch he'd dropped off the floor, and ran headlong down the tunnel even as the dead man behind him was crushed beneath the feet of the rest of the undead rushing forward.

When Logan reached the cliff face his team had descended, he found those above rapidly pulling the ropes up behind them.

"Hey!" he shouted. "You can't leave me here! Throw me the rope!"

A glance back down the tunnel showed the horde closing in on him.

"Hey!"

There was no reply from above; they continued working in silence, ignoring his pleas.

Fuck!

Logan looked frantically about, searching for another way up. He grabbed the rock face in front of him, tried to pull himself up with his bare strength, but there were too few handholds, and he slid back down in seconds.

Turning, he put his back to the wall and watched the pack of mummified warriors getting closer with every step. If he didn't get out of here, he was a dead man!

The Mayans were less than twenty feet away when he

spotted it—a small hole in the wall at floor level to his left. He hurried over and bent down to check it out; it was a tunnel, leading heaven knew where, but wide enough that he could probably fit in it if he squeezed his shoulders tight.

Without another thought he threw himself into the opening, squirming forward as quickly as he could, reaching out and pulling himself forward with his hands while pushing with his feet.

The Mayans didn't hesitate, either. The lead warrior followed him right into the tunnel; Logan could hear it scrambling along in his wake.

If he didn't do something, the creature was going to grab his feet, and it would all be over pretty quickly after that. Even as the thought occurred to him, he felt the thing's fingers scramble across the sole of his boot; another few inches and it would have had him.

Logan did the only thing he could think of. He relinquished his hold on the spell illuminating his torch, pointed his hands back down the tunnel behind him, and sent a bolt of power into the ceiling just above his feet.

The walls shook around him as the little tunnel was plunged into darkness, and Logan prayed to every dark god he could think of that the entire rock wouldn't come crashing down on his head. He scrambled forward as the ground beneath him bucked and swayed and the tunnel was filled with the rushing roar of falling rock.

And then, silence.

Logan lay still, the neck of his shirt pressed over his mouth, doing his best not to breathe in all the dust filling the narrow tunnel around him. He listened for pursuit but didn't hear anything beyond the occasional settling of the stone behind him. He could see nothing.

Hopefully this tunnel went somewhere and he hadn't just entombed himself beneath hundreds of feet of solid rock. Escaping one horrible death to suffer another wasn't his idea of a good time.

First things first; he needed light again. He felt around ahead of him until he located the torch he'd been carrying, then reached deep inside and tried to call forth a bit more power to light it up.

Nothing happened.

Uh-oh . . .

He tried again, but the well had run dry. The bolt of power had depleted his energy reserves. He wouldn't be able to conjure up a light for some hours now, not until his body had a chance to rest and regenerate its energy stores.

Crawling around down there in the dark was not his idea of fun, but at the same time he didn't want to just sit still and wait for his mojo to return. If any of the Mayans had survived the rock fall—and why not, they were already dead, right?—they could have been digging through to him at that very moment. He didn't want to be there when they managed to dig themselves out from under.

Best to keep going and look for a way out while he still had the strength to do so.

Inch by inch, foot by foot, Logan slithered forward as best he was able. The darkness was absolute, and he began to feel like it was a living thing, surrounding him, hemming him in, pressing against every inch of his body until he wasn't certain where it ended and he began. He wanted to scream and shout in fear and frustration but was afraid the second he opened his mouth the darkness would swoop down inside him, diving deep into the depths of his very soul, and that would be the end of him.

So he gritted his teeth and clamped his mouth shut and kept crawling, ever forward.

After what seemed like forever, the tunnel slowly grew wider, enough that he could get up on his hands and knees and move forward a bit more expeditiously, but the lack of fresh air combined with his physical exertions soon pushed him into a haze of dizziness despite the extra space. All he wanted to do was lie down in the middle of the tunnel and go to sleep, but something inside told him that if he gave in to that urge, he might never rise again, so he pushed on, moving forward little by little. He lost track of time and then lost track of the fact that he'd lost track of it, until it felt like all he'd ever done was crawl forward on his hands and knees, feeling for a way out.

When the tunnel floor disappeared from beneath him, it was almost a relief.

He reached forward with his left hand, just as he had a thousand, maybe ten thousand times before, except this time there wasn't anything there to hold him up. His hand went down, down, down farther still, and by that time the weight of his body had tipped forward and he fell right out of the end of the tunnel he'd been crawling along and dropped into nothingness.

He let out one short, sharp cry and then slammed into the stone floor many feet below, knocking himself unconscious in the process.

Logan woke to excruciating pain, his right leg broken in two places. He screamed when his hand accidentally brushed against the shaft of bone sticking out of his shin and promptly passed out again.

Time passed.

When he came to a second—*third?*—time, he found that though his leg was still broken, his pain had settled into a low-grade hum in the back of his mind. He wondered, briefly, if he was dying. Had he perhaps lost so much blood that his body no longer had the capacity to feel the pain? If that was the case, then why was he thinking so clearly?

It didn't make sense, and so, with no facility to puzzle it out, he just let it go.

He focused instead on the cavern around him, which, he realized with no small shock, he could actually see. A thin shaft of moonlight was shining into the chamber from a hole in the ceiling high above. He glanced upward to its source and then followed it down as it slashed through the darkness to land on the face of a figure seated on the other side of the room. Logan jerked in surprise at the sight and was struck with such an overwhelming sense of danger that he raised his hand in front of his face to shield himself.

When several seconds passed and the figure failed to move or speak, he sheepishly lowered his hand and gave the other a longer look.

Whoever he'd been, it was clear he'd been dead a long time. Like the warriors in the hall of the necklace, this man's corpse had shriveled and blackened with age. His lips had pulled back from his teeth in a death's-head rictus, and his eyes had sunk so deep in his skull that they were all but invisible. He was dressed in the remains of some kind of primitive robe, and a necklace of small round stones hung across his chest.

Logan stared at the necklace, a suspicion growing in the back of his mind.

Those aren't stones . . .

The notion that he'd found the missing eyeballs of the dead Mayan warriors in the hall above wouldn't go away.

His gaze drifted from the necklace to the throne on which the man sat. What he'd first taken as whitish stone revealed itself in the moonlight to be a massive collection of human skulls. Iron bands, looking strangely fresh after what was certainly ages beneath the surface, bound the man's extremities to the throne itself.

He might once have been a king, but he ended his life as a prisoner, Logan thought, *trapped down here where the darkness dwells, just like I am now.*

He must have drifted off for a bit, for when Logan came to again he found that he was a bit closer to the throne than he'd been before. Had he crawled forward in his sleep?

The idea was a bit unnerving, he had to admit, but not as unnerving as the sense that the man—thing?—on the throne seemed to have moved since he'd last looked at it. Where before it had appeared to be sitting up and staring straight ahead, now it appeared to be leaning forward, its head cocked a bit to the side so that it could look directly at him.

It's a trick of the light, he told himself, but deep in his heart he didn't quite believe that.

Not really.

But as with his injuries, his mind didn't really want to dwell on who, or what, he thought the thing on the throne really was.

Logan was looking about in the dim light, searching for another way out besides the hole in the ceiling three stories above, when he heard the voice.

Simon . . .

It was faint, almost at the edge of his hearing.

At first he thought he'd imagined it, but after a moment he heard it again.

Simon . . .

"Who's there?" he called out, and was shocked at how weak his voice sounded even to his own ears. It was little more than a whisper itself.

I'm here, Simon.

"Hale? Is that you?"

No. That murdering bastard deserted you, Simon, left you to suffer for his own mistake.

The thought sent a spike of red-hot anger pouring through Logan's frame, jolting him a bit into greater awareness.

"That fucking bastard," he mumbled to himself, no longer wondering just who he was talking to, but focusing instead on the subject of the conversation.

Yesssss. He must be punished for what he's done to you, stranding you here.

Logan laughed, a high, cackling sort of laugh with more than a touch of madness in it.

"Punished?" he said. "I'm not going to punish him. I'm going to rip his lungs out and kill him."

The voice was silent as Logan went on mumbling for a bit, ranting really, talking about how he was going to fuck one Jonathan Hale nine different ways from Sunday if he ever made it out of this godforsaken place . . .

I can help you with that, you know.

"Help me with what?"

Getting out of this forsaken place. Isn't that what you just said you wanted? To get out of this place so you can make that bastard pay . . .

Another laugh. "In case you haven't noticed, my leg's pretty messed up. I'm probably bleeding to death right now and I don't even know it. Probably making you and everything else in this place up in my mind, just figments of my imagination as my brain gets starved for oxygen and my veins pour out on the ground."

I assure you, I am quite real.

For whatever reason, Logan believed him. And he played the only hand he saw before him.

"Okay, then; pop my bones back into place, knit my flesh back together, and we'll get out of here. The two of us, together. You help me, I'll help you. Deal?"

There was the sound of a gasp in the darkness, as if the other couldn't quite believe what he'd just heard, and then a quick succession of rapid pops.

Almost like iron clasps being broken under immense force . . .

Logan had a second to wonder just what he'd done, and then the figure from the throne was bending over him, its bony teeth shining in the darkness, the eyes on the necklace around its throat all turning as one to stare at him in horror.

This won't hurt a bit, the other said, and then a hand clamped itself over one side of his face as a searing heat burned itself deep into his flesh and his head was filled with the triumphant laughter of a being who should have remained locked in its prison deep beneath the earth until time itself passed all meaning, but was now free to wreak havoc wherever and whenever it wanted . . .

The Adversary was a prisoner no more.

Six Months Later

The door to the mansion in the swamps outside New Orleans crashed inward from a savage blow, and then Simon Logan strode into the room, staring with satisfaction at the surprised occupants and disrupting the ritual that they'd just begun.

One of them stepped forward.

"What's the meaning of this?" he cried. "How dare you intrude on—"

The speaker, one of the senior mages of the Council of Nine that Simon Logan had once longed to emulate so badly, never got any further. Logan waved a hand, and the man began choking to death, his throat collapsing inward upon itself as if it had been struck by a great weight.

As the man struggled to escape the fate he'd called down upon himself, the other men in the room fell silent, stunned into inaction by the power of the man they thought long dead, the man who had once been nothing more than an eager acolyte but had now returned to them as a powerful sorcerer in his own right.

Just the reaction Logan was hoping for.

He searched their faces one by one, looking for his target. Not seeing him, he addressed the closest man. "Where's Hale?"

This man was perhaps a bit smarter than his colleague, for rather than protesting he simply turned and pointed into the ranks of those behind him.

Sensing where this was going, the men standing in that part of the room quickly separated, leaving Logan staring at the man he had come here to kill.

Hale's mistake was in not attacking the moment Logan entered the room. The extra time gave his opponent the opportunity to prepare his defenses, so when the attack came, it crashed against a wave of arcane force far more powerful than Hale had anticipated.

Logan gazed calmly at Hale as the other stood there, bewildered by his onetime apprentice's newly found power.

"My turn," Logan said with a smile.

When he was finished, there wasn't much left of the former necromancer but a few bloody bits of flesh clinging to the walls.

Logan addressed those still standing in the room.

"I hereby claim leadership of the Council of Nine, its power and authority granted to me by the rite of trial by combat. Any objections?"

There were none.

As he turned, intending to seek out his former master's study and see just what artifacts and books of power he had hidden away, the voice of the Adversary spoke into his mind from hundreds of miles distant.

Oh, we are going to have so much fun, you and I.

So much fun.

Simon Logan, now the most powerful necromancer in the United States, merely chuckled in agreement.

BELLUM ROMANUM

CARRIE VAUGHN

In the Kitty Norville series, werewolf Kitty hosts a talk-radio advice show for the supernaturally disadvantaged. At first the show is all about consoling lovelorn women whose vampire boyfriends have become pains in the neck. But the farther Kitty delves into the supernatural world, meeting powerful vampires and sinister magicians, the more she realizes the world isn't what it seems and a deep, dangerous conspiracy is afoot. At the center of this conspiracy is a mysterious vampire named Roman. Before he became Kitty's nemesis, Roman was Gaius Albinus, a centurion of Rome, and two thousand years ago he was dragged into the supernatural world against his will. He's been seeking revenge ever since.

Gaius Albinus stood before the locked gates of Diocletian's Palace. Fifteen hundred years of planning, and he could not get to where he needed to go because of a chain and padlock, an electronic security system, and a modern sense of reasonable working hours, helpfully marked out on a placard bolted to the stone. What had once been a palace was now a museum, and it was closed.

So many obstacles in this modern era did not involve armies, weapons, or violence. No, they were barriers of bureaucracy and officious politeness. Another venerable institution of old Rome he ought to have known well, passed down to successive civilizations.

He couldn't help but smile, amused. To come so far, and to be confronted now by a sign telling him the site had closed several hours before and that he could not enter until daylight. Impossible for him.

Well. He would simply have to find another way. There was *always* another way.

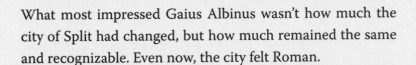

What most impressed Gaius Albinus wasn't how much the city of Split had changed, but how much remained the same and recognizable. Even now, the city felt Roman.

The central palace complex still stood, amidst the sprawl that had grown up around it. The temple walls were identifiable. Many pitted stone blocks had fallen long ago and were now arranged in artistic piles in the interest of archaeological curiosity. At some point, cast-off stones had become valuable, worthy of admiration. Entire towns had turned into relics, museum pieces. And the roads—the roads still marked out routes across the Empire. The great engineers of Rome remained triumphant.

These days the onetime retirement retreat of Emperor Diocletian was a university and tourist town, raucous with nightlife, young people crowding into cafés, spilling onto the beach, drinking hard under strings of electric lights.

Not so different from youths cavorting under suspended oil lamps back in the day, letting clothing slip off shoulders while pretending not to notice, making eyes at each other, offering invitations. That hadn't changed either, not in all his years.

Now, as then, tourists were easy to spot by how they wandered through it all with startled, awestruck expressions, most likely not understanding the local language. Gaius remembered going to Palestine as a young soldier, expecting to hear a cacophony of languages yet not being prepared for the sense of displacement, a kind of intellectual vertigo, that came from standing in the middle of a market and hearing people shout at one another using strange words, laughing at jokes he couldn't understand. The way people became subdued when he spoke his native Latin. More often than not they understood him, even when they pretended not to. They marked him as a foreigner, a conqueror.

Since then, he had learned not to particularly care what people thought of him.

Outside the old Roman center, the city was comprised of the blend of modernity and semimodernity along narrow medieval streets that marked so many European cities. After traveling out by car, he stopped at a squat town house of middling modern construction: aluminum and plywood. Clearly a product of the time when this country was part of Yugoslavia, communist, and short on resources. That era had lasted less than a century. The blink of an eye. Hardly worth remembering.

The hour was late. Gaius knocked on the door anyway, and a mousy-looking man answered. In his thirties, he had tousled black hair and wore dark-rimmed glasses and a plain T-shirt with sweats. An average man dressed for a night in. He blinked, uncertain and ready to close the door on the stranger.

"I need your help," Gaius said in the local Croatian.

"What is it?" The guy looked over Gaius's shoulder as if searching for a broken-down car. There wasn't one.

"If you could just step out for a moment." The man did, coming out to the concrete stoop in front of the door. People were so trusting.

Gaius needed him outside his house, across the protection of his threshold. In the open, under a wide sky, the Roman could step into the man's line of sight and catch his gaze, then draw that attention close, wrap his own will around the small mortal's mind, and pull. In the space of three of the man's own heartbeats, Gaius possessed him.

Gaius's heart hadn't beat once in two thousand years.

"Professor Dimic, I need to get inside the palace. You have access. You'll help me."

He didn't even question how Gaius knew his name. "Yes, of course."

Gaius drove the archaeologist back to the city center and navigated the crowds to the quiet alley where the gate to the lower level of the palace was located. Gaius could have broken in himself—picked the lock, disabled the security system. But this was simpler and would leave no evidence. No one must track him. No one must know what he did.

Dimic unlocked the gate and keyed in the security code, and they were inside.

"Anything else?" he asked, almost eagerly. His gaze was

intent but vacant, focused on Gaius without really seeing anything.

"Show me how to reset all this when I leave."

"Certainly."

The archaeologist gave him the code, showed him the lock, and even left a key. He helpfully pointed out restrooms at the far end of the hallway.

"Go home now," Gaius instructed the man. "Go inside. Sit in the first chair you come to and close your eyes. When you open them again you won't remember any of this. Do you understand?"

"I do." He nodded firmly, as if he'd just been given a dangerous mission and was determined to see it through.

"Go."

The archaeologist, a man who had dedicated his life to studying the detritus Gaius's people had left behind, turned and walked away, without ever knowing he'd been in the presence of a onetime Roman centurion. He'd weep if he ever found out.

Gaius made sure the gates were closed behind him and went into the tunnels beneath the palace. The vaulted spaces were lit only by faint emergency lights at the intersections. Columns made forests of shadows.

He had to orient himself. The main gallery had been turned into some kind of gift shop or market. The eastern chambers had become an art gallery, scattered with unremarkable modern sculptures, indulgent satire. But along the western corridor, he found a familiar passageway, and from there was able to locate the series of chambers he needed. He reached the farthest, not taking time to glance at any of the exhibits—he knew it all already. Then he counted seven stones along the floor to the right spot on the wall, two bricks up. Anyone who'd come along this passage and happened to knock on this row of stones would have noticed that one made a slightly different sound. A more hollow sound. But in all that time, it seemed that no one had ever done so.

He drew a crowbar from inside his jacket and used it to scrape out mortar and grime from around the brick, then worked to pry the brick free. He had to lean his body into it; the wall had settled over the centuries. Dust had sealed the cracks. But he was strong, very strong, and with a couple of great shoves and a grunt, the brick slipped out and thudded to the ground at his feet.

Gaius reached inside the exposed alcove.

A thousand disasters could have befallen this site. A dozen wars had crossed this country since the last time he'd been here. But he'd chosen his hiding place well. The palace area had been continually lived in and not left for ruin. The town was off the main crossroads of Europe. Armies generally didn't have a reason to level a coastal village with no strategic value. The place was still mostly intact, mostly preserved. Even better, over the last couple of centuries it had been cleaned up and maintained.

And in all that time, no one had discovered what he'd left buried. He drew out his prize and held it up to check its condition.

The artifact was a clay lamp, terra-cotta orange, small enough to fit in the palm of his hand. A spout at one end would hold a wick; oil would be poured in through the top. It was a poor man's lamp, too plain and commonplace for wealth. The designs imprinted around the top were of fire. The thing was dusty, covered in grime, but otherwise in good shape. Just as he'd left it. A couple of swipes with his gloved hand cleared some of the dirt. There'd be plenty of time later to clean it more thoroughly. It didn't need to be clean, it needed to be intact, safe in hand. The Manus Herculei. The Hand of Hercules, which he would use to bring fire down upon the Earth.

If archaeologists had found it, they'd have tagged it, cataloged it. Stuck it behind glass or simply put it on a shelf in some climate-controlled archival storage. He might have had a harder time claiming it then, and some of the artifact's power might have diminished. But this . . . this was the best outcome he could have hoped for, and it made him wonder if there wasn't in fact some weight of destiny on his side. He was meant to do this, and he was being guided.

He had been on this path, unwavering, for two thousand years.

———————————>◦<———————————

79 CE

When Gaius Albinus arrived in Pompeii, he had not aged in eighty years. He still looked a hale man in his thirties. A bright centurion of Rome, though he'd left his armor behind decades before. Who needed armor, when one was practically immortal?

He'd never wanted to be immortal. He'd wanted to die for

Rome. That chance had been taken from him by a monster. Since then, he had looked for purpose. Some kind of revenge against the one who had done this. Unfortunately, Kumarbis was as indestructible as he was.

The force of Gaius's rage surprised him. He'd never had a reason to be angry before. When he looked for an outlet, something he could break or destroy to somehow quiet his fury, he found one worthy target: the world. If one was going to be immortal, one might as well use that time to attempt the impossible.

In Herculaneum, he rented a house. This was a port village up the coast from the more decadent, raucous Pompeii. Here, he'd have quiet and not have to answer so many questions. The place was small, just a couple of rooms on the outside of town, but it had a courtyard behind high walls. In privacy, he could burn herbs and write on the flagstones in charcoal, washing them off when he finished.

Then he learned to make lamps.

He couldn't simply buy one in a market and have it be pure, so he went out one night to a pottery workshop and persuaded the master there to help him. The potter was skeptical, even with Gaius's particular brand of persuasion. Gaius was well dressed and held himself like a soldier—why would he need to learn to make lamps? "It's a hobby," Gaius said, and the man seemed to accept that. The potter taught him to fashion objects from clay, bake them, fire them. His first few efforts were rough, lopsided. One shattered in the kiln.

"Practice," the potter said. "Even a simple thing takes practice. Keep trying."

Gaius understood that, and at the end of a week of working long nights he had a lamp, all of his own making. He paid the potter well, which seemed to confuse the man.

That was the first step. Next: the inscription.

He washed; wore a light, undyed tunic; and went barefoot. The summer air was thick, sticky, but his skin was cool, was always cool. He'd taken blood from his servant, who now slept in the house, out of the way. The borrowed strength buoyed him and would be enough to carry him through the night.

A full moon rose as dusk fell, and the smallest hint of sunset still touched the deep blue sky when Gaius arranged his tools in the courtyard. Charcoal, candles, string, braziers, and incense. His lamp. He had a hundred incantations to learn, a hundred symbols to memorize and write, then write again, until he had them perfect. Practice, as the potter had told him.

Such good advice.

He had a lamp to infuse with power.

Kneeling, tools in hand and bright moonlight silvering the courtyard, he hesitated. The hair on his arms stood up, and a sudden tension knotted his shoulders. It was the sensation of being stalked by a lion. He resisted the urge to look over his shoulder.

The danger was outside the courtyard, approaching. If he quieted himself, he could sense every beating heart in the town, he could follow the scent of warm blood and the sound of breathing to every hidden soul. But the thing approaching had no heartbeat, and its blood was cold. The hold it had on Gaius Albinus was difficult to define, but even after decades, the bond remained and called to him.

He set down his tools and marched to the courtyard door, wrenched it open, and looked.

An old man, his skin shriveled, his bones bent, pulled himself along the alley wall, creeping from one shadow to the next on crooked limbs. Hairless, joints bulging, he should not have been alive. His ragged linen tunic hung off him like a crucified body. This was the source of nightmare tales that kept children awake, the stories of ghouls and demons that hid under beds and in wells.

Frozen, Gaius watched him approach. His teeth ground, his jaw clenched with rage, but he couldn't move, he couldn't flee. He ought to murder this monster. But he couldn't.

The shriveled old man heaved up against the wall and stared back at him. Laughing, he pointed a crooked finger. "*Salve*, Gaius Albinus, *salve*! I found you. Given enough time, I knew I would find you. And, my dear son, all I have is time."

"I am not your son," Gaius said reflexively, as he had done a hundred times before, uselessly. He glanced around the street; he didn't want anyone to witness this.

"Yes, you are. I made you. You are my son."

The old man, Kumarbis, looked desiccated, as if he had been wandering in a desert, baked by the sun. Which was impossible for one like him. This meant he had not been eating, going weeks between feeding on blood instead of days. He was starved; he was weak. How was he still existing?

Something dug hooks into Gaius, a connection between them that he'd never be able to deny, however much he wanted to. A feeling: compassion. Gratitude. A tangle emanating from this creature, binding them together. Gaius had tried to escape these lines of power, fed through blood and woven with terrible magic, created when Kumarbis transformed him.

"No! I disavow you. I broke from you!"

"You are my son—"

"You are a mockery—you are not my father!" Gaius's father had died decades ago, never knowing what had become of his son, who'd vanished into the service of Rome.

The old man stepped forward, reaching an angular hand, grinning skull-like. "You owe me . . . hospitality. The tribute due to a master from his progeny. You owe me . . . sustenance." Horribly, he licked his peeling lips.

"You fended for yourself for a millennium before you ruined me. I will give you nothing."

Perversely, the old man chuckled, the sound of cracking papyrus. "I knew you were a strong man, able to resist our bond. Very strong. I knew it. I chose you well."

"*Leave* here. Leave. I never want to see you again."

"Never? *Never?* Do you know what that means? You are only just beginning to realize what that means. We will always be here, we will always be bound."

"Come in, get off the street." Gaius grabbed the old man's tunic—he refused to touch that leathered skin—and pulled him into the courtyard, slamming the door behind him. The ancient fabric of the tunic tore under the pressure, as if it had rotted in place.

Kumarbis slumped against the wall and grinned at Gaius as if he'd won a prize. "You have servants."

"They're mine, not yours."

"You are mine."

"I am not." He sounded like a mewling child.

What he ought to do was drink the old man dry. Suck whatever used-up blood was left in him, destroying him and taking all his power. But he would have to touch the monster for that. And . . . that pull. That bond. It made the very idea of harming the man repulsive. He couldn't even bear the thought of stabbing him through the heart with a length of wood, putting him out of his misery. The terrible magic of his curse, that he could not bring himself to kill the one being in the universe he most wanted to.

"I don't have time for this," Gaius said, turning back to his tools, the mission. He should just buy a slave for the old man to drain and be done with him.

Kumarbis pressed himself against the stone. "What are you doing here, Gaius?"

"Showing my strength. Proving a point."

Wincing, craning his neck forward, the old man studied what Gaius had prepared, the writing he had begun. "This magic . . . Have I seen anything like it?"

Gaius spared a moment to glare. "I wouldn't know."

"Explain this to me." He seemed genuinely confused, his brow furrowed, a hand plucking at the hem of his garment. "You're working a spell . . . a spell made of fire?"

"No! I owe you nothing!" He stomped forward, raised his hand to the old man—and could not strike. Fist trembling, he snarled.

A knock came at the door. Both Gaius and Kumarbis froze, looking at each other as if to ask, *Were you expecting someone?* This night was cursed with disruptions. Gaius went to the door and cracked it open.

"What?"

"May I enter? Am I interrupting anything important?" He seemed like a young man, but Gaius had learned not to trust appearances of age. With his bright eyes set in finely wrought features and the confident stance of a patrician, this man would have been at home in the Forum in Rome. The kind of man who always had a curl at the corner of his lip, as if all he gazed on amused him. His tunic and wrap were expensive, trimmed with gold thread.

"Who are you?" Gaius demanded, and seemingly of its own will the door opened and the stranger stepped inside.

At the same time, Kumarbis dropped to his knees, which cracked on the flagstones.

"Hello there," the stranger said amiably to him.

"You! It was always you!" the old man cried. "Your voice in the dark, drawing me forward. I tried! Don't you know I tried to build your army? I tried!"

The stranger's mouth cracked into a grin, and he turned to Gaius. "Is this man bothering you?"

Some sort of balance tipped in that moment. Gaius felt it in the prickling of skin on the back of his neck. In the way this stranger drew the eye, held the attention, though there seemed to be nothing noteworthy about him.

"Please! Why have you forsaken me?" Kumarbis had prostrated himself and was weeping. It was . . . almost sad.

The stranger said, "I found a stronger man. Or, you did. Thank you for that." He looked Gaius up and down, as if surveying livestock.

"For thousands of years I've—"

"And? Do you expect pity from me?"

"Perhaps . . . perhaps . . . mercy?"

The stranger laughed. "Oh, no, old man. No. Not from me."

"But—"

"Get out. Go." The stranger took Kumarbis by the arm and hauled him to his feet. He had no care for brittle bones or bent back. Why should he, when the old man didn't seem inclined to break? Only to weep.

He pushed the old man out and gently closed the door. Almost, Gaius worried. Where would Kumarbis go? Would he find shelter by daybreak? Would he find sustenance? But no, Kumarbis had survived this long; he didn't need help. He didn't need pity.

The stranger turned back to Gaius. "There. Where were we?"

Gaius stood amazed. "Who *are* you?"

"Call me Lucien," the man said, smiling like he had something to sell.

"What do you want?"

The man paced around the courtyard, studying the stone walls, looking over the charcoal and candles Gaius had laid out. "That's not the question. The question is this: What do *you* want?"

His words held a largeness, a vastness to them that expanded far beyond mere sound. They spoke to the depth of Gaius's anger, his urge to grab Kumarbis's skull and smash it against the wall. To break everything that would break, to shatter it all. But a dozen skulls would not satisfy. And rage was unbecoming to a soldier of Rome.

He said, "I want to see how much of the world I can change with my actions."

"Change?" Lucien said. "Or destroy? I see what you're doing here—this isn't change."

"Destruction is a kind of change."

"So it is." His pacing brought him in a spiral to the middle of the courtyard. To the candles, the charcoal, the wax tablet with the symbols Gaius had copied for practice. The precious lamp. For a moment, he was afraid Lucien would break it. That he was some crusader who had somehow gotten wind of his plan.

Lucien had just tossed a two-thousand-year-old vampire out onto the street. Gaius was fairly certain he wasn't powerful enough to stop this man—this whatever-he-was—from doing whatever he wanted.

Lucien turned to him and stopped smiling. "I know your plan. I support your plan. Be my general, Gaius Albinus. Gather my army for me. And you will have power."

"What . . . what army?" Gaius asked.

"Ones like you. There are more than you think, and by rights they should serve me. Also the werewolves, the demons, the succubi—"

"Werewolves?"

Lucien smiled. "You'll meet them soon enough. Use that army, destroy what you must. And hand it all over to me at the end of days. Agreed?"

A cause to march with. Gaius had missed the structure of direction, of orders delivered for a righteous cause. And here this man appeared. This easy, smiling patrician with an answer and quip for everything. Gaius could see a moment, some years or decades—or even centuries—in the future, when Lucien would turn his back on him. Literally throw him onto the street as he had done with Kumarbis. This man used and disposed of tools as needed.

But at least Gaius understood his role here.

Lucien offered his hand. "Come, my friend. I can make sure your talents don't go to waste."

Stepping forward, Gaius placed his hands between Lucien's and pledged his loyalty. He was surprised at how warm Lucien's skin was against his own chilled, bloodless hands. As if the man were made of fire.

And then he was at the door, a light of victory in his face. "Good journeys to you, until next we meet."

"When will that be?"

Lucien shrugged, his lips pursed. He might have known, he might not have. Maybe he wanted to keep secrets.

Gaius said, "Then I will simply go on as I see fit. Gather this army for you. Gather power."

"And this," Lucien said, "proves that I have chosen well this time. *Vale*, my Dux Bellorum."

"*Vale*," Gaius said softly, but the man was already gone.

Gaius had work to do.

He assumed that Kumarbis still rested in Herculaneum. That he had somehow found a safe place to sleep out the day, as he had every day for the last many hundreds of years. Gaius couldn't confirm this, and he had no desire to waste time looking for the old man, however much a thread of worry tugged at him. That thread was false, and Gaius owed it nothing. But the suspicion determined the target of his strike. Of his masterpiece.

The next night, he woke at dusk and gathered his tools: flint and steel, chalk and charcoal and ash for making marks, candles for light, his own will for power. The lamp to ignite it all. He slung the bag containing everything over his shoulder, wrapped his cloak around himself, and took the road out of town.

A half hour of walking brought him to a field where goats grazed in the day, at the foot of the great mountain Vesuvius. The eaten-down scrub gave him a surface on which to write, after he kicked away stones and goat droppings. The open space gave him a vista in almost every direction: the lamplight of the towns along the coast, the bulge of the mountain blocking out stars behind him. He had some six hours of night in which to work. He moved quickly but carefully—he had limited time but needed perfection.

Once he began he could not stop. No different than any other campaign march. He cleared a space around twenty cubits across. Marked the center with a stake. Then he began writing in powdered charcoal carefully poured out from a funnel.

The first circle of characters was an anchoring to drive the spell deep underground, hundreds of feet, to the molten fissures that fueled the mountain. The next ring of symbols built potential, stoked fires that already existed within the mountain. The third ring directed those energies outward. Then the next, and the next. Thirteen layers of spells on top of the work he'd already sealed within the lamp. The casting took all night. He would barely have time before the sun rose and destroyed him. He didn't think so much of the time that passed, only of the work that needed to be done, methodically and precisely. The good work of a Roman engineer.

The thirteenth circle, the outermost ring, was for containment, protection. The power he raised here would not dissipate, but would instead burst out at once, and only at his signal. As great a show of power as any god could produce.

A deep irony: magic provided him with the knowledge that gods did not operate the Earth and Heavens. A volcano's fury was not the anger of Vulcan making itself known. No, it was a natural process, pieces of the world crashing together and breaking apart. The resulting energies caused disasters. Sparks from the striking of flint and steel, writ large. The fires of the Earth bursting forth under pressure.

Magic didn't create. It manipulated what was already there. Placed the power of the gods in human hands. Or vampire hands.

At last the text was done. The moon reached its apex; dawn approached. He had finished in time, but only just. He went to the center of his great canvas and placed the lamp.

The object served as a focus and a fuse. A battle of primal elements and energies, a physical poetry. Words only captured a shadow of the true forces. Many languages, symbolic conventions, all of them together were still an imperfect representation and only approached the sublime. Magic was the art of trying.

In the middle of it all remained a need for brute force. The inchoate power of the Earth itself. He lit the lamp and waited a moment. Another moment. The lamp burned with a single buttery flame. The terra-cotta orange of the clay seemed to glow, and he couldn't tell if this was the natural light or burgeoning magic. The slight, rounded shadow of the lamp on the ground shuddered, then vanished as a circle of illumination spread out, stretching along the pasture and up the side of Vesuvius. The scrub-covered ground seemed to glow with the same light. People in the town would think the hillside had caught on fire.

Gaius waited, the nails of his hands digging welts into his palms. He didn't know what would happen, what signal he should wait for. He knew only what he wanted to happen, and waiting for that was agonizing. To the east the sky faded with a hint of the gray of dawn. He had to get out of the open, but he wanted to see the spell ignite.

The faint glow on the hillside disappeared. It didn't fade, didn't dissipate. Gaius swore he saw the light itself sink into the ground. Then the earth rumbled. Just an earthquake. Tiny, inconsequential. The kind anyone living near a volcano must sense from time to time.

But this—he had triggered it. He was sure of it. And he was sure this was just the start. He laughed. Put up his arms in triumph and brayed like a fool.

The lamp in the middle of his circle had burned out. The clay was cold. Its power had all gone into the mountain. It was *working*!

He scooped up the lamp, the charcoal, the candles, knife, wicks, and other tools and shoved them into the bag. Then, before the sun rose, he raced back to Herculaneum, and from there to safety.

He had arranged for a boat to wait for him. He had given careful instructions to the captain: however strange and chaotic the world became, they should not leave until Gaius Albinus was on board, or they would forfeit their very large fee. The galley had a cabin belowdecks, a cupboard that Gaius sealed up with waxed leather and blankets until the place was perfectly dark. He paid enough that the captain asked no questions.

In the middle of that day, Vesuvius exploded. While he was sorry he'd missed the main of the eruption, asleep in his sealed cabin, that night from the safety of the boat at sea he watched the fires light up the darkness. It was glorious.

In the centuries after, he collected eyewitness testimonies. Pliny the Younger and other historians gave a great accounting of the disaster that buried Pompeii and Herculaneum. Some eighteen hundred years later, the first excavations of the cities revealed grotesqueries, shapes of despair frozen in ash and preserved in plaster by archaeologists. Gray husks of mothers bent over children, of dogs chained helplessly to walls. They had known they were going to die. They'd had moments to prepare, to wait. Squeeze shut their eyes, hold their breath, and hope that they would survive the flood of ash. Seeing photographs of those cast figures so many years later, Gaius felt that stab of triumph all over again. That thrill of realization: he had done it, he had caused this terrible thing to happen, this explosion of the Earth.

And he could do it again.

Gaius Albinus emerged from the basement of Diocletian's palace with the lamp, which he had named the Manus Herculei, safely in hand.

He had heard and read the speculation of philosophers on the topic of immortality. Did humankind need the challenge of mortality? A limited span of time in order to feel the drive of ambition? Would ambition even exist without the need to leave one's mark on the world before one died? If granted immortality, would a person become bored? Would they long for death? Would they cease to even remember all the time they had experienced? Would they become little more than ghosts?

Gaius held the two-thousand-year-old clay lamp in his hand and could declare that immortality did not cause forgetfulness, did not dampen ambition. He remembered everything. He could smell the musk of goat and the tang of dried grass of that field; he remembered the fires of Vesuvius lighting up the night, the last of the screams that came from the town as the ash flow settled. The satisfaction, knowing that hideous old vampire was likely burned to nothing and buried under a ton of ash. The touch of clay against his skin was like a spark that transported him through time.

The power of the lamp had not diminished. No, by hiding it he had allowed it to sleep as its power grew. The next disaster he triggered with this artifact would make Vesuvius seem like a candle.

He was securing the gates as the archaeologist had instructed when he sensed a presence, an eddy of power in the night. Several of them. Enemies.

A call echoed on stone and through shadow. "Dux Bellorum! Your time is done!" Arrogant laughter followed.

Gaius knew the voice, though he had not heard it in decades. Not every vampire chose to follow Gaius, to join his army. Some rebelled. This man was an upstart, Master of the city of Barcelona with centuries of power pressing from him. Still a child, really. Nothing to worry about for Gaius Albinus, known as Dux Bellorum, also called Roman. Last of his people.

Gaius slapped the crowbar against his hand and waited, mindful of the precious artifact wrapped in cloth and tucked in his pocket.

Early on, there had been those who recognized what he was doing and opposed his quest. Even if they didn't entirely understand the nature of his quest and its origins. That he was merely a general, following orders from his Caesar. Everyone who had opposed him, mortal or monster, full of power or merely earnest and naive, had failed. They would fail now, and he would enjoy putting them down.

One more hurdle, then, before leaving Split. Then he could begin his journey to the park called Yellowstone, in North America.

ALTAR BOY

JONATHAN MABERRY

"Altar Boy" is set in the world of the Joe Ledger weird science thrillers. The series began with Patient Zero, *and the more recent* Dogs of War *is the ninth volume. Joe Ledger is a former Baltimore cop recruited into a covert Special Ops group tasked with confronting terrorists who have cutting-edge science weapons. This story, however, does not feature Ledger but instead focuses on Toys, a character introduced in the first volume as a villain and who continues in the series as a "recovering bad guy," fighting for his soul every step along the rocky path to redemption. Toys is no one's idea of a hero, but he isn't quite the villain he used to be. Maybe . . .*

1.

Saint John of Patmos Catholic Church
Pacific Beach, California

It was a small church, which was good because he felt small. It was old, and that was also good because the young man felt old. Used up, spent, wasted, overdrawn, weathered, and past his sell-by date.

It was a Catholic church, and that was good. Not only because he was Catholic—or had been, once upon a time—but because the Catholics kept the doors open all day. Anyone could come in and sit. Anyone.

Even someone like him.

Even one of the damned.

2.

His name was Alexander Chismer, though everyone called him Toys.

He hated the nickname because it belonged to another man, to another life. But like a bad smell, the name stuck to him. He wore it without complaint. Toys complained about very little these days. It wasn't that everything satisfied him or that he was too timid to speak his mind. No; it was that he felt he no longer had any right to complain. If he hated his nickname but other, better people wanted to use it, then that was fine. It was a small thread in the cloak of punishment that he wore. That's how he saw it. Any unkind word, any unfortunate accident, any bit of physical damage that came his way was, in some overarching way, his due.

The damned don't have the right to complain. Not about anything.

And Toys did believe that he was damned. His Catholicism, long absent from his life, had come flooding back with irresistible force, bringing with it all of the guilt, the weight of sins, the visions of the Pit, the certainty of his own fall into hell. Things he had scoffed at only a few years ago, things he jeered and made jokes about, were now burning lights in his inner darkness.

He preferred to be alone as often as possible. When he went to work, he spent most of his time in his office with the door shut. Most of the people who worked for him at Free-Tech didn't. They were happy in one another's company, and the whole building was alive with their chatter and laughter. To them he was a moody, eccentric, misanthropic loner who seldom smiled, though he never spoke harshly to anyone. Ever.

If they only knew, he often thought. *If they knew who they worked for, that happy crowd would transform into a mob of villagers with torches and pitchforks.*

A few did know, of course, and an even smaller handful knew all of it.

Junie Flynn was aware. She was Toys's partner in the FreeTech venture. He was the money, the logistics, the big-picture planning. Junie was the one who actually oversaw all of the projects. The company was built around the deliberate and specific repurposing of radical, cutting-edge technologies obtained by the Department of Military Sciences. In short, the DMS took very nasty toys away from terrorist groups, teams of rogue scientists, and utter madmen and then gave the science to FreeTech. It was amazing how much of that deadly science could be realigned to do measurable good. FreeTech deployed teams all over the world to help with water purification, sustainable farming, renewable energy, education, health, and more. They did it very efficiently and they did it very quietly.

That was another part of Toys's job—to keep his company out of the press and to let groups like Doctors Without

Borders, Habitat for Humanity, and scores of others take the credit. It would actually have killed Toys if his name somehow wound up on a short list for a Nobel Prize. There was no amount of good he could accomplish that would wash his soul clean. He knew that with absolute certainty.

So he did his job and went home. On the way home, he often stopped at the church. Sometimes for mass. Sometimes to light candles for the souls of everyone that he had killed—directly or by enabling the actions of his former employers. Sometimes he sat in a quiet pew in the most remote corner of the church and wept. He never prayed for forgiveness, because he did not believe he deserved any and because he did not think God was that tolerant. He lived alone, except for a battered old stray cat he'd named Job. He did not have friends. He did not date. He ate alone and he lived his life and he waited for the day he would grow old and die. Toys was a young man, he was fit and healthy, and he understood that the purgatory of being alive was likely to last a long, long time.

So it was in that church, in that pew, on a random Tuesday on another of San Diego's relentlessly sunny days, that he met the woman.

3.

She came and sat down in the next pew up and a little apart. Not next to him, but close enough so that her presence there had to draw his eye.

It did.

He looked at her, assessed her, instinctively ticked off the pertinent details, then looked away. She was in her early thirties. Very thin, very pale, with coal-black hair pulled back into a severe ponytail. Minimal makeup. Middle Eastern features. She looked vaguely familiar, but in the way someone is when they look a little bit like a famous person. A borrowed familiarity.

Toys did not react to her as a woman, merely as a person. She was pretty enough, and fell into the category of the kind he used to go for. Women and men of the subgenre that had once been called *heroin chic*: borderline emaciated but actually filled with a raw and intense sexual energy. Like him. Or, like he had been once upon a time. That was all past-tense now, and Toys hadn't been with anyone in more than four years. Not that he couldn't have found willing partners, but he was equally aware that he exuded a toxic vibe. *Hands off.* Or, maybe, *unclean.* People who began to make passes at him quickly changed their minds and moved off with looks of uncertain disapproval twisting their mouths. That was fine with him. The last thing on earth he wanted was a girlfriend or boyfriend, or even a fling. Living like a monk was more appropriate somehow.

He caught the woman looking at him. He glanced at her and then away, but the memory of dark eyes made him cut another look. This time she smiled. A small, sad little smile.

He nodded to her. She nodded back, her smile fragile. And again there was the flicker of almost-but-not-quite recognition. He'd known so many people in so many places around the world, and he'd spent an enormous amount of time in the Middle East with his former employer, Sebastian

Gault. This woman could not have been part of that crowd. Most of them were dead, and the rest were of a life Toys had stepped away from. They called themselves either warriors of God or freedom fighters; the rest of the world called them terrorists. The woman's face touched an old memory, but not in a way that set off his alarm bells.

Toys bent to read from his Bible. Something about someone doing something to someone else. He couldn't concentrate, though. He could feel the woman looking at him, but when he glanced up, she was focused on the pages of a hymnal. Toys tried to read more of the passage but realized that he'd repeated the same verses three times and still had no idea what they said. It was one of Paul's epistles. Dense, pedantic stuff.

"Can I ask you a question?"

He jerked in surprise to find that the woman was no longer sitting in the next pew but was now standing but a few feet away. He could smell her. Some kind of inexpensive perfume. Roses. And soap. She smelled clean. She wore floral shorts and the kind of sandals that were good for walking.

"Sorry, love, did I make too much noise, or—?"

She smiled. "You're English?"

He nodded.

"I was in England for a while. In college."

"Oh."

"I've seen you in here a few times."

"Oh?" He had not noticed her before, though he had not been trying to notice anyone.

"I moved to San Diego a few months ago," she said. "Got a place in Pacific Beach, near that restaurant? You know the one right on the boardwalk? World Famous? I see you in there almost every morning." Her accent was definitely Middle Eastern. Iraqi, he thought, but with a heavy veneer of London English and generic TV American.

"Oh?" he said again, trying not to feed the conversation.

Undeterred, she came and sat down in his pew. He almost flinched, almost slid away from her.

Almost.

4.

Catamaran Resort Hotel and Spa
3999 Mission Boulevard

Her name was Aayun.

"It means 'eyes,'" she said.

"I know," said Toys.

She was surprised. "You speak Arabic?"

"A bit. Traveler's Arabic. I don't know much."

It was a lie, but it was enough. They were sitting at World Famous. It was the third time they'd talked since meeting in the church. Toys had tried very hard not to be interested, but she *was* interesting. Smart, filled with energy and life, but also a little sad. It was the sadness that drew him to her. He understood sadness in all of its many shapes and flavors. Their conversations were never personal, which seemed to be by mutual consent. She was as intensely private as he was, except for her desire to talk. So they talked. They talked about art and music, about movies and places they'd been.

He was careful not to talk too much about his travels in Iraq, Afghanistan, Iran, and other troubled places. She spoke of growing up in a small village near Baghdad, and of moving away with her family in the early days of the war. They did not talk politics. They did talk religion, though, and it became clear that she was not a Catholic. He asked her why she'd been in the church.

Aayun blushed. "I . . . I followed you in."

"Why?"

She shrugged. "I don't know why. I just did."

Toys felt enormously uncomfortable about that, but he let it go. Aayun was interesting, articulate, amusing, and insightful. He could talk to her about things that had no connection at all to who, and what, he had been or who, and what, he was now. She called him Alexander because she had no idea that the world called him Toys. One day she touched his hand at the table and he didn't pull away. It surprised him. And he liked it.

They met for meals and talked their way through food they barely ate and tea they consumed by the gallon.

He had no intention of taking her to bed. They went to bed anyway.

It was a sultry night, and he had brought her to the small ground-floor apartment on the grounds of the Catamaran Resort Hotel where he lived. She was delighted as he showed her around. The resort was gorgeous, with sculptured gardens in which stands of green bamboo framed ponds of brightly colored koi. Parrots in lovely ornate cages chattered to one another, and ducks waddled in and out of a series of lazy streams that were also home to turtles and bullfrogs.

Totem poles hand-carved in Bali seemed to encourage meditation in the gardens. And guests could wander beneath the cool canopy of leaves formed by over a hundred species of palm trees, with a thousand species of flowers and plants filling the air with a subtle olio of fragrances.

Toys's apartment was the least ostentatious of the rooms, with the least enchanting view. That had always been fine with him. It was remote and it was quiet. The fact that he owned the hotel was something no one at the Catamaran knew, nor did he tell Aayun. The staff knew that he was a permanent resident—the only such person at the place—and they mutually assumed that he was a relative of the owners.

But Toys was related to no one. The staff at FreeTech knew he lived there, but Junie Flynn was the only one of them who knew he owned it. And that he owned large chunks of San Diego real estate. Not his own money, really, but close enough.

The money had come to him along with a challenge to do some good with it. However, it was blood money, and Toys felt stained by it.

The British pharmaceutical magnate Sebastian Gault had been Toys's employer as well as his best friend. It had been Gault who had pulled Toys out of the squalor of his younger life, seen the potential beneath the veneer of poverty and bad habits, provided him with the best education, and given him a chance to prove himself. Toys had risen to the challenge, becoming a fixer in his own right. When problems arose, Toys sorted them out. Sometimes that meant arranging a bribe, sometimes it meant cutting a throat. Toys had never been squeamish about it, and soon had a reputation in certain circles as a ruthless, efficient, fiercely loyal enabler of Gault's excesses. Even when that meant supporting Gault's big-ticket play to manipulate the political and religious extremes of El Mujahid and his terrorist network.

The plan was built around a weaponized disease pathogen called *Seif al Din* that had been designed by the brilliant scientist Amirah—who was also El Mujahid's wife. *Seif al Din* had been engineered to be virtually 100 percent contagious, and it turned any infected person into a mindless engine of destructive rage. Zombies, or at least the real-world approximation. The plan had not been global destruction. No, Gault wanted to scare the superpowers, notably America, into shifting the bulk of their defense budgets away from mechanized warfare and into research and development for prophylactic drugs that would protect the population from the disease. Gault was well positioned within the pharmaceutical community, and although everyone in the industry would benefit, it was his own profits that were of primary concern.

The problem was that El Mujahid and Amirah were never really under Gault's thumb. They saw the pathogen as a weapon of God, something that would do what decades of terrorist attacks and suicide bombers had failed to do: tear down America.

Toys had bullied Gault into trying to stop it. Together they had destroyed Amirah's lab but nearly died in the process.

Ultimately it was all too much for Toys. He was a murderer, but he did not want to become one of the Four Horsemen of the bloody apocalypse. His Catholic upbringing, so long abandoned, reemerged, and he realized that he was an irredeemable sinner with hell as his only destination.

He had hoped to fade into obscurity and live out his years as a nothing, doing no more harm. But Mr. Church, head of the black-ops group that destroyed the *Seif al Din* program, found him and made him an astounding offer. He gave Toys access to the vast fortune Church had recovered from numbered accounts connected to various terrorist groups, and Church challenged Toys to use some of that money to do good in the world.

Why Church had selected him, of all people, for that role was beyond Toys. He was evil. He was a mass murderer, an enabler of horrors, a lost soul. He was damned and doomed.

But he took the challenge, even though it meant often interacting with Joe Ledger and feeling the acid burn of the man's contempt. Ledger was Junie Flynn's lover, so there were complications at every turn. Toys found no forgiveness there, and he understood that he deserved none. Not a drop. A sinner with so many black marks against his soul was not allowed the right to despise the devils who tormented him in hell.

And yet . . .

Every day, he felt that he was failing. Every day he could feel the darkness inside calling to him, pulling at him, silencing the voices of his better angels. And over and over again that malicious bitch Fate shoved him in the direction of new violence, new killings, new crimes. New sins.

All of this bubbled like a witches' brew in Toys's mind as he strolled with Aayun through the gardens. It was still there when they returned to his rooms and sat on lawn chairs with cold beers and watched the hummingbirds. His scruffy cat, Job, came and stared at Aayun for a long time. She tried to pet him, but the cat walked away.

"He's not a very social animal," said Toys.

"Are you?" she asked. Her eyes were large and beautiful and they awakened something in him that Toys had long since thought dead. Not just passion, but a desire to *feel* passion. To allow it.

"I . . . I need to say something," he found himself saying.

She set her bottle down and swung her legs over so she sat sideways on the chair, facing him. "What?" she asked, her voice smoky and soft.

"I'm damaged goods."

Aayun smiled. "Who isn't?"

He saw it in her eyes. Pain, old and worn like calluses into the soft flesh of her life. He had no idea what species of pain it was, or why it had come to her. He assumed it had something to do with the wars that followed 9/11. He didn't ask, though. The pain was there and it was hers, and he could understand it without having to know a single detail. As she, clearly, understood him.

There was no more conversation for a long time. He stood up, and she rose with him. They kissed beneath the fires of a dying sun. The kiss was tentative at first. Careful, as if each was afraid of breaking the other. That moment held in sweetness, and then everything became incredibly intense.

They tore buttons and fabric on the way inside to his narrow bed. When she was naked, he could see that she was beautifully made but far too thin. It did not matter. She was so alive. They kissed with volcanic heat. There was a kind of tenderness between them, if layered beneath need and urgency and fumbling of a kind that happens when things are so new, or so newly intense; the hands tremble and the body shudders and the blood roars.

He came too quickly because it had been so long. It didn't matter. She came a heartbeat later. And then after half an hour they both climbed the long hill together, sweating, crying out, gasping, and as one they plunged over the edge.

When there was no more for either of them to give, when they were spent and languid, and exhausted, he held her in his arms and buried his face in her hair and tried not to weep.

But when he heard her first small sobs, he lost all control. They clung together like drowning people.

5.

Dawn was still hours away when she leaned close and kissed his cheek, then whispered softly into his ear.

"I'm sorry," she said.

He swam upward through lingering dreams toward the surface and wakefulness. He wanted to tell her that it was all okay, that there was never going to be any reason for either of them to say that they were sorry. For anything.

Then he felt the sting on the side of his neck. A little bee sting.

He tried to say something, anything, but even "ouch" was

beyond him. Once more he seemed to fall off a cliff, but now he fell down, down, down into a bottomless black hole.

6.

He woke naked, bound to a wooden chair by duct tape, sick and terrified.

"You're awake," she said.

Toys forced his eyelids up. It took effort. The darkness wanted to pull him back down, to keep him. He almost let it take him.

Almost.

Instead he looked at her.

Aayun sat on the edge of a metal equipment case. The last time he had seen her she was naked. Now she wore a white lab coat over jeans and a T-shirt. Her hair was loose around her shoulders. No makeup. No smile.

"What the bloody hell are you playing at?" he mumbled, his voice thick, his lips rubbery. "And what the hell did you do to me?"

"It's a synthetic compound developed by the Iranian military. A ketamine base with some other elements. Very fast-acting. They use it for abductions when they want no noise, no fuss."

He nodded, accepting and absorbing that. He licked his dry lips and sucked enough spit from his cheeks to allow himself to swallow. It helped, but only a little.

"Why?"

Aayun shrugged. "You don't know? Haven't you figured it out yet?"

"Sorry, but no. Why would I understand anything about something like this? You drugged me and brought me . . . where?" The room was a concrete box, big and dark, with bare walls but crowded with packing crates of all sizes. The stencils on the closest crates indicated that they were machine parts from Canada. "Am I still in America?"

"Maybe you're in the last place you'll ever be, Toys," she said.

Toys.

There it was. She knew who he was, and suddenly the fragile construction of their chance meeting cracked and fell to the ground, leaving behind a lot of possibilities. All of them were ugly.

He straightened and reappraised her, and as he did so, the chair to which he was bound creaked. The tape held him fast to it, with his hands behind the back slat and his ankles tight to the front legs.

"Who are you?" he asked.

"Who do you think I am?"

"A wicked bitch who needs her throat cut. But that's just my wishful thinking."

She got up and walked over to him, smiled, and then slapped him across the face. She did it forehand and backhand. Hard blows that tore his lips and rattled his head. She knew how to hit and how to hurt.

Then, still smiling, she went back to her seat. "Try again."

He spat blood onto the floor between them. "Is Aayun even your real name?"

Her dark eyes glittered with strange light. "Yes. Does it ring any bells? It should."

Toys thought about it. Over the years he'd met a lot of people, and a fair number were from the Middle East. Sebastian Gault and Hugo Vox both had extensive dealings throughout that part of the world. How many women named Aayun had he known? One? But she was an old woman and probably dead. How many had he known *of*? That took more thought, and he could come up with only two. One was the young wife of an antiquities broker in Cairo. He'd seen her only briefly once, and this woman was the wrong physical type. Who was the other? He had to fish for it. A niece of someone? No . . . a younger sister. Seen only once in a family photo but spoken of often. The sister of . . .

He froze and felt the blood drain from his face. Aayun was watching him, and she nodded when she saw that he remembered.

"You're *her* sister?" he said.

"Yes," she said.

And then all of the memories that had tugged at him whenever he'd looked at Aayun clicked into place. If he had seen her somewhere other than a Catholic church, if they'd met under any circumstance that might have tied her more firmly to her family, then he might have understood sooner. Now he felt like a fool, and very possibly a suicidally stupid one.

"You're Amirah's sister," he breathed.

"Yes," she said again.

"Dear God . . ."

"I've looked for you for such a long time, Toys," she said. "First I chased rumors, and twice I thought you were dead. People have been saying that you went soft. That you found God. That you lost your nerve."

"Is that what people say?"

"They do. People have been looking closely at you. You used to be a careful person, but now you've become predictable, even clumsy. You live at that resort, you eat in the same diner every day. You go for long walks on the beach. You go to church nearly every day. You make no ripples. So . . . yes, the people who file reports on you say that you've lost your nerve, that you've become weak. That you're no one."

She paused, but Toys said nothing.

"So I had to come and see for myself. I had to know for sure."

"Know what?" asked Toys.

Aayun smiled. "I had to see for myself if you were broken."

"Oh?"

"I had to see if you've really become some kind of altar boy. And if so, why?"

His heart was pounding now. "What have you learned, Aayun?"

Aayun said, "I don't really know, and that's my dilemma. You could be broken, but you could also be licking your wounds and lying low until you figure out your next move. After all, you've had bad luck in picking patrons. Gault failed you. Twice, by my count. And Hugo Vox outlived his relevance."

"Doesn't say much for my effing judgment, though, does it?" muttered Toys.

"Oh, if we're to talk about judgment, let's start with why you killed my sister."

He spat more blood. "Your sister was insane."

"She was *brilliant*."

"She was a classic example of the mad scientist, sweetie, let's face it. She created an actual doomsday weapon."

"It was because she believed in—"

"Stop," he said. "Just stop. You can effing kill me if you like, but please don't subject me to a lecture on the virtues of Dr. Amirah Malaki. She and Sebastian made quite the pair. He was a self-absorbed narcissist with delusions of economic grandeur, and she was a brilliant back-stabbing soulless witch. And let's add El Mujahid to that mix. He let his wife whore herself to Sebastian in order to fool him into thinking they were a team."

"Sex is a very useful weapon," Aayun said flatly. "It makes men unbelievably stupid."

"Okay, touché, love, but it doesn't whitewash anyone in-volved. We're all whores of one kind or another. Amirah fucked Sebastian stupid, and he believed that she was his ally. The *Seif al Din* pathogen was only ever supposed to be used as a scare tactic, as part of the biggest extortion gambit the world has ever seen. But your sister and her husband actually tried to release it and start a global pandemic. They would have killed everyone. You do grasp that, don't you? *Seif al Din* could not be stopped once it was out. And don't give me that claptrap about them wanting to use it to preserve their twisted version of Islam. They would have killed billions of Muslims with it."

"They wanted to save the faithful and—"

"Bullshit. They turned themselves into fucking zombies! Sure, they were smarter and could speak, unlike the rest of the infected, but they were still effing *zombies*. Think about that, Aayun. They perverted their own bodies and were willing to destroy the whole world. Do you think Allah would have approved? 'Cause I bloody well don't."

Aayun shook her head. "I don't care about that. I'm not a Muslim. Not anymore. I don't believe in that any more than I believe in your idiot who got nailed to a tree with a promise of salvation on his lips, which, I should point out, was a failed promise. Has anyone ever been saved by Christianity? Or Islam? Or anything? No."

"So this is what? Revenge?"

The smile on Aayun's face changed. Twisted. Became darker and stranger.

"Of a sort," she said softly.

Aayun got up and walked a few yards away, stopping in front of a packing case that was about the size and shape of an old-fashioned phone booth. A crowbar stood against it and she picked it up, weighed it thoughtfully in her hands, and then fitted the crow's foot into the gap between the front of the box and the closest side.

"What are you doing?" Toys asked quickly.

"Oh, you'll see," she said between grunts of effort. The green wood squealed as she pried the box open.

"Aayun," he called, and he hated the sound of fear in his

own voice. "Aayun, whatever you're doing . . . *don't*. Come back. Let's talk this through."

She paused in her work and looked at him over her shoulder. Her face was flushed with effort. "You are a murderer, Toys. My sister killed a lot of people, but you're right . . . she was actually insane. She was always insane. I think God drove her mad, or at least the twisted vision of God that she always clung to. Her and El Mujahid. That was no loving God. They worshipped a monster. They believed in fatwa and jihad and all of that bullshit. They thought they were still fighting the Crusaders to protect the Holy Land. No matter what any of us tried to tell her, she would never listen. It was 'Allah wills this' and 'Allah wills that.' And I've seen people like her all over the world. I've traveled, Toys. I didn't lie about that. I actually went looking for God, for hope, for something to believe in, but no matter where I looked all I found was lies, propaganda, false hopes, and more insanity."

She gave another pull, and the wood cracked a little but didn't give way. She repositioned her crowbar.

"Maybe you weren't looking in the right places," said Toys. His heart was still hammering, but it hurt. Not physically, but for her.

Aayun shook her head. "Oh, please. Spare me the proselytizing. I was never the audience for that kind of thing. Not even at home. Not even when I pretended to be a good and dutiful little Muslim and went to the mosque and pretended to pray. I *wanted* to be, but God kept disappointing me. I was hoping that you were haunting the church as some kind of dodge, some kind of protective coloration, but you're not.

You actually believe. You actually think you're going to be saved."

"No," he said. "I don't think that at all."

"What . . . you don't believe in God?"

"No, darling, I don't believe I'll be saved. If you know so much about me, then you know that I'm beyond redemption."

"I thought Jesus was all about cleansing sins."

"Surely there's a limit, and I can say without fear of contradiction that I'm well over the mark."

She studied him, and he saw something flicker in her eyes. It looked like sadness, like the kind of raw emotion he'd seen in her before. But it was there and gone.

"Do you know what I've been doing all this time?" she asked.

"Other than following me? No."

"Oh, I mean what I've been doing my whole life. Since before you even met my sister."

"What . . . ah . . . *field* of study?"

The sadness in her face shifted, darkened. "I followed in my sister's footsteps."

"Oh, God . . ."

"There's no real name for the field. Amirah was pioneering new ground. She called it 'transformative biology,' but that was for lack of something else to call it." Aayun paused and shrugged. "As good a name as any, I suppose."

She gave the crowbar another fierce pull, and the front of the packing case leaned outward, seemed to pause for a moment, and then fell with a crash.

The case was filled with madness.

7.

Toys had to fight back the scream that rose to his mouth.

Inside the crate was a cylinder of heavy reinforced glass seated in a metal base upon which was a computer control pad. Wires and thick cables snaked up to the lid, and hoses dangled down inside. The lights on the control panel glowed in vibrant shades of red and green. A monitor beeped softly.

The cylinder was filled with liquid, and inside the liquid, standing like a golem from some mad story, was a naked figure. A man.

A man Toys recognized.

His name was—or had been—Abdul Fazir. Like Amirah, he was a scientist, and a good one, specializing in virology and infectious diseases. He had helped Amirah modify *Seif al Din* to bring its level of communicability to near 100 percent. The last time Toys had seen Fazir was the day he and Sebastian had sabotaged the geothermal vents in Amirah's lab beneath the sands in Iraq. Fazir had already been infected with the latest generation of the pathogen. Not the version that created the mindless and murderous living dead, but the strain that let the victims retain their personalities, even at the cost of their sanity and humanity. It was the strain that Amirah had used on herself and that had given El Mujahid the power to nearly kill Joe Ledger.

And now here Fazir was. Suspended in liquid, but awake. Dead, but not dead. Living dead. Staring with milky eyes through the curved wall of glass at Toys.

"What have you done . . . ?" he whispered.

Aayun bent and rested her forehead against the glass. Fazir's hand moved and touched the inside of the cylinder. His fingers twitched as if caressing her hair. She spoke without looking at Toys. "He's the last of my family," she murmured. "Uncle Abdul . . ."

There must have been some kind of speaker attached to the tube, because when she mentioned his name, the dead man smiled. His teeth were rotted to jagged green stumps, and there was a look of dreadful, bottomless hunger in his eyes. His bloodless lips formed a single word.

Aayun.

He said it to her, but he was looking at Toys. Then his eyes shifted away, and Toys turned to follow his gaze. At least half of the crates were of the same size and shape as the box in which Fazir's cylinder stood. Toys's mouth went dry. There were at least forty of them. Maybe more.

"No . . . ," he breathed.

When he looked back at Fazir, the dead man was grinning at him. A tongue the color of an old mushroom lolled out from between those jagged teeth and licked the rubbery lips with great, slow relish.

"Aayun!" cried Toys. "Aayun, what is all this? Why did you bring them here? Why did you bring *me* here?"

She pushed off from the cylinder, walked back to him, and stood so close that he could smell dried sweat and sex on her from last night. Aayun caressed his cheek with the backs of her fingers.

"I'm dying," she said.

He gaped at her. "What . . . ?"

"Yes. Cancer. I've had it for years. My hair just grew back

from the last round of chemo and radiation. They thought they'd gotten it all, but it's back. I can feel it growing inside me. Imagine what that feels like, Toys, to have something consuming you from the inside out. My uterus, my breasts. The doctors said that they could try radical surgeries, but what's the point? It'll come back. They said that I have a twenty percent chance of remission this time. Twenty."

Despite everything, he felt tears burn in the corners of his eyes. She saw them, too, and shook her head.

"Amirah wanted to transform the world, Toys," said Aayun, leaning into the words, using the urgent tension in her body for emphasis. "She wanted to create a new kind of life using Generation Twelve of the *Seif al Din* pathogen. Transformation into a new state of existence. Not alive, not dead, but rather living death. A kind of immortality. Alive forever, but different, changed. Think about it, Toys. To never grow old, to never get sick again. To never die. It's a wonderful thought."

Toys shook his head. "You have it wrong. Amirah turned herself into a monster. She was going to kill most of the world and turn the survivors into monsters like her. Like Fazir. *That* was the price of immortality."

"Yes," agreed Aayun. "And if you're alive, like you are, and healthy, like you are, with a future, like you have, it's too high a price to pay. But think about it from where I stand. I'm dying. If I allow them to cut me open and scrape out my uterus and cut off my breasts, I'll buy myself maybe another year. Maybe. Which means that in eighteen months I'll be dead anyway. Dead forever. Dead and forgotten."

"Oh, please . . ."

Aayun spread her arms wide. "If I embrace the transformation, I'll live forever."

"As a *monster*!" he cried.

"So what?" she snapped. "You're a monster. You're a soulless monster, Toys, and you know it. You're no better than Amirah. You *enabled* what she did. You share in every one of her crimes, and you own so many more of your own. You're a far greater monster than she ever was."

"She wanted to kill the world."

"She wanted to remake it."

"No."

"*Yes!*" said Aayun, pounding her thigh with a tight fist. "Not into the kind of world where someone like you would want to live. No. There wouldn't be a place for monsters like you. For the damned."

Toys closed his eyes.

"But it would be a world that would survive," said Aayun softly, almost gently. "And that's what I'm going to do. To finish her work, to ensure that her dream becomes the only enduring reality. I will build my lab right here. My uncle and the others I've already infected with his blood will provide me with all of the biological materials I need to perfect the pathogen, to bring it to Generation Thirteen, or higher. To remove some of the cognitive side effects, to create something that will help me bring about a wonderful new world. I mean . . . if God can't or won't save the world, if Jesus and Mohammad and all of those frauds can't do it, then I will. Science is, after all, the only god whose existence can be proved."

Toys shook his head. "Aayun, please, you can't *do* this."

"I've already started, Toys. It's taken me years, but everything I need is in these boxes. I'll have the lab set up in a month and I'll have a working Generation Thirteen within weeks. Amirah's lab was destroyed, but all of her research was backed up in the cloud. I have everything I need, and I have just enough time to do it before I'm too sick to work. And then . . . then I won't be sick ever again. No one will. All disease will end for those who survive the *Seif al Din* release. No birth defects, no cancer, no Alzheimer's, no anything. The world will be purified of all of that."

He struggled against the duct tape, drawing shrieks of protest from the wooden chair. "Why tell me this, goddamn you? Why bring me here? Why not just cut my throat in bed? You could have, Aayun."

She looked surprised. "What? No . . . you don't understand, Toys. I don't want you dead."

"Then what, for fuck's sake? Are you looking for a confessor? Sorry, sweetheart, but I'm no priest."

"Not that, either."

"Well, I'm running out of ideas. If you wanted to gloat or if you want a cheerleader, sorry, I'm the wrong choice for those, too."

Aayun took his face in both hands. "No, you idiot," she said fiercely. "I want you to *join* me."

"What?"

"I want you to be one with me. To become immortal. Let's leave everything behind. God, sin, damnation, redemption. You can't go to hell if you never ever die. I brought you here this way because I didn't think you'd *listen* unless I made you. I wanted you to know that I was serious, that this is real, that I know what I'm doing. You're like me, Toys—you're damaged goods. You used up whatever this version of the world had to offer, so I'm offering something else. A new chance. A clean slate in a new world."

He stared at her, his mouth wide. There was such earnestness in her face, such deep pleading in her eyes, such total need, that it froze the world for a long, long moment.

Toys leaned toward her as far as the tape would allow.

"God . . . ," he whispered, "*yes*."

It came out so fierce, so hot.

"Yes . . . ?" she asked, her voice small, tremulous. Uncertain and afraid. There was hope, too, but it was tiny, fragile.

"Yes, yes, yes," he said. "Please, yes. I . . . need this. More than anything else in the world, I *need* this. To step back from the edge of the Pit. I . . . I . . . oh, please . . . yes."

Tears sprang into her eyes and rolled down her thin cheeks, and a strange, twisted, delighted laugh bubbled out of her. She showered his face with a hundred small kisses.

And then she was tearing at the duct tape, ripping it, sometimes bending to bite it. When he was free she pulled him to her with surprising strength, kissing him, touching him. Her need burned furnace hot, and Toys felt himself getting hard despite the eyes of the monster in the tube.

He stopped her as she shrugged off her lab coat. Toys took her face in his hands and kissed her long and deeply and sweetly.

"Aayun," he murmured. "I want you to be happy."

"I am now."

"Shhh, listen," he said, still holding her face so that she had to look at him. "I was so lost before I met you. So lost.

You brought light into my life when I thought that kind of thing was fairy-tale bullshit. You're real, though. Talking with you over these last few weeks, making love with you last night . . . that's made me feel more alive than anything has for years. I've been dead for so long. I just haven't had the courage to lie down. I've been afraid of ending it all because of what I believe—what I *know*—is waiting for me. You, though, you made me realize why I need to be alive. To stay alive. To continue to live."

"I—"

"I'm already a monster, Aayun," he said.

And with a savage twist of his hands, he snapped her neck.

Inside the glass cylinder Abdul Fazir screamed a long and silent scream.

Toys sat down on the wooden chair, leaned his forearms on his naked thighs, and stared at Aayun. He tried so hard to weep but could not.

For him the tears did not start until after the place was burning.

Until after he walked the seven blocks from the warehouse Aayun had leased to use as her lab.

Until after he was in his lonely pew in the most remote corner of the church. The tears started then. He put his face in his hands and wept.

And he lived for years and years and years.

MAKE IT SNAPPY

FAITH HUNTER

"Make It Snappy" is set in the modern-day world of Jane Yellowrock, a Cherokee skinwalker, but a few years before Jane and Leo Pellissier meet. Leo, the vampire Master of the City of New Orleans, is attacked from a direction and by an enemy he never expected. This story introduces Katie (Leo's vampire heir), George (his human primo), the outclan priestess Bethany, and Leo, before Jane and her Beast begin to tame the MOC. It is a time when Leo's hubris runs free and his humans are little but cattle.

"Make It Snappy" is a rare look at the backstory of Leo, one of the heroes . . . or villains . . . who started it all.

Leo eased the girl's blond head off his shoulder. She was asleep, dreaming blissfully about their encounter, his mesmerism and the power of his blood assuring her happiness. He ran a hand over her hip. Her body was rounded and plump, the perfect vision of beauty until modern times. Now when he visited those sworn to his service, he was often offered scrawny, bony creatures with no curves, no soft and pleasing warmth. She murmured in her sleep, pleasure in her voice and on her face.

Many of his kind preferred the scent of fear, the unwilling, the blood-bound. He preferred his meals willing, even if only by bargain. This one came to him at dusk, when he woke, offering herself in return for a simple favor. He tried to remember her name as he dressed. Cynthia? Sharon? Simone? She had been an easy read, offering all of her past but for one small corner of her thoughts that was closed off and darkened, perhaps some trauma, some childhood fear. He'd left it there, in the depths of her mind, silent and untouched.

He strapped a small blade to each wrist, positioning the hilts in their spring-loaded scabbards. Shrugged into his crisp dove-gray shirt and black suit. Tied the contrasting charcoal tie. No denim or T-shirts for him. He had worked too hard for too many centuries to dress down in casual clothing, using comfort as an excuse for a crass lack of style. His uncle had taught him the social advantages of education, intelligence, and elegance, and while he was delighted the old Master of the City was dead, he wouldn't toss out the lessons learned at the knee of a dominant, successful Mithran, particularly his sire.

He smoothed back his hair as he walked toward the door. The sheets on the bed shifted when he reached the entrance, and he paused to look back. The young woman was sitting up, watching him, a hand at her throat where his fangs had pierced her as he fed. Her face was wan and uncertain. "You won't forget?"

Forget? His brow quirked up in amusement. The woman was his, with or without his compliance in her little family matter, her useless bargain. Women were such an easy indulgence. But still, he was concerned with her "favor" for business reasons, and it would not take him long to resolve it. "I shall do more than remember. I shall accomplish your request before the sun, *ma chérie.* Marcoise will no longer have the power to cause pain." A small smile lifted his lips. "Perhaps we may meet for dinner, just before dawn, *d'accord*?"

"C'est possible," she said in a schoolgirl French accent. She ducked her head, her long hair sliding forward to curl around her breast. "You know where to find me."

"I do." She had recently come to work in the Royal Mojo Blues Company, a music, dance, and cocktail bar catering to Mithrans, the vampire masters of New Orleans. As the Master of the City, he had right of first taste of all the new blood. Mixed with wine, he had found hers to be piquant, saucy, with undertones of currants and laughter. When she had begged a favor in return for a night in his arms, he had readily agreed.

Leo tapped down the stairs of the townhouse she shared with another girl from Royal Mojo Blues and out the door, into the street. His guards gathered close, summoned on the cellular telephone used by George, his primo blood-servant. Security was much easier since the invention of the devices, though at some point his enemies would discover them, he was certain.

The limousine approached quietly from down the street, riding low, the weight of the armor holding it close to the asphalt. Once inside, Leo said, "One more stop tonight. Back to the club." The club where Marcoise worked as head bartender. Where his bargain with the girl would be satisfied.

"Why, boss?" George asked, his upper-class London accent deliberately coarsened to fit his new persona, his new identity. Like most blood-servants, George had outlived his natural life, his papers and his past reinvented again and again.

"The sister of *ma petite fleur* received an inappropriate and unwanted advance from Marcoise."

George's brows drew down.

"According to *la fille*, several of the other girls were similarly approached, with the implication that they would lose their employment if they refused his attention, a clear violation of his service to me."

George shifted his eyes from the street to meet Leo's. "Inappropriate and unwanted advances? And that becomes problematic to you, my master?"

Leo lifted an eyebrow at what might have been censure in the tone. "They are mine. When would I not protect what belongs to me?"

George bowed his head, the gesture formal, the gaze between them broken. "My apologies, my master. It's of no matter."

Leo thought otherwise. George was conflicted and wished to speak, but was holding his tongue, his scent burning with an internal struggle. He was known to have a tender heart for females, having seen his sister abused and his mother killed by those who used them. They would speak of this later, after the situation with Marcoise was addressed. "Her sister acquiesced and has not been seen since their date. I shall attend to the issue."

George scanned the street and the sidewalks to either side as they drove, searching for enemies, problems, threats. Such loyalty as existed between them was rare, but their relationship began in death and violence and had joined them closer than most. Leo knew his primo's mind and heart; they were bound, body and soul.

They pulled up in front of the club, the lights bright inside as the cleanup crew attended to post-closing duties. Leo lifted his cuff and checked the time on his Versace Reve Chrono, though he knew, almost to the second, when the sun would rise. His kind always did. "I'll be only a moment. Security will wait outside."

George opened his mouth to protest. George was always protesting something. Leo lifted his finger, silencing his primo. "I will speak to Marcoise alone. You may cover the outer exits. You may not enter. The cleaning crew will be working and, as former military, they will be armed. I will calm them. I will not have a bloodbath in my club."

George hesitated, clearly thinking about the number of potential victims and hostages. "Derek Lee's company is new," George said. "I'm not certain of the extent of his knowledge, or of his biases."

He did not need to add, *Many have refused to work for the vampire Master of the City of New Orleans.*

He raked through his hair with his long fingers, worried.

"Alone," Leo insisted and tapped on the window. The chauffeur opened his door. "Thank you, Alfonse," Leo said. He was always polite to the help. Into the night, he exited with all the grace of his kind, part ballerina, part snake, part spider, all predator. The night smelled of humans and blood. Saliva filled his mouth, hunger riding him. The girl earlier had been a tasty diversion, her body a delight as she used it to seal his promise, but this . . . this was the hunt. There was nothing like it, and even civilized Mithrans such as himself knew the desire, the overriding craving for shadowing and stalking prey.

Leo leaped to the door, his speed creating a pop of sound as the air around him was displaced. He keyed open the lock and entered. His men, left behind, rushed to provide the protection his kind seldom needed. He slipped into the shadows. Standing behind a brick pillar, he watched the cleaning crew, scenting them. The men were all dressed alike, in one-piece gray uniforms; they were healthy, their blood touched with alcohol and marijuana. He had known it for centuries as hemp, MJ, ganja, and by a hundred other names and grades and varieties.

He took in a slow breath and parsed the chemicals in their blood. The marijuana smelled . . . odd. Impure. He watched as a small man, no more than five feet, five inches tall, lifted a bucket and then, oddly, dropped it. The pail landed with a clatter and splash of water on the concrete floor, and the man stood, hunched over, staring at the mess as if mesmerized. Certainly confused.

Leo sniffed again. There was something mixed with the marijuana, some chemical he did not recognize. The small man took a breath, a faint gasp of sound. He fell.

Leo held still, as only undeath allowed. The other men rushed to help. Another fell, his head bouncing on the floor. A third dropped. And another. Only Derek was still standing, the boss of the crew. Leo had hired Derek Lee's fledgling company because of his service in the military, though the man was destined for far more. Derek pulled a weapon and backed to the bar, the brass rail at his spine, analyzing the room, the short hallways.

Leo said, "You did not partake of the smoke offered to the others."

Derek swung his weapon toward the column hiding Leo. "Who's there?"

"Leo Pellissier, Master of the City. The smoke? The *weed*?"

"Owner of the Royal Mojo. Fanghead. And no, to the weed," Derek said, his weapon steady on the brick pillar. "One of the guys brought it. Said his brother had gotten a deal on the streets."

"Mmmm. And a gift is always a good thing."

"No."

"And what shall you do to the man who injured your cohorts?"

"Better you don't know." Derek's voice was harsh, unyielding.

Leo chuckled. "There is more here than meets the eyes."

"No shit, dude. I got free weed, four downed boys, and the Master of the City hiding behind a brick column. How 'bout you come out. Make nice-nice wid me."

"How about we take down whoever is waiting for us in the office? I smell six. One is a Mithran, one is female and bleeding, one is a dead human."

"My men?"

"They are breathing. I will offer them healing blood if they are not awake before dawn."

Derek considered. "You take the fanghead. I'll take the others."

Leo stepped from behind the column, hands where they could be seen.

"You seem certain that you can contain the humans," he said. "Three against one?"

"This trap wasn't for me. Makes sense it was for you. I'm supposed to be down and out, so they won't be expecting me."

"Better things, indeed," Leo murmured to himself, reevaluating the young man. "You are correct that this is a trap for me. I was sent here by a woman, to chastise an employee named Marcoise. You don't perhaps know if he is with the others?"

"Beats the hell outta me."

Leo chuckled. "I shall enter at speed and engage the Mithran. If there are humans held against their will . . ."

"Understood. No collateral damage. After this, I suggest you get a better security system. Cameras woulda gone a long way to keeping this place safe."

"Undeniably so." Behind him, he heard the door open and George's scent blew in. George seldom followed orders he felt were unwise. "Do not shoot my primo. He follows," Leo instructed Derek. Silently, he led the way to the back, Derek following, and George behind.

At the door to the office, Leo paused, pressed his ear to the crack and listened. There was silence on the other side, the scent of blood and pain and gun oil wafting from beneath the door, but no scent of a fired weapon. He gently attempted to turn the knob. It was locked.

He nodded to Derek and to George, both armed, weapons at the ready.

He stood back, positioned his body, lightly balanced on both feet, and kicked out with all the strength of a well-trained Mithran. His foot impacted the door where the lock's bolt entered the strike plate. The frame splintered, the door banging open. Moving with faster-than-human speed, Leo leaped inside. Still in the air, he took in the room's layout in an instant.

Three humans bracketed the doorway. Two with cudgels, one with a long rifle, the battlefield kind, fully automatic, created to bring down multiple enemies. If it hadn't been pointed at him, he might have approved of the choice. And the girl, in the center of the room. Fastened to a chair with duct tape. Unconscious. Bleeding. Near death. No Marcoise in sight.

The true enemy stood in the back of the room, holding two silvered blades, his fangs down, eyes scarlet and black in fighting form. Shock sped through Leo in recognition. *El Mago.* Leo had left the mage on the fighting floor, his body in pieces, over three hundred years ago on a visit to Madrid. The fiend was dead. Or should be.

Leo snarled, bending his legs to touch down. Heard three shots from the door. Derek, behind cover, taking down the shooter. George screamed, a battlefield roar, intended to shock the other two humans. Leo landed, let his body fall forward over the chair, taking it and the girl with him, into a roll, and shoving her and the chair across the room, out of the line of fire. He drew two small steel blades and rose upright, into El Mago's face. Inside his reach. Thrust both blades into his abdomen, twice each. Stab-stab, high, low. He withdrew the blades for another double thrust.

Pain ratcheted up and through his body. He looked down. El Mago had dropped the longswords and performed the same maneuver on him—two shorter blades were buried inside him. Agony shredded his belly. The blades were silvered.

And then El Mago yanked upward, the blades slicing into his core, then out to the sides.

Leo fell to the floor, the blades still buried in his body.

Standing above him, El Mago extended an arm and turned over his hand. White crystals poured from a black bag. *Salt?* Sea salt? Crystalline flakes of a brilliant white fell over him. El Mago removed his blades, wiped them on a cloth. Darkness descended upon Leo, his vision telescoping down into nothingness. The sound of gunshots was a muffled hollow drumming as the darkness stole even that.

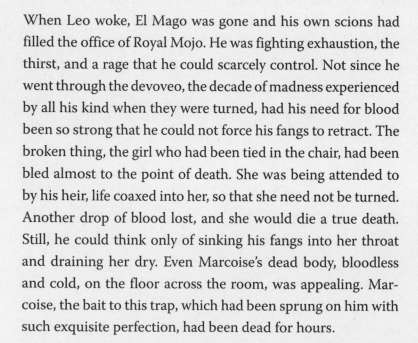

When Leo woke, El Mago was gone and his own scions had filled the office of Royal Mojo. He was fighting exhaustion, the thirst, and a rage that he could scarcely control. Not since he went through the devoveo, the decade of madness experienced by all his kind when they were turned, had his need for blood been so strong that he could not force his fangs to retract. The broken thing, the girl who had been tied in the chair, had been bled almost to the point of death. She was being attended to by his heir, life coaxed into her, so that she need not be turned. Another drop of blood lost, and she would die a true death. Still, he could think only of sinking his fangs into her throat and draining her dry. Even Marcoise's dead body, bloodless and cold, on the floor across the room, was appealing. Marcoise, the bait to this trap, which had been sprung on him with such exquisite perfection, had been dead for hours.

"Master?"

George stood behind him, his heart strong and pounding. He had been honed into a weapon so perfect his body was little more than a sheath for the blade he was. Hot, perfect blood, pumping through his primo. *Son sang est rempli d'énergie, puissant, merveilleux sang.*

Leo spun up from the floor like a snake striking, too fast for George to dodge. He sank his fangs into George's throat.

He heard gunshots. Felt the impacts. Whirled to confront his enemies and took a stake to the belly. Leo fell to his knees at the feet of his assailant. His own heir. Katherine.

He slid to the floor, where he lay in a spreading pool of his own blood, paralyzed by the ash wood that pierced him. Above him, around him, other Mithrans, his scions, rushed to heal George, whose blood was spurting across the room.

Heal George.

He had attacked his own primo, the human blood-servant who most trusted him. The human he most trusted. Shock flowed through him, filling the empty veins that had been drained out on the cement. Katie bent over him, her silvery-blond hair upswept, her long teal gown split up the side, a bastard sword at her hip.

She toed him, cocked her head far to the side, her eyes luminous and thoughtful. Very, very quietly, she murmured, "I know you can hear me. Understand this, *my master.* If I wished your lands and hunting grounds, I could take them this night. If I wished to be forsworn and yet powerful enough that such treachery was no matter, I could take your head.

"You attacked your primo without provocation and mortally wounded him. Had I not been informed that things had gone wrong and seemed off-kilter this night, your George would now be turned and in *my* scion lair, not yours. Had I not been here, you might have died at the hands of your humans.

"Now you are at my mercy. However, I am loyal still, and do not wish to rule. This bargain we shall strike. Someday I may require all your power and influence to save me, to protect me, keep me in my undeath and not true-dead. At such time, you will remember this moment and provide such assistance as I might need. Until then you are in my debt." She stood straight, her body positioned so that he might see up her split skirt. "Think on this as you bleed, my lord and master."

If he had been able to draw breath, Leo might have laughed, knowing that Katie meant both her threat and what she displayed. Had he been able to move at all, he would have run a questing hand up her leg. His heir ran a bordello in the French Quarter, and half the state's elected and law enforcement officials had visited her at one time or another. Her peep show was a reminder of her strengths—human friends in high places and a sexual libido and prowess unmatched in his centuries of experience.

She drifted from view, her grace and balance impeccable in her five-inch stilettos. Katie had been a small woman in human life, and, after so many centuries, with each generation of humans growing taller than the last, she was apt to be taken as defenseless and vulnerable. But his lover and heir was never that. He was truly in her debt. After this night, he would be in the debt of many.

His blood ceased to flow. His hunger was growing prodigious. His eyes were drying out—perhaps the most uncomfortable of his small miseries. The cleanup was well under way, his people moving around him, working silently. No one had attempted to remove the stake embedded in his belly, not with Katherine wearing her *duel sang* bastard-sword. It had been forty-two years since Katherine Fonteneau had dueled for position in his clan, but no one who had seen it would ever doubt her wicked expertise with the blade nor her cunning strategy.

Leo Pellissier, Master of the City, owed his heir much this night. Though he would make her pay for the paralysis, humiliation, and discomfiture. It was the kind of punishment that would take place in his bed.

One good thing came of the enforced immobility: the time to remember, to reflect. El Mago had been on the far side of the room when he entered. There had been a sword in each hand. The sorcerer had been wearing long sleeves that hid his arms, likely places to conceal weapons, such as the short blades he had used. Hidden blades were Leo's own strategy. Clearly El Mago remembered from the last time the tactic had been used against him, when Leo had killed him. *Almost* killed him.

Leo had been predictable. The mage had *expected* him to step inside his reach. He had dropped the swords, incapacitating him with the blades in his own sleeves. He had carved his way deeply into Leo's entrails.

It was time to rethink his dueling methods. But . . .

Silver should have rendered him incapable of healing without massive amounts of blood. Yet when he awoke, his belly was uninjured. There had been a scent like silver and marzipan. The scent of bitter almonds. Cyanide was not lethal to Mithrans, but when coating a silvered blade, unable to purge from his body after entry, and allowed to fester with an unknown spell that both healed and fettered him . . . Leo did not know what effect that might have. His ancient enemy had intended to disable him, not kill him. Or, at least, not right away.

It was clever: the bag of white powder upended over him had healed his flesh over the wounds, so that he and others might not know what had happened. Buried within his body was poison, silver, and a spell—the spell that was perhaps the reason he had attacked his primo. Either one he might have defeated, but all together were deadly, had he not been stopped with a stake to the same damaged area.

The bag El Mago had emptied on him seemed to contain a white powder—crystalline flakes like salt. It had made a quiet *shushing* as it left the cloth sack and fell upon him. When Leo stood after he awoke, nothing had fallen from his clothing or his person. He remembered the sound of Katie's shoes on the floor as she walked through the room. There had been nothing between her soles and the concrete, no grinding or crushing or near soundless compression of some softer material.

He was poisoned. Likely dying. What seemed a minor inconvenience only moments past loomed large. If his heir didn't remove the stake, and soon, so that he might ask for aid, it might be too late.

Another hour passed. Pain had begun to grow in his belly, cold and harsh and remorseless, spreading through his empty veins and arteries. By the time Katie meandered back, he knew with certainty that he was dying.

She knelt beside him, aligning their faces. Her eyes, hazel gray, met his. She had applied fresh scarlet lipstick, and when she smiled it was the smile of a court courtesan, practiced and perfect and only slightly sadistic. "My master, you look miserable," she said. "But perhaps it will cheer your un-beating heart to know that our George is once again fully alive and will neither perish nor be forced to take our curse. No? No comment?" She shook her head, making a small *tsk-ing* sound.

Katie bent and kissed him, her lips as cold as his own. She held the kiss before pulling away, and as she did, she took a breath, then froze. Her remarkable eyes widened. "Bitter al-monds."

She ripped his shirt open, revealing his abdomen and torso. "*Mon dieu.*" Katie yanked the wood from his belly and ripped the flesh of her left fingers with her fangs, her healing blood spurting. She dug her fingers into his flesh, inserting her blood at the point of the original damage. She ripped her right wrist and placed it at his mouth. "Drink, sire. *Drink!*" When he did not swallow, Katie shouted, "Get the priestess!" Then, to herself, "Oh, no."

Astonishment flashing across her face, Katie staggered back and fell to the floor beside him. She held up her left hand. The fingers she'd tried to heal him with were blackened and smoking. "Poison. I am poisoned. How is this possi—" She swooned.

Leo's body was lifted and carried to the front of the club. He was placed on the bar, where he could see only the bottles and the brass-backed mirrored wall behind them. Not a silver-backed mirror, but one in which his kind might be seen as more than a blur. Katie's body was placed on two tables shoved together.

The outclan priestess, Bethany, floated into the room and stood over him, her dark skin catching the lights, her skirts swirling in brilliant shades of blue. She sniffed his small wound, then Katie's hand, which appeared in the mirror as blackened and smoking. Bethany pointed at three humans and said, "Feed her copious amounts of blood. Bring in more servants. Tonight Katherine is a Naturaleza." Which meant she would drink humans down if they were not careful. Returning to the bar, she tore her own throat and climbed over Leo, her limbs moving like a praying mantis on the hunt, elbows and hips high. She placed her ripped flesh at his mouth and began to chant softly in her native tongue.

Magic swirled over him like a dense fog from the Mississippi River, a coiling mist of light, whirling and twisting, enveloping him. Sliding down his throat. Convulsively, he swallowed. Again. And again. Magic and blood twined and flowed down his throat. Magic pressed into his abdominal wound and snaked through him and curled tight with the blood of the priestess.

The magic of the assault spell that had woven itself into him parted before the onslaught of the priestess's own power. He felt strands of El Mago's spell snap. Agony speared through him. He gasped. Lifted one hand and gripped Bethany close, drank, sucking down her healing blood. He lost track of time before she peeled herself away and another took her place. And then another. Trying to heal the damage of the poison, the silver, and the magic with blood.

After the third human was wrenched away, he gasped out to the nearest blood-servant: "George?"

"He is well, my master."

"Katie?"

"Healing, my master."

"The two human girls? Bring them to me. Now."

"Yes, my master," the voice replied. "You and you. Go get the girl from the apartment. You and you, bring the one from the office."

"What's happening?" someone asked.

"Better you don't know, dude," Derek said, moving for the door.

Leo closed his fangs gently, slowly, on a blood-servant's throat. And drank.

The pain was bearable but the rage was still hot within him. He had drunk from Bethany and from ten humans, taking a little over a pint from each. He had ingested over a gallon of blood, and he could have taken more, but he had an enemy to find before dawn. El Mago. The mage would not be allowed to reside in his city if he had to cut a swath through the populace to find him.

In the private restroom of the office, Leo washed his face and brushed his teeth, his fangs, and the hinge structure that operated them. He combed his black hair and tied it into a queue, then took a moment to inspect his abdomen and torso. They should have displayed dreadful wounds, but they were unmarked. He dressed in the clean clothes that had been brought from his clan home on the west side of the river, but this time he strapped a small weapon to his right leg. The Smith & Wesson .380 semiautomatic pistol was loaded with silver/lead rounds. He belted his dueling swords around his waist and checked himself in the brass-backed mirror. Human customers in the bar hated it, but for Mithrans it was the only way to see a reflection. His flesh picked up the golden tones from the brass, looking far more human than his pale skin in the bright lights. Satisfied, Leo rifled through the zippered bag holding his clothes and pocketed a cell phone. Some wise person had placed a folded sheet of paper between the clam-shell halves with instructions on how to use it. Fortified, Leo stepped from the restroom and walked across the room through the lines of his humans to the girls.

The one who had been tied to the chair was stretched out on a chaise, her head in the lap of the other one. The victim was named Audrey Salick, and she looked vaguely Asian. Her sister, the blond temptress who had shared Leo's bed earlier in the night, was named Margaret Coin. The same mother. Very different fathers.

"Audrey," Leo said softly, his voice a low purr as he wielded his mesmerism. "You have been healed. The memories of your abuse muted. Are you well?"

Audrey lifted her head off her sister's thigh and blinked blearily around the room. "I'm fine, I think." She focused on the Mithran behind Leo who had healed her and pointed a finger. "I know you. You're Estavan." Her brows came down in a scowl. "Hey! Did you . . . ? Did we—"

Estavan moved to the back of the couch and took her hand. "All is well, *mi hermosa ave.*" My beautiful bird. Leo's lips lifted at the endearment. Estavan loved women and he was already half in love with this new one. "All is well," Estavan finished. He lifted her hand and bowed over it to kiss her fingers. The woman sighed. "She is well, my sire. And she knew nothing about tonight's ambush."

Leo set his eyes on Margaret. "But this one. She knew much," he said.

Margaret pressed her body into the couch, her blond hair coiling about her. Her blue eyes filled with tears. "He had my sister. I didn't have a choice."

"We all have choices, my dear. Estavan, take your new blood-servant."

"No!" Margaret screamed, even as Estavan leaned across the couch and lifted Audrey into his arms. He whisked her through the door, into the bar. "No," Margaret sobbed, one arm out as if to drag her sister back. "I was supposed to be saving her."

"In return for . . . ?" Leo asked.

"A week of . . ." She drew in a sobbing breath and her mouth pulled down in shame. "Servitude."

"A week in a Mithran's bed," Leo clarified. "A vampire who called himself El Mago."

Margaret nodded, tears reddening her pale skin.

"Then you shall have five weeks in mine, as payment for the trouble you have caused. For now, we will start in small sips. Give me your wrist. And this time you will withhold nothing, not even the trifling dark place in your soul that hid the knowledge of my enemy from me. The trivial dark spot that I should have forced my way into when you were compliant."

"No. No, no, no, no."

"She's wearing an engagement ring, boss."

Leo turned slowly and looked at his primo. His voice took an edge. "So she is. Had she come to me and told her story, I would have saved her sister and set them both free. I have been magnanimous to all human cattle in my city. I have made it clear that they may come to me at any time. She did not. She chose to fear an enemy, to become one herself. You would have me punish her according to a law older than my own?" According to the *Vampira Carta*, the written laws that all Mithrans adhered to, he could have taken her life for such an infraction.

"No." George shook his head. "I'm not—"

"This is about your sister and the shame she was dealt. I understand. And for this reason alone, I will not banish you, nor strip you of power. But for now, leave me." Leo smelled Alfonse in the room. "Alfonse, take my primo home. See that he stays there. The rest of you, wait in the main room. Drink. Enjoy yourselves. I'll be an hour."

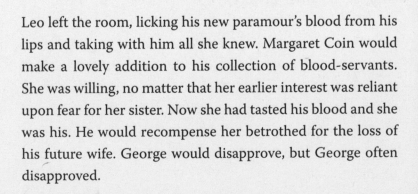

Leo left the room, licking his new paramour's blood from his lips and taking with him all she knew. Margaret Coin would make a lovely addition to his collection of blood-servants. She was willing, no matter that her earlier interest was reliant upon fear for her sister. Now she had tasted his blood and she was his. He would recompense her betrothed for the loss of his future wife. George would disapprove, but George often disapproved.

Leo stepped silently into the main room of Royal Mojo and said, "My enemy is at the Hotel Monteleone, in the Ernest Hemingway suite. He has magic, spells of confusion and obfuscation and false health. He has silver and poison. I will compel no one to fight at my side, nor will I condemn any who walk away. But I ask for aid and fighters who might join me."

Katie made a soft sound with her lips, *Pfttt*. "I am yours to call. You need no one else."

"You are my heir. This is not your fight."

"And if you die true-dead? You would leave me shackled with the city and its restive Mithrans? Dreadful responsibility for one such as I, who has dedicated her life to pleasure. Such boredom, tied to the boardroom of negotiation and mediation." Katie tilted her head and gave him the same smile she had offered him when he lay on the floor, paralyzed. "It has been long since we fought your old . . . *enemy* together. Since the day he turned on you, breaking his blood bond to his sire and yours. All recall when he used magic on Amaury Pellissier rather than a blade, the day he broke his word, broke his vows. Proving his blood and birthright was the lesser, tainted by dishonor." She drew her sword, the sound like a caress as it left the decorative scabbard. "Let us go to the Monteleone and play with your wily nemesis."

Bethany said, "I carry a trinket that will allow a Mithran to see magic as I do." From a finger, she removed a wooden ring, carved from a tree from her homeland in Africa. She had worn it as long as Leo had known her, which was many centuries. "Capture the mage who forced you to attack my George. And before he dies, tell him that his death would have been infinitely more painful at my hand. Catch. And go."

She tossed the ring. Leo's hand swept up and he caught the ring. He slid it onto his finger and instantly saw a purple haze about the priestess, her magics swarming for a moment with darker-purple particles before she inhaled and pulled it all back inside her.

Leo paused outside the elevator, the Hemingway suite at the end of the hallway. It was one of the most elegant in the extravagant hotel, with two bedrooms and a large sitting room for social engagements. He glanced at his cohort and grinned, fangs down, remembering the last time they had entered this suite. It had been a week of revelry at Mardi Gras, a dozen young tourists, far too much alcohol, and ceaseless sexual escapades.

Katie chuckled, a wicked sound, and ran her fingers up his back. "If we are back in your lair before the sun, my love, we might reenact in great detail. For now, you shall inform me what you see in the seating area and engage our enemy if he is there. If he is not, then we shall clear the parlor, the bedroom on the right, then the room to the left. Oh. And Leo, *mon amour*, will you please demolish the door? These are new Jimmy Choos." Katie swept back her split skirt, displaying the stilettos and a great deal of leg.

"Of course, my darling, though what I had in mind is perhaps more anticlimactic than you might wish." Leo strode to the door, pulling a room card from his pocket. He swiped it and the door clicked open. "I borrowed it from the front desk."

"I do believe that I adore you."

"As I do you," Leo said, easing the door open a crack, clenching his fist around the ring. "No magic."

The door opened silently to reveal the large parlor, the pale green of its walls, long upholstered couch, and heavy draperies producing a sense of serenity. The antiques, tall ceiling, crystal chandelier, and heavy moldings established elegance. The merrily burning fire generated a comfortable ambience for the three humans standing before it on the room-sized Persian rug. They were well-armed toughs, incompatible with the luxury, far more suited to a barroom or pool-hall brawl. They were not expecting Katherine Fonteneau.

His heir blew past him at speed, and in three perfect cuts, slashed the throats of all three. Before he was dispatched, the last one shouted, giving away their attack, though Leo had never supposed they might enter without such a warning.

"You could have left one for me," Leo said.

"I have never been called generous except in the bedroom."

"True, my love. But in bed you are Hathor, Aphrodite, and Venus all together."

"I am," she agreed.

They raced into the bedroom on the right. It was empty, though it smelled of sex and fear and the bedcovers were rumpled and smeared with blood.

The marble bathroom was empty. Leo followed Katie to the bedroom on the left. At the doorway, he placed a hand on her shoulder, stopping her. Into her ear, he whispered, "Magic."

"Where?" she mouthed.

Leo pointed into the corner behind the door. There was room for only one of them. The other would have to clear the room and provide protection from rear assault. Katie pouted, her lips pursing around her canines. "Poo," she said. She inserted her sword in its scabbard, out of the way, and slammed back the door. She tucked, dropped, and rolled past it, into the room.

Leo followed her through and then kicked the door closed behind them, revealing the space behind the door. Empty. Except for a haze of reddish magics with particles of black swarming through it. And the faintest haze of a Mithran hidden within. With a single thrust, Leo speared through El Mago's heart, whipped his flat-blade left and right. With a single backhand cut, he slashed his old adversary's throat. The fog of magics dissipated, revealing El Mago, falling to his knees, blood spouting from his throat. His black eyes flashing in shock, his long black hair up in a fighting queue.

Leo dropped his swords and grabbed up his ancient rival. Covered the torn throat with his own mouth, and began to drink. He slid his mind into the mind of El Mago, following the pathways of their earlier years, before their conflicts. He drank down the old jealousy, the hatred, and the betrayal they had given birth to. He absorbed the plans and the hopes and the future as El Mago wished it to be. He understood.

The European Mithrans were coming for the Americans, as soon as fifty years. They wanted his land, his Mithrans, his cattle. They wanted to rule the world; what better place to do so than from the United States of America? *His land.*

He would not give it up.

Leo dropped El Mago and, with an economical swipe of the sword, removed his head.

Katie bent down, inspecting the body. "You killed him before we left for the Americas. Only someone powerful might have healed him from the mortal wound you administered." She tilted her head to Leo. "You have enemies. Will you grieve again, for his death?"

"I will not." Leo pulled out the cellular phone and followed the instructions. "Pellissier Clan Home," a woman answered.

"This is Leo. Send a cleanup crew to the Hemingway suite of the Hotel Monteleone."

"Leo. The Master of the City?"

"Of course. Who else would make such a call? And send a car to collect the heir and me. We shall be walking down Royal toward St. Louis Street. We require a male blood-servant and the human Margaret Coin, champagne, and privacy in the limo. And . . ." He considered the odd phrase he had heard his people use, "make it snappy."

Leo Pellissier, Master of the City of New Orleans, dropped the cellular phone and held out his arm to his beloved. "Come. Let us take in the city before the sun rises."

Together they left the Hemingway suite and the body on the floor of the bedroom. Perhaps this time El Mago—Miguel Pellissier—would stay down.

Re-killing his brother was tiring.

CHASE THE FIRE

JON F. MERZ

What if vampires weren't undead, but had evolved in secret alongside humanity, protected by an elite cadre known as Fixers? In the Lawson Vampire series, Lawson is one of the elite, constantly battling rogue vampires, terrorists, spies, and more. "Chase the Fire" is a glimpse at an insidious plot brewing from within the vampire governing body, one which Lawson will soon have to deal with.

Amsterdam, Netherlands

We found him in one of the brothels on De Wallen."

Shiraz Aziz eyed the tiny man before him and smiled. As always, the temptations of vice worked for those who knew how to use them to their advantage. He scratched at his bristling beard, which he'd started growing to help conceal his identity. At day eleven, it was almost relentlessly itchy.

But that would pass soon enough.

The tiny man shivered in the cool night air, clad only in a flannel shirt and jeans, teeth chattering as he kept glancing around. Shiraz's men eyed him like he was already dead. But Shiraz gave him a warm smile.

"And how are you tonight, my new friend?"

The man looked up at him. "Do I know you?"

"No," said Shiraz. "You do not. But I know you, and that is far more important. In fact, you might say that it's perhaps the most important thing of all." He smiled some more and then leaned forward to the man crouched on the floor. "I'm going to ask you some questions now. Be a good lad and answer them."

The man said nothing, just continued to look up at Shiraz.

"You are what is known as a Ferret. Is this true?"

The man shook his head and stuttered a quick denial. "I don't know what you're talking about."

Shiraz allowed his smile to fade for dramatic effect and then looked at his men. "Perhaps we have the wrong man here? Maybe you got confused when I asked you to bring him to me? Maybe it is not really who I was looking for after all? Hmmm?"

Hassan, his right-hand man, frowned. "It *is* possible, I suppose. There was a great deal of confusion when we arrived there. Clothes strewn about everywhere. Perhaps we were mistaken." He nodded toward the man. "But if he is not the one we want, then what should we do with him?"

Shiraz waved his hand. "I don't care. Kill him, so no one tracks his location back to us." He stood to leave and almost immediately, the tiny man reacted as Shiraz knew he would.

"No, don't kill me!" He grabbed at Shiraz's leg. "I'm the Ferret. It's true. Don't kill me. It's really me."

Shiraz eyed him with mock suspicion. "And how do I know you're telling me the truth? You could just be saying that to save your own skin."

The tiny man gulped and then looked back up at Shiraz. For a moment, he said nothing. And then the words tumbled from his lips. Guttural. A mongrel amalgamation of hundreds of forgotten languages. *"Haz letand min shako."*

Taluk. The ancient tongue of the vampire race. And the Ferret had apparently given a recognition code that only another Ferret would know the answer phrase to. Shiraz did not know what the correct response was, but it didn't matter. The Ferret had admitted he was indeed one of the intelligence specialists assigned to work for the Council, and that was enough for Shiraz to ply him with questions.

But he still made the small man wait another two minutes before resuming his seat. "Your name?"

"Wilkins. Roger Wilkins."

Shiraz looked him over. Unlike the Fixers—the elite spy commandos dedicated to preserving the secret existence of the vampire race—Ferrets were decidedly unremarkable. Wilkins looked like a rail-thin college professor with squinty eyes buried beneath thick glasses and a pimple-ridden face that defied his age. Tufts of hair sprouted at weird places on his scalp, but he was clearly going bald. As far as vampires went, Wilkins was about as un-bloodsucker-looking as you could possibly get. No doubt he never hunted, but just subsisted on the shipments from the Council for his daily allotment.

"Very well, then. As I said, I am going to ask you some questions," said Shiraz finally. "Some of them I already know the answers to. Some of them I do not. You will not know which is which. Do you understand what this means?"

Wilkins blinked. "You'll know if I'm lying."

Shiraz smiled. "Very good, my friend. Very good." He clapped his hands together. The interior of the warehouse was cold, deliberately so. The more uncomfortable the environment, the easier it was to get someone to talk.

"Where is the Fixer known as Lawson?"

Wilkins didn't hesitate. "Boston."

"He has several homes. Do you know which one of them he is staying in?"

Wilkins shook his head. "No. I only know the locations of two of them."

"And what happened when he returned from Syria? How did the Council receive his after-action briefing?"

"From what I heard," said Wilkins, "he is not liked by the majority of the Council. But he is tolerated because of the results he gets. Ava, one of the leaders of the Council, despises him."

"Indeed," said Shiraz. "And why does she despise him so?"

Wilkins shrugged. "I don't know. No one seems to know why she hates him, she just does. She goes out of her way to make things hard on Lawson."

"Interesting." Shiraz scratched at his face. "And where does Ava live? In Boston also?"

Wilkins nodded. "Not technically Boston. One town over. She has an estate in Brookline."

"An estate? How nice." They might have been chatting over coffee. "Is she married?"

"No. I think he died. They had one daughter."

"Fascinating," said Shiraz. "And you're absolutely certain Lawson is currently in Boston?"

"The last time I saw the agent dispatches, he was listed as being in the city, yes."

Shiraz leaned back. "How often do you see those?"

"At least twice each week," said Wilkins. "I need to know who is available in case we have immediate action intel come through that requires a response."

"Very good. And the last time you saw the dispatches was . . . ?"

"Yesterday."

Shiraz smiled. "I must say, this has gone far better than I thought it would. I halfway expected a man such as yourself would be loath to give up his secrets. And yet here you are, freely speaking with me as if we are two of the closest friends in the world."

Wilkins rubbed his arms and looked around. "Well, you'd know if I was lying."

"Indeed." Shiraz leaned forward. "And tell me one more thing: what do you think of Lawson?"

"I don't mind him," said Wilkins. "He's always been pleasant to me—"

The word died on his lips as Shiraz stabbed him through the heart with a length of wood. He watched without interest as Wilkins's incisors lengthened and then retracted as death came for the reedy vampire. Wilkins took a final gasp and then slumped over to one side.

"That was rather the wrong answer," said Shiraz. He looked at Hassan. "Get him out of here and then come back. We have a lot to talk about."

Hassan returned an hour later. Shiraz eyed him. "Where did you dispose of the body?"

"In the garbage compactor at the local junkyard. He won't be found."

"In any other intelligence service, it wouldn't matter. They would assume Wilkins's vices had caught up with him. But the Council must always know what happens to its people lest they think they've been compromised and the humans know about their existence." Shiraz sighed. "They'll come looking for him."

"They'll never be successful," said Hassan. "Are we leaving for Boston?"

Shiraz smiled. "I like your enthusiasm, my friend, but this must be planned carefully. Lawson has not gotten to be as good as he is without many years of experience. He managed to squirm out of our trap in Syria and he no doubt knows that I will come for him."

"But the sooner we act, the better. Our other plans . . ." Hassan's voice trailed off.

Shiraz held up his hand. "I am well aware of the need to remove Lawson prior to beginning our other work. But again, if we move too fast, he will sense us coming."

"Sense us?" Hassan sniffed. "He is only a Fixer."

"And a seasoned one at that. While they might not have any supernatural abilities, he is combat hardened and his sensory perception is above what a normal vampire is endowed with. As I said, Fixers don't survive as long as Lawson has unless they are quite good at their job. Lawson is perhaps the best Fixer in history, even though much of the Council would disagree with that statement."

Hassan shrugged. "So what do we do in the meantime?"

Shiraz smiled at his trusted henchman. "We will leave for Boston. Our other work necessitates our presence there, anyway. And if the gods smile upon us, then an opportunity will present itself and we will kill Lawson."

Boston, Twelve Days Later

Shiraz's face was now almost entirely obscured by the beard he'd let grow in. As he sat on the park bench in the Boston Public Garden, he smiled to himself. He was sitting only a few blocks away from the Council building headquarters—the governing body of the entire vampire race—and if they only knew how close he was, they would summon every Fixer around to kill him.

Well, perhaps not *everyone* on the Council would want him dead. Shiraz watched as a man in a wool overcoat made his way toward the park bench. He was careful not to look as though he was heading straight for the bench, but even still, Shiraz knew it was him immediately. He'd only seen him once before in person when they had hatched a plan together to ambush Lawson in Syria. That plan had failed and the man who was now sitting a few feet away had been forced to lay low for a while to avoid suspicion.

"It is a beautiful day," said Shiraz. "One for the ages."

"The leaves are in full bloom," said the man, "and the world is full of life."

It was better and safer to speak in code than using Taluk.

The recognition sequence completed, Shiraz held a phone up to his ear and pretended to speak into it.

"You've been well?"

"As well as can be expected," said the man. "The blowback from the failed op was harsh. We were all subjected to intense scrutiny. But I think they are satisfied that the leak did not come from me."

"That is good. Then you are free to continue our work?"

"Of course. I've never stopped planning. But in order to be successful, Lawson still needs to be taken care of."

"He will be," said Shiraz. "But only when the time is right. If we act too hastily he will escape again. And we have other matters to attend to."

Despite the warmth of the sun, the man next to him shivered in the stiff breeze. "What do you need?"

Shiraz glanced around and watched as a couple of young lovers strolled by hand in hand. An older man picked his way across the path in search of used bottles he could recycle for a nickel each. Across the park, a child and his mother played.

"One of your colleagues has a home in Brookline. It is an old estate, one of the oldest in Boston."

"What about it?"

"I need the layout. Floor plans preferably. Security systems. Computer network access. Any uninterrupted power supply systems, the like."

The man said nothing for several moments. "You're asking for quite a lot. I don't know if I can get my hands on that information without risking exposure."

"You're going to have to. The item we need to continue our work is buried beneath the estate."

The man actually turned to face him before forcing himself to look away again. "How do you know this?"

Shiraz smiled. "The Council tries so hard to keep its secrets hidden. But we're not so different from humans; many of us crave power and will do whatever it takes to acquire it. Pay off people in the know. Intimidate others. Even kill to find out what we need. I have done all of that and more in my quest. Rest assured I will not stop now. So please tell me you will be up to the task at hand. Otherwise, I will be forced to find someone else who can deliver what I need."

"I can do it," said the man finally. "How can I reach you?"

Shiraz stood. "You don't. I'll be in touch. Wait for my call." And then he walked away, leaving the man behind on the bench in the cool spring afternoon air.

"I have it."

It was three days later when Shiraz called the man. "Excellent."

"How do you want me to get the information to you?"

"There is a pay phone—"

"A pay phone? Are you kidding? No one uses pay phones these days."

Shiraz sighed. "And yet, despite the fact that we are in the twenty-first century, there remains a pay phone at the commuter rail station called Norwood Depot. It has been used as a dead drop for many years and still functions as one. That is one reason why it has never been removed. You will ride the commuter rail train to that stop, make a phone call from that phone and while doing so, deposit the material on the underside of the phone tray using a magnetic box that you can acquire at any hardware store. When you've made the drop, mark the ground with a piece of purple chalk, surreptitiously of course. Then ride the train back into the city. One of my associates will recover the dead drop. That is all I require from you at this moment."

He paused. "I've never done any of this type of stuff before. Won't it look weird that I'm using a pay phone?"

Shiraz sighed. "Not as much as you think. Just act natural and you'll be fine. And be sure you don't have any ticks on you."

"Ticks?"

"Surveillance," said Shiraz. "If you do, you'll need to lose them prior to making the dead drop."

"Okay, I'll do my best."

"Do better than that," said Shiraz. "Otherwise all of this will have been for naught." He hung up the phone and turned to Hassan.

Hassan looked up from his laptop. "Did he get what we need?"

Shiraz nodded. "Do me a favor and be a guardian angel to our amateurish friend, would you? While he claims the Council is done looking at him as a traitor, I would hate for him to have any unwanted attention when he goes to bring us the information."

Hassan nodded. "What should I do when he has made the drop?"

"Nothing. Let him go. We still require his presence in our

plans. Once he has outlived his usefulness, then we'll dispose of him."

Two Days Later

The estate covered twenty acres in the midst of the city. Trees cloistered around the house like a protective shield, warding off any indication of urban sprawl. *If you didn't know any better,* thought Shiraz, *you would simply assume you'd woken up in some place in the country.*

The long winding drive up to the house did a good job of hushing much of the noise, but Shiraz's ears were well trained and every once in a while, he could make out the sound of traffic from the streets.

Still, for a place that was a mere three miles from downtown Boston, it was hard to match.

The floor plan showed that the house covered roughly ten thousand square feet, with seven bedrooms and an indoor swimming pool among its many amenities. Shiraz shook his head when he gazed upon the mansion bathed in the soft glow of exterior lights. Vampires might have to live in the shadows, but they certainly lived well in this house.

The Council saw to that, of course. Vampire society had evolved from one of hunting to one of existing in prosperity. With vampires having infiltrated every portion of human society, they could steer plenty of money toward the vampire race. Whole blood banks existed to feed them; investments made years ago helped ensure future generational wealth.

And blue-blooded Boston vampires—scions who had helped settle the new world and begin the governing body itself, especially aristocrats like Council member Ava—had the greatest wealth.

Shiraz wondered what her problem might be with Lawson. Not that it truly mattered to him, although he was the curious type and he enjoyed knowing things. What mattered more to Shiraz at that moment was getting inside the house and down into the subbasement that lay underneath the basement itself.

The estate was old. It had been remodeled and expanded in ensuing generations, its brick and mortar replaced and given a fresh look, but the framework of the place still dated back to the early 1800s.

Hassan nudged him. "We are prepared to disrupt the power as soon as you give us the word."

Shiraz nodded and looked at the moon above them. Ideally, this would have waited until a new moon for a better infiltration. But then again, time was of the essence and it didn't really matter since they now possessed the security configuration. He still did not know if Ava was inside. She had another home on Beacon Hill, steps away from the Council building. Perhaps she was staying there tonight.

Or perhaps not.

It mattered little. Shiraz nodded at Hassan. "Do it."

Hassan spoke into his phone and within seconds, the floodlights illuminating the exterior went dark.

It was time to move.

Hassan trotted ahead of him, a suppressed MP5 submachine gun held at the ready. Ava wasn't supposed to have much in the way of security, but that didn't stop Shiraz from expecting the worst. Experience had taught him that if things could go wrong during an operation, they inevitably would.

At the main door of the house, two more of Shiraz's men got to work on the lock. In seconds they had the door open. Such a better option than blowing it off its hinges, Shiraz observed. Although, they could have catered for that eventuality as well, given the backpack that Hassan wore.

Inside the foyer the house was quiet. Shiraz frowned. Shouldn't there be someone here? A butler perhaps? After all, would a woman like Ava live alone in all of this incredible space? It didn't make sense.

"Search the house," he said quietly.

"As you wish," said Hassan. He nodded at the two other men to break off and start checking rooms. Within ten minutes they were both back with nothing to report.

"Interesting," said Shiraz. "Well, let's get to work, then. Leave one of your men up here to keep watch. If anything comes down that drive, I want to know about it immediately."

"Of course," said Hassan.

Shiraz walked toward the huge chef's kitchen and found the door leading down to the basement. The carpeted stairs muffled his footsteps as he descended, his vampiric eyesight helping him see without the need for a flashlight. Deeper down, though, he would need to use one to find the secret entrance he suspected existed here somewhere.

Hassan appeared at his side. "Now what?"

"Give me a moment and let me get a feel for the place,"

said Shiraz. His eyes roamed over the walls, sectionals, and chairs. An enormous wide-screen television that would have looked more at home inside a movie theater hung on the wall. On the opposite side, Shiraz saw a popcorn stand and a bar. He wondered if Ava had blood on tap for herself and her guests while they watched the latest Hollywood blockbuster.

He looked at Hassan. "How long until the power comes back?"

"Thirty seconds. But are you sure we want it back on?"

Shiraz nodded. "We cut it so that we could get in and take control of the place before she had a chance to raise an alarm. But since she is not here, there's no sense not having any lights on. Plus, if she happens to come home, she'll be expecting to see lights."

"Very well," said Hassan. He spoke into his phone and almost immediately the lights came back on.

Shiraz blinked and looked at the basement in the light. He was right: Ava had had the place decorated to resemble a movie theater. Heavy curtains hung on the walls to better insulate the sound. And judging by the look of the projector mounted on a shelf coming out of the ceiling, she must have spent a good deal of money on it.

Shiraz ran his hand along the curtained walls, ruffling the heavy maroon material. Somewhere here there had to be another door.

He found it on the second time around, a vague outline that slowly revealed the shape of a thin door as he pressed in on it. "Here," he said more to himself than to Hassan.

Hassan heard him anyway, as expected. "You found it."

Shiraz nodded. "Get it open."

Hassan bent and examined the lock. "Simple." Within seconds, Shiraz heard the click. The door opened with a soft hiss of escaping air and slid back into a recessed portion of the wall. Hassan stepped back and allowed Shiraz to take a look.

The door revealed a cold concrete corridor sloping down at an angle. "It would appear this is the way we go from here."

He stepped through the doorway and glanced around. The high-quality recessed lighting of the proper basement gave way to a string of simple bulbs whose light led the way downward. He and Hassan walked in single file. The corridor broke left at a strange angle and they followed that for perhaps another twenty feet, still descending. At the end, another door—this one much older—stood in front of them.

Shiraz ran his hand over the surface, feeling the weight of the wood before him. The door had obviously been carved long ago. It could have been hundreds of years old for all he knew. But the door itself didn't matter nearly as much as what lay beyond it.

He glanced at Hassan. "What do you think?"

Hassan eyed the door and the keyhole. He shrugged. "I can pick it, but it will take time."

Shiraz glanced at his watch. Time was the one thing they did not have. If Ava came home and found them here, then they would have to deal with a huge liability. "We don't have much time."

Hassan nodded. "The other option is to breach."

"How loud will the explosion be?"

Hassan glanced around. "Down here? Hardly anything.

Between the walls and the makeup of the basement above us, the noise should be pretty much muffled. You might hear a vague *whomp* upstairs, but even that will be negligible."

Shiraz smiled. "Excellent. Get to it, please."

Hassan removed the backpack and started assembling the door charge and placed it around the frame. When that was done, he connected the det cord to a small detonator and then turned to Shiraz. "We'll need to move back since there's no place to stack on either side of the door."

Shiraz nodded. "Very well."

Shiraz moved back to the basement door and Hassan followed, trailing out the cord that led to the charge.

Back in the home theater area, Hassan looked at Shiraz and nodded. "We're ready."

"Do it."

The blast was quick and Shiraz felt the concussive wave rush up into the basement. But most of it had been directed into the door. Hassan's skill with explosives placed him well above the level of just another demolitions man. He could penetrate a steel bunker given enough time and the right resources.

Shiraz walked back down the corridor to survey the damage. Smoke and debris littered the ground and he coughed once as he tasted the air.

But remarkably, the door still stood.

Intact.

"Hassan."

Hassan stood behind him. "What the—?" He moved forward and checked over the door. But from where Shiraz stood, he could see that the breaching charge had done no damage to the door itself. He frowned. Hassan was not the type to screw something up.

Even still, his right-hand man looked back at him with fear in his eyes, as if scared Shiraz would punish him for his failure. Shiraz waved his hand.

"It happens. Prepare another charge."

Hassan nodded and got to work. He took his time and placed significantly more explosives around the frame. When he was done, Shiraz noticed a line of sweat breaking out along Hassan's hairline.

"All set?"

Hassan faced him. "I do not know what happened the first time, but I swear this time it will blow open."

Shiraz smiled and clapped him on the shoulder. "As I said, it happens. Now let us see what your next charge will do."

They moved back to the basement and Hassan initiated the charge. This time, the boom was significantly louder and the room around them shook. More smoke clouded the hallway and Shiraz heard a shower of debris fall. He nodded to himself. This time the door was certainly destroyed.

Except, it wasn't.

And when the smoke cleared, Hassan let out an audible gasp. "It cannot be."

He started to move closer to the door, but Shiraz stayed him with a hand to his shoulder. "Wait. Let me go forward."

Hassan stood aside as Shiraz passed him.

As he approached the door, he could see that the second explosion had done nothing more to the door than the first. It was unscathed. Shiraz frowned. How could this be? Hassan was as reliable as they came with his explosives.

But this.

This was . . . unnatural.

"Magic," he breathed. The door had to be protected by something. Some arcane ritual was at work so that no one could pass without the proper authority.

That was the only possible answer.

But what sort of magic? He knew the vampire race had experts on the old rituals. Invokers could conjure the spirits of dead vampires. And there were others he'd heard whispers of . . . those who could work with magic as easily as they drew a breath.

Indeed, the relic Shiraz sought was rumored to be magical. And full of the sort of power that he so desperately wanted for himself.

But he hadn't expected to run into a magical barrier keeping him from his quest.

He turned back to Hassan and shook his head. "Unless you happen to know any magic, I think we are not going to be able to retrieve anything tonight."

Hassan bowed his head. "The explosives . . . perhaps they were less potent than we required."

"It's not your fault," said Shiraz. "I underestimated this woman. I thought her impetuous enough to keep the relic hidden behind a simple door. The fault is mine alone. Now the only problem we have before us is finding out who we can get to help us through the door."

"But who?" asked Hassan. "Who can we get to help us?"

"An Enchanter," said Shiraz. "I've heard rumors of their existence. But I never thought they might be actively employed by the Council to help protect things like this."

"They won't agree to help us, though, will they?"

Shiraz smiled. "Everyone has a price. Everyone has something they are willing to die for. It's simply a matter of finding out what that something is and then using it to gain leverage over them."

"First we need to find one of these Enchanters," said Hassan. "Do you even know where to look?"

Shiraz nodded. "I would assume right here in Boston would be a safe bet. After all, if this was protected using magic, then the person who cast the spell must be nearby."

"Why so?"

Shiraz cocked his head. "From what I've heard, the spells are stronger if they are cast by someone local to the area. Something about drawing power from the geography of the environment. But then again, I am not well versed in magic. I'm much more at ease dealing with people using a gun."

"Same," said Hassan. "What do you want me to do?"

"Get the men together. We're leaving. I don't want to be anywhere around when Ava returns. She'll know someone was here."

Hassan nodded and turned to head back to the basement before he realized Shiraz wasn't following and stopped. "Are you coming?"

Shiraz waved him off. "I want another minute with the door. Go. I will catch up with you upstairs."

"Very well."

Shiraz turned back to the door and ran his hands over its surface. The wood felt solid. Old. And there, near the top, in script so small he hadn't noticed it earlier, Shiraz saw the Taluk inscriptions.

He tried reading them, but couldn't even make out what the first word was. Taluk was such an ancient language that it had a myriad of variations that no one but the Elders of the vampire society could hope to read.

Shiraz smiled. This only confirmed what he had suspected: that the relic was a truly powerful weapon in the right hands.

Shiraz's hands.

He patted the door once more. "Very soon you will give up what I seek and you will belong to me forever."

Just then the lights went out.

He frowned and turned. He'd given Hassan no such order to kill the power. Unless one of the other men had done it. The fools. He sighed and started back up the corridor toward the basement, stopping to take one final glance at the door with wistful eyes.

"Soon."

He stepped into the basement and then froze.

Something was wrong.

He drew his pistol and slid the safety off.

Blood.

His nostrils flared at the scent that tinged the air. Not close, though. Upstairs? If it had been close, the scent would be more cloying. Heavy.

Tangible.

Shiraz moved into the basement and stopped close to the stairs leading up to the kitchen. He heard the muffled pops and then a loud thud as something dropped to the floor. He resisted the urge to call out for Hassan.

He moved smoothly up the stairs, his senses primed as

he brought the pistol up and then swung around the corner of the door into the kitchen.

One of the men he had left here lay on the floor, a smear of blood already staining the tile. He was dead.

Shiraz sank to his knees as he approached another doorway. He'd learned from his brothers that you never stood at normal height and looked around a corner. You always got smaller. And if you could lie down on the floor and do it, all the better. No sense risking getting your head blown off.

With one eye, Shiraz peeked around the corner.

The living room that led back to the foyer was dark. But a shape lay on the Persian carpet. And Shiraz knew that it was the other man they had brought with them.

With two of his men killed and Hassan nowhere to be seen, Shiraz wished he had known these men. They'd served him well. The least he could do was know their names.

Perhaps another time, he thought.

He slid into the living room, keeping the pistol ready to bring up if a target presented itself. He thought he heard a noise behind him and pivoted easily, raising the gun and taking aim.

He very nearly fired, too. But then froze.

No.

Not there.

They'd made the noise to make him think that was where the threat was going to come from. But no—

He pivoted again and squeezed off a single round.

And watched as it punched directly into the sternum of Hassan.

"No!"

Hassan's face showed shock as he dropped to his knees. He looked down at his chest. The wood-tipped bullet had torn his heart open and the wooden fragments in his blood were already killing him.

Hassan might well have cried out in pain.

But he couldn't.

His mouth was secured with duct tape. He stayed upright on his knees for another moment before falling forward on his face. Shiraz saw now that Hassan's hands had been bound behind his back using more of the same tape.

Shiraz blinked. What had just happened?

A small object bounced into the room directly between him and Hassan and even as Shiraz started to bring his gun up to fire again, the object exploded in a brilliant flash of light and sound.

The effect was instantaneous. Shiraz lost his eyesight and hearing. His head swam. He tried to breathe. Tried to blink. Tried to get his head right.

But to no avail.

And then he felt his weapon being fleeced away, his wrist turned back in as a painful joint lock pinned him down on the ground. His vision started to clear but even as it did, he saw a large object coming straight for his head.

It impacted with such force that Shiraz felt his teeth rattle.

And then everything went black.

———————————⟫⟨———————————

"Welcome back."

Everything was still black. There was a blindfold around

his eyes. He quickly took stock of himself. His head thundered from a serious bruise to his skull. He tasted copper in his mouth, which meant that he'd been bleeding. His arms were pinned behind him and he sat in some sort of chair. He couldn't move his feet, either. He guessed that he'd been immobilized with the same duct tape that they used on Hassan.

Bastards.

Shiraz frowned and resolved to kill whoever had done this.

"Would you like some water? Perhaps it will help clear out that bad taste in your mouth. After all, it can't feel very good to be where you are right now."

A woman's voice. Shiraz cleared his throat, tasting the blood and sputum, and then swallowed hard. "Who are you?"

"I'm the person who got the drop on you. And I'm the person who killed your men. Rather easily, I might add."

"How did you know we would be here?"

Laughter echoed across the room. "Do you think you are really so much a genius that a preschooler couldn't figure out what your plans would be? After Syria, it was rather obvious you'd be coming for Lawson. And for the relic."

"What do you know of the relic?"

"I know plenty. And I know that you are not going to get your hands on it. Ever."

"Big words from someone who doesn't even have the courage to look me in the eye when she talks to me."

There was a pause and then without warning, the blindfold was ripped off. Shiraz blinked in the bright light that greeted him and made his head throb all the more.

A woman.

And he knew then who she was without even needing to think about it.

"Ava."

She smiled, revealing her gleaming white teeth. She was dressed from head to toe in some sort of black coverall that was taut enough to show off her curves. Shiraz estimated that she would have been somewhere around fifty to fifty-five in human years. But she looked very good for her age.

Very good, indeed.

"Why did you kill my men?"

"Because they were in the way," said Ava. "And frankly, I can't have a bunch of rogue vampires bumbling around and threatening to upset my grand plans. Can't have that at all. No chance."

"Grand plans?"

Ava bent forward and looked Shiraz in the eyes. "My plans." She leaned back and laughed lightly. "That's the problem with men. One of the problems. You always think so small. You're all shortsighted. I can imagine that you only thought it through to the point where you got your hands on the relic. It would only be later that you would think about what to do with it. And by then, you would have drawn so much heat from the Council that it would be suicide to show your face anywhere."

Shiraz frowned. "And I suppose you've thought things through?"

"Well, far more than you did," said Ava. "That's one of the benefits to being underestimated. People leave you alone. They don't ever think that you're capable of doing things, planning things. They think they can manipulate you, without ever seeing that you're the one who's been controlling their actions from the get-go. You allow them to think they've won, when in fact all they're doing is simply playing into your hands. Most people are tragically susceptible to manipulation. It's an art form, and one that I happen to be a master of. Much to the consternation of those I've destroyed over the course of my years in the service of my people."

Shiraz swallowed again. "So why keep me alive? You could easily kill me and be done with it."

Ava sighed and then pulled up another chair, settling herself on it before considering Shiraz for several moments. Then she folded her arms across her lap and pursed her lips. "Yes, well, that is the million-dollar question, isn't it? Why did I choose to keep you alive? Why on earth would I risk exposing myself like this?"

"Indeed," said Shiraz. "From a security standpoint, it might not be your wisest move. After all, I'm fairly certain you are going against the Council by doing whatever it is that you are doing."

"The Council doesn't know what is best for our people."

"And you do?"

Ava smiled. "Of course. I have seen the Council wrecked by stodgy old fools whose only intent is preserving the status quo. I know what our kind requires. What it will mean to move us forward into the next millennium by assuming our rightful place here on this planet."

Shiraz shrugged. "Vampires have existed for thousands of years in secret. Now, all of a sudden, you're going to move us out of the shadows into the light and let the humans know we exist? You'll never make it. Any type of maneuvering like that would warrant your immediate sanction by the Council. You'd be dead before you even left the building."

"Only if they know about it. I've spent years putting the pieces into place. Moving assets that I will need when the time is right. It has taken me a great deal longer than I thought, mainly because every time I get close to implementing my plans, that bastard Lawson gets in the way. He hates me even if he doesn't realize my true motives. He can't move against me, either. Not while I am one of the most powerful members of the Council. I imagine I am as much a pain in the ass to him as he is to me."

"We both have our reasons."

"Of course," said Ava. "He killed your two brothers. You are the only one left in your family."

"He will die by my hand," said Shiraz.

"You do realize that he was only carrying out orders from the Council?" asked Ava. "I doubt it was ever personal."

"The circle must be closed," said Shiraz. "It is the only way to restore the honor of my family. I must be the one to kill him."

"The question now becomes: can I trust you?" Ava eyed Shiraz. "Because frankly, it's fairly miraculous that I've let you live to this point. My instincts are all telling me to kill you and be done with it."

Shiraz grinned. "But you need someone to remove Lawson for you. If you do it yourself, there will be too many questions, you'll be too exposed, and your plans will be revealed. But if I do it, then you will remain safely obscured. You can continue to plan your grand schemes without worry of discovery or of Lawson interfering."

Ava said nothing, but continued to look at Shiraz.

Shiraz allowed his smile to widen. "My question to you is this: what do I get out of it if I agree to help you?"

Ava raised an eyebrow. "Did I give you the impression that this was a negotiation?"

"Everything is negotiation," said Shiraz. "It's just a matter of finding out what terms we will both find agreeable so that we can work together."

"That implies a partnership," said Ava.

Shiraz shrugged as much as he was able to do being bound to the chair. "Call it whatever you wish. I want to kill Lawson. And honestly, I would like to know what you plan to do with the relic and what you are planning to do to our people."

"Not what I will do 'to' our people, but what I will do 'for' our people. It's a very important distinction. One I would hope you would recognize."

Shiraz nodded. "Fair enough. So, what will you give me in exchange for killing Lawson?"

"The honor, as you said, of closing the circle for your family."

Shiraz shook his head. "That's not enough. I need something more."

Ava stood and placed the chair back against the wall. "You'll still have your life as well. I imagine that counts for a great deal."

Shiraz smiled. "I'm doing your dirty work, Ava. I deserve something for that. A piece of the pie, so to speak."

Ava sighed. "I suppose you're right." She moved closer to Shiraz, bringing her face inches away from his.

Shiraz watched her approach. There was no denying her beauty. Her power radiated out from her pores, intoxicating the air and making him heady.

"We could figure out a way to seal the deal," said Ava as her lips brushed across Shiraz's.

"We could," said Shiraz thickly. He swallowed and watched as Ava's lips brushed his cheek and then continued toward his ear.

She licked at his lobe. He could feel her hot breath against his skin.

And then he felt the most indescribably poignant sensation, like a searing heat in his chest. He looked down as Ava moved away and saw something that didn't seem to jibe with his expectations: a slim shaft of wood jutted from just below his sternum.

Shiraz felt his breath coming in spurts as blood spilled from where the shaft had pierced his heart. He looked up at Ava.

"Why?"

Ava shook her head. "You're too much of a liability to me. And you'd have leverage over me if I did choose to keep you around."

"But . . . I can kill Lawson . . . for you."

Ava laughed. "My dear fool, after everything you've witnessed here today, do you really think I need your help to take out one Fixer?"

Shiraz felt his breathing coming slower now. His incisors had lengthened as well.

Death was . . . close.

He looked up at Ava one last time even as darkness came for him. "I will . . . have . . . vengeance."

Blackness came for him then and the very last sound he heard was of Ava laughing.

"Not in this lifetime," she said. "Not ever."

UNEXPECTED CHOICES

DIANA PHARAOH FRANCIS

In the Horngate Witches series, the magical apocalypse has struck. Destructive wild magic has washed over the earth, unleashed by the Guardians—a group of elemental beings with extraordinary power—in order to restore the balance of magic and magical creatures in the world. Giselle is a witch who established the Horngate covenstead to help preserve those humans she can, though her methods are often brutal. Shoftiel is an angel of justice. Centuries before, he was imprisoned in the Mistlands after passing a death sentence on an innocent woman. Free again, he finds himself repeating his mistake, seeking vengeance on Max—one of Giselle's supernatural warriors—who he mistakenly believes has imprisoned two of his angel brethren. Now he faces eternity in the bleak, unchanging Mistlands.

Both Giselle and Shoftiel are villains in their own ways. Both seek redemption. "Unexpected Choices" brings them together once again. The question is, can either of them overcome their hatred and suspicion of each other to save the world and themselves?

He felt no pain in the Mistlands, even when he tried to harm himself. The wounds gaped bloody and then healed, all without the slightest ache.

No hunger. No weight of exhaustion. No cold. Nothing. No change at all. How long would he remain this time? Five hundred years? Double that maybe, for failing a second time?

It was his own damned fault. The knowledge burned. He'd been prideful, so sure of his judgment. How could his brother angels have *willingly* bound themselves to a witch's coven? The idea was ludicrous. No, it was *insane*, a betrayal of their race, of everything they were. Like putting themselves in service to dung beetles.

All the same, he should have known. He was better than they. He was stronger, smarter, and more powerful. Yet here he was, once again trapped in the Mistlands, brought down by an ancient curse, the very same one that had brought him here before. For all his abilities, he'd made an error, one that would cost him centuries more in this hellish place.

There was nothing in this realm but thick white mists. No sun, no moon, no landmarks. Shoftiel had no way to judge the passage of time. His mind clawed for something, anything, to do. He decided to use this time to learn perfection. He must learn so he never again made a mistake of judgment.

How had he been so wrong?

The answer repulsed him. His pride made him blind, unwilling to see what was, unwilling to question, to consider he might be wrong.

He'd been made to be perfect. An angel. He *could not* be fallible like the cockroaches swarming the earth. But the facts were unimpeachable. He was not perfect at all. Not even close. Now he reaped what he'd sowed.

A change.

Shoftiel instantly noticed the subtle shift in the air. A faint scent of stone, fire. A melody of magic whispering across his skin, ruffling through his gold-edged crimson covert feathers as they shifted from solid to smoke and back again.

Somewhere a door had opened.

Another impossibility. Still, his entire being riveted on the feeling of something new, something different.

The scents faded, but the melody remained. It called him. Teased him. Taunted slyly in the opaque mist.

His heart sped, his wings flaring to lift him. The blood-red feathers turned to smoke as Shoftiel flew blindly. The song grew merrier as he drew closer to the source of the siren call.

Then song and sensation died.

Shoftiel faltered, his heart splitting in two. "No!" he howled and a sword of red smoke appeared in his hand. He slashed it back and forth through the mist as if he could cut it apart. It stirred and quieted, silently obdurate as ever.

Shoftiel howled again. If he could have found a rock in the emptiness, he'd have beaten his idiot head against it.

Something hard pelted his naked chest. He snatched it from the air with preternatural speed. "Ask and you shall receive," he muttered with mordant humor.

It was a polished oval half the size of his palm. Indigo and gold flashed within black. Labradorite. He turned it over, looking for something to tell where it had come from. He was sure it was a message of some kind, if he only had the wit to read it.

The rock stabbed his palm. He swore and dropped the labradorite cabochon. Before it could fall far, he snatched it out of the air again. Blood pooled in his hand from a puncture wound. Realizing what was wanted, he set the stone in the blood.

A cloud of blue puffed from the stone, then a streamer of blue smoke unraveled from it. It rose in the air before him, twisting and curling into a smiley face.

Shoftiel scowled. He'd used the same face to taunt the Shadowblade warrior as he brought her to her knees. What was she up to?

The mouth of the smiley face opened and more indigo smoke poured forth, forming into words:

A choice.
To serve or rot.
The term is one week
then freedom.
Say yes and you are bound.
Say no and all is nothing again.

Not exactly poetry, but succinct and to the point. What kind of service? What degradation would he be forced to endure? Was this revenge? The concept of agreeing to serve a mortal sent rage boiling through his veins.

He opened his mouth to refuse. "Yes."

The smiley face and words vanished. The labradorite oval flared brightly. Silver filaments wriggled out of it. They lengthened and wove together into flat straps before closing around Shoftiel's wrist, snugging tightly, though not uncomfortably. Arcane symbols glowed on the metal, then faded.

By his own hand, he was bound.

Panic exploded like a rabid porcupine inside him, sending quills of terror drilling deep into his soul. He panted as adrenaline spiked. Before he could come to terms with his sudden slavery, the bracelet grew heavy and pulled him downward. He beat his wings to stay aloft, but to no avail.

He plummeted. The white mist dissolved. The real world blurred into a kaleidoscope of blue, green, gray, and yellow.

He jerked to a halt in midair. His surroundings came into focus.

He hung a foot above a broad meadow. Green shoots pushed up between winter-dried grasses. Obsidian mountain peaks rose up from behind a turquoise forest a short distance away. The sky was cobalt and clear.

Just before him, a complicated pattern of sigils and symbols coiled within a brilliantly lit witch circle, perhaps twenty feet in diameter. It consisted of an outer circle with a five-pointed star inside, and in the center of that, a triangle, and inside that, the witch. Her hands were bandaged, indicating she'd drawn the circle in her own blood.

Shoftiel's lip curled at the sight of Giselle, though he'd known the message could have come only from her. She was the only witch who both knew of his banishment and was strong enough to summon and bind him.

A petite woman with long chestnut hair worn in two pig-tail braids that hung down below her breasts, she wore torn jeans and a long-sleeved blue plaid shirt. Her feet were bare, despite the chill. She was the lead witch of the Horngate coven-stead in Montana, where his two brothers had inexplicably bound themselves in service.

It was hard to imagine this diminutive insect had the kind of power to establish and hold her own coven, much less convince two powerful angels to submit to her service. *Three* now, at least for a week, he corrected himself. Sitting cross-legged with a smudge of dirt on her cheek, she looked like a homeless waif, hardly more than a child.

Power crackled in the air, a purple sheen rising up in a column from the witch circle. One by one, the inner triangle, the star, and the exterior circle winked out along with the sig-ils and symbols. The purple sheen evaporated and the magic scattered like sparks on the wind.

Giselle stood. She dusted off her backside then turned her attention to Shoftiel, scanning him from head to toe. He slowly drifted to the ground.

"We don't have much time," she said, kicking at the rem-nants of her spell circle. When she'd destroyed any evidence of its existence, she walked away. Shoftiel burned at her si-lence and lack of deference, which fought against the feeling of unholy joy at his freedom from the Mistlands. Whatever the witch wanted of him, it was surely worth the price to es-cape that hellish place.

He flew to catch up with her, dropping down to match her stride.

"What do you want of me?"

"Protection." She didn't bother to look at him.

Shoftiel bit back hard on his annoyance. "From what?"

"Bad guys."

The answer was entirely unsatisfactory. "Explain. You have Shadowblades and Sunspears of excellent quality." She couldn't argue that. The best of them was Max, the warrior he'd mistakenly punished for crimes she hadn't committed. "*And* you have two other angels in service to you."

"I don't want to risk any of them. They'll die."

"And I won't?"

She shrugged. "Maybe. I don't really care."

Shoftiel smiled with reluctant appreciation. Brutal honesty. He liked that. "What kind of witch worries about losing her warriors? You can make others."

She stopped and looked at him, her gaze piercing and fierce. "I want to risk *you*. Who knows? Maybe I'll get to see you die a painful, horrible death."

"I am immortal."

"Technicality. Everything can be destroyed if you try hard enough." She gave him a taunting smile. "You motivate me."

He couldn't help his own slight smile. Sparring with her was vastly more entertaining than the Mistlands. But then, so was watching mountains erode. His standards had gone ridiculously low. He yawned. "What is this venture you need my help for?"

"A snatch and grab."

He frowned. "What?"

"Stealing something that doesn't belong to us."

That sounded intriguing. "What is it?"

Without giving an answer, Giselle started walking again,

following a packed-dirt animal track. Once more, Shoftiel fell in beside her.

"Are you going to tell me?"

"You don't need to know. Your job is keeping me alive."

They came to the lip where the land dropped twenty feet and rolled away to the mountains. Below, a Jeep was parked next to a clump of pink trees. Their limbs moved in the pair's direction as Giselle jogged down and grabbed a pair of socks and boots off the backseat and put them on.

"You can fly if you want," she said, getting into the driver's seat.

Since it seemed she'd prefer not being saddled with his company, he went around to climb in the other side. Riding in vehicles wasn't easy for an angel. Wings didn't usually fit. He was surprised to find that Giselle had removed the front and rear passenger seats and replaced them with cushions. There was a bench that lowered and adjusted to allow him to sit or kneel, and the roof had been raised to give his folded wings space. The single extra-long door slid open to allow easier access. All in all, it was surprisingly comfortable.

He'd barely shut the door when the witch hit the accelerator. Powered by magic, the vehicle jumped forward.

She steered them southward. Any road that might once have been there was gone. The waves of wild magic released by the Guardians had transmuted the world in fantastical ways. The Jeep rode smoothly, despite the often strange and difficult terrain. Giselle skirted a sudden desert of pure red sand. It rippled and moved and Shoftiel realized that it wasn't so much a desert as a lake.

Something rose and fell in the sands. It had a smooth

green body with hook-like protrusions running down its slim length. The tip of its tail was akin to the fletching on an arrow or dart. More creatures squirmed across the surface and burrowed under. Twenty, fifty, a hundred—all of varying sizes.

All of a sudden, the sky darkened and beasts dropped out from the clouds. They were feathered and furred and looked like hyenas with talons and razor-toothed beaks. They were ridden by small figures Shoftiel couldn't make out. They dove, driving spears, teeth, and talons through the hides of the sand serpents. As soon as they made a capture, the hunters rose into the sky, the serpents whipping and flailing. They flew off to the west with their prizes.

Shoftiel watched the event, fascinated, even as suspicion crept up his spine.

"How long was I in the Mistlands?"

"Almost three and a half years."

So long? And yet it had seemed like a century. Before he'd been sent to the Mistlands, wild magic had already begun to twist and change the earth. Or rather, returned to a starving land. The enchanted forests of old grew back a hundred times as big. Fields of flowers became blood hungry. All the creatures of fairy tales that had left or retreated into hiding began to return. "The world has undergone more changes. A bounty of curiosities."

"You don't know the half of it," Giselle muttered.

"Explain."

"You know, you have a habit of snapping out orders like I'm going to obey them. You should probably rethink that approach."

"Or what?"

"You'll make me angry. You wouldn't like me when I'm angry." She smiled as if at some secret joke.

"I don't like you now. As for your anger—is that supposed to be a threat? I am exponentially more powerful than you. I would crush you."

She laughed like he'd threatened her with nothing greater than a snowball fight, saying, "Not for seven days," when she finally collected herself.

Fury spun through him. Curls of red smoke wreathed his hands and arms. He was achingly tempted to teach her a lesson, despite the blood oath he'd taken to bind himself to her service. He did not tolerate being laughed at. "I don't see the humor."

"That's because, as usual, you think you're all that and a bag of chips. Do you ever get tired of worshipping yourself?"

"I see no reason to pretend I am less than I am."

"You also see no reason to think you could possibly be wrong about anything or anyone. How's that been working out for you, by the way? Been enjoying your vacation in the great white beyond?"

Shoftiel's rage exploded the windows of the vehicle. A gust of chill wind rushed through.

"Oops, did I touch a nerve?"

Shoftiel snarled, summoning the glass back and fixing the damage. He did *not* lose control. "Very well. Suppose you tell me why I should fear your anger?"

"Because I'm not stupid, though you obviously think that I am."

He did not. He'd spied on her and her coven enough to know the witch was devious. The fact that she'd created Max and earned the faith of two angels only proved her strength and capability.

"Perhaps you should enlighten me."

"I don't know. Might be fun to surprise you."

She was toying with him. "Explain," he demanded again.

"There you go, snapping orders again." She shook her head. "I guess you and old dogs have a lot in common. All right. I'll play. I'm not so stupid as to release you from the Mistlands without the ability to protect myself and my coven-stead from you. The 'how' of that I'll leave for you to find out on your own. As for what you missed in the last few years, the short answer is, a lot.

"You were here when the Guardians dumped magic into the world to cull humanity and bring magic-kin back into the world. They figured if they didn't get rid of a lot of the human infestation, they'd be right back where they started in nothing flat, since humans have a knack for doing things that null out magic. What you missed is that it didn't work. The cities didn't suffer much and a lot more humans survived than expected. The Guardians hadn't realized how much the metal infrastructures of cities and industrial areas would resist the flood of wild magic.

"'If a little doesn't work, then use a lot more' seemed to be their motto. The Guardians let loose another deluge. That was probably a year or so after you went back into the Mistlands. When that didn't work any better than the first time, they went another route and forced a war between magic-kin and humans. Some of us chose the human side. Anyway, the fighting went on for a year, and then stopped cold. The Guardians stood down, the magic-kin went home.

No one knows why, but now there's a truce between magic-kin and the cities, and the Guardians have backed off. The earth is pretty much saturated with magic, and we get these storms every so often that twist things up again. When that happens, a lot of people evacuate to the cities, including a lot of magic-kin. Since we need humans and they need us, we protect each other."

Shoftiel sat silent, absorbing the information. The miles reeled away. He stared out the window, as fascinated as a blind man newly cured. He hated the Mistlands. There was no worse hell. He should know. He was one of seven angels of punishment—the Malake Habbalah—doling out punishments to those who deserved it.

Unless they were wrong.

His lip curled at the unfamiliar doubt that knifed through him. He had twice proven fallible in his judgments. How many more mistakes could be laid at his door? Injustices he'd committed?

Unfamiliar doubt sank into him and nothing he did drove it away.

They'd driven up into a row of spongy brown and white hills. Their pebbly surfaces were slick with a yellow syrupy substance. Orange moss grew thickly in the creases between. On the other side of the hummocks, the land dropped deeply down into a vast plain. A black ocean spread as far as he could see to the west. It narrowed and thinned into a long dogleg going eastward. Small hummocks and islands broke the matte surface.

"That used to be the Great Salt Lake," Giselle said, braking to gaze out over the vista. "It's a tar bog now. Runs from

Salt Lake City over there"—she pointed—"nearly to Nevada over there. Still stinks like an outhouse in August, too."

As they descended, they began to see other travelers heading for what appeared to be a road bridging the tar bog. Or so he assumed. He couldn't see the far side. Some came in wagons hauled by animals or in cars or trucks. Others came on a spectrum of pedaled bikes, or in strangely shaped floating balloons. There were also flying contraptions and winged creatures, plus the unlucky who were forced to go on foot.

"What's on the other end?"

For once the witch gave him a better-than-terse answer. "A city of sorts. Not a lot of permanent structures. People come from all over the west to trade, buy, and sell whatever they've got. There's also a kind of shrine there. Some people go there looking for miracles."

"Do they find them?"

"They find something."

"That's cryptic."

"It's a cryptic kind of place," she said. "You'll see soon."

"This thing you plan to steal—it's here?"

"That's what my visions said."

"And if you don't succeed?"

"Human sacrifice, dogs and cats living together, mass hysteria," she said.

He glowered at her. "What the hell is that supposed to mean?"

"Oh, for fuck's sake. You're as bad as Xaphan. Don't you angels ever get out to the movies? I mean, *Ghostbusters*. One of the best all-time funny movies. You really need to get out more."

"I have had better things to do with my time," he said loftily.

"Right. Like torture and enabling a serial killer. Good times."

Her sarcasm annoyed him more than it should have.

"Don't pretend you haven't tortured and killed," he said. "You say it's in the name of righteousness, but it's all ambition and hunger for power, isn't it? You are just as ruthless, savage, and pitiless as I am. More so, because you are driven by greed."

"I don't get off on it like you do. You probably blow a load every time you hurt someone."

"Why shouldn't I enjoy giving justice?"

"Are you sure it's always justice?"

The lash of that whip silenced him. He had been wrong twice. *That he knew of.*

"You never said what you have come to steal," he said, changing the subject.

She stared ahead, her face set. "That's because I don't know."

He studied her, trying to decide if she was lying or toying with him. She appeared to be genuine. "Explain." After a moment he added, "please."

A hint of a smile flickered over her lips. His reward for his effort at politeness was an actual answer, rather than more prevarication.

"My visions said there's something inside I have to get. I don't know what, and before you ask, I don't know why, or what to do with whatever it is once I do find it."

"How will you know when you have?"

"I'm hoping for a big neon sign and maybe trumpets or dancing girls," she said. "Maybe a big *X* marking the spot. Isn't that the way this sort of thing works?"

"You're the reason the Guardians want to eradicate humans," Shoftiel said, irritation getting the best of him.

"Me? Personally? Wow. Do I get a trophy for that? Or just one of those participant ribbons everybody gets?"

"A gag would be more appropriate."

She shrugged. "You want me to shut up? You got it. And witches don't count as human."

They got into the long line waiting to cross the bridge. Heat waves rose from the tar bog, distorting the air. On either side of the road were fields, the dirt turned and ready for planting. The sun was starting its descent into the west, its light shedding fire on the bog's black surface. Shoftiel doubted they'd cross to the other side of the bridge before dusk. For a moment he considered taking a short surveillance flight, but dismissed the idea. He was bound to protect Giselle and couldn't if he wasn't by her side. He cast a sideways glance at the witch. She had a fertile imagination and she despised him. He had no doubt the cost for breaking his binding would be worse than the Mistlands.

The trip across the river was slow and hot. They crept along between a magic-powered semi and a wood-topped wagon pulled by a giant anteater with horns. The bridge extended at least ten miles with only two lanes. Boats poled through the tarways between hummocks and islands, some populated. Fumes made it difficult to breathe.

On the other shore, a city sprawled. A mix of tents, ramshackle buildings, and magical constructions, it must have covered several square miles. A mass of humans and magic-kin filled it to bursting. In the distance on a rise in the center, slender white pillars that looked no bigger than Shoftiel's arm rose high into the air like a ghostly forest of limbless trees. Above them spiraled a vast cloud of lavender smoke.

"What's that?"

"That's where the miracles happen," Giselle said, but her grim expression was anything but hopeful.

They drove the meandering streets. Giselle seemed to have a goal in mind, following a map only she could see.

"The streets move all the time," she offered up. "The far-ther away from there"—she jerked her chin toward the center swirl of lavender smoke—"the more stable things are. The outer fringes near the bog are where most of the traders set up and where more of the permanent structures tend to be. We're headed to one of those. We'll get something to eat be-fore we hike in closer to the shrine."

She pointed out a couple of landmarks—a series of steel buildings large enough to house a dozen leviathans each. "That's equipment for a conglomerate of growers. Tractors, harrows, bailers, threshers, all that kind of thing. Magic does a lot of things, but good old-fashioned technology can be a lot cheaper and more efficient."

The steel corrals they passed covered thirty or forty acres and contained a variety of livestock, many of which Shoftiel had never seen before. One area looked like an aviary.

"That's where they keep the pigs." She grinned. "They re-ally do fly now."

Eventually she pulled up in front of a pair of rippled-glass gates. They were set in a tall, thick wall made of stone layered in more glass, like ice. Giselle rolled her window down and tapped the button on a speaker.

"Yes?" came the instant response.

"Giselle from Horngate. I've got an angel with me. Need a place to park, food, and rooms for a couple of days. Usual payment, plus some extra goodies for Merri."

"Enter and be welcome."

The gates slid apart just wide enough for them to pass. A curtain of magic continued to guard the entrance. It sizzled over Shoftiel with unexpected—and familiar—power.

"Your spell?" he asked Giselle.

She nodded. "Money's no good anywhere, but witch services are always in demand. I laid down the wards and recharge and strengthen them whenever I come down."

"All this in just three and a half years?" He waved his hand in the direction of the rest of the city.

She shrugged. "People want to survive. They got their shit together fast. Humans are resilient that way. They worked with magic-kin to develop farms and continued with a lot of city-based industry. Electricity still works there, along with most trappings of life like refrigerators and air-conditioning and streetlights. Gasoline is harder to come by, but magic works just as well as any motor. Trains still operate. Planes do, too, though warding them is tricky. Same with ships on the ocean. If the Guardians meant to knock us back to the Stone Age, they didn't realize what they were up against."

Inside the compound, she drove to a parking barn and was directed to a spot by a wizened woman with a shock of white hair who gave Shoftiel's wings a startled look. Once parked, Giselle pulled a backpack out of the back along with a heavy coat.

"Let's go. I'm starved."

Shoftiel was, too. His mouth watered at the thought of eating, of chewing and tasting. He'd gone years in the Mistlands without. His stomach actually growled.

They entered a rambling two-story inn. Giselle made a beeline for the front desk. A young man waited on the other side. He had pointed ears, smooth black hair, and a narrow jaw. Delicate green designs wrapped every inch of exposed skin. His eyes, when he looked up from his ledgers, were almond shaped with slit pupils. An elf. Probably one of the Irish variety, but he could very well have come from any number of places.

He smiled at Giselle, and bowed his head in greeting. "Welcome back, mistress."

"Hello, Nior. It's good to be here."

With little ceremony, he provided her with a blue crystal key on a chain with a number tab on it. "It's an honor to serve you. May your endeavors be successful."

He bowed again and Giselle led Shoftiel away. He expected her to drop her gear in the room she'd rented, but instead she wound her way to the restaurant at the back of the inn. It was three-quarters full, with a couple dozen diners wearing lavender robes and white-and-black face paint.

"Supplicants," Giselle said before Shoftiel could ask. "They must have come in on a bus." Her frown indicated disapproval.

"What's wrong with them?"

She gave a little shrug and found a table in the corner.

Shoftiel followed, ignoring the gasps and rising voices his presence generated.

"You're causing a lot of excitement," Giselle said. "Most people never get to see an angel and there's still a bunch that believe you guys are holy."

His gaze sliced across the watchers and then dismissed them. He speared the witch with his eyes instead. "Why don't you like the supplicants?"

"They come for miracles at the shrine. Most of them get heartache in one shape or another—at least, those who come out. A lot don't."

He considered her words. "What happens to them?"

"Who knows? Enough come out with their prayers answered that people keep pouring in. They don't seem to care that their odds aren't very good. Or maybe they think they get whisked up to heaven."

"And yet you plan to go inside."

"I'll have you to guard me. Or don't you think you can handle it?"

"I don't think I can handle *you*," he muttered, and was irritated to find that despite his dislike of her, she interested him. She wasn't a typical witch and that snared his curiosity. He blamed his sojourn in the Mistlands. At any rate, protecting her wouldn't be an issue. Between the two of them, he doubted there was much they couldn't handle.

"What did you say?"

He was certain she'd heard. "I said I'm perfectly confident in my ability to protect you." From outer harm. Whether he could protect her from herself—that was another question altogether.

He'd had time these last years in the Mistlands to remember every detail about Horngate and had concluded
that whatever else the motley group were, they were unusual. They sacrificed themselves for others, even strangers.
Giselle could very well do something stupidly altruistic and
get herself killed. But if she did, would the spell binding him
send him back to the Mistlands for the duration of the
curse?

He wasn't about to find out.

The pillars rose before them like giant skeletal reeds. Phan-
tom mist twisted between them. Shoftiel couldn't tell what
they were made of. Salt, perhaps. The area had been known
as the salt flats once. Some of the stalks were the size of a finger. Others as big around as a barrel.

Unnatural silence smothered the sound of their footsteps
and the rustle of their clothing. Giselle had said little since
they departed the hotel in the predawn hours. He'd surprised
himself by offering to fly them to their destination. She'd surprised him by accepting. Normally he'd have cut his arm off
before lowering himself to such menial work, but he wished
to see the sprawl of the city from the air and could not leave
her side. Now they walked.

"Why did my brothers bind themselves to your coven-
stead?" he asked. The question had burned in him since he'd
learned what Tutresiel and Xaphan had done.

"Self-preservation," Giselle said. "They didn't want to be
pawns for the Guardians any more than we did."

He frowned. "How could binding themselves to Horngate allow them to escape?"

"It's a long story, but the upshot is Max received a wish as a gift and used it to make the Guardians forget Horngate, including every member of the covenstead. Since they thought we were a better option than the Guardians, Tutresiel and Xaphan pledged themselves to Horngate."

His brows rose. "Clever." Her explanation only stimulated his curiosity about Horngate's denizens. Max could have used that wish on herself, but instead she'd protected her covenstead. A fact that reinforced how very wrong his judgment and punishment of her had been.

Witches who established their own covensteads created supernatural warriors out of ordinary humans to protect the covenstead. Each had a squad called Sunspears, composed of those who could come out only during the day, and a second squad composed of those who could survive only in the dark, called Shadowblades. Max was one of the latter, the Prime, or captain, of her fellow Blades.

They came to the inner edge of the ghostly towers surrounding the shrine. Shoftiel put a hand on Giselle's arm to halt her. He could see nothing through the smoke, but he felt a *presence*. Many of them. And enormous magic.

"What's wrong?"

"There's more here than I suspected."

"How so?"

He frowned, trying to sort out his impressions. "This is no mere shrine."

"Well, whatever it is, we're running out of time." The witch tugged away and strode in between two bone-white columns. Magic rippled and sent brilliant threads to wrap her legs and wind around her body until she was covered from head to toe in a golden net of power.

Shoftiel launched into the air and hovered beside her. "How can you have lived this long with shit for brains? I thought you were smart, but you're being dumber than a bucket of dirt right now." Crimson magic wreathed his hands as he reached out to break the spell.

She waved him off. "Don't."

His eyes narrowed. "You knew what would happen."

"Yep."

"You saw this in a vision?"

"Yep."

"You might have mentioned it."

"Across all the visions, this never changed. I figured it was bound to happen, so why wait? Now, let's stop wasting time."

He floated back a few feet, studying her, then shrugged. "Suit yourself."

Shoftiel fumed. He was unused to doing nothing, and the magic net covering Giselle could quite well kill her before he had a chance to stop it. In which case, he'd be jerked back to the Mistlands.

He dipped closer. Any sign of attack and he'd snatch her up and fly her clear of the place. He didn't care how much she fought him.

"Look," Giselle said as a path cleared in front of her. It pulsed with radiant light. "I guess that would be our invitation to the ball." She started walking.

Shoftiel shielded himself, then prepared another shield to

throw around Giselle should she need it. He readied another spell to destroy the magic encasing her. As they went deeper into the smoke, the hair on his body prickled. The throb of power continued to deepen and expand. The *presences* he sensed gathered closer. Everything about this venture felt like a trap.

He closed the gap between them so that his wings brushed the witch's shoulders. She shivered at his touch and quickened her pace. He sped up to maintain contact. Instinct told him it was necessary, but he also took great satisfaction in her obvious discomfort.

The path meandered in looping curves. The lavender smoke disguised any landmarks. They'd walked nearly an hour when movement boiled on the left and a figure flowed onto the path, blocking the way.

It wore robes like the supplicants at the restaurant. Its face was black shadow with pearl eyes. Though its shape was human, Shoftiel could tell it was not. Giselle stopped a few feet away. The figure neither moved nor spoke.

"What do you want?" Giselle demanded.

No answer.

She started to go around, but Shoftiel stopped her. "Don't leave the path."

To his surprise, she obeyed. Then, before he could stop her, she lunged forward, passing through the figure. It burst apart into tatters of smoke and vanished. The motion made Giselle break contact with Shoftiel. Before he could overtake her again, lavender smoke swirled between them and she vanished.

"Giselle!" he shouted, but the only answer was silence.

Shoftiel darted forward, but she was gone. There was no sign of the path. He might as well have been back in the Mistlands for all he could see. He released a burning swell of magic, cutting a swath through the smoke. For a moment, a space maybe thirty feet in diameter cleared. Dozens of lavender-robed figures stood about like statues, all facing different directions. He could see no sign of the witch.

Within a few seconds, the cleared space filled again. Shoftiel focused his senses on the binding between Giselle and him. Nothing. That he still remained in this place proved she was alive. But for how long? And how to find her?

He flung himself at a spot where he'd seen a robed watcher. Nothing was there. He released another burst of magic. The figures had all shifted places. Shoftiel snatched one, yanking its hood back.

"Where is she?" the angel demanded, shaking the creature.

Its only response was to shiver and collapse into smoke. Shoftiel flung aside the robe. Something akin to panic spooled tight in his belly.

He released another blast and flew across the exposed space. He repeated the exercise again and again. It was a lousy way to search, but he had little choice. He did have an excellent sense of direction, however, and knew without a doubt that he was moving deeper into this land of smoke. Whatever was hiding here had to be at the center. That's where Giselle would go. She was too stupidly stubborn to be stopped.

Shoftiel hovered, letting his senses play outward, sliding back and forth until he pinpointed the place of strongest power. He arrowed blindly toward it.

A force hit him like a hammer of god, smashing him out

of the air. He slammed to the ground. His brain fogged and blackened around the edges as he gasped for breath. Bones had broken. He felt them knitting together. He flung himself upright, hardly aware of the explosions of pain racking his body. His wings shimmered into a crimson-and-gold mist, then resettled into feathers.

Shoftiel's shield spell had protected him from the magic he sensed in the ground beyond the pathway. Now he rocketed into the sky. This time he felt the blow coming before it struck. He dodged. He flung a bolt of magic in the direction from which the attack had come.

Another hammer strike. He twisted, but the blow caught his side, sending him tumbling until he finally caught himself with strong sweeps of his wings. An awareness searched for him. He could feel it. More sought him from below.

Shoftiel recognized the moment his opponent located him. He strengthened his shield and plunged back on his original path. When the strike came, he met it with a blast of magic that for a moment outlined a giant beast with a gaping mouth, hulking shoulders, and arms like sequoia redwoods. It had a multitude of fingers, each tipped with short, hooked claws. It screamed in pain and rage as white fire ran over its body.

Shoftiel took advantage of its distraction to wing past it. He homed in on the massed pulse of power and flew there with lightning speed.

The air thickened and he had to fight to get through. His ribs bellowed. Sweat slicked his skin. Abruptly he came out of the lavender smoke into a clear, round space, like the eye at the center of a hurricane. Golden lines of magic spilled out across the ground, weaving together into a brilliant tapestry. The spell was too complex for Shoftiel to understand without seeing it all.

Crossing the field of gold were suppliants of all shapes and sizes, all wearing lavender robes and wrapped in cocoons of golden light. They walked toward the center of the field where an open-roofed temple surrounded a squat pedestal, its round base wrapped in the spell's gold filaments. Something sat on top. Without a doubt, the angel knew that this was what Giselle had come to steal.

Shoftiel flew lower, gliding above the shuffling suppliants. As he watched, several fell. The light encasing them flared and they vanished. A moment later, he caught sight of Giselle. She'd nearly reached the temple. He raced to overtake her. He caught her by the shoulder just before she stepped within the alabaster pillars.

"Giselle."

She turned her face to look at him. Her skin was bloody, striped with cuts and blistered from burns. Her hair was little more than stubble. Her clothes hung in tatters and her backpack had disappeared. For a moment, Shoftiel didn't think she recognized him. Then one side of her mouth quirked. "Just in time for the grand finale," she said.

"Do you know what's happening here?"

"No." Then, "I think whatever this is, it's the reason the Guardians abandoned the war and have left us alone."

Shoftiel frowned. She leaned against his arresting grip as if unable to resist the pull of the temple. He felt its draw as well, though not as strongly as he suspected those caught in the spell nets did.

"Then if you succeed in your mission, the war will begin again."

She grimaced. "I don't think it's that simple. Let go of me. Standing here isn't doing any good."

He considered plucking her up and flying her out. Breaking the spell that held her was the problem. If he did, pulling that one thread could short-circuit the rest of the massed spell. The explosion could wipe out the entire continent.

He loosened his grip slightly, curiosity getting the better of him. There would still be time to flee. "I'll stay with you."

The moment they stepped through the pillars into the temple, the air turned warm and thick as honey. It was hard to move, even with the protection of his shield magic. Giselle moved easily, no doubt facilitated by the spell wrapping her. Supplicants entered from every side. They formed a circle around the pedestal. Each laid their hands on the smooth white surface. As they did, the spell strands ensnaring them flared bright as sunshine. When it died away, most of the supplicants had disappeared. The few left standing would bow their heads and then turn to walk robotically away.

Rarely—he only saw one as Giselle lined up for her turn—the radiance didn't die away. The supplicant would rise in a golden bubble and float out through the top of the temple and away. A miracle recipient.

All around them, the supplicants whispered and muttered, mostly to themselves. Mostly prayers, but some were invocations, and others were spells. Shoftiel still couldn't make out what was on top of the pedestal. Opalescent light disguised it. What could stop the Guardians in their tracks? A weapon?

Finally Giselle was next. He moved behind her, settling both hands on her shoulders. "You're going to do this?"

"The stupid is strong in me," she said without turning to look at him.

"What happens if you don't?"

He'd not asked her that. Hadn't really cared. But the situation was far bigger than he'd imagined, and given her coven-stead's penchant for sacrifice, he had a feeling this could end very badly for her . . . and him.

"I told you—"

"Truthfully," he interjected before she could repeat the movie line she'd given him last time.

Her back stiffened and her shoulders squared beneath his hands. "Something like the apocalypse. Only worse."

That she believed it, Shoftiel didn't doubt. Whether it was true, he didn't know. Before he could ask anything else or even think of a question, she stepped forward and laid her hands flat on the pedestal. Light coruscated over her and up his arms, washing over him until he was engulfed.

The temple and supplicants vanished. They stood inside a white salt circle. Another one surrounded it and another. Thirteen altogether. Between each were inscribed symbols and sigils glowing golden. The ground where they stood was black obsidian except for a small silver plinth in the center. On top, balanced on the point of a pin, was a crystal sphere the size of his head.

On the other side of the plinth was a shadowed figure, and another two, one on the left, the other on the right. Ethereal blue light limned all three.

For a long moment no one moved. Shoftiel spread his

wings to be sure he could, his fingers tightening on Giselle's shoulders.

"Time to fish or cut bait," she said softly, and then stepped toward the plinth. That the sphere was the object she'd come to steal seemed obvious. Whether she could was another story. The magic emanating from the three champions guarding the object was greater than Shoftiel's own. He and Giselle would not win a battle. That left trickery. He'd have to follow the witch's lead, a fact that made him want to beat his head against a rock. How had he allowed her this kind of power over him?

The three shadow opponents vanished and reappeared in front of them, blocking their path to the pedestal.

"This has to end," Giselle said, stopping. "This is no longer a good solution."

"We cannot go back to war," the center figure answered, its voice deep and hollow, as if the ancient stones of the world spoke.

"They saved our world, and then they tried to kill it," came the one on the right. Its voice was lighter and made Shoftiel's bones ache like a winter wind cutting through his flesh.

"There is no other way," the third one said, its voice booming like thunder over the mountains.

"Let me talk to her?" Giselle asked in a respectful tone. "If we must fight one another, let us know the reason why."

More secrets. Shoftiel's fingers dug deeply into her shoulders until they touched bone. Giselle neither flinched nor cried out in pain. "Who is *she*?" he gritted in her ear. He didn't expect an answer and he got none.

The shadow figures exchanged looks, and then nodded. They stepped aside, the center one gesturing for Giselle to approach. None of them paid any attention to Shoftiel.

Giselle stopped before the plinth and looked from side to side. "Join me," she said. Shadow fingers wrapped around her arms and then she reached out, placing her hand on top of the sphere.

Light flashed and a scream tore through the world. It was all Shoftiel could do to keep from dropping to his knees. He felt Giselle tremble and wobble, and he slid his arms around her to keep her upright. Her head lolled forward. Magic crackled over her skin, lighting her on fire. Shoftiel felt her heart stutter as she whimpered.

Without thinking, he pulled her tighter to him, encircling her in his aura. The fierce magic jumped into him. It burrowed, trying to pull him apart. He fought it, burning it out and shearing off the tentacles that returned. His power melded with Giselle's and together they pushed it back, putting up a wall between them and the invasion.

Abruptly the attack stopped.

"Who are you?" The voice chimed like a bell, reverberating through their bodies and sending spiderweb cracks across their shield. As one, they reinforced it.

"A witch. An angel. Your wardens."

"You were not invited."

The condemning words hit his heart, squeezing it in a deadly grip. Shoftiel's arms tightened on Giselle as he spread his wings. Could he get her away? Fly her to safety? He told himself it was because of the binding, because he didn't want to go back to the Mistlands. It was true, but he feared she might have infected him with her peculiar brand of honor, one that put sacrifice above self-preservation. It seemed he didn't want her dead.

"You must hear me," Giselle said, her body shuddering, blood trickling from her nose and ears.

"What do you want?"

"Your imprisonment ended the Guardian war against the humans," Giselle said. "The truce has been celebrated by magic-kin and humans alike. No one wants the return of the war, except maybe the other Guardians."

Other?

Her statement was met with silence. Eventually the voice spoke again. "This is true."

"You are dying," Giselle said baldly.

Another silence. "This may also be true. I am growing different."

"If you die, the world will burn as the other Guardians take revenge."

Another considering silence. "It is likely."

"The same will happen if you are freed."

The light around them shimmered and turned a shell pink. A figure emerged. She was slight and small, perhaps four feet tall. Her form blurred and shifted, then concentrated together to solidify, then shifted again, much in the same way Shoftiel's wings did.

She was lovely, but not human. She was like nothing he'd seen before. One moment she looked like a woman. Then a bear, an eagle, a praying mantis—it was like she was everything and nothing. A Guardian.

Shoftiel felt a mix of awe, fear, and anger. The Guardians

had much to answer for, both good and bad. But to imprison one—that was pure evil. "How did they capture you?"

She smiled and melted into a silver-winged moth. "I came because I was needed."

"You're not a prisoner," Giselle said, and shook her head. "I am supposed to steal you from yourself," she said. "The universe has a rotten sense of humor, doesn't it?"

"I hoped my sisters and brothers would decide they'd done enough," the Guardian said. "War hurts those we wanted to save and protect the most. But the others have not changed. I cannot leave."

"You can't stay," Giselle said. "I've seen what happens. It will make war look like a kid's ice-cream party."

"I must stay."

"Oh, for fuck's sake. You guys are all alike. You, too," she said, casting a disparaging look over her shoulder at Shoftiel. "You all know better than anyone else. You never make mistakes, except when you do. The rest of us aren't idiots, you know. Sure, we make mistakes and we're going to make a fuckton more. But that's *our* problem, not yours. Your problem is that you need to back off and keep your superiority to yourselves. You need to go home and leave us the fuck alone."

Shoftiel growled and suddenly the labradorite binding fell from his wrist. He was free. Despite his shock, he wasn't so befuddled that he lost contact with Giselle when she lunged forward and grabbed the Guardian by the ankle.

The world went nova. Shoftiel held tight to Giselle as reality shattered and every molecule in his body separated from the rest. He shielded himself, extending the spell to hold Giselle and the Guardian. Not that the latter needed it, but he couldn't close the spell around Giselle without cutting the Guardian's leg off.

Guardians were elementals of the universe, physical expressions of the creation magic that had formed the worlds and everything on them. They were shepherds and police. They couldn't die, and he wasn't sure he actually could cut off her leg, but there was a fragility to her that he didn't want to test.

They spun wildly out into nothingness. He felt Giselle cast a spell. Amazingly, it wrenched them back into the temple. They sprawled onto the alabaster pedestal. Pain radiated through him as bones cracked and joints pulled apart. He absorbed most of the fall, keeping the witch and the Guardian on top of him.

All three lay there a moment, then without a word, Giselle stood and picked the Guardian up in a fireman's carry. She leaped from the pedestal, pushing out past the crowd of supplicants, and then sprinted across the open space to the wall of lavender smoke. By the time Shoftiel found his feet, they'd disappeared.

He sought them on foot, and then by air as he healed himself. The magic running through the golden patterns on the ground tarnished and faded, but the smoke remained.

After a while of fruitless searching, he returned to the inn. He peeled open the security web with little effort, repairing it before looking for Giselle. She wasn't there.

Emotion churned in his gut. She'd had ample time to return. He tried not to think about what the Guardian might have done to her. Even fragile, she could pulverize the witch with just a thought. He didn't examine too closely why he cared. His business with Giselle was certainly done. The removal of the labradorite cuff had freed him from their deal. Likely because the fool thought she'd die and wanted to release him before that, which made no sense whatsoever. She'd pulled him from the Mistlands to protect her. Why would she release him before she'd escaped with the Guardian?

When he found her, he'd make her answer if he had to light her on fire to get her to talk.

He'd worked himself into a volcanic fury by the time he found her four hours later. She limped along a snaking road, several miles from the inn. Her body was a welter of wounds, her clothes rags. She had no shoes, nor did she have the Guardian. He dove out of the air and snatched her up, flying high in the sky. She shivered from the icy chill of the wind at this height.

"What the hell are you doing?" she demanded, and despite the shaky weakness in her voice, she sent a substantial jolt of power through his arms. "Let me go."

He dropped her, then caught her just feet above the ground.

"Asshole," she said, trembling with fear she couldn't hide.

"Careful. I might drop you again."

"Why haven't you gone off to inflict yourself on someone else? I'd have thought you'd hightail it for the hills the moment I took off the binding."

He'd have thought so, too. He wasn't ready to examine why he hadn't.

"I want to repay your kindness to me," he mocked. "In rescuing me from the Mistlands."

"I gave you a choice and besides that, you deserved to be there for what you did to Max. You still do."

He couldn't argue that. The poison of being wrong burned like acid in his veins.

"So where are you taking me?"

"I thought I might drop you in the tar bog."

"Then you overshot. We passed that ten minutes ago."

"What did you do with the Guardian?" he asked.

She didn't answer right away. Shoftiel continued to fly. He was going north, and though he'd not chosen a destination deliberately, he knew where he was headed. Depending on her answer.

"You realize this is none of your business," she said.

"I'm making it my business," he said, considering dropping her again.

She sighed. "Whatever. Once we got outside the shrine, she and I had a talk. Then she left."

Now Shoftiel did drop her. She swore a blue streak when he retrieved her. "Now tell me the real story," he said.

Giselle sighed. "Doing what she was doing was killing her. If she died, the other Guardians would destroy the earth in revenge. Once she was out of her prison, she couldn't go back inside it. She doesn't have enough strength anymore. The supplicants have been feeding the spell, but she couldn't have lasted much longer."

"So, what does she do now?"

Giselle shrugged in his embrace. "Go home, I guess. Maybe the rest of them will listen to her. Maybe not. I'm not in a hurry to find out. Now can you take me back to the inn? I'm freezing, I'm hurt, I'm tired, and I'm hungry."

He pretended to consider. "No."

He thought she'd be angry, but instead she seemed resigned, like she'd expected him to turn on her. They flew through the night. Her shivering grew more pronounced, but she made no effort to use magic to warm herself. It was like she had given up. That irritated Shoftiel. But then he smiled. No doubt that was the point. Ruin his fun by dying before he could torture her. The angel wrapped her in a warming spell, her wordless protest confirming his conclusion.

Hours passed and at some point the witch fell asleep. She'd mostly stopped bleeding, and her heart beat strongly. What wounds she had wouldn't kill her before they reached their destination.

The sun was just rising when they arrived. Shoftiel circled. He dismissed the idea of dropping her again to wake her up, as amusing as it would be. Instead he nudged her awake with his knee. She stiffened as awareness returned.

"Where are we?"

"Home," he said.

She scowled. "Whose home?"

"Yours. And mine. I am moving in to Horngate for a while."

She twisted to gape at him. "What the hell are you talking about?" Then shook her head fiercely. "No way. Nobody wants you here."

"Which will only make me enjoy my stay more," he said. He smiled, anticipating the furor his arrival would cause. He had an ulterior motive, however. Horngate intrigued him, and he had a debt to pay to Max. It was the only way to clean his soul of unjust punishment. His smile taunted the witch.

"Do you think you can stop me? Didn't you say you're now prepared for my attack?"

She flushed. It was a bluff, then. She lifted her chin, meeting his gaze. "I won't let you hurt my people."

It was what he'd thought she'd say.

"Then we agree. It will be fun."

"Fun?" She glared in disbelief and then shook her head. "You're insane. Max is going to make mincemeat out of you. I'm going to enjoy watching the whole thing."

"I may grow on you."

"Like mold."

"Make your choice. I can drop you off here, or both of us can walk in the front doors."

She considered. No doubt she was actually considering the death option. She wanted what was best for her covenstead. Nothing about her was selfish. Nothing about her was typical for a witch. He wanted to know why, whether she liked it or not, and for that he needed her alive. He was done giving her choices.

"You couldn't keep me out before, and your wards won't keep me out now. I'm moving in. Get used to having me around."

With that, he took them home.

REEL LIFE

A Glass Town Story

STEVEN SAVILE

There are monstrous creatures in Glass Town, but the worst of them by far is an ordinary man, Seth Lockwood, whose envy of his brother drove him to kidnap the love of his life—a beautiful young actress, Eleanor Raines—over a century ago, because he couldn't stand the thought of his brother being happy. Glass Town spans generations of obsession. Seth lives in a world where one hundred years pass as one, and he has lifetimes of being unlucky enough to get what he thought he wanted lying ahead of him . . . but there are cracks beginning to appear now as Damiola's great illusion is failing, allowing Seth to slip between then and now. Without Seth, there is no Glass Town. Without Seth, our young lovers might just have been the Hollywood happy ending after all. "Reel Life" follows Seth through the cracks as he comes to grips with a century's worth of obsession, looking for a way to win once and for all, and damning himself in the process. . . .

Seth Lockwood was in Hell. It had a lot of other names, but that didn't change Glass Town's fundamental nature. With Damiola's magic he thought he was buying a ticket to his own personal heaven. A kingdom to rival any glory he could have dreamed of. But this place was Hell, even if it lacked the reek of brimstone and the streets of fire of its more traditional renditions. Hell for Seth Lockwood looked like an abandoned movie set filled with false façades and painted windows that looked out onto streets pretending to be normal.

It was hard to imagine that even a few months ago this was what he wanted more than anything else in the world; to be here, in this place, alone with the woman of his obsessive dreams. He had won the fair maiden, but theirs wasn't a love affair for the ages. It began in covetous lust, slid slowly into jealous obsession, and finally consummated in violence. He wasn't sure love had ever come into the picture, but that didn't matter to Seth because in his world, winning was everything, and he'd won.

For once, though, winning wasn't enough. The prize was bittersweet because she'd given up, and to Seth, something given freely had no worth.

That wasn't to say he didn't enjoy her begging. He did. He loved those moments when she pleaded, tears streaking her rouged cheeks. He delighted at the feeling of her hot breath against his neck as it came in ragged, frightened gasps. He savored the sensation of taking what wasn't his to take, of reaching up to pull aside the gusset of her panties with no pretense at seduction. But what Seth took the most joy out of was his brother's imagined pain. Isaiah truly loved Eleanor Raines. That, more than anything else, was the reason for

Seth's obsession. Like everything else, the pleasure he took from ownership was fleeting and he was left feeling hollow as he walked away, leaving Eleanor Raines curled up on the ground, the two-dimensional street painted around her. She looked like a broken doll cast aside by a petulant child.

He looked down at his bloody knuckles and flexed his fist.

It was the only way he touched her now.

Part of him still wanted to believe that, given enough time, she would learn to love him, but that part was a naive fool. The best he could hope for was acceptance, that this place would beat her into submission and she'd finally resign herself to the reality that these few make-believe streets were the be-all and end-all of her world now.

He heard the baby crying behind one of the thin plywood walls.

The boy wasn't his. The mathematics of conception didn't add up, meaning this was his brother's parting gift to him. The first time he held the boy in his hands, just a couple of hours ago when he still hadn't known what he was going to do with him, Seth found himself imagining squeezing the soft plates of the child's skull until the bones broke.

He couldn't do it.

Eleanor didn't need to know that, though. So he left her on the ground, bleeding and believing he really was capable of crushing the life out of her baby. The last thing he did to her was promise to bury the kid beneath the dirt somewhere in the old film lot; she could play a grim game of hide-and-seek if she wanted to. His lips flickered into the approximation of a smile, but even that was fleeting. He pulled open a door into nowhere and stepped through into the backstage world of two-by-fours and unpainted Masonite boards. His nephew, barely a few hours old and with his forehead still flaked with the dried blood from his welcome to the world, lay beneath a wooden brace holding up the painted wall. His pudgy little legs kicked at the air. "Hush your noise, child. Uncle Seth's here to take care of everything," he said, taking his jacket off to swaddle the infant. Taking him out of this place was the easiest way he knew how to hurt Eleanor. Robbing her of the baby was the most obvious way to break her spirit. It went beyond anything physical he could subject her to.

Seth had never been driven by a need to procreate. Whatever biological imperative nature intended to see him share his seed was missing in him. In Seth's London, children were a weakness to be exploited by bastards like him. They were leverage.

He'd found the fissure a couple of weeks ago, but resisted the temptation to step back through into the London he'd left behind, until now. He clenched his fist, dark thoughts running away with his mind as he imagined finding his brother and throat-punching him, then standing over the little bastard as he choked to death.

But all it took was half a dozen steps on the other side of the fissure to put an end to that particular fantasy. That was all it took to see how much had changed in the time they'd been gone.

He started to understand the magician's miracle.

Everything was different out here.

A biting wind blew across the cobbled streets around

him. There was ice in the air coming up from the Thames, and smoke with it. The horizon shimmered red. The city was burning. He didn't understand what he was seeing. Huge spotlights strafed the night sky, adding to the stars. The worst of it, though, was the damage close at hand. There was a deep crater where three terraced houses had been, rubble piled up around the street where rescuers had tried vainly to find some sort of life in the ruin. He knew the street from before he'd left. He was on the outskirts of the East End and his old stomping ground. The first bloke he'd truly fucked over had lived in one of those missing houses. He'd broken one of his knuckles on the kid's jaw, but it had been worth all of the pain that followed because it marked his rise from nobody to someone not to be fucked with, and on these streets, that was everything. He realized he'd made a fist. Reflex memory. He walked on, picking a path through the debris.

The first person he saw in the new world was an urchin in a threadbare blazer, and short trousers that exposed his knocked knees. He clutched a wax paper–wrapped parcel in filthy fingers. His shoes were scuffed, the sole peeling away from the toe, and his socks were down around his ankles. There was an equally scruffy dog at his side, some sort of terrier, all slack skin and protruding bone. The animal was starving. So was the kid.

"What's happening?"

The boy looked at him like he'd just crawled out from under a rock and spat a wad of dirty phlegm at his feet. "Same things as yesterday. Same things as tomorrow," the boy said dismissively. "The Jerries." He looked up at the sky. That was the only explanation Seth was going to get.

"What have you got there?" Seth looked at the grubby parcel in the boy's equally grubby hands.

"None of yours, mister."

"Less of your lip, sunshine," Seth said. "A smart mouth only encourages someone like me to give you a fat lip."

"I didn't—" The back of Seth's hand silenced the rest of the boy's objection and left him spitting blood.

"You can't say I didn't warn you. Now let me have it." He held out his free hand.

Tears in his eyes, the lad managed a surly, "Fuck yourself," which earned him a second slap and a "No, fuck *you*," from Seth as he took the package with his free hand. The terrier growled, but didn't attack. It knew its place.

Unwrapping the parcel while holding the baby wasn't easy. "Get yourself gone before I decide to hurt you properly, boy." The way he said it left no room for misunderstanding. The boy spat again, the phlegm thick with blood, and wiped the back of a soot-smeared hand across his lips. He backed off. It was only a couple of steps, just enough to put some distance between himself and Seth's fist.

Ignoring the kid, Seth teased apart the knot of string tying the parcel, and peeled back the layer of brown wax paper to reveal a second layer of wrapping—old newspaper— and inside that a link of a dozen pork sausages as fat—or thin as the case may be—as the dog's legs. "That's all we've got, mister. Me, my folks, my little sister. Take a couple if you have to, but give the rest back. Please."

Seth wasn't really listening to the kid's lament; he was staring at the date above the headlines that promised an incredible seventeen years had passed since the night Damiola and Glass had helped them disappear; 14th February 1941. There was no room for Saint Valentine in this world of bombs and burning streets he walked into. That didn't matter to him. The Germans could rain holy hell down from the heavens for all he cared. The only thing that did matter was that seventeen years had passed. No one was going to be looking for them now.

"Please," the boy wheedled.

"Shut up, lad. I'm trying to think."

"We'll starve if you don't give 'em back. We ain't eaten in two days."

"And I'm supposed to care?" Seth said, upending the contents of the paper onto the slush-covered cobbles. He watched the boy throw himself to his knees and scrabble about, desperately trying to gather them before his mangy mutt could scarf them down.

Seth left them to it.

1941.

Part of a sign still hung over the door of an empty ironmonger's; the only words left legible after the fire damage proclaimed: GIDEON SMITH PURV. That was it, the rest of the gold paint was charred beyond reading. Gideon was a good name. He looked down at the baby in his arms. Maybe he'd grow into a name like Gideon?

The streets he walked had borne the brunt of the bombing. The fallout was devastating. These were the same streets the world's most notorious murderer had prowled in the days just before Seth had been born. The famous church bells rang out. *At least the old church survived*, he thought, not in the least bit sentimental for the place. He hadn't realized where he was walking until he stood outside the old gates and looked up at the nunnery. He rang the bell and waited for the lined face of a world-weary sister to peer through the small hatch. "Got a little 'un here," Seth said. "His mum didn't make it last night." He looked up at the sky as if to blame her passing on the invisible enemy. The old woman leaped to the conclusion he wanted her to leap to and ushered him inside without a word. She led him across the courtyard to the main building. "I figured you'd be best placed to find someone who might be able to nurse 'im, poor scrap. I can't look after 'im." He exaggerated his accent, laying it on thick, then caught his reflection in the mirror and stopped cold. He could have sworn he'd aged a decade since he'd walked between worlds. Gray had crept in at his temple, his crow's-feet deepened around his eyes, and his complexion had gone from ruddy to waxen. The transformation just highlighted how unnatural Damiola's magic had been. Now, looking at his grim reflection, he knew his hours here were marked if he didn't want time to catch up with itself and leave him old before his time. Seth gathered his wits and pushed on. "Maybe some unfortunate mum who lost her little 'un? It'd be good if some good could come out of this." Again he lifted his gaze heavenward.

The old woman nodded. "Of course. We'll do everything we can. We're here to help you and the child." She offered him a practiced smile of sympathy. "Please, sit yourself down. You must be desperate. Let me take the little one." She held out her hands for the swaddled babe.

"I'm not staying," Seth said, handing the boy over. "Take him, find him a good home. I need to go. I can't bear to drag this out, you understand? Just find the boy a good home. I don't want to think of him suffering."

"What's his name?"

"Gideon," Seth told her. "Gideon Lockwood."

"Pleased to meet you, little Gideon," she said. "I'm Sister Anne. I'm going to take good care of you, I promise." She fussed over the little bundle of joy. Seth left the old woman and the boy, knowing he needed to go home.

He was already halfway down the street before he realized he'd started running.

It struck him then that he didn't even know if he'd be able to step back through the fissure into Damiola's great illusion or if he'd locked himself out of it forever. For just a moment, the silence between heartbeats, when the blood wasn't pounding through his skull, allowed him to think that maybe that wouldn't be such a bad thing. He could make a new life for himself here.

Finding the fissure was easy enough when you knew what you were looking for—and from this side it was obvious how it had come to be. It wasn't some flaw in Damiola's design; it came down to the damage of the German bombs. The building the illusion was anchored to had taken a battering in the most recent wave of blanket bombs, weakening it so much that time had begun to flow back toward the crack, trying to fill it in. Without knowing what you were looking at you'd have been forgiven for thinking it was a smudge on your glasses or a bit of grit in the corner of your eye, making your vision blur ever so slightly. Watching the flight of a bumblebee gave it away, the way the insect's flight stalled then juddered backward as it struggled to escape the gravitational pull of the fissure. The image of the bumblebee repeated itself over and over and then it was gone. Seth wiped his mouth with the back of his hand, looking at the damage the German bombs had done. He felt dread form in the back of his throat, thick with the taste of iron, and sink to the bottom of his gut as he walked on into the rubble. Balancing on the broken bricks was difficult because the ground kept shifting beneath his feet, but he made it across the gap, reaching out a hand to touch the shimmering movie light spilling out of the fissure. He couldn't leave it like this. Someone would see it, even if they didn't understand what they were seeing, and once seen it wouldn't be forgotten. Seth needed people to forget if he was going to truly disappear and ever stand a chance of re-emerging from Glass Town into anything approximating his old life.

What could he do, though? It wasn't as if he could rebuild the wall and hide the fissure away, could he?

Even as the thought occurred to him, Seth was on his hands and knees scrabbling around in the debris for pieces of brickwork that might fit together, but like all of the king's horses and all of the king's men, he couldn't put the building together again.

He hurled a huge chunk of plaster at the sliver of glittering blue light and watched it disappear. That answered one of his questions. He could step through, but then what? Find some building tools left over from when Glass Town had been a failed movie set and look to build a fake façade here? That was beyond his ability. But he had money. Money could solve a lot of the world's ills; surely it could hide away a fissure in the fabric of the city from prying eyes.

Seth went to the nearest pub, a seedy little place a couple of streets away, and found a couple of desperate men willing to re-create the front of the Georgian terrace for the promise of good money. Opportunities for men not on the Front were few, so there were plenty of willing souls to bite his hand off when the color of his money proved to be green.

Seth didn't stay in the city to supervise the work. He had to trust them to do what they were paid to do, and gamble that they wouldn't grasp the true nature of that slight smudge that caught every so often in their line of sight. If they did, then he would be waiting for them on the other side, and that would be bad for them.

He didn't return to London proper again for more than twenty years.

They'd kept his secret intact.

The culture shock of returning this next time was extreme. He'd barely changed. For Seth, only a couple of months had passed since he'd last ventured out, but as he slipped between the oblique—that was what he'd taken to calling the fissure, an oblique, as it was like some angle where one world brushed up against the other, allowing him to slip through—he was confronted by an almost alien landscape. All manner of cars lined the road. Streetlights shone down amber on the rooftops. There was a phone booth across the road, a girl in a brightly colored swirl of a miniskirt making a call. Her blond hair was cut savagely straight in a short bob that swished about her shoulders as she laughed at some unheard joke. Seth watched her through the glass wall, but she gave no indication that she'd seen him slip through the oblique from Glass Town, so he put her from his mind. In all the time he'd been gone, the building he'd paid to rebuild hadn't changed very much at all, but then when he looked past the superficial modernization all around him, so much of the other buildings were essentially the same. The more the things changed, the more they stayed the same.

He had limited time here if he didn't want to return to his prison an old man.

He needed to find Cadmus Damiola, if he was still alive, and get him to undo his damnable illusion without costing him his unlived life. There was only one place he could think of that might offer a thread back to the old man and his tricks: the Magic Circle.

Magicians weren't the only ones with tricks; ordinary decent criminals like Seth Lockwood had their own, and when it came to getting into locked buildings, theirs were far more effective than a few mirrors and a bit of smoke for distraction. He'd scavenged a decent set of tools from the back of the movie lot he called home, including the glass cutter he'd used to enter with as little breaking as possible. Now, creeping through the dark corridors, it was about finding whatever clues he could to the whereabouts of that damned magician, and getting out again without seeing another ten years of his life slip away unlived. The building didn't live up to his expectations; it was more like a museum than a home of magic. But then, 99 percent of the illusions housed in it were nothing more than cheap chicanery. Wooden crates lined one of the walls, stamped FRAGILE and THIS WAY UP with arrows pointing at the ceiling, exhibitions yet to be laid out. He made his way through the various displays, reading names he didn't recognize and looking at the tricks that had made them famous, things like the Mismade Girl and Asrah Levitation, the Devil's Torture Chamber and Sands of the Nile, as well as Chen Lee's Water Suspension and the Dagger Head Box. The props offered a candid look up the magician's metaphorical sleeve, but Seth had no interest in the workings of a few old tricks. He moved through the displays, looking for Cadmus Damiola's name on one of the small plaques. Display after display offered up the equipment of the deceased, Thurston and Robert-Houdin, Harry Blackstone, junior and senior, Chung Ling Soo, Sorcar and Kellar, Maskelyne and the great Houdini himself.

He was at the point of giving up and getting out of there when he saw a table with an ancient praxinoscope on it. There was a screen set up beside it and a number of cards cut out in the shapes of various scenes the device would animate on the screen. On the wall beside the display he saw Damiola's face. He had forgotten just how much he loathed the miserable little man; seeing him brought it all flooding back. The short biography ended with the lines: *Damiola failed to perform what would have been the last show of his tour, disappearing on the night of January 13, 1924, never to be seen or heard from again. It is believed he fell afoul of notorious figures from London's criminal underworld. His disappearance was linked with that of a young actress, Eleanor Raines, who went missing on the same night. The commonly held belief is that the pair ended their days in unmarked graves somewhere outside the city limits.*

If only they knew the half of it, he thought.

It answered the most obvious question, though: forty years on, it wasn't going to be as simple as walking up to

Cadmus Damiola's door and demanding he reverse what he'd done. If he wasn't dead, Damiola had done a bloody good job of making it look that way to the rest of the world.

Seth lashed out in anger, toppling part of the display. The praxinoscope lurched, starting to fall. He caught it as the rest of the setup fell and set it down gently. He spun the carousel, watching the figures flicker to life on the screen. They took a couple of faltering steps in a chiaroscuro ballet before the light burned out and left the wall in darkness. He spun it a second time, watching the couple dance on. It was a neat little trick, but nothing close to the kind of thing Hitchcock had been doing in *Number 13*. The description of the trick was dry, detailing how it had been first invented by Charles-Émile Reynaud in France and how it worked by inserting a strip of pictures around the inner cylinder, the motion of the praxinoscope bringing them to life. He couldn't understand why a piece of junk like this was on display until he saw the twist Damiola had brought to the trick, bringing the animations to three-dimensional life detached from the screen. He had called them the Reels, which sounded positively monstrous to Seth.

Aside from a single inconsequential journal, it was the only thing of Damiola's in the place. The brief biographical sketch described some of his other great illusions, including the Opticron, but suggested they had all been lost or destroyed and that aside from the Reels none of Damiola's other illusions survived.

He didn't realize what he was hearing at first, as the sirens wailed out in the street, but even out of his own time, it didn't take a criminal mastermind to know he needed to get out of there. Fast. He hadn't intended to steal the carousel and its cards, but that was exactly what he did. The cutouts were brittle with age. He slipped them into a manila envelope and took the praxinoscope by the base, making his way back toward the open window up in the gods.

The police could run around like rats down below, Seth thought with a wry smile as he made his escape across the rooftops. Today wasn't the day they'd finally catch up with him. He moved from rooftop to rooftop, following an elaborate pathway of planks he'd put in place to take him out of harm's way. By the time the police emerged, scratching their heads at the bizarre theft of an old trick, Seth Lockwood was long gone.

He needed to think, make an alternative plan.

He couldn't simply wait it out in the '60s—that meant aging forty years if he couldn't find a way to reverse what Damiola had done. Without the magician that wasn't a viable option, not with time catching up with him faster than he could run. No, like it or not, he was going to have to go back, regroup, come up with another plan. In the meantime it wouldn't hurt to work out what, exactly, he had just stolen.

Seth took no joy from Eleanor's company. Frequently he found her presence a drain on his composure and once his temper was frayed he'd lash out either verbally or physically. The bruises healed quickly enough. She cowered in his presence, preferring to hide rather than risk getting on the foul side of his moods, but Glass Town was a small place, and staying out of each other's way only led to a crushing sense of loneliness that was in many ways the true curse of Damiola's trickery. There was only so much of his own company a man like Seth could take, so inevitably he'd seek her out. The only reasonable conversation they had in weeks was when he admitted that he had made a mistake in bringing her here. Not that he was sorry, just that he'd been wrong. Seth Lockwood didn't say sorry.

"You don't get it," he said, ignoring the loathing behind her eyes. "But why should you? I can't just let you go. There's no way out. This is it. From now, forever. These few streets. Me and you. I'm stuck with you. That's what the reality of beating that idiot brother of mine means. This. Forever. Slowly driving me out of my mind. Even if I could just open a door out of here you wouldn't last a week if you walked through it. Too much time has passed now. Believe me, it's crossed my mind, but tearing the place apart, sending you back out there doesn't just kill you, it condemns me to fifty, maybe sixty years of solitude. A man can't live alone without losing his mind. He just can't. So like it or not, I'm stuck with you."

She was beautiful in all the ways a woman could be, truly beautiful, but looking at her, Seth found every single contour and pore repugnant. He couldn't imagine being forced to look at her for the rest of his life, slowly watching her age and knowing they could never escape each other. Hell was getting what you wanted, he realized bitterly. Seth clenched his fist. His breathing hitched in his throat as his chest rose, and he had to force himself to let his anger go before he slammed his fist into her face and left it looking anything but beautiful.

She followed him around after that. He'd catch glimpses of her in the background, spying on him. She didn't believe they were trapped here, that much was obvious. He'd have walked her to the oblique and kicked her out into the '70s if he'd thought it would do anything other than damn him. He needed to find a way to undo Damiola's illusion, and that meant understanding the mechanism behind it as much as the nature of it. And, should he somehow solve it, or find a way to circumvent the side effects and essentially find a way to live a lifetime that spanned centuries, he needed to know it was safe to emerge from Glass Town. Not that he feared the police. They couldn't touch him. No one would look at a thirtysomething and assume he could possibly be behind crimes over half a century old. That was the one good thing about Damiola's mess. A thirtysomething? Only weeks ago in the timeline of his life he'd been a twentysomething. That time was gone, robbed from him.

He crouched down, setting the praxinoscope on solid ground, and took a moment to pick an appropriate inlay. He eased it into place on the carousel and, lighting a candle in the centerpiece, began to crank the handle, causing the drum to spin faster and faster and the flickering image of the kid from the Charlie Chaplin movie begin to take on substance in the street in front of him.

It wasn't as realistic as he might have hoped. The image was good, if a little disjointed and blurred around the edges, but as the candle flickered within the carousel so, too, did the figure of the kid in the street, appearing to phase into and out of existence as the drum slowed.

He cranked the handle again, faster this time, and something incredible happened: the figure of the kid took on a more substantial form, becoming more realistic the faster the drum turned until it was fully formed and seemed to detach itself from the background that spun around it.

Seth stared at the Reel for a moment, not sure what he was seeing, and then it turned its back on him and loped away toward the edge of Glass Town with a curious, juddering gait. The kid turned to look at him, hesitant, as though waiting for orders. "Aren't you a peculiar thing," Seth muttered, pushing himself up to his feet. He walked up to where the thing waited, and reached out tentatively to touch it. His fingers slipped easily through the projection, causing the kid's body to ripple around his hand. The effect was curiously hypnotic. The illusion was almost convincing, but like most tricks failed at the last. Above all else, it was a projection. Something conjured from film, tied somehow to a reel of film. He started to think of it as a Reel, linking the two things together in his mind.

A burst of static echoed out of the tortured figure's mouth as its jaw dropped wide open.

It was quite the worst thing Seth Lockwood had ever heard, and he'd stood over people soiling themselves as they begged for their lives. That desperation didn't come close to this. He felt a twinge of pity for the thing, then laughed at his own stupidity. "It's not like you're real," he muttered, shaking his head. "Go on, get out of here." The apparition of the kid inclined its head, giving an eerily accurate impression of listening and thinking, then turned and dashed off down the street. Seth couldn't help it: he laughed and set off after the apparition, while behind him the drum rattled on and on, the candle's flame keeping the Reel alive.

He followed the kid to a painted doorway. He'd walked

past the spot more than a thousand times. He knew that it didn't open. He knew that there was nothing behind it. Yet, the kid walked straight through, its body crackling with static discharge as it disappeared. Seth stood there stupidly, hands on his knees, shaking his head. He thought about calling it back like some sort of runaway dog, but for some reason he couldn't explain, he reached out for the door handle and it opened.

Seth was confronted by a wall of mist so thick he could only see a dozen or so yards into it before shadows became diffuse and lost all definition. He saw the kid scurrying away and chased after it, more out of curiosity at this new facet of his prison that the Reel had led him to than anything else. But two steps over the threshold was more than enough. The ground felt like shifting sand beneath his feet. He stopped. A chill gathered around his heart. The kid was already far out there in the mist, slipping out and back into focus as it moved. Out beyond the kid he saw another shape. A woman dressed head to toe in white, a lantern in her hand, beckoning to the kid to follow her as she turned and walked away into the mist. She faded from view like dust motes drifting across his eyes. For a few minutes he watched the yellow light of the lantern slowly fade to nothing, swallowed, as she walked into the distance. He heard the gentle lap of water against an unseen shore. The kid cried out with another burst of static. The mist answered with a melancholy cry of its own that seemed to come from everywhere and nowhere at once.

For the first time in his life, Seth Lockwood was frightened—properly frightened.

Nothing about this place was *right*.

There was nothing of substance out there. No landscape to speak of. The world was reduced to the gray of the mist banks. Nothing existed beyond them. He watched the kid phase out of sight once again. This time a few moments passed before it reappeared, and when it did its head lolled awkwardly on its neck as though it had regressed and, like a baby, its neck couldn't support its weight. The kid lolloped toward him, arms dragging lifelessly. Something had happened to it out there. As if to emphasize this point the baleful cry came from the mists again. The kid slouched on, dragging its feet. Seth couldn't hear the drag-scuff of the Reel's worn-out shoes because ghosts—if that was what it truly was—made no sound in any world they inhabited. Coming into range, the Reel stiffened, straightening its body and bringing its head up slowly until it looked at him somewhere close to his eyes. Had he been a religious man Seth Lockwood would have offered a prayer then, but there wasn't a bone in his body that believed in anything he couldn't control. "What are you looking at?" Seth demanded. The Reel inclined its head again, a couple of inches to the right, as though considering him. "I'm talking to you."

The kid offered no answer.

He realized then that it was considerably more substantial than it had been. He could no longer see through its black-and-white "flesh" to the mist beyond. Something had happened to give the Reel solidity. There was intelligence behind its movie-star eyes that hadn't been there before.

The kid tried to talk to him, another shriek of white noise crackling out of its mouth as it spoke.

Inexplicably, Seth understood what it was trying to say to him.

It existed to serve him. Whatever it had been before was forgotten. The Reel had given it a body of its own so that it might finally leave this place between places. It was no longer simply the ghostly twitch of light Damiola had harnessed for his trick, there was more to the thing before him than that. By letting it loose in this place, hidden away between two worlds, the place for gods and monsters both, something had taken possession of the Reel and rode in it now like a hermit crab, using Damiola's conjuring to escape this Hell. He felt the weight of eternity looking back at him through the kid's eyes and couldn't begin to imagine how long it had waited for a chance to be free of the mist.

Forever felt like an appropriate word.

He wasn't sure how he might best harness the Reel now, or how he might use it to his advantage, but there was no doubt in his mind he was in possession of a weapon unlike any other, and that excited Seth. When he looked back over his shoulder there was no sign of the fake building or painted door. Instead he saw the stone walls of a high tower, like something out of a pseudo-medieval Errol Flynn flick full of swash and buckle. He backed up first one step then another, back into the safety of Glass Town. The kid followed him.

The candle had burned down to a stub when he returned to the praxinoscope, and the drum had long since come to rest—and yet still the Reel existed in this place, no longer dependent upon Damiola's device for its ungodly life.

That was interesting.

Did that mean he could conjure the Reel in one place

only to unleash it in another? That he could send it forth with instructions to do his bidding?

He snuffed out the candle, and with it the kid flickered and failed.

Interesting again. He struck a match to light what remained of the candle's wick, and cranked the handle to send the drum spinning faster and faster until the Reel began to take shape in the street before him again. Even before it had fully materialized the words formed in his head: *what do you want from me?* It wasn't exactly a genie in a lamp offering three wishes, but there was no denying the fact that the thing was communicating with him.

"You'll know soon enough," Seth promised, snuffing out the tiny flame once again.

The door, he realized, was no longer a door. It was back to being a badly painted prop. Part of the black around the golden door handle had begun to blister and peel away from the wood where his hand had rested on it.

He didn't understand what had happened here, or what that place was, but his mind was alive with the possibilities the Reel presented. Maybe, just maybe, it was the answer to finding Damiola? Could he unleash it like some preternatural bloodhound?

It might have even worked if Eleanor hadn't found the fissure and slipped through into London. That changed everything. January 12, 1994. A Wednesday that was unremarkable in every other way. He followed her into an alleyway off Spitalfields—which had changed so much in the time he had been gone. It was at once familiar and utterly different. Kids in plaid shirts and torn jeans walked hand in hand, the men with longer hair than the women. Eleanor was easy to follow as she pushed her way through the people coming and going from the market; her red dress was a beacon. Seth stopped dead in his tracks. Less than half a dozen paces away from him, out of the mouth of the alleyway and across the narrow, cobbled street, an old man stared at Eleanor like he'd just seen a ghost.

He crossed himself.

He couldn't look away.

Seth watched him from the shadows, all the resentments he thought he'd outgrown bubbling up again. The years hadn't been kind to Isaiah. Death walked a step behind him, just waiting to introduce himself to the old man. His brother had transformed into a statue in the midst of all of the shoppers. He was absolutely still for the longest time, then he began to shake.

Seth needed to get her out of there.

He cursed the stupid, stupid woman as he ghosted up behind her and whispered into her ear, "Just keep walking. Don't turn around. Don't look back." He felt her stiffen as he placed his hand on the small of her back and steered Eleanor away from the safety of people.

"You might as well kill me," she told him as he pushed her into a passageway so narrow both of her shoulders scraped against the walls on either side when she stumbled forward. "I'm not going back there."

"Then you die," he told her. There was no anger in his voice, only resignation. It was easier to let her see the effects of remaining where they didn't belong than it was trying to drag her back by the hair, kicking and screaming. He had to trust that despite her defiant words, when she was confronted by the reality of watching herself age, her self-preservation instinct would kick in.

He pushed her forward, her heel catching on the uneven cobbles, but he didn't let her fall. He kept on pushing her until she stood outside the blacked-out window of an old cinema on Latimer Road, and saw her reflection. For a moment it was obvious she didn't know what she was supposed to be looking at, but when he wouldn't let her walk away she had no choice but to study her reflection and slowly recognize the changes creeping in between memory and the reality standing in front of the cinema.

She looked down at her hands then back up at him through the backward landscape of their reflections.

"What's happening to me?"

"Time," he said. "Look around you. This isn't the city we left. This isn't 1924. It's not even 1941 or 1965. Everything's different now. We don't belong here. Time is doing what it's supposed to do. It's catching up with you. Stay here and you'll be an old woman before long."

She looked like she wanted to argue with him, but the truth of his words was writing itself on her skin.

"How . . . ? Why?"

"I wanted you to myself."

"You're a monster."

"Probably," Seth agreed. "And if not now, soon enough, given the things I'm going to have to do if we ever want a normal life. So if you really want to die, all you have to do is stay here a little while longer. The years will catch up with you and you will save my soul in the process. Or you can return with me to that place and give me time to try and work out how to undo the mess that damned magician made. Right now I don't care either way. I'm done with considering you a prize. If I could I'd take you back to where you came from and dump you on my brother's doorstep and be done with you. But I can't."

She looked at him then, realizing something. "Is this where you took my baby?"

He nodded. "Yes. Although he's old enough to be your father now."

There was a moment as the pain registered and the loss settled in, then Eleanor shook her head, not in disagreement so much as in denial.

And because of her one moment of stupidity, they couldn't come back here again, not safely. Isaiah had seen her. He knew she was still alive, even if he couldn't explain how she could have lived so many years without aging a day. He had seen her. He wouldn't let that go now. Even if no one believed him, and dismissed his claims as the ravings of a senile mind lost too long in grief, it didn't matter. It would stir it all up again: the beautiful young actress who had disappeared, the jealous brother who was anything but an ordinary criminal, and the magician who had disappeared off the face of the earth. It might feel like a lifetime ago, but bringing that shit back into the public consciousness after all this time was just going to make any hope of living here more problematic than simply undoing Damiola's curse.

There were options, of course. The most obvious one was

that it was time for the Reel to claim its first victim. The creature had made no secret of its hunger. It needed to feed to sustain itself, and the longer it burned the fiercer its appetite became. He was still learning how his monster functioned, but he was beginning to think that if it didn't feed, it would burn forever, unquenched, unsatisfied. It would feed. It would *have* to. So it was only fitting that the first blood it tasted should be the blood of his blood.

"So?"

He knew he'd never be able to trust her again, no matter what she said now. There would come a time when she'd slip through the fissure again, stepping back into this world, unable to resist the draw of the place and the life she'd lost— without understanding it wasn't here to be found. That unforgettable need would eventually be their undoing. There was no getting around that. It was that, or cast her out now and let time unravel her. "Take me back," she said, becoming a willing prisoner this time.

"Wise choice."

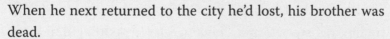

When he next returned to the city he'd lost, his brother was dead.

Minutes had passed for Seth, months for the others. He'd intended to put the frighteners on Isaiah, lean on him, maybe crack a few bones to be sure he forgot what he'd seen at the market, but instead he had been the uninvited ghost at the family funeral. Seth watched the relatives who'd long since forgotten he existed pay their respects to his brother.

The whole charade left a sour taste in his mouth. They had no idea who Isaiah really was. His boy, Boone, delivered the eulogy with customary tears and trembling. As they lowered the coffin into the ground he talked about hoping his father could finally find the woman he had spent his entire life looking for, and if not her, then at least peace. He gave the dead man his own promise that he'd never stop trying to work out what had happened that night in 1924. It would become his obsession, handed down from generation to generation like some twisted heirloom. Seth hawked and spat in the direction of the open grave. Boone's own son was next to pay his respects, kneeling at the graveside to place what looked like a wooden rattle on the top of the coffin. Some sort of memento that no doubt meant something deeply significant, even if it looked cheap and childish.

Seth watched them mourn, the Reel kid beside him fidgeting like a real boy might.

Just because he couldn't scare Isaiah anymore didn't mean he couldn't end this now. With that in mind, a plan slowly formed in his mind. Seth dismissed the Reel, sending it back through the fissure to Glass Town, and followed Boone to the memorial.

He watched him for an hour, talking with his friends, trading his stories, and chinking glasses as they drank another one down. Music played in the background. No one was singing. Finally, when the old man had drunk enough, he wandered over to introduce himself, a spare glass of diluted whiskey in his hand. "Sorry for your loss," he said, holding out the second glass.

It was as easy as that.

They shared a drink, face-to-face with the blood of his blood, in the smoke-filled bar of the workingman's club, no flicker of recognition passing between them. He was almost disappointed. He listened to the son tell tall stories about his old man, unable to tell truth from lie as the exaggerated life of a man he never really knew took life around him. He waited for the story of Eleanor to come up, knowing it would. How could any night in honor of Isaiah Lockwood—though he'd taken the name Raines, it would seem, from the order of service someone had left lying on the table amid the beer rings and ashtrays—not revolve around the great tragedy of his life?

"Did he ever come close, do you think? To finding her?"

Boone shook his head. "It was a fool's errand. She's dead. They both are. Long gone. You ask me, the magician was behind it. Look at the stuff we know. He canceled his last ever show, disappeared the night they vanished. What you've got to remember is it was different back then. Much easier to get away with things. I always figured they were dumped somewhere like the Hackney Marshes or Leyton Marshes, Rainham or Erith, plenty of places you could make a couple of bodies disappear with little risk of them turning up to haunt you."

"So, you're not going to carry on looking for the truth? I thought you said—"

"The old man was only ever looking for the truth. He knew they were dead. He wasn't an idiot. Well, not until his last days, at least. He left me this." He took an envelope from inside his jacket pocket. Seth assumed it was his eulogy. "I'm not sure what to do with it."

"What is it?"

"His dying declaration. It's all in here, his story, everything that happened to him, everything he'd worked out about what happened, all of it."

"That's got to be some read," Seth said, measuring his words carefully.

"He swears that only a couple of weeks ago he'd finally seen her, in the same red dress she'd been wearing the day she disappeared. He swore she hadn't aged a day."

"Well, that's hardly likely, is it?"

"I don't know what to think anymore."

"You want my opinion? Sometimes things are better left forgotten," Seth said.

"Maybe. I just can't shake the feeling there's something . . ."

"May I?"

Boone shook his head. "I don't think so." And then his brow furrowed. "You know, I don't recognize you. I feel like I should. . . . How did you say you knew my father again?"

"We go way back. We were like brothers once upon a time." The other man looked at him then, and he realized he'd said too much. "He looked after me when I needed looking after. He was a good man."

"He was anything but," Boone disagreed. "He was obsessed with finding Eleanor, with seeing his brother, Seth, brought to justice. Nothing else mattered. He ignored my mother. He only married her because she was Eleanor's sister, and if he couldn't have her, then he'd have the next best thing. He didn't care about us. He didn't care about anything in the end. And judging by his letter, it damned near drove him crazy by the end. That one night tore his life apart. He never got over it."

Which is music to my ears, Seth thought. But that wasn't what he said. "So, why do that to yourself? Do you really want your boy looking at you the way you obviously looked at *your* father?" Seth turned to look across the room at Barclay Raines, young, handsome, and almost a twin for Isaiah, proving the apple didn't fall far from the biological tree. "Walk away while you can. Make a clean break from the past. Do what's right for your family."

Boone took a swig from the half-empty pint glass in his hand, knocking back more than half of what remained.

"He looks like a good kid," Seth said.

"He's hurting. He worshipped his grandfather."

"Most boys do."

"He didn't deserve it."

"Can I be frank, Boone? I feel like I can be. We're talking man to man here. We're both men of the world."

"Spit it out," Boone said with an amused smile.

"Here's the thing. Take a good look at that boy of yours and ask yourself this: if you knew that chasing this fool's errand of your father's would end up getting him hurt, would you still be hell-bent on doing it?"

"What do you mean?"

"Exactly what I'm saying. You wouldn't want anything to happen to your boy, would you?"

"Who are you? And don't give me some crap about being a friend of the family. You're not."

"No, I'm not. But you know me. Or my name at least."

"Who are you?"

"What if I told you that we're related. Family."

"I'd ask you how."

"And I'd say through your father," Seth said, playing the game.

"Again, I'd ask how."

"Then I'd tell you how your father was my brother."

Boone shook his head. "Not funny. Now stop taking the piss and fuck off out of here, you're not welcome anymore."

Seth nodded his head, his smile almost affable. "Shame. I was hoping it wouldn't come to this. I'm only going to say this once, no second chances, Boone. My name is Seth Lockwood. I am a lot older than I look, you *are* my nephew. If you don't forget everything you read in that letter, your boy will die, because I want this chain broken. I want to come home. And I'm prepared to do whatever it takes to make that happen. This doesn't have to get any worse than it already is, that's the thing. All you need to do is walk away. Burn that letter. Move on and live happily ever fucking after. Do we have an understanding?"

"Fuck you. Just fuck you." Boone's voice spiraled. People started looking their way through the corkscrew curls of cigarette smoke. "Get the fuck out of here before I lose my temper and do something you'll regret."

"I take it that's a no? All right." Seth shook his head. He looked across the bar at the young Barclay. He really didn't want any more blood on his hands, not if it could be avoided. Looking at the kid was like looking at himself. "Last chance," he said. "Agree that this ends here and I'll walk away. Promise that you will stop looking for us, Eleanor and me, and I'll go happily."

"Are you out of your fucking mind?"

"Probably," he said. "I'll even give you this to seal the deal." Seth took a set of keys out of his pocket and offered them to Boone. He hadn't thought it through, but it made sense. Sometimes it wasn't about breaking bones, just getting people to see things your way. Money tended to make that happen. "It's a flat, in Rotherhithe. I haven't been back there in a long time, but I've gone to great pains to keep it, even paying a housekeeper to clean once a month, although nothing is ever out of place. It's across the street from The Angel. You'll recognize the name on the door. Think of it as an inheritance you didn't know was coming to you. It's got to be worth a lot of money now."

He dropped the keys in Boone's hand even as his nephew said, "I don't want them."

"Do the smart thing. Close your fingers around them. Make a fist. Hold them really tight. Drink to your dad, then walk out of here and forget the letter, forget his obsession with Eleanor, forget me, move into your nice new place down by the water, hell, give it to your boy as a wedding present when the time comes, just walk out of here and *live*. You can do that, can't you?"

But of course he couldn't. He could no more let go of the family obsession than Seth could turn over a new leaf and live the life of a virtuous man. The rot had eaten into him a long time ago. He wasn't about to change now. He walked out of that place, through the rain-drenched streets of London, thinking how little stuff had really changed, how things were only different on the surface despite all of the flashing lights and fast cars and the endless circus of noise, back to the oblique and slipped back through the fissure into Glass Town. He was only there a few moments, long enough to summon the Reel. All he'd needed to do was feed the kid a name, as the candle flickered inside the spinning drum, and visualize the face of his victim, planting it in what passed for the Reel's mind. He sealed the pact with blood, drawing a few drops from his wrist with a piece of broken glass before he turned the Reel loose.

A couple of years had passed in the time it took him to return, long enough for Boone to have forgotten his threat, long enough for Barclay to have started his own family, ensuring the bloodline would live on. Even with Barclay Raines dead there would be kin in London.

He could live with that.

Seth followed the Reel kid as it prowled from street to street, sniffing the air like some ghostly bloodhound. Static roared out of its mouth as it called a challenge to the rising sun. Each fresh burst of white noise reminded Seth of the Reel's true nature. The pair attracted strange looks from those not too busy to see them, but Seth didn't let that bother him. This was about buying himself a chance at a normal life; about breaking the chain; about ending his exile and starting life anew; it was about finding peace, finally. But more than anything—and this was hard for him to admit to himself—it was about winning. About beating his brother once and forever. Because Seth Lockwood did not lose. Not now. Not ever.

The kid walked into a new part of town, a housing estate filled with hopes and dreams of fresh starts, neatly parceled-off lawns and paved garden paths. The sign on the green welcomed visitors to The Rothery. Seth followed the kid as the Reel phased into and out of existence like a flickering flame.

So, this was where Boone had ended up?

He'd seen worse places.

The front door to one of the houses in the horseshoe of bright and shiny glass doors and leaded windows on Albion Close opened and Barclay Raines emerged, shouting over his shoulder that he was just nipping out for a packet of cigarettes.

"They'll be the death of you," Seth said, much to his own amusement as the kid followed Barclay to the corner store. He followed a couple of steps behind, and watched as the young man went in.

"Wait," he told the Reel. It inclined its head, listening, obeying. Seth went inside. It was a small shop, with jars of candies and toffees and striped mints on display, newspapers laid out on the counter, and a few everyday essentials on the shelves. Barclay was in conversation with the shopkeeper. For last words they were inconsequential, a back-and-forth about the game the night before. Something and nothing. Seth joined them at the counter.

"Can I help you, mate?" the shopkeeper asked with a welcoming smile.

"Just a copy of today's paper. I want to remember everything about today."

"Then maybe you want tomorrow's instead," Barclay Raines said. He tapped two fingers on top of the headlines. "This is all yesterday."

Seth smiled at that. "Maybe I do. Sorry, don't I know you?

You're Boone's lad, right?" He nodded. "Thought so. I want you to know something before you die. I'm not the monster here. He is. It's all on him. He had a chance to make this all go away. I begged him to, for your sake. But he didn't think you were worth it."

"I don't understand. . . ."

"That's okay, you don't need to. You just need to die today. That's more than enough for you to worry about." Seth took the top copy of the newspaper and left without paying. At the threshold, he looked back to see the two men looking at him. Neither moved to stop him from stealing the paper.

Seth sent the kid in to kill his nephew's only child while he made his way back to Hell. And as he walked those lonely streets, he caught repeated reflections of himself in the windows, and saw again how many years had been stolen from him by that damned illusion, by Glass Town, and knew that the only hope he had of ever having anything approaching a real life would be if that damned magician could do the impossible and give them back to him. And that was the problem with impossible things, they were impossible.

He wasn't sure he'd ever make his peace with that.

THE DIFFERENCE BETWEEN DECEIT AND DELUSION

DOMINO FINN

Black Magic Outlaw kicks off with a hero in trouble and on the run through the blood-soaked streets of Miami. Those particular events, however, were set into motion many years earlier. Various criminal elements, some not altogether human, have long flourished in a city ripe with vice. "The Difference Between Deceit and Delusion" is a rare look at the backstory of one of the villains who started it all.

The man sobbed. His thin mustache was sticky with phlegm, the tender skin around his eye swollen and purple. Dribble ran down his chin as he pleaded for his miserable life.

It was my life now.

"My name is Tunji Malu," I said. Measured, calm, patient. As if speaking to a third-grade classroom. "There. You see? That's how easy it is to give a name."

"I don't know any names."

"Let's start with yours."

The man paused, wary of betraying any information.

Given his dire situation, he must have decided cooperation couldn't hurt. "Marco," he confided. "Please, just kill me."

His arms were bound together above his head. A shimmering line hung from the ceiling and wrapped his wrists so tight it bit into his flesh. The man's toes barely scraped the floor if he extended himself. An hour hanging like that will leave a man a wreck.

And that was without the torture.

"Now why would I kill you," I growled, "*before* you've answered my questions?"

The attic was dark. A hastily constructed cubby above a warehouse loft. The wood floor creaked and groaned under my weight as I paced back and forth. It was past midnight and there were no lightbulbs up here, so a single candle rested on the floor by his feet. It lit the room dramatically, the two of us in a circle of light with the walls and ceiling left ominously black. It was my kind of room.

I came to a stop, towering over the human, flexing my muscles. Then I leaned in and bared my metal fangs.

"Oh, God," he said. "What are you?"

I smiled, which only unsettled him more. I was a scary sight by any measure. Broad shoulders and barrel chest. Thick, leathery arms and legs. For all this man knew I was an ogre.

But that was only half-right.

I glanced at the open bite wound on his neck. "I can give you another demonstration if you require."

He shook his head furiously.

Interrogating humans was easy. Getting in their heads was easy. But my compulsions were having trouble with this one. This guy was making me work. This guy was special.

Not spectacular, mind you. But special. Marco wasn't like everyday humans. He was an animist. A tapper of spirits and user of spellcraft. Not the most powerful I'd seen, but not altogether useless. He could project force fields of a sort. Great for gunfights. Horribly lacking when confronted by a West African vampire and his trickster pet.

Still, the man himself had been unexpected. Miami is an international city, but one with tendencies. One particular infestation is the new-world voodoo, a perversion of my mother country's mysticism. *That* was the kind of bastardized magic I'd expected. Not this.

But the type of spellcraft was academic. What mattered was animists were often able to resist my vampiric compulsions. At least for a time.

"I swear," he sputtered. "I told you what I know. It was only about Namadi."

Namadi Obazuaye. Esteemed Nigerian businessman. My boss. I was his bodyguard, but it was me who had picked him rather than the other way around. His was a rags-to-riches story, and I needed a foot in this world. I clung to him, protected him, and rode his good fortune all the way to America. He'd found great success with the small African community here. And my work had been easy. To date I'd only needed to threaten a Haitian gangbanger or two. Kid stuff. At least until this guy.

"What is Namadi to you?" I demanded.

"I told you."

My voice went low. "Tell me again."

He took a few stuttered breaths and nodded. He'd given me the story before, but he didn't mind a repeat performance; it was either story time or sharp metal teeth.

"We just wanted your boss to clean our money through his businesses."

"*Legitimate* businesses," I reminded. "You wanted your filthy drug money to come through the esteemed Nigerian community."

The drugs were something I *had* expected from Miami. International port of call for the Caribbean and Latin America. This man certainly fit the bill. South American with a heavy accent. Bronzed skin, wild hair.

"Wrecking Namadi's storefronts. *My* storefronts."

I paced a lap around him so he had to spin on the line to keep sight of me. He gritted his teeth with the effort. The man's shadow encompassed me on his far side. I lingered there just long enough to make him wonder what I was doing. Just long enough to let his imagination do the torture for me.

I emerged from the darkness, but turned and addressed the black corner. "I wonder what he planned to do with us?" I curled my lip and laughed at the ensuing silence. "I have an idea. He was gonna shove us around a little. Piss all over our people, like we wronged him."

I caught the glint of light from my teeth in the reflection of his eyes.

"Who are you talking to?" he asked.

I waited a laborious breath. "I bet you were gonna offer us a way out. A way to get on your good side. After your boss declared war on us, you were gonna have us make it up to you by laundering your cash at rock-bottom rates. You were gonna make it seem like you were doing us a favor while we took a ridiculously low percentage for our trouble."

"The terms are negotiable," he said with a hint of hope in his voice.

That was disappointing. That meant I hadn't broken him yet.

"Not with you," I countered. "It would be your boss we'd be negotiating with, no?"

"S-sure."

More pitiful hope.

I snarled. "How do you expect me to do that without telling me who he is?"

The mage flinched away from me. His eyes blinked quickly as he pondered his words. "H-he . . . doesn't have a name."

I didn't move. I waited for Marco to retract his statement. To read my face and realize he made a mistake. But the man just stood there on his tiptoes, sticking to his story. A line of blood trailed down his arm from a cut on his wrist.

"You know what I hate?" I asked placidly. I leaned in so the wavering light illuminated my face. Black eyes. Sweaty skin the color of bark. I pulled my lips clear of my metal fangs. "Tough guys," I said.

"It's true—it's true."

I turned to the dark attic corner again. Clenched my jaw in a scowl. "He would have us believe his boss is a ghost. As incorporeal as the spirits he channels for his spellcraft."

The man's eyes darted to the dark area.

I walked to the opposite wall and stopped with my back

to him. I hefted two hooked blades. Near-complete loops of sharp metal, perfectly balanced with a small handle. One for each hand. With his eyes on my back, I scraped the knives together. Metal on metal. There's something visceral about that sound. Primal.

I took my time, too. That's one thing he had, at least. Not the kind of time to enjoy a long, fulfilling life. But enough to reflect on his predicament. To come clean. Enough for me to not misstep in haste. So I used that time to sharpen the blades against each other and let them do the talking for me.

When I finally turned around, the South American was sweating profusely. That hope of his was evaporating. Giving way to my venom. It would only be a matter of time.

I crossed my arms over my broad chest, resting each blade on a shoulder, and regarded the man coldly.

"Do you know the difference between deceit and delusion?" I asked.

"W-what?" he stammered.

"It's a simple question," I said plainly. "Deceit and delusion. Have you ever thought about the difference?"

The man's eyes fixed on my blades and he shivered.

"Deceit," I explained, "is when a man lies to others. Delusion is when he lies to himself."

I watched his face expectantly. He was too scared to ask.

"Like right now, for instance. Is it true you don't know the name of the man who sent you? Are you lying to me? Or is it that you're somehow convinced that whatever your boss will do to you if you talk is worse than what you're facing right now? Because *that*, little human, is pure delusion."

I tapped into my innate magic and charged. In a fraction of a second, I moved from the wall to inches away from his face. It took him longer to register my motion than it had taken me to complete it. I waited until he jumped, startled by my sudden shift, calm and methodical though it was. Faster than humanly possible.

Marco let out a scream as sure as if I'd buried my blade in his chest.

But that was too easy for this one. He'd long ago relieved himself of the right to a quick death. I let him shake and sniffle until he opened his eyes a peek, disappointed to see he was still alive and unharmed.

"I could flay you alive, mageling. Stem the flow of your blood with my magic so you wouldn't bleed out. I could get in your head and convince you to beg for it. I could make you chew your own fingers off. Believe me, anything your boss can dream up is a pale comparison to what I can do."

"I believe you!" he cried. "I'll tell you what you want to know—I'll tell you everything."

I grinned, metal teeth inches from the open wound on his neck. I inhaled deeply, taking in the sweet scent of his beating heart. His blood was fouled now. Poison from my bite pumped into every inch of his quivering body. It was biological betrayal. His own flesh and blood working against him.

His mind was the last holdout. Sheer willpower, emboldened by the practiced channeling of spirit energy. But even that defense was crumbling before my eyes.

"What is his name?"

He swallowed hard. "I don't know that. I swear to Christ."

I lifted a blade to his ear.

"But I know where he is," he hastened to add.

I paused. New information, at last.

Marco nodded his head conspiratorially, overeager to make a deal. "He's expecting me. Waiting for my return. I'll tell you where he is if you let me go. You have to let me go."

I grinned. Delusion again. But I supposed fair was fair.

"If you tell me true, I won't kill you. You have my word."

An intake of air caught in his throat. He couldn't believe his good fortune. He was afraid to let that hope back in for fear it would betray him, too. He spoke before I could renege my offer.

"He keeps properties along the coast for when he needs them. He doesn't come often, but he's here now. For a couple of days at least. He's here."

For the next several minutes, I pumped the broken mage for information. Location. Security. Procedure. Expectations. It all sounded professional enough. Concerning, even. Exactly the type of thing I needed to personally take a look at myself.

"So, you're gonna let me go?" Marco finally asked.

I leaned in and dangled my black tongue over my teeth. I lapped at the blood pouring from his neck. Already coagulating. It would get infected, perhaps, but it wouldn't bleed out. "I would've liked to drink your life into mine."

"No. You said you wouldn't kill me."

I pulled away and licked my lips. "He wants to live," I announced to the room. "And a deal's a deal."

I watched him and waited for it. That glimmer of hope to return. That twinkle in the eye. I waited and when I saw it, I ground it to dust: "I won't be killing you, because I've already promised you to the Anansi."

I stepped away from the man. Backward. Watched the fear dawn on his face. He spun on the tight wire holding him up. Laser focus on the darkest corner of the room. The thing I'd been talking to.

"Don't worry." I backed away farther. "He won't kill you immediately. Just chew on you a little."

Marco spun to the other corner, then wildly to me again, kicking over the candle by mistake. The fire flickered in the dark, lighting us with a menacing sway.

"His venom is very different from mine," I continued. "It will liquefy your insides. Make a good soup out of your bones and organs. Then he'll drink you in over the course of days until you're nothing more than a dried husk."

The man swiveled around, taking in all of the attic, trying to keep whatever was in the darkness at bay. He pulled frantically at the invisible line ensnaring his wrists. It bit into his flesh, threatening to slice the skin off like a glove.

But there was nothing in the room to see. Just him and the candle and me, leaning against the open doorway on my way out.

He forced a nervous chuckle. "Oh, damn, you're kidding. Right? Please tell me you're kidding."

I disappeared into the shadow. "Delusion," I said. "He thinks we're kidding."

A chittering sound above the man snapped his head upward. Eight bulbous eyes of uneven size reflected his screaming face back at him. A tarantula larger than his head crept down the translucent spiderweb binding his arms. When the first furry appendage brushed his skin, Marco recoiled, nearly severing his hand.

It was too late for that.

The trickster spider lunged onto the man's head, extending spindly appendages. Fangs swung open like switchblades and sunk deep into soft flesh.

My boots stomped down the creaky attic steps, a sound overpowered by the man's terrified howls. A moment ago, his worst fear had been the curved blades in my hand. Now he realized those would've been a mercy.

"You sure about this, Tunji?"

My eyes narrowed as I studied the dock. It was bright tonight. Biscayne Bay reflected the full moon. That complicated things a bit. The two armed mercenaries outside the boat complicated things a hand more.

Jaja and Pim huddled at my side. They were West African, like myself. Only human, of course, but they were both capable. Obeah men. Not the voodoo charlatans of Haiti who worship Christian idols in the names of their gods. Obeah men were true spiritualists. Respectful of the land and the ways of the Old World.

"You afraid of automatic weapons, Jaja?" I asked.

He snickered and adjusted his feathered top hat. It was a concession to the New World. His only one. The rest of Jaja was rough and drab. A brown leather vest over a midnight-black chest. Strong in a lean kind of way. Capable without being showy.

"I don't like boats," was all he said in reply.

I smiled. The salt water would interfere with their spell-craft. But the boat, I reminded myself, wasn't the destination. Just the means to it.

We were ready for war. As such, I had my full battle dress on. Metal breast- and shoulder-plates. My blades. Even my boots were metal, with long shin guards that ran up to my knees and ended in sharp protruding spikes.

"Do your thing," I commanded.

Jaja lifted a wooden figure to his lips. A one-legged idol. His spellcraft fetish. He kissed it and spoke a word of Igbo, his mother tongue. The air surrounding us grew unusually muggy, even for Miami. It crossed the grassy clearing on an unnatural breeze and hit the dock with a gentle roll. The two gunmen trembled.

"They are weak," I observed with satisfaction.

The gunmen looked around and traded sharp words. Then they gave each other hard stares. A curse. Another. A shove. Within half a minute they were in a heated argument.

I nodded for Jaja and Pim to go. They skittered along the sidewalk in a half crouch before starting down the marina driveway.

I stood from behind the bush, vaulted over it, and made a steady gait for the boat. It was a straight line, right over the public lawn, trampling the flowers in manicured pockets of dirt.

The arguing guards spun at the sounds of laughter to find Jaja and Pim stumbling drunkenly, leaning on each other for support, booming voices carefree in the wind. The spellcraft had distracted the guards enough for the obeah men to get halfway down the driveway. Now that they were noticed, the gunmen straightened up and addressed the problem.

"Private marina," announced one of them. "The dock's closed."

Pim lifted his eyebrows and spoke in Igbo. The tone of his voice was appeasing and confused, but the words were a common Nigerian insult involving a mother and a donkey. I grinned, because the obeah men were only a distraction themselves.

"Hey!" barked the other guard, raising his compact weapon against the intruders. "This is your final warning. Back off."

I leaned forward, almost into a fall. Then I kicked my boots under me and went from zero to sixty in a blink. The first guard had his gun halfway pointed at my companions when I took both their heads clean off. Two curved blades, two slashes that spread my arms into an impressive wing-span. The headless bodies listed momentarily before crumpling to the floor.

I knelt beside one of them and washed my hand in the pumping blood. I ran the wet palm down my face, over my closed eyes, and brushed it clean with my tongue.

"Tunji!" cried Jaja, lifting his fetish in alarm.

I spun on my knees and let my blade fly. The circle of steel sliced through the air at the captain of the boat. A third man, his pistol already raised and ready to fire, lasered onto my center mass. A twitch of a finger away.

He wasn't fast enough.

The open part of the blade slipped around the man's

neck. I closed the fingers of my empty hand and the weapon froze midair, hooked around the man like a collar. An invisible tether of magic led from it to my palm. I pulled violently. The boatman dropped the pistol and it lurched through the air, pitching over the gunwale and flying into my hands.

"*That* would've been a mistake," I growled.

I checked the boat. A well-used and inconspicuous thing. It didn't look like a drug dealer ride. The stern displayed the vessel's name: *Risky Proposition*. I liked that.

"You're going to take us to your boss," I said.

The captain swallowed hard and jerked his head up and down. "Okay," he said. "Then you let me go."

"Relax," I assured. "You have my personal guarantee that *I* won't kill you."

I smiled at Jaja and Pim as they rolled the bodies into the water and boarded the boat. I unhooked my blade from around the captain's neck and shoved him into Pim's headlock. Then I punted a loose head far into the bay. It skipped once like a stone.

The captain took us to Star Island, one of several man-made islands between the beach and the mainland, a place affordable only for the rich and famous. A high-profile kind of place, but one with the luxury of bushy yards and privacy-seeking residents. Mansions lined the water, each with a private dock. Most had yachts and cruisers much nicer and newer than the *Risky Proposition*.

That's when I realized the boat was a throwaway. I

wouldn't be surprised if the house we were headed to was as well.

"Right there," called the captain.

Many of the houses were well lit, but not the one he pointed to. The accent lights on the lawn were dark. The sconces on the outside walls, too. Some ambient flashing within the large first-floor windows, but dim. Only a second-floor bedroom had a proper light on.

They were keeping attention away from the house. From the dock. That kind of darkness would've worked against them, too, if it wasn't for the bright moon. We could've snuck right to their doorstep in the absence of moonlight. Instead, a silverish azure highlighted everything with a monotone glow. I easily spotted the pacing guards. Confirmation this was the right place.

I considered docking elsewhere but there was a good chance we had already been spotted from a distance. Besides, my patience was wearing thin.

"Cut the engine," I said.

The boat went silent and the captain guided us to the dark wood structure. Before we stopped, two men approached from the side of the house. I fixed the spotlight on them, keeping it low enough not to alert anyone inside the home but high enough to blind the guards.

Without bothering to face him, I said, "Thank you for your service, Captain."

He only had time for a sharp intake of breath before Pim tackled him overboard. Both men splashed into the shallows. The captain's fingers clawed at the hull as the obeah man held his head beneath the lapping water.

"Showtime," I said.

Jaja nodded and raised his idol.

The first approaching guard paused on the lawn. His attention suddenly diverted to his feet. To something on the ground. He flinched away.

"What the—?"

The spirits were in his mind. They would drive him crazy.

The other guard was unaffected and stepped forward onto the dock. His eyes squinted against the spotlight.

"They're all over the place!" yelled the first one, trampling the ground. The panicked man pointed his automatic weapon at his feet and fired. Lead thunked into dirt and stirred blades of grass into the air.

The other guard swung around with his gun, ready for an ambush. All he saw was his partner emptying a magazine into the lawn.

He stood on the dock, bewildered, until Pim launched out of the water below and grabbed his legs from behind, tugging hard. The gunman slipped on the dock and fell to his knees, a short burst of bullets releasing into the sky.

I stretched my jaw in anticipation. Stealth was overrated. Now that the whole neighborhood had woken from the automatic reports, the only thing left to do was to finish this. I swung around the spotlight, stepped on the gunwale, and hopped to the dock. My metal boots landed heavy.

Stomp. Stomp. Stomp.

I marched forward, eyes on the house. The faint light on the first floor went dark. A television, likely.

Pim swung his machete. It glanced off the gun of the guard, who had resisted being dragged into the water. Now he was kicking the obeah man away to keep the blade from doing damage. At the same time, his gun hand struggled against Pim's grip, trying to shake loose so he could pump a few rounds into his attacker.

The gun yanked up and away from Pim, who lacked leverage. The guard smiled as his arm was loosed, reaching for the sky.

I slashed viciously as I passed, staying focused on the house. The man's forearm sliced clean off, gun and hand alike bouncing into the bay. His eyes widened as he took in his stump. He screamed loudly until a machete buried itself into his head like it was a coconut.

Pim tugged his blade into the water and pulled the corpse down with it.

Stomp. Stomp. Stomp.

My metal boots rang out on the dock. The back door of the house opened. A woman with short blond curls and purple eyeliner emerged onto the patio. She locked eyes with me.

Stomp. Stomp. Swiff. Swiff.

I didn't hurry my pace as I hit the grass. I didn't stutter. My steps evenly and consistently pressed ahead, savoring the challenge.

"They're all over me!" yelled the remaining guard. He'd dropped his weapon and was clawing at his skin, his back to me as I passed. This time I used my left hand and swung the blade downward, rending his back open along the spine. All the while, I kept my eyes on the woman at the door.

Swiff. Swiff. Swiff.

Purple eyeliner tightened into shrewd slits. The woman barked orders inside. Two mercenaries rushed out to stand beside her, waiting for her command. When she called them idiots and pointed at me, a light-skinned man ran at me with his weapon up and fired.

In a blur of motion, I dropped down on a knee spike and swung both blades ahead of me. The trail in their wake formed a protective shell. The bullets ricocheted against sharpened steel.

The man was stuck for a moment with his jaw open. When he hurried to reload, a machete lobbed through the air plunged into his gut.

Pim came up on my right to recover his weapon. Jaja was already advancing through the trees on my left.

And me? I didn't run. I didn't hurry. I rose steadily to my feet and made a straight line for the blond woman and her second mercenary.

Swiff. Swiff. Swiff.

The pair traded a worried glance and retreated into the house. The dead bolt clicked loudly. I made my way across the yard and Jaja slipped around to the front. Behind me, Pim's machete chopped at bone.

Two left, at least. South American ex-military and Florida trailer trash. Interesting that she was leading them. Hadn't even seen a gun. This led me to a single conclusion: she was an animist, like Marco.

I marched onto the cement patio, past the hot tub and wicker furniture. The back door was made of heavy wood. A solid piece of carpentry.

Stomp. Stomp. Thunk.

My hooked blades bit deep into the old wood. With a grunt, I heaved the door off its hinges.

The deafening blast surprised me. A solid blow punched me in the side of the gut, just beneath my breastplate. I didn't have time to inspect the damage because the South American was hiding in the laundry room, gun ready.

As he pulled the trigger, I swung the door in front of me, holding it like a shield. Bullets peppered the large surface but failed to penetrate. When the barrage ended, I held the blades tight and planted my boot in the center of the door, kicking it loose in the gunman's direction. He scrambled out of the way and came up for another volley.

I hurled my blade into his chest.

I paused a moment. Stumbled a step forward. Slipped and fell to a knee. My armor spike cracked the tile.

Running my fingers along my side, I found the torn gouge of flesh. My hand came away with black blood.

Which is when I noticed the spent double-barreled shotgun that had been rigged to the door. A primitive booby trap.

"Trailer trash," I muttered.

I ground my teeth in annoyance at the oversight. I winced and pushed to my feet. Placed my boot on the dead man's chest and yanked my blade free. I moved into the living room, favoring my side.

Stomp-stomp. Stomp-stomp.

"So, you're *not* bulletproof," drawled the blond woman.

Waiting for me on the far side of the couch, she didn't look like much up close. A loose T-shirt. Cargo pants. But her pink skin was plump like a peach. A bonus for my trouble.

"I'm disappointed," I said. "I was hoping you'd present a more original challenge."

The woman didn't hold any spell tokens. She didn't wear

an amulet or have magic spilling from her eyes. Instead, she held a single Beretta 9mm.

Someone pounded on the front door. A voice inside yelled something in Spanish. So there was one more mercenary, at least. The woman and I returned our eyes to each other, content to let the others fight their own battle.

I twirled the blade deftly in my fingers. "What are you going to do with that toy?"

"You'd be surprised," she said defiantly.

"I do hope so."

I caught the blade by its grip and reared back to throw it. She fired the pistol as I knew she would. Not careful or precise. Not especially well aimed. The blade arced before me in a flash to batter away the spray.

The spray never came.

The rounds didn't hit me or the blade. They missed my breastplate and the floor and the walls behind me. My surprise went cold and calculating. I zeroed in on the slightest movement: fifteen rounds hovering unmolested in the air, all by themselves. A swarm of wasps positioning to strike.

The animist smiled and tossed the spent Beretta to the floor. Her open hands engaged the Intrinsics now, the manifest energies that make up the world, the building blocks of magic. She focused and teased the bullets to her will. They spread around me in a cloud. Surrounded me from multiple angles.

I stood tall and readied my weapons at each side. "You only get fifteen chances," I warned.

She smirked. "I'm an all-or-nothing kinda gal."

She clapped her hands together and the bullets all rocketed toward me at once. I spun with my blades, deflecting some and dodging others. I moved so fast I was a blur. Faster than a speeding bullet.

But these weren't normal bullets. They weren't obeying the laws of physics. I deflected a few for good, but the remaining rounds pivoted and changed course. The hornet's nest was angry and the insects converged on me with unerring accuracy. I twisted out of their path and battered more away with superhuman speed.

It wasn't enough. As I planted my foot for another spin, eight bullets punched into my back and side.

I roared and buckled to all fours. One of my blades clanked to the tile. The pain was excruciating.

Out of sight, another aftermath was playing out. The pounding on the door stopped. The South American screamed violently. The blond animist stepped aside to make sure her back wasn't exposed to whatever was coming from that end.

That's when Pim struck from behind me. He charged in and raised his machete overhead.

"Stop!" shouted the mage.

Pim's weapon froze midair, as the bullets had. Stuck. He tugged at it, unwilling to give it up to the woman. It barely budged. He put his weight into it. She strained to hold him off.

I laughed. A deep, throaty laugh. It resonated in my lungs. My shoulders heaved and the pain from the bullet wounds seared across my back. Then I laughed harder. A booming and boisterous thing that made more noise than the pain.

I grabbed the dropped weapon and pulled it toward me slowly, blade scraping against tile.

"Bulletproof or not," I grunted, "your weapons cannot kill me."

I got my feet under me and stood. The woman's eyes quivered as she watched, locked in a mental struggle with Pim. Jaja rushed in from the front of the house. She spun as he tackled her. Pim broke free and charged her as well, raising his blade for a killing blow.

"No!" I boomed.

Everybody froze. Jaja on top of the whimpering animist. Pim towering over her mid-strike. In the background somewhere, a man quietly begged to die.

Once again I didn't hurry. I studied the black blood on my hands. Wiped my blades clean on my pants. When I spoke, my voice was colored by annoyance.

"All night I have promised my kills to others, or left them behind to be scavenged. But not with you." I strolled around the furniture and ran my eyes over the pathetic woman. "Now I finally get to feast. What a delight."

I knelt over her, opened my jaw, and crunched down on the tendons in her neck. They ripped easily between my metal teeth. Human blood washed into my mouth, warm and full.

The obeah men waited as I ate. It didn't take long. I wasn't a trickster spider who meticulously wrapped my victims in webbing. This was primal and naturalistic and raw. I drank the essence of the woman and chewed whatever flesh and bone got in the way. Then I rolled her lifeless body over and wiped my mouth.

The house on Star Island was silent now. No heavy steps. No gunshots. No yelling or sirens. It was as if life had never existed here at all.

We made our way through the house. The first floor was clear. The stairwell by the front door the last holdout. The final South American mercenary lay there, dead. He was propped up against the steps, knife still in one hand, a deep scoop of flesh and intestines tugged out with his other. Self-inflicted. Jaja had dreamed up a real nightmare for that one.

I nodded to the obeah men and made my way up the stairs. They crept silently behind me and fanned out in the hallway. I nudged a door open with my weapon. An empty bedroom. Jaja and Pim cleared another and a bathroom. All our eyes fixed on the single door at the end of the hall, a sliver of bright light shining through underneath. The last place to hide.

Stomp. Stomp. Stomp.

Pim was the closest. As he reached for the doorknob, a stream of light blazed right past him. The obeah man grunted and was knocked to the floor.

Behind me, Jaja yelped. I spun around to see him being flung through the air. He bowled through a wide second-story window and careened to the ground below.

I stepped forward and felt it coming. The hairs on the back of my neck stood straight. Every open wound on my back tingled.

I dove into a roll. The wall where I'd been smashed apart. I swung my blade backward in an expeditious arc. It whiffed and dug into the hardwood floor.

The ghostly attack didn't let up. A punch to my shotgun wound. But I was fast as well. I dashed away and defended with a sweep of my metal boot. Again I hit nothing.

Pim cursed in Igbo and swiped at something with his machete. The blade sunk into the wall and he stopped short with a gurgle. He looked at me, eyes wide, and then suddenly burst into flames. The obeah man screamed and kicked until he toppled over the banister and plummeted to the floor below, ashes in his wake.

I scanned the hall, both weapons ready. The darkness was alleviated by the unnatural fire below.

I could see I was alone.

I breathed silently, patiently. Waited for another attack. It never came.

I peeked downstairs. Pim was a charred crisp. The magic that had done him in was powerful. Efficient. I smelled something in it that I hadn't encountered in a long time. As the flames died to a smolder, the hall darkened. The bright sliver of light under the bedroom door taunted me.

I am here, it said. *I am waiting*.

I snarled and barged inside.

"In Nigeria, Ghana, and all along the Ivory Coast," came a disembodied voice, "they speak of a creature with hooked arms and legs. One impervious to weapons, who sinks sharp metal fangs into unwary wanderers. Those without homes or futures. The asanbosam, they call you."

My boots stomped heavily on the floor. I studied the bedroom. Large by most standards. A king-sized platform bed opposite a fireplace. Desk and writing chair in the corner. Long balcony with a view of sparkling Biscayne Bay, the lawn, and the dock.

But no man.

"If this display is meant to cow me," I announced, "it is inadequate." I lowered my blades and waited.

"An asanbosam," repeated the voice. "That means you're not actually African at all. Not really. You're from the Nether. You scurry out from the holes between worlds to feed on humans foolish enough to tempt the dark."

Hands clapped together behind me. I whirled around to see a man studying me. Bright-orange hair. Sharp cheeks and a pointed nose resting above a thick beard.

The grip on my weapons tightened, but the figure barely registered them. He was too busy taking stock of me.

"My, but you are fearless," he observed. "Aren't you?"

I waited, amused by his smugness but concerned with his smell.

He looked normal enough. Unimpressive, really. The loose sports coat over the wrinkled polo did a poor job hiding his belly. He was hardly daunting by conventional means.

"You aren't human, either," I returned.

"All the more reason for us to deal in a civilized manner."

My face darkened. "You killed my obeah men."

"The one outside will live. The other one, I'm sorry to say, forced my hand. But then you've killed many more of mine. I won't hold that against you during our negotiations."

I sidestepped to the balcony window. Jaja lay in the grass, unconscious but breathing.

"You're a jinn," I spat. "A primal being. There are legends about your kind as well." I stared him in the eye. "Deals with jinns are foolish business."

He widened his eyes almost imperceptibly. "Smart. Doubly fearless, too, given that knowledge. Tell me, aren't you scared of me even a little?"

"Should I be?"

"Oh, yes." Flames danced in his eyes. "I've lived a long time and I've never met a Nether creature who didn't cower at my presence."

"You've never met an asanbosam."

He frowned in consideration. "Too true. And I admit to being impressed so far, despite your lowly birth. Powerful and candid, but reckless as well. Wouldn't you agree?"

I didn't answer.

"A deal with a jinn," he said. "A dangerous thing, to be sure. What you fail to realize is that I've met your obeah men before." He smiled. "Don't worry. They didn't betray you. We merely bargained over turf. They did their jobs without realizing who they were dealing with."

The jinn raised an open palm and a ball of fire burst into being. "You know, the human protections don't apply to you. I could incinerate you with a flick of my wrist."

I showed my teeth. He could try. "Get on with it," I said. "Speak plainly or fight."

"In a rush to die, I see," he said with a chuckle. "But it doesn't have to be that way. I could use someone with your talents."

"Nobody uses me."

"What about the Nigerian?"

"I work for Namadi Obazuaye."

Now the jinn laughed outright. "A weak-minded man. A charming smile and good business sense, perhaps, but no formidable talent to speak of. And here you are. An asanbosam. Once lurking in the trees of the Third World, feeding on the desolate and the lost. Desperately looking for a permanent escape from the dark pits that bore you. That's why you're here, is it not?"

I worked my jaw. This one had a silver tongue. I considered slicing it off and eating it first.

"Tell me, Tunji Malu," he started, "do you know the difference between deceit and delusion?"

My breath stopped. I narrowed my eyes slowly. "How did—"

"It's a simple question," he said plainly. "Deceit and delusion. Have you ever thought about the difference?"

"You were there," I said, a statement not a question, but incredulous nonetheless. "In the attic."

The jinn vanished in a blink and appeared on the other side of me. "I am made of fire and air, Nether one. I am everywhere."

I snorted. "Then why didn't you stop me? Why didn't you save your mage?"

The jinn grinned hungrily. "Where would be the fun in that?"

I blinked and took a hesitant step away. When I realized I was showing weakness, I stopped.

"Deceit and delusion, Tunji. Are you deluding yourself? That you serve this man. That you aren't clawing out from your cesspit and trying to reach heights your brothers never dreamed of. Or were you merely employing deceit? Telling Namadi you were his loyal servant while hitching on his coattails, keeping your true identity and intentions hidden."

"This was a job interview," I concluded.

"Perceptive, again."

The threatening ball of flame in his palm winked out. The jinn slipped his hands into his pockets and leaned against the wall, abandoning any pretense that I could kill him. In truth, I wasn't so sure I could. But he was giving me an opening.

"I'll triple your salary," he said, closing the deal. "Plus bonuses for special jobs. I have other people in place, but Miami's a surprising city. A gateway into this country, loose and wild and corrupt in all the best ways. But also a tough nut to crack. I could use someone with your skill set to speed along my influence."

I relaxed my posture and held my blades loose. As he spoke I moved closer.

"You'll keep your current job, too," he said. "An influential businessman like Namadi is a good one to have under hand. You made a wise choice there. And we'll launder my money through him, of course. Keep those details from him, and do it without a percentage. You'll earn plenty through other means, including what the fool will continue to pay you as his bodyguard. Is that understood?"

I waited a beat. "You're serious."

"Deadly. I have big plans for this city. You could be a part of them."

I licked my lips and wondered if his big plans had included the dead mageling downstairs. Then again, her death had been her own fault.

The jinn stepped forward and offered me an outstretched hand. "What will it be, Tunji? Death or glory?"

He waited for my reply, a statue of unwavering resolve. I considered his hard eyes carefully. He was different from Namadi. More shrewd, more dangerous. Wasn't that the game I was playing?

I worked my jaw again. Considered Pim still smoldering downstairs. Then I recalled the long, endless tunnels of the Nether. The wide-open nothingness of Africa. I recounted how far I'd already come, and foresaw how much further I could still go.

It was all within reach. I just had to take it.

I clasped his hand into mine. "We have a deal."

Delusion. That was one problem I didn't have.

BALANCE

SEANAN McGUIRE

When monsters and men are one and the same, it's up to the cryptozoologists to keep the peace, and keep humanity from understanding that we are not alone. Most of the cryptids in the InCryptid universe are perfectly lovely people. But then there are the cuckoos—telepathic ambush predators who will steal everything you are, and laugh while your world falls apart around you. They live for math. They live for malice. In "Balance," we see that these two things are not always at odds . . .

"Please. For the sake of humanity, watch for the absences. Watch for the holes. Know the threat is real, and guard against it with your life."

—ALEXANDER HEALY

A small outdoor café in Burbank, California

Now

The server waited for me to take my first sip of pink-tinged tea, every line of his trim cater-waiter body vibrating with the need to know that I was satisfied, that he hadn't somehow managed to disappoint the most important person in the industry. He was hoping for his big break, and when he looked at me, he saw his name in lights.

Fool. Still, for the moment, a useful fool, and eliding a corpse is almost always more trouble than it's worth. I took the sip.

"Tangy," I said, and felt him swell with pride. "But a bit under-seasoned, don't you think? Really, I expected better from a place with this sort of reputation."

His shoulders sagged. Humans are so senselessly demonstrative, like they're afraid their emotions will lose all meaning if not painted constantly on a billboard. Noisy, nasty things.

"I am *so* sorry," he babbled. He began to reach for the tea, then froze, apparently realizing that taking it would mean snatching the cup out of my hands. "I'll remove it from your bill immediately. Honestly, I don't know what happened—"

"Bring me a glass of V8," I said. The café didn't sell the stuff, but the bodega across the street did, and I knew my eager attendant would make an unauthorized jaunt to get me what I asked for.

"Right away," he said, and turned and fled before I could change my mind about losing my temper. Mammalian fool.

I leaned back in my seat, considering the minds around me. They were all mammalian, hot and swift and teeming with untidy hormones. Most were human. A chupacabra actress held court at the table one over from mine, talking about making the transition between telenovelas and American drama.

It would be a small, easy thing to twist the part of her

mind that allowed her to regulate her shape. How many of her fawning sycophants would stay in her company if she turned inside out and revealed herself as the glorious monster that she was? The screaming would be amusing, if nothing else—the chaos would be *delicious*.

But I would never get my V8. More, in this age of cell phones and cameras everywhere, the footage might attract the sort of people I didn't want to deal with. Monster-hunters are tedious at the best of times. Drama queens and ambulance chasers, the lot of them, driven by the fear that perhaps humans aren't at the top of the food chain after all.

As if they ever were. I sipped my tea, sighing with transitory contentment. It would have been difficult not to enjoy the delicate interplay of jasmine and tomato puree mixed with honey. It wasn't a blend a café catering to a human clientele would ever think to put on a menu, but menus have little meaning for me. Truly, it was a lovely afternoon.

Maybe the V8 would be overkill. The tea was improving as it had time to fully mature. Jasmine is like that. I stood, taking my teacup with me.

My server was running back across the street, my requested beverage in hand. There was a truck heading his way, slowing to let the pedestrian pass. The driver was close enough for me to taste his thoughts, the slow, murky consideration of the world around him. One more boring man, living a boring life in a boring world, never making headlines, never doing anything worth remembering.

I could fix that.

The driver slammed his foot down on the gas, barreling forward fast enough to catch the unwary waiter square across the ribs. He went flying, V8 shooting out of his hand and smacking into the windshield. The truck continued onward before turning sharply and plowing into the front of the café. The chupacabra was fast enough to get up and out of the way before her table was driven through the window and into the dining room. Her companions were . . . less fortunate.

Humming to myself, still sipping my tea, I walked away. There must be something to do in a town like this on such a beautiful day. All I had to do was find it.

———————⟫⟪———————

What possessed evolution to make something in such a practical form with no functional defenses, I may never know. Humans are fascinating creatures. They look like cuckoos: two arms, two legs, moderate sexual dimorphism. They have more variation in their appearance, but that only makes sense, as they have no other way of distinguishing one another. They can't read minds or feel thoughts like we do; they lack the true understanding of their peers that every cuckoo is born with.

Perhaps that's why they gather in such dismayingly large hives. Put a million cuckoos in one place and you'd get a riot the likes of which this world has never seen. We can't abide each other, save under very specific circumstances, when the need is greater than the desire to be left alone. Humans, though, they pile themselves up like locusts devouring a field, until their bodies are the greater part of their environment, and when they close the doors to their homes, they think themselves alone.

Humans are bees. Cuckoos are wasps. Even in this backward dimension where evolution clearly went wrong, bees exist to feed the wasps who move among them. They feed us in whatever way they can, and we show them the mercy of remaining solitary creatures. If we gathered in swarms like they do, we would destroy them inside of a season.

I walked. I sipped my tea. A man pulled a knife in the shadow of a parking garage, intending to take the purse of a young woman with two small children. He stabbed himself in the throat instead. His intended victims screamed in terrible harmony as I walked on.

The youngest of them would never recover. I could taste the shape of her trauma knitting together, one loop at a time. It would be a beautiful equation when it was finished, as long as no one interfered. I was nearly out of range of their minds, yet still close enough to reach out, tinker, and suggest. I'm no cuckoo queen, to completely modify memories. Pleasant as the power would be, it comes with a fate I have no interest in coveting.

Still, if I can't take a memory away, I can tone it down, wear off its edges, make it seem less important when set against the complicated mathematics of a life. The woman and her older child would forget this day more quickly than they would have believed possible, while the youngest would dwell on it, wrap herself around it, *become* it, until the stress of carrying that burden exploded in some fascinating new way.

I would be a hundred miles away by the time her equation reached its inevitable, explosive end. That was fine. Part of the fun of surrendering a piece of territory is in leaving presents for whoever takes control of it after me. Let the next cuckoo contend with whatever delicious atrocity this child grew up to commit. I would read about it in the papers, and have a pleasant memory to brighten a dull afternoon.

Still humming to myself and sipping my tea, I walked on.

The effort of altering their memories had been enough to leave me weary. I paused to look around and consider my options. Burbank is a lovely town for shopping, snacking, and playing with people, but its hotels tend toward the lower end of the scale, and most of the truly interesting people spend all their time behind gated walls protected by tedious security systems. Damned electronic eyes don't yield properly to psychic pressure.

There was a woman walking toward me on the sidewalk, her car keys in one hand and a Starbucks latte in the other, her thoughts filled with vague errands and emptiness. She would do. I waited for her to reach me, fell into step beside her, and smiled sweetly.

"There you are," I said. "I've been waiting *ages*."

There was a pause while her perception of reality adjusted to the changes I was feeding it. I felt her relax, and knew from the shape of her thoughts that she was smiling back, sheepishly, as if she had let someone terribly important down.

"Sorry, Eliza," she said. "The line at the Starbucks was awful, and you know how I get when I don't have my coffee."

"Next time, why don't we drive someplace less crowded, rather than waiting?"

"What a good idea." She unlocked her car, a mid-range

BMW, unremarkable for the neighborhood but nice enough for me to feel confident in my choice. I *hate* the conditions some humans live in. Squalor is one thing, but there's no reason to wallow in it. "Do you want to drive?"

Clearly she thought I was the dominant half of this friendship. That was good: sometimes people write themselves into the role of my protector or keeper, and those can be difficult to get away from. I allowed my smile to turn gracious, following the cues from her mental response to get the shape of it exactly right. Our acquaintance was still new enough that I needed to be careful if I wanted it to deepen properly.

"Now, Barb, you know I don't drive when the sun's up," I said. "My eyes, you know. You go ahead."

Her cheeks reddened. "I'm sorry. We'll go straight home."

"Thank you," I said, and got into the car, balancing my teacup on my knee as I closed my eyes and settled deep into the buttery leather seat. Yes. This was definitely an improvement.

Barb chattered idly as she drove, and I didn't interrupt or try to stop her. She was contradicting herself almost constantly, first pointing out a landmark and then recounting a story about a time she and I had gone there together and done some festive thing or other. I paid her little attention, letting her work through all the snarls of our "relationship" without input from me.

This is what it is to be a cuckoo: people who look at me will always see what they want to see, what they *need* to see in order to be drawn to protect me. I can shape the flavor of their response, turning it familial or fawning, but for the most part, I don't bother. The human mind is elastic and impressionable. I've found that if I simply hurl myself into their psyches and embed myself there, they'll heal around me, finding the most stable formation to support my needs.

People who don't appreciate the simple elegance of what we do call us parasites, say that the way we reshape the world is outside the natural order of things. They're wrong, of course. We're as natural as anything else the universe has to offer. It's not our fault that we're more effective predators than anything else on *this* world.

Humans, especially, don't like to remember that their world isn't the only one around.

Barb pulled into the driveway of a pleasant two-story house: not as palatial as some I had commandeered, but sufficient for an afternoon. I smiled at her as I got out of the car.

"I'm so glad you could drive me home."

Her thoughts roiled, confusion kicking up the silt at the bottom of her mind. That was important. She had settled into the framework of our relationship all by herself, and now it was time for me to quash anything that would contradict it. I mentally reached out and pressed down on the parts of her that wanted to object, to rebel. It took only a few seconds for her thoughts to settle, her face going blank enough that even I could see the lack of animation.

Humans and their *faces*. If they could share their emotions silently, like civilized people, they wouldn't need so many expressions.

"Of course, Eliza," she said. "You know I'd do anything for a friend."

"I know," I said, and held out my hand. "My keys, please?"

She tossed them to me without objection.

The walkway was clean and well maintained. Barb trailed behind me like a puppy eager for approval, and I allowed it. If nothing else, having her around would mean not needing to search for anything, and unless I wanted to order her to drive off the nearest available cliff—not out of the question if she got annoying enough—I could have her chauffeur me around for a few days while she "slept over" with the friend she thought I was.

The door opened on an airy foyer with a domed ceiling that must have been hell to cool during the height of the summer, given humans' narrow range of comfortable temperatures. Truly, it's a miracle they were able to survive long enough to develop central air. They should have died off long before their technology progressed to such a point, leaving the world to a dominant species capable of enjoying it properly.

Still, the windows were thick enough to keep the place nicely insulated, and the curtains I'd seen from the outside had looked heavy. Light-blocking. That meant I'd have all the things a modern cuckoo needs to sleep peacefully. "I think I'll lie down for a little while," I said. "Feel free to make yourself at home until I wake up."

Barb nodded, thoughts turning painfully grateful, as if this weren't her house and I hadn't just taken it over as easily as plucking an apple from a tree. That's another problem with humans: they bounce back so quickly that sometimes they scar over damage that any other thinking species would have been able to eventually route around and recover from.

If my ancestors had been looking for the perfect prey, they couldn't have done better than humanity. They'll love us all the way to their own graves, and if they leave ghosts when they go, they'll keep on loving us forever. We win. Every time, we win.

Barb's bedroom was on the second floor. I walked a circuit around it, considering the size of the bed—queen—the lack of pictures of family members or pets, even the stuffed bunny on the pillow. Excellent. She'd been a casual acquisition, the minion equivalent of grabbing takeout when it was too late to get a proper dinner, but it seemed like she might be something worth keeping for a little longer than I'd originally planned.

Humans are fragile. If one is going to be in the business of cultivating them, one must also accept that they will occasionally need to be replaced—and that the good ones should be kept for as long as possible, to make those replacements less frequent.

The linens smelled of lavender. I put my teacup down on the bedside table, crawled beneath the covers, and closed my eyes. Sleep would do more than simply restore my body. It would consolidate my hold on Barb, and through her, on her neighbors. It would make this my home, and not simply a house I happened to occupy, until I was prepared to move along.

Sleep came swiftly. It always does, when things are going well.

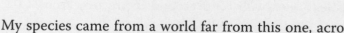

My species came from a world far from this one, across the gulf of a dozen dimensions, each with their own delights and dangers to offer. I was born on earth, as were all the cuckoos of my generation, and the generation before us, going back to our arrival in this world some five hundred years ago. We had exhausted the world that had been sheltering us, sucking it dry and denuding it of entertainments. A change had been necessary. A change will almost always do us good. So a hive had come together, and working together, had lifted up a queen and used her to do what queens do best. They had used her to find us something new to devour.

Our shatter point had formed in Qingyáng in China. I sometimes wish I could have been there. Thousands died, humans and yōkai alike, as they tried to beat back the waves of what must have seemed like an alien invasion—not quite right, but not quite wrong, either. They couldn't win, of course. We're unstoppable, when we want to be. When the dust settled, the rift was closed, and the cuckoos were masters of a new world.

Really, if we could work together with one another, we would have devoured this place centuries ago. That's the secret. That's the gift evolution gave us, and through us, gave to everyone else. We hate each other so completely that we can't stand to keep one another company. That means it takes us time to eat our bright new hives from the inside out. Our hatred for one another is the way we get the time to breathe . . . and when we have time, everyone else has time. Even if it's only borrowed. We grant you all a stay of execution every time we decline to get along.

In a world of mammals, a single cuckoo might as well be all-powerful. We can go where we want, do what we want, *take* what we want, and few humans will ever realize they've been manipulated, much less become aware of our presence. We can eat a swath across a continent, and it's only by looking at the seemingly senseless crimes in our wake that anyone will ever know that we were there.

Which isn't to say that we're malicious. All we do is exploit what's available to us. Does a human who makes their dog work for its supper consider themselves malicious? Do they feel like terrible people because they enjoy a good piece of steak on occasion? No. They recognize themselves as the higher creature, and they use the lesser as they see fit. We simply do the same.

We simply do it to *them*.

One day, when we finish draining this place dry, we'll move on to something new, something fat and slow and unwary, like this world was before we came. We'll close the door behind us, and we'll set the sky on fire, because who would want to live in a world after we've taken everything good it had to offer? Really, if anything should prove that we're not monsters, it's that. We're willing to put the sick dog down, rather than walking away and calling it "mercy."

Mercy is for people who don't understand what it is to balance the equation and let the numbers speak for themselves.

———————————⇒⇐———————————

I woke at sunset, in a room filled with warm amber light, warm and bright. I sat up, yawning languidly as I stretched the kinks out of my shoulders. Barb had clearly replaced her mattress within the last year: my back felt better than it had in days. I added another number to the "stay here awhile" column.

Some of my kind believe in planning, making elaborate itineraries and schedules, moving around the world according to a checklist. To be fair, they tend to have a great deal of fun, and better yet, they do very well at avoiding accidental encounters with our own kind. Knowing exactly when you're going to be somewhere makes it easier to hang out the KEEP AWAY sign.

But planning creates patterns, and patterns are how human hunters find us, the bastards. We may be an invasive species, but that doesn't mean we don't serve a purpose in the ecosystem. This world welcomed us during a time when it was bleeding predators, slaughtered by careless humans who didn't understand what they were doing. There have to be checks and balances, or else the equation of the world falls apart. Just look at what humanity's doing, now that it doesn't have anything bigger to keep it from spreading like a plague across the planet. They didn't learn *anything* from killing the dragons and the manticores and the sirens.

We keep the planet from collapsing under the weight of its own occupants, and how do those occupants repay us? By hunting us when they have the opportunity, because we're "unnatural" and "cruel" and all those other things that could just as easily be said about the human race. Really, it's only fair for us to play with them a little before we destroy them. They've earned it. Unquestionably, they've earned it.

The doorbell rang. I stopped mid-stretch. Barb wouldn't answer the door, not when she believed herself to be a guest in my home. I don't like humans who take initiative.

Indeed, a few seconds later, I heard footsteps on the stairs. Barb crept close to the partially open door before asking, sotto voce, "Eliza? Are you awake?"

I considered chastising her for risking waking me, and decided against it. She had company, and whoever it was hadn't been close to me long enough for my telepathy to begin revising their memories of this house. Under the circumstances, she'd done the right thing.

"The doorbell woke me," I said. I didn't have to work to sound irritated. "Please answer it, and let whoever's there know that I'll be down in a moment."

Barb looked surprised. "You don't want me to get rid of them?"

"Oh, no." I smiled as I emerged from the room. "Let's say hello."

Whoever this was didn't live here, or they wouldn't have rung the bell, and they weren't expected, or Barb would have remembered that they were coming and would assume they were here for both of us. My victims can justify almost anything within the framework of the world I construct for them. The fact that she'd come to wake me instead told me that this was a surprise for both of us.

I don't like surprises. They're messy. I slipped my shoes back on and smoothed my hair down with my fingers, aware that both humans would think I was the most beautiful thing they'd ever seen regardless of what I actually looked like.

Really, humans are so suggestible that they're lucky it was us who found them, and not something with a bigger appetite and a smaller sense of humor. We do a great deal of damage within our limited spheres, but the key word there is "limited." We are small equations moving the sum of humanity toward balance.

I could feel the second mind when I was halfway down the stairs. It was a human male, unreasonably excited, broadcasting his enthusiasm like glitter in the air. Barb was radiating confusion. Whoever this was, it was a stranger to her as well as to me. But there was no malicious intent in his thoughts: this was no hunter come looking for a cuckoo to kill.

I reached the bottom of the stairs and walked down the short hall to the living room. Our "guest" was standing just inside the door, wearing a high-collared coat that should have had him roasting in this heat. He turned toward the sound of my footsteps, and his thoughts exploded into relief and delight.

"Victoria," he said. "I *knew* it was you. I just *knew* it."

I froze.

Humans have a great deal of variety in their physical appearance: necessary, when recognition is visual, and not blessedly mental. It's all very messy as far as I'm concerned. Unfortunately, because their recognition is purely based on what they see, they find cuckoos to be virtually indistinguishable from one another. I'd stumbled into another cuckoo's hunting grounds, and now I had one of her . . . victims? Servants? Not lovers: his delight was elemental and light, not mired down with physical desire. It didn't matter. Whoever he was, he'd spent enough time around this "Victoria" to reek of her now that I was looking for the signs of her interference.

Working around another cuckoo's changes is difficult and time-consuming, and not something to be done without preparation. I needed him gone.

"I'm sorry," I said stiffly. "You have the wrong house."

"No, I don't," he said. "Victoria, come on. It's *me*."

He wanted so badly for this Victoria to know who he was, to recognize him and accept him back into her life. The wanting was enough to put a crack in the walls she had constructed around him, leaving me an opening. Not enough to modify, sadly, but enough to *learn*. I shaped my mind into a needle and darted through the opening before his mental shielding—surprisingly good, for a human—recognized the danger and slammed closed again.

There she was. Victoria. A cuckoo in a long skirt, with a butterfly clip in her hair. She was on her knees in front of a cardboard box, flipping through its contents as she laughed at something the man had said to her. *Laughing.* We're excellent liars—nature designed us to be the best—but the sound in his memory was sincere. She sounded happy. She sounded entertained.

I stared at him, too perplexed by what I was seeing in his memory to know how to respond. He stepped around Barb and threw his arms around my shoulders, pulling me into a human-style embrace.

"I *knew* it was you," he said. "I just knew it. God, Victoria, where have you *been*?"

Arguing with him would be harder and more time-consuming than changing my name. I pulled away, already smiling sweetly, noting as I did that he had managed to hug me without touching my bare skin, damn the luck. The kind of revisions I'd been doing on Barb were easy, even from a distance, and didn't require any conscious effort on my part. The longer she spent around me, the more I would rewire her to my liking. If I decided to remain in this house until I got tired of it, I'd leave her drained dry and unable to function without me, too wedded to the version of reality I had spun for her to know what to do when it disappeared.

Conscious adjustments are harder. Cuckoos evolved to be ambush predators, not hunters. On the rare occasions where we make skin contact with our prey, however, it gets easier. If he'd touched me, or if the collar of his coat hadn't blocked me from touching him, I could have blasted this "Victoria" right out of his head, and harvested her location from his memory in the process.

Only room for one cuckoo in a city, even one the size of Burbank. If she was here, she had to go.

"Oh, around," I said. "I go by 'Eliza' now. It sounds better, don't you think?"

Confusion and displeasure surrounded him. "No," he said. "It's not your name, and it doesn't sound better. Did something happen? Did those people you were always worried about catch up with you? God, Victoria, we would have helped."

Now there was a "we"? This kept getting worse. I must have been radiating distress, because Barb—dear Barb, who would die for me if she felt it was necessary—was suddenly beside me, every inch of her screaming caution at our unwanted visitor. He took a step back, startled. Good. The more distance between us, the better.

I wanted skin contact, so I could learn what he knew, and

I wanted him to stay away from me. It was a contradiction: most things are. I angled my body, putting Barb between us. If things got worse, she could intervene. She *would* intervene. She had already been my loyal friend, and now that I was scared and filling the room with that fear, she loved me enough to die for me. That's how things work.

"I don't know what you're talking about," I said.

The stranger's eyes darted to Barb. "Is she one of them?" he asked. "Is she keeping you here against your will? Victoria—"

"Her name is *Eliza*," snarled Barb.

"Eliza, then," said the man. "It's me. It's Jesse. If something is wrong, you can tell me. I want to help you. I've missed you. We've all missed you."

"Barb?" I whispered.

She nodded, and then she moved.

Humans, by and large, are aware that they're fragile things. They're also smart, an attribute which has served them incredibly well when it comes to dominating their environment, but which turns against them when they're dealing with a predator that works best against smart things. Every ounce of Barb's intelligence was mine to use, and I was twisting it into a tangled mass of protective instinct and utter terror.

Better yet, because they're so fragile, humans have taken steps to make themselves better prepared to fight for their own survival. Barb moved like a striking snake, the side of her hand lashing toward the stranger's throat, and I knew that she'd undergone some of the quaint "self-defense" training so popular with human females.

The stranger dodged. Barb kept pressing forward, and he kept dodging. The concern and confusion that had been rolling off of him was abruptly gone, replaced by a chilly satisfaction that required no translation. I took a step back.

"You're all Victoria to me," said the man, and pulled what looked like a pellet gun from his pocket. He pulled the trigger. There was a soft puffing sound like air being pushed out of a balloon, and Barb stopped fighting. She went still, her face losing its incomprehensible animation, before slumping to the floor, leaving me alone with the stranger.

The chilly satisfaction he exuded was somehow shallow, like there was an artificial floor to his emotions. I took another step back. The satisfaction spiked, deepening into something terrible. I tried to push against it, and found nothing I could grab onto. His thoughts were shielded from me. I couldn't touch his mind.

With Barb unconscious, I couldn't access her memory of a back door—I didn't know how to get out of here. I was trapped.

"She'll be fine," he said. "Not that you care."

He was right: I didn't. If Barb was dead, I could still keep her house, still take advantage of the things she'd left behind. The banks would come eventually—damned humans and their computerized systems for every little thing—but until then, whatever she'd had would be mine, without the added complication of having Barb herself fawning over me every time I turned around.

But Barb wasn't dead. Her mind was still sparking under a thick layer of cottony haze. She might even wake up eventually.

Not fast enough to help me. I needed to stall.

"Who are you?" I demanded. "Why are you here?"

"Because, *Victoria*, I've been looking for you." He dropped his pellet gun and pulled another from inside his jacket, aiming it squarely at me. His hands were shaking slightly. The shallow pool of his satisfaction deepened again, for an instant, and I saw the way out, if I was quick enough to take it. He wanted to talk. He could have shot me already, if he'd wanted to, but he wanted to talk more than he wanted to see me dead, because he wanted me to *understand*.

That was his mistake. That was his smartness getting in the way.

"My name's not Victoria," I whispered.

"But you look like her," he said. "You sound like her. You take over the minds of innocent people like her." He nudged Barb's fallen body with his foot. "How long has this one known you? An hour? A day? How long does she *think* she's known you?"

"We met this afternoon."

"Uh-huh. This is her house, isn't it? You just decided to take it over."

I didn't say anything. It was clear that he knew more about me—about us—than was safe, and I wanted him to reveal exactly how much that was. Answering his questions would allow him to shut down his mind, taking in information without handing any back to me. Forcing him to answer those questions for himself would make him think about what he was saying. I could learn from that.

"Of course you did," he said, disgust coating his words. "That's what you do. You take. You're monsters."

"How did you find me?"

"I pay someone. To watch the traffic cameras for women who look like you."

He thought we were an all-female species. Not uncommon. We have so little physical variation within genders that sometimes people assume we're even more like earth wasps than we actually are. He could have missed a dozen male cuckoos while waiting for a shot at me.

"This 'Victoria' hurt you," I said. "That's funny. The memory you showed me was a warm one. I wouldn't expect you to feel so warm about someone who'd hurt you."

"I bought that memory from a witch who'd seen one of your kind at a comic-book convention," he said. "I've never met that Victoria in my life. I'd kill her if I could. But the memory loves her."

"Charming." He was willing to modify his own mind to be a better hunter. That was . . . not good. Humans are so picky about what goes into their heads. They feel like thought can be pure only if it originates with them. That's why they hate us so much. Well, that and our tendency to kill them when it suits us.

Something inside me snapped closed, a circuit I was barely aware of completing itself. The math of the moment said that he was a threat to the hive, with his new technique for hunting us. We might be scattered, we might hate each other's company with a hot passion we rarely felt for anything else, but the continuation of the species was more important than any individual. I took a breath, broadcasting alarm as loudly as I could on all the frequencies my mind knew how to reach. I might die here. I hated that thought. I didn't want the world to exist beyond me. But the cuckoos, the Johrlac . . .

We would endure. No matter what happened, we would endure.

"It got me close to you." He trained the gun more firmly on my chest. "I won't show you Victoria. She'd like that. She'd enjoy knowing she was remembered. So I won't give her the satisfaction. Do you know what's in this gun?"

He was thinking of Halloween, children in masks running down the sidewalk with pillowcases clutched in their hands. It didn't make any sense. I didn't answer him.

"Victoria was my first love."

Of course she was. Humans were almost as infatuated with the idea of love as they were with the idea of their thoughts being their own. I didn't move.

"She said she'd stay with me forever."

Of course she did. What would be the point in acquiring a toy if it already knew it was going to be thrown away? Humans did the same. Their animal shelters are always full. I didn't speak.

"She made me a murderer."

Well. That was interesting. "Who did you kill?"

"*I* didn't kill anyone," he snarled. "*She* did. She used me as a weapon, and she killed my parents, and she stole everything they had, and she ran."

"Were they wealthy, then?" He nodded silently, and I smiled. "What a smart girl. She found a good target."

He pulled the trigger.

His little toy gun spat a dart into my chest. I gasped and yanked it free, dropping it on the floor. He grinned.

"Theobromine," he said. "That's something you have in common with a dog: it's poison to you. I guess the worst thing in the world had to have something in common with the best."

I glared at him.

"You'll stop breathing soon. But why didn't you stop *me*?"

Because by the time I'd realized he was a threat, Barb had been down and I hadn't known how to get away. Because my species was designed to hide and go unseen, not to stand and fight. Because I wasn't important. I would miss so many things about being alive. I would miss so many things about being *me*. But I am—I was—a cuckoo, and to be a cuckoo is to be part of a hive.

Wheels screeched outside the house. Doors slammed. The cavalry was coming, too late for me, but not too late for this fool, who'd thought he could play games with something bigger than himself. I smiled.

"Victoria," I said. "Did you kill her?"

"What? No. I took what I knew, and I learned how, so that when I saw her again, I could."

"Good," I said. My chest was getting tight. Breathing was getting difficult. I closed my eyes. "Perhaps now you can try again."

I fell.

The last thing I heard was my assailant screaming as the rest of the cuckoos in and around Los Angeles—all the ones close enough to have heard my call—swarmed into the house with their own Barbs, mowing down the man who had come, who had killed me. They were my siblings and my enemies and my family, and they had never been my friends, but they would avenge me.

Oh, yes. They would avenge me. The math has to balance in the end.

The math always has to balance.

EVERYWHERE

A Pitchfork County Story

SAM WITT

The Pitchfork County series follows the struggle of the Night Marshal, Joe Hark, against the forces of darkness that threaten the world at every turn. When Joe discovered the Long Man, his mentor and long-time ally, had become one of the horrors they'd battled, he had no choice but to turn against his old boss. "Everywhere" pits the battered foes against one another once again, and sets the table for the final war against the darkness.

The Long Man was dead.

Mostly.

The Night Marshal, whom for decades the Long Man had trained and empowered to fight evil, had turned on the Long Man and shattered his body. After centuries of manipulating men and women for their own good, the Long Man's plans had finally become too convoluted for even one so ancient and wise as he to control.

He'd failed in his mission to protect humanity from the coming darkness, just as he'd failed to keep a leash on his most powerful and promising allies. He'd paid the price for his mistakes.

The Long Man was dead.

Mostly.

The Long Man crawled across the broken plain, his only companion the taste of failure's bitter ashes. He was debased and defiled, a broken shadow of his former glory. In his struggle to save those placed in his charge, the Long Man had become the very thing he fought against. All he wanted was to rest.

But, first, he had to return to the Father to confess his sins and accept solace among the ranks of the fallen.

The moon of mankind came and went a half-dozen times before the Long Man glimpsed the gates of the Father's home. The stumps of the Long Man's scorched wings twitched against his back and the many gaping sockets of his ruined eyes wept black tears. He had returned and he would, at last, know rest.

Time jumped and jerked and froze and then lurched forward again like a frame stuck in an old movie projector. The Father's voice fell over the Long Man like a shadow, at once ominous and soothing.

"You failed in your most sacred mission, my child," the Father intoned. "Like your siblings, you underestimated the sons and daughters of dust."

The Father swept his broken child up from the dirt and cradled the wounded wreckage to his bosom. The Long Man fought back tears as the Father's gentle hand swept ash and filth from his brow. Their hearts beat as one, and the Long Man's failure crushed him into the Father's embrace.

"I tried." The Long Man's words slithered through the vaulted hall of the Father's mansion. Their echoes bounced through the great entryway where his siblings hung, and their ruined eyes rolled in bleeding sockets as they sought out the last of their kind.

The prodigal son averted his gaze from his sisters and brothers. Shame and horror at what he'd done, what he'd allowed to happen, made him yearn for the peace of endless rest. He could not bear the weight of his failure any longer.

The Father lifted him like a doll and nestled him into a niche above the Eternal Throne. The golden stones embraced the Long Man. This was his home, entombed among his siblings. Together, they would watch the Father's world end in blood and shadows. Finally, they would rest.

Forever.

The Father lifted the golden raiment to clothe the Long Man, but his hands froze in midair. "What have you become, child?"

The Long Man would not meet the Father's gaze. The centuries had shaped him with the cruelties of necessity. He was not the creature who had left this place to protect the children of dust. "There is a darkness in the world of dust. It consumes everything."

The Father let the golden cloth fall from his fingers. It burned as it brushed the floor. "Even you, my child?"

The Long Man wrapped himself in grief to hide his shame. "I had no choice. The war never ends. My attempts to win it marked me with its darkness."

"My child, there is no place for you here." The Father pressed his fingers into the Long Man's chest, forcing him deeper into the niche. The golden stones grew cold and hard against the Long Man's back, and crystalline spines pierced his flesh. "You are an abomination."

The tortured monster's pride flared like the last lash of a dying sun. "I did it for *you*. I became this defiled *thing* to save your precious *men*. I sacrificed myself to save them—and they destroyed me. They stole my power and cast me out. Father, I have earned this rest."

The Father's eyes turned hard and cold as the stone impaling the twisted being he had once embraced as his own child. "You have earned nothing. You took the gifts I gave you and corrupted them. You are of the shadow now, and this is light's home."

The Long Man's remaining eyes burned with unshed tears. "You may cast me out, Father, but I will return. I will reclaim what was mine and prove this is my place *by right*."

The Father turned his face away and the Long Man found himself crawling once more upon the broken plain. The jagged earth bit into his palms and the caustic dust clawed at his throat.

The Long Man crawled back to the world of men, back to the place of his death.

"So it begins, so it begins . . ." he chanted to himself in a language dead long before the sun first burned above the world of dust, "and so will it end."

The Long Man glared at the world through the remnants of his body: a single feather-rimmed eye. Its pupil as wide as a grown man's hand, the eye all that remained of the flesh that once carried him through the world of men. Only this scrap of his majesty survived the Night Marshal's betrayal.

It wasn't much, but it was enough.

His ancient power was as crippled as his physical form. The Night Marshal had stolen most of it away in their final confrontation, leaving him with a few sad dregs of his ancient strength.

It wasn't much, but it was enough.

The Long Man waited for days following his return to this world. He watched the sun rise and fall and rise again in a cycle that tormented him with its unchanging regularity. His sole eye lay on the floor of the Black Lodge. Shadows covered it, the sun shone upon its oily surface, and night fell on it again. Nothing else changed.

Until a lone squirrel hopped through the broken window and scampered across the ash-strewn floor in search of an acorn.

It wasn't much, but it was enough.

The Long Man blinked and a single tear oozed from his eye. He flicked his feathered lashes and the salty bead splashed against the squirrel's face.

The rodent screamed and shuddered from nose to tail as the Long Man burrowed into its flesh.

And then the Long Man was in the eye, but also within the squirrel.

A part of him scurried out of the Black Lodge, bushy tail twitching and beady eyes darting. The squirrel was a start, but he needed more.

He found the sow soon after. The squirrel dropped

acorns in front of the great pink mother, one after another, a few inches of trail at a time.

The gravid pig happily followed the trail through the fire-cracked doors and ignored the slipping of her hooves on the Lodge's slick marble floors. The scent of death was in the air, but the scent of death was always in the air around this place. The sow's hunger was all that was important, and she would not stop until she'd stuffed her belly full.

The last acorn dropped from the squirrel's jaws and landed before the eye. The Long Man shed more tears and his essence flowed out to embrace the acorn.

The sow snuffled after the tasty morsel, and she gulped it down before sensing the danger. The Long Man pinned her primitive thoughts beneath his own. Her body quivered, struggling to resist his command, but she was far too weak to stand against him.

The sow walked on stiff legs. She stood before the eye, trembling. Her head lowered, inch by inch, until her snuffling nose pressed against the orb's bulging surface.

Her lips peeled back from her teeth and the sow ate, filling her belly with the Long Man's essence.

Then she ran, screaming, and the Long Man was within her, too.

Sean heard a pig's panicked squeals and imagined the feral hog bacon he'd make in the drum smoker behind his house. Killing the damned thing would make him late for his shift at the mill, but he gave no fucks.

A whole hog's worth of meat would more than make up for the lost wages, and killing the porker would save somebody's yard from getting ripped up. He rolled down the window to hear the hog better and slowed the truck to a crawl. There was something in the pig's cry, some panic-stricken note that struck a chord of unease deep in the reptilian core of Sean's brain. For a moment, he considered leaving the hunt for some other lucky bastard.

And then he saw the sow.

"Well, I'll be goddamned."

The fat pig squatted in the center of the road with its head thrown back to unleash one full-throated cry after another.

The hog didn't react when Sean killed the truck, scooped his hunting rifle out of the rack in the cab's rear window, and hopped onto the asphalt.

Sean shouldered the rifle and drew a bead on the pig's outstretched throat.

The damned thing kept on screaming even when Sean was ten feet away.

Sean squeezed the trigger and the bullet ripped through the pig's neck, then blasted through the little bulb of brain nestled at the base of her skull. Blood and shards of bone exploded from the back of the sow's neck, and she pitched over onto the street with a quiet sigh.

"Got you, sumbitch," Sean crowed. He stowed the old rifle on the gun rack and dug an oil-stained tarp from the truck's bed. He didn't have time to field dress the beast. He'd just wrap it up and throw it in the pickup's bed and deal with the mess later.

Sean unfurled the tarp on the gravel road next to the pig and smoothed it with the toes of his work boots. "Good enough," he declared, and knelt down to haul the pig onto the tarp.

The Long Man whipped the sow's head around and latched its teeth, *his* teeth, onto Sean's wrist.

"Get off!" Sean screamed. He smashed his fist into the side of the pig's head, to no effect. The efforts to free his arm from the pig's jaws opened Sean's injury ever wider.

The Long Man slithered out of the hog and into the wound. Threads of dark essence wriggled into Sean's blood. They streaked along his veins and arteries, seeking his heart, his brain.

Sean's body cracked and stretched, his bones lengthened as his skin buckled and expanded to accommodate its new occupant. Nubs of cartilage twitched alongside his spine, and Sean was no more.

The body's new owner staggered onto its feet and flexed its arms and knees. A twisted grin split its face.

"I'll be goddamned," the Long Man crowed. "It's good to be back."

———————⟶⟵———————

The Long Man's new body annoyed him. The thick band of beer-soaked fat around its center made it hard to move, and the layer of suet coating its organs made it slow and weaker than he'd imagined possible. He could still feel the part of himself left in the squirrel. It, at least, wasn't slow.

The possessing spirit watched the Night Marshal, Joe

Hark, through the bar's front window with stolen eyes. The asshole rolled a bottle of beer between his palms. He twisted it this way and that, like a child trying to figure out how to operate a pistol found in his daddy's nightstand.

He watched Joe wrestle with the demons baked into his very soul. The Night Marshal had fought and killed a hundred different monsters, but none held a candle to the one inside him. All the power he'd stolen from the Long Man was useless in fighting his thirst for another drink of the booze that had nearly killed him.

The Long Man waited in the cab of Joe's truck for hours. It was boring and fascinating. Did his old enemy struggle with this weakness every day? The bottle of beer in his hands had the trappings of ritual, a spell woven to ward off the darkness.

The Night Marshal's former master wondered if it worked.

When Hark left the tavern, the Long Man hunkered down in the passenger's seat. He half turned toward the driver's door and levered Sean's stolen rifle up at a slight angle.

Joe's eyes went wide when he opened the door and saw the weapon aimed at his chest. A cold rage settled into those eyes. "The fuck're you doing in my truck?"

For a moment, the monster hesitated. Power rolled off the Night Marshal in heavy waves. Power stolen through bonds Pitchfork's onetime guardian had forged between them himself.

The moment passed and it was evident his old enemy didn't recognize him. "Get in the truck. Close the door."

The monster wearing Sean's skin wondered if the Night Marshal would follow orders. Joe wasn't an easy man to scare, and even the rifle aimed at his heart didn't make much of an impression.

"This better be good," Joe said. He hauled his lanky frame into the truck and slammed the door. "Now what?"

The gun hung between them, a promise of violence whose time hadn't quite come to pass. "Drive."

"Anywhere in particular?" Joe leaned on the steering wheel and shrugged. "I mean, I got plenty of gas, we can go wherever your heart desires. Just speak up."

The Long Man flicked his eyes toward the road. "Head north on 44."

They rode in silence for half an hour, until Joe's captor had to ask, "Do you even recognize me?"

The Night Marshal chuckled. The sound was as cold and dry as winter's first frost. The glow from the dash cast an unhealthy green glow onto the Night Marshal's face. His eyes sank into deep pockets of shadow and his teeth glinted like knives when he spoke.

"You got no idea how many people might want to point a gun at me. It's a long list, and no way I can keep all their names straight."

A stolen tongue rasped over stolen lips. For three decades he'd kept an eye on the Night Marshal, watching him grow from a rebellious young man into a useful tool and then into a dangerous adversary. And yet, he'd always held out a slim shred of hope they would find themselves once again on the same side of the war.

"Why couldn't you just follow orders?"

The question got Joe's attention and triggered a cold memory. "Didn't I kill you a while back?"

The possessed body smiled. "Almost all of me. But just almost."

Joe considered the original question. "It's my job to kill the monsters. Somewhere along the line, you forgot that. Turned into one. Weren't no going back after that."

The Long Man sighed. "The war is still out there, Joe. That power you stole won't do you any good if you don't know how to use it. Someone bigger and meaner is going to come along and rip it out of you if you aren't careful.

"Just give it back to me. Let me carry the burden. You're too weak for it."

Joe laughed. He steered the old truck onto the highway. "Wasn't too weak to kill you. Hell, if what I did didn't put an end to you, somethin' tells me you can't kill me with a bullet."

The rifle's barrel dug into Joe's ribs. The monster ground the cold metal against the bone and smiled as the Marshal's features twisted with pain. "Believe me when I tell you it will still hurt."

The Night Marshal shook his head. "Maybe. But I'm not letting you get back in the saddle."

They rolled along in silence for another twenty minutes before they approached an exit. "Get off the highway here. Something I want to show you."

Joe shrugged. "Whatever. I'm running out of patience, though, and you won't like me very much once that happens."

The Long Man knew this was his last desperate stroke. There was a much greater darkness coming, one that would wipe them all out, and he aimed to stop it. Winning this war was his ticket back home, and he wasn't about to let it slip through his fingers. "Don't make me kill you, Joe."

The Night Marshal laughed. "The bonds between our sorry excuses for souls were severed the day I stuck that knife in your withered old heart. There's no way for you to get back what I swiped. You kill me, all the mojo I stole from you goes straight to Hell with me."

"Maybe I don't care. Maybe just seeing you die will be enough."

Joe grinned. "Shit, boss, if that was true, you'da done pulled the trigger on my ass as soon as I opened that door."

Joe's ancient truck rattled down the access road to the rear entrance of a world-famous brewery. Security cameras mounted on tall silver poles swiveled to follow the truck's progress. "Nobody's gonna stop us?"

The Long Man chuckled. "No, the people watching us know who we are. At least, they know who I am."

The Long Man had owned this place for almost two centuries. He'd helped his first servants plant the foundation for the original building, and he'd overseen the first thousand batches of beer himself. This was one of the cornerstones of his kingdom, a part of the network of wealth and power that fueled his plans and guarded him from his enemies. Most of them, anyway.

But how long since he'd last come here? Two decades? Three? Time slipped away from him when he wasn't looking.

They reached a security gate and the Long Man barked

out four digits. His enemy, his onetime ally, maybe even his once-a-friend, punched in the numbers. "You can't wield the power you've stolen, Joe. You don't have the knowledge. You don't know what's coming or how to stop it."

More than anything, the Long Man needed Joe to see the truth of this. They'd worked together for a long time, and he'd worked with Joe's father for even longer, to hold back the rising tide of evil. Together they'd killed an army of demons.

Then things changed and new tactics were required to win the battles. The Long Man wanted to keep the world pure and untainted, but he'd had to make compromises. Joe had gone off the path, then, unable or unwilling to adapt to the realities of their fight. The Night Marshal had rebelled, and taken up arms against the Long Man.

The Night Marshal drummed his fingers against the steering wheel. "All I know is when you had this power, you brought evil to Pitchfork. If I hadn't stopped you, the whole place would've gone to shit." Joe turned his attention back to the road and steered the truck deeper into the brewery's guts. "You lost sight of what you were fighting to save, and became the very monster you were fighting to destroy. Maybe you're convinced you did the right thing, but I know evil when I see it."

The Long Man pointed at a tall building and the parking spot in front of it. One way or another, this had to end. He hoped Joe would see reason, but there were other plans if he didn't.

The Long Man stowed the rifle in the gun rack in the truck's rear window. He needed Joe to relax, and pointing a gun at him wasn't going to help ease the tension. He had another surprise stowed away in the back of his belt, just in case, anyway.

"Let's go inside, Joe. There's something you need to see."

The building's guts reeked of yeast and hops. Great kettles of beer bubbled above a profusion of copper tubes that led into a vast refrigerated filtration system. Beyond that, a series of nozzles dispensed the heavy, amber brew into an endless parade of thick-walled brown bottles sliding across a chain of steel rollers. The technology was old, but it worked just fine to keep the beer flowing and the crates of bottles moving out into the world.

The rich, earthy perfume of wild yeast dragged the Long Man back through the years to those early days when he'd run this place himself. "This was the first brewery west of the Mississippi," he said. "And now it's the oldest and the biggest."

Joe didn't seem impressed, but he followed the Long Man up onto the catwalk overlooking the roiling fermentation kettles.

"This place doesn't look like it would pass a health inspection," the Night Marshal quipped.

The Long Man waggled his finger at Joe. "You always were a stickler for the rules. You're right, of course, but this little corner of the business isn't for public consumption. What gets brewed here is from my secret recipe, and it goes to a very exclusive clientele. They're willing to pay very, very well for what gets bottled in this part of the plant."

Joe snorted. "What're you selling? Eternal youth? Ulti-mate wisdom? A little bit of your blood in every bottle?"

"Just the best beer known to man, Joe. Nothing more. Nothing less."

The Long Man caught Joe licking his lips and suppressed a smile. He hoped his choice of venue for his pitch would soften the man's obstinate resistance.

He took a long breath and swept his arm in an expansive gesture that encompassed everything they could see. "I don't need any of this, not anymore. I have enough money squir-reled away to last me a dozen lifetimes. Honestly, I could never spend all my money no matter how grandiose my plans."

Joe leaned against the railing and shook his head. "That's it? That's your big play? You brought me out all this way to try and bribe me with a brewery? Shit, what would I want with this place?"

The monster hiding under Sean's skin folded his stolen arms over his swollen belly. "Not the whole brewery, just this label. With no effort on your part, this little chunk of my em-pire will put tens, maybe hundreds, of thousands of dollars in your pocket each and every month. There's nothing you could do with that kind of money?"

Joe's former boss and ally knew he could use the money. The Night Marshal's wife was dead, killed in the same battle that killed the Long Man. But, even worse, his children had vanished in the aftermath, gone as if scrubbed from the face of the earth. There'd been no trace of them in the weeks since, and their disappearance was a millstone around Joe's neck.

The Long Man held his tongue, knowing he couldn't broach the subject of the Night Marshal's family without setting off a fight. He waited and watched Joe struggle with the proffered bait.

A handful of long seconds crawled past, and then the Night Marshal pinched the bridge of his nose. "No amount of money will bring Stevie back."

"True," the Long Man whispered. "But it could hire a lot of private investigators. A lot of bounty hunters who could search for the rest of your family."

Joe gnawed on the idea of hiring an army of men and women to bring back his wayward children, his thoughts plain on his face to his enemy. But, in the end, the Long Man saw his offer wasn't enough to entice Joe off the path he'd chosen.

The Night Marshal shook his head. "If that's all you got, I'm afraid I'm going to have to turn you down."

The ancient entity trapped in borrowed flesh cursed himself for underestimating the Marshal, again. He'd gambled on a way to reclaim what Joe had stolen without violence. That bet hadn't paid off. Now it was time to end the game in a different way.

He lunged forward with the hunting knife he'd taken from Sean's truck.

———————————⇒⇐———————————

The Long Man knew his attack had missed the second he threw it. The stolen body was too old, weak, and clumsy to do what he needed. Without the ancient power he'd always enjoyed, he was like a puppeteer trying to control a cheap marionette with tangled strings.

The Night Marshal leaned away from the clumsy slash and then punched his assailant, once in the ribs, and then a second harder hook to the jaw. The Long Man sank to his knees and looped one arm over the railing to keep from falling onto his face. Blood drooled from his mouth, thick and sticky.

The Long Man levered himself up onto his feet and wiped the blood from his face with the back of his hand. He showed Joe the red smear across the pale flesh and shook his head. "Pathetic, isn't it? It wasn't so long ago I could've crushed you like a bug. Now? I'm nothing. Less than nothing. Put me out of my misery, Joe."

He wiggled the knife at Joe. He was weak, and he sorely missed the power this mortal had stolen from him, but this fight was far from over. He faked a lunge at Joe's middle, then dodged back as the Marshal threw a punch at his face.

The knife darted up and ripped through the flesh on the underside of Joe's wrist. The tip came away gleaming with blood, and the Long Man lifted it to his nostrils. He breathed deeply and the heady perfume of his stolen power curled into his sinuses and burrowed into his memories. The power was right there; he could taste it.

But it was no longer his. It belonged to this thief.

Joe bobbed from left foot to right foot, hands raised in a boxer's stance. Under the brim of his cowboy hat, the Marshal's eyes glinted like embers in a dying fire. "Neat trick with the knife, but it won't save you this time. I don't know how you came back, but your little vacation from Hell ends now."

The Long Man dodged back, stumbling over his own feet as the Marshal unleashed a blistering flurry of jabs and roundhouses. Hard knuckles rocked his head back on the knobs of his spine and the Long Man felt the strength drain from his legs. The railing bit into his back as Joe blasted body shots under his ribs one after another.

The Long Man couldn't breathe, couldn't think.

The pain was horrible . . .

But invigorating.

He sucked it up and converted it to rage.

This man, this pathetic *insect,* had stolen from him. He'd cost the Long Man his pride and made him look a fool before the Father. It was time to put things to rights.

The Long Man pushed Joe back and whipped the knife back and forth with wild abandon. The defensive tactic gave him the breathing room he needed to get his wits back and his legs under him. He darted forward and flicked the knife's tip at Joe's face.

The blade opened the Night Marshal's cheek from the corner of his left eye down to the edge of his jaw.

The Long Man's strength was flagging, but the pieces of his plan were coming together. He could still win this. "I didn't come all this way to take a beating. I gave you a chance to end this without pain. You don't want to be rid of me? Fine. I'll never be far from you again."

The Long Man lunged and flailed the blade left to right, then right to left, then back again in a relentless sweeping arc.

The Marshal took a step back, then a second, and a third. The catwalk was a long skeleton of beams and steel lattice that stretched the length of the brewery's old bottling plant.

Every step carried the combatants across open containers of ale that filled the room with a rich, earthy perfume.

The Long Man pressed the attack, forcing the Marshal back with one wild swing after another, but his vigor was flagging. He wasn't strong enough to keep this up all night, his reserves of endurance were limited by the body he was trapped in. *I should've chosen someone else, someone fitter.*

But he hadn't. That was all right, he could still do what needed doing.

The Long Man let the knife's tip drop and the Marshal took advantage of the opening. He stepped forward and threw a straight punch into his opponent's flabby chest.

The monster took the blow full in the sternum. His eyes bulged with surprise at just how much the attack hurt. The Marshal had fueled his attack with the power he'd stolen from the Long Man, adding insult to the injury. The stolen body's ribs crackled and separated from the muscle holding them closed around heart and lungs.

Joe's former boss fell over the savage blow. He angled his left arm around Joe's right, twisting them together and pulling the Marshal close. It was easy to get inside your enemy's defenses if you didn't worry about surviving.

"Give me what is mine."

Joe snorted and slammed a head butt into the center of the sneering, demanding face before him. Blood splattered from the Long Man's shattered nose and his thoughts splintered into jagged shards of rage.

The Long Man fell against Joe. He used his greater weight to push the Night Marshal back into the railing. The Long Man held fast to Joe's arm and leaned in close. His mouth opened wide and his teeth gnashed the air an inch from Joe's cheek.

Just one bite, he thought. He just needed one bite and he would be inside Joe. Like he'd been inside the squirrel, the pig, and now Sean. If he couldn't beat Joe, he'd become him.

The Long Man growled and snarled, snapping his teeth like a rabid dog. His incisors grazed the Marshal's cheek, but couldn't find purchase. His tongue dragged across razor stubble and he tasted sweat and stale bar smoke, but he couldn't get the bite he needed to possess his enemy.

Joe shoved the Long Man back. He punched the old bastard, a downward strike across the jaw that shattered teeth into bloody enameled chunks. "I done killed you once, it's time for you to go back where you come from."

Another punch loosened more of the Long Man's stolen teeth and rattled his brain like a pea in a gourd. Through a concussed haze, the once-powerful spirit saw his future. There was still a way to do this. He should have seen it earlier.

He raised his knife to strike.

Joe grabbed his adversary, his onetime ally, his former mentor, by the hair and hauled him to his feet. He spun the old monster around and hooked a wiry forearm across the stolen body's throat. Joe's words were an intimate whisper. "This ends now," he growled, crushing the Long Man's windpipe.

The broken spirit gripped his knife with both hands, and turned the tip up and in. "Yes, it does."

The Long Man convulsed as the knife punched up under his ribs. The weapon's tip plunged through his diaphragm and into his heart.

With the last of his strength, the Long Man ripped the knife from his chest and flung it into the kettles below. A gushing torrent of blood followed the blade, splashing into the beer along with the shattered remains of the Long Man's essence.

The Long Man watched the Cubs win the World Series through the eyes of a trucker with a mouth stuffed with chewing tobacco. He watched them win from inside a meth junkie swigging black-labeled beer in a desperate attempt to stave off the tremors of withdrawal. He heard that last game in Chicago through the ears of a cop listening to the game instead of keeping an eye on the pimps and prostitutes strolling down the alley outside his car.

The Long Man was no more, but he was also much more than he'd been before. The blood-tainted beer had gone out to his customers and they'd served it in bars, taverns, and restaurants across the Midwest.

He'd lost his body, but now there were pieces of him, scattered remnants of his personality and power, lodged inside the minds and bodies of the weak and the hopeless and the angry who guzzled beer in the vain hopes it would smooth out the ragged edges of their doomed lives. None of them were a match for the Night Marshal, but that was all right.

The Long Man lived inside each of these boozy disciples, and he had plans for each. His hosts smiled when they saw one another, secretive smirks that signaled a deep, dark knowledge the rest of the world wouldn't share until it was far too late.

Weeks passed, and the Long Man's spirit spread far and wide. His hidden army grew, their numbers swelling as bottle after bottle of tainted beer vanished down unsuspecting gullets. Some threw off his influence, but more—many more—welcomed him into their lives and bodies.

He gave them something they needed, even if they couldn't articulate what had been missing from their useless existences.

He gave them a tribe to call their own. He gave them purpose. These bodies, each one weak on its own, would do what the Long Man, in all his glorious power, had not been able to accomplish. He would guide them on their missions, and they would do the dark deeds that would save the world. Thousands, perhaps tens of thousands, would die, but the rest would be saved.

One day, perhaps, people would remember him not as a monster, but as the hero who saved them against a darkness much greater than their puny minds could comprehend.

Then, his power restored, the Long Man would return home.

He would show the Father.

Around Christmas, the Long Man decided it was time. A part of him wedged into the brain of a traveling salesman stopped at a pay phone alongside I-44. That piece of him fished out a fistful of quarters and fed them into the decrepit device, listening as each one clunked into the near empty coin box. Then he dialed the number burned into his memory from years of using it. It rang and rang and he began to wonder if Joe would bother to pick up the phone only the Long Man had ever called.

And then . . .

"How?" Joe asked. That one word held a multitude of questions the Long Man didn't feel like answering.

How was he still alive? How was there enough of him left to make this phone call? What did he want?

Instead, the Long Man smiled. "I just wanted you to know, I'm still out here."

The Night Marshal's voice crackled through the line like a blazing whip of rage. "Where are you, motherfucker?"

He tutted into the phone. "Such language. Don't worry, you won't be seeing me again for a while. Maybe we won't ever cross paths again. You did give me quite a beating last time, didn't you?"

The Long Man relished the echoes of pain from that fight. More than that, he loved to relive the moment when he'd outsmarted the Night Marshal one last time. This hadn't been his plan, but it proved to be more successful than he'd imagined.

"Where?" The Night Marshal's voice cracked with rage and something else. Fear? "Let's finish this. Tell me where you are."

The old monster laughed, a long, loud peal that sent a flock of birds screaming into flight. "I'll tell you where I am, Joe. Listen carefully."

He looked at the pay phone in front of him. He watched a long string of unbroken highway unspool under his headlights somewhere in the heart of Montana. His eyes fixed on the clouds below him as she soared in a plane headed for

Tokyo. He watched juicy bugs splatter against his motorcycle's windshield as he roared down a strip of gravel road somewhere on the edge of Kansas. He sipped from a bottle wrapped in a brown paper bag and watched children playing in a park outside Seattle. In a thousand places, in a thousand different bodies, he smiled as the world ticked on around him, unsuspecting.

The Night Marshal's voice creaked through the phone line, frayed with fear and anger and confusion. "Where are you?"

The Long Man took a deep breath, and smiled so wide his cheeks ached. He whispered, from a thousand mouths, "Everywhere."

ABOUT THE AUTHORS

KELLEY ARMSTRONG, The Cainsville Series

Kelley Armstrong graduated with a degree in psychology and then studied computer programming. Now she is a full-time writer and parent, and she lives with her husband and three children in rural Ontario, Canada. Find her at Kelleyarmstrong.com and @Kelleyarmstrong on Twitter.

JIM BUTCHER, The Dresden Files

#1 *New York Times* bestselling author Jim Butcher turned to writing as a career because anything else probably would have driven him insane. He lives mostly inside his own head so that he can write down the conversations of his imaginary friends, but his head can generally be found in Independence, Missouri. Find him at Jim-Butcher.com and @Longshotauthor on Twitter.

DOMINO FINN, Black Magic Outlaw Series

Domino Finn is an entertainment industry veteran, a contributor to award-winning video games, and the grizzled urban fantasy author of the bestselling Black Magic Outlaw series. His stories are equal parts spit, beer, and blood, and are notable for treating weighty issues with a supernatural veneer. If Domino has one rallying cry for the world, it's that fantasy is serious business. Take up arms at Dominofinn.com and @Dominofinn on Twitter.

KEVIN HEARNE, The Iron Druid Chronicles

Kevin Hearne lives with his wife, son, and doggies in Colorado. He hugs trees, rocks out to heavy metal, and will happily geek out over comics with you. He also thinks tacos are a pretty nifty idea. Find him at Kevinhearne.com and @Kevinhearne on Twitter.

FAITH HUNTER, Jane Yellowrock Series

Faith Hunter is the *New York Times* bestselling author of the Jane Yellowrock series, the Soulwood series, and the Rogue Mage series. She loves to paddle Class III rivers, travel, and make jewelry. She is mama to two rescue Pomeranians; they have learned that when mama is writing, she will laugh or burst into tears for no reason. Mama is weird. Find her at Faithhunter.net and @Hunterfaith on Twitter.

CAITLIN KITTREDGE, The Hellhound Chronicles

Caitlin Kittredge spends her time creating novels and comics, including the Hellhound Chronicles, Black London series, the YA novel *The Iron Thorn* (a YALSA Best Fiction finalist), and the comic series *Throwaways* and *Coffin Hill*. She lives in Massachusetts and spends her free time reading (mostly nonfiction), binge-watching Netflix, and hunting for weird stuff in thrift stores. Find her at Caitlinkittredge.com and @Caitkitt on Twitter.

JONATHAN MABERRY, The Joe Ledger Series

Jonathan Maberry is a *New York Times* bestseller and multiple Bram Stoker Award–winning author of *Code Zero, Fall of Night, Patient Zero*, the *Pine Deep Trilogy, The Wolfman, Zombie CSU*, and *They Bite*. His work for Marvel Comics includes *The Punisher, Wolverine, DoomWar, Marvel Zombie Return*, and *Black Panther*. His Joe Ledger series has been optioned for television. Find him at Jonathanmaberry.com and @Jonathanmaberry on Twitter.

SEANAN McGUIRE, The InCryptid Series

Seanan McGuire is a Washington State–based author with a strong penchant for travel and can regularly be found just about any place capable of supporting human life (as well as a few places that probably aren't). She writes the October Daye series and the InCryptid series, both published by DAW. *Rosemary and Rue*, the first novel in the October Daye series, was named one of the Top 20 Paranormal Fantasy Novels of the Past Decade; and her novel *Feed*, written under the pseudonym Mira Grant, was named as one of *Publishers Weekly*'s Best Books of 2010. She also won a Hugo for her podcast, and is the first person to be nominated for five Hugo Awards in a single year. You can visit her at Seananmcguire.com and @Seananmcguire on Twitter.

JON F. MERZ, The Lawson Vampire Series

Jon F. Merz is the bestselling author of more than thirty novels, including his Lawson Vampire series and the Shadow Warrior series, as well as many stand-alone thrillers. A veteran of the United States Air Force, he holds a 5th degree black belt in Togakure-ryū Ninjutsu, is an avid CrossFitter and GORUCK enthusiast, and also models and acts in many television commercials. He lives by the motto "Who Dares Lives," is an avid adventurer, husband, and father to two amazing sons. He lives outside of Boston, Massachusetts. Find him at Jonfmerz.net and on Instagram @Jonfmerzofficial.

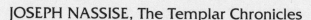

JOSEPH NASSISE, The Templar Chronicles

Joseph Nassise is the *New York Times* and *USA Today* best-selling author of more than thirty-five novels, including the Templar Chronicles series, the Jeremiah Hunt trilogy, and the Great Undead War series. He also writes epic fantasy under the pseudonym Matthew Caine. He is a former president of the Horror Writers Association, the world's largest organization of professional horror writers, and a multiple Bram Stoker Award and International Horror Guild Award nominee. Find him at Josephnassise.com and @Jnassise on Twitter.

DIANA PHARAOH FRANCIS, The Horngate Witches Series

Bestselling writer Diana Pharaoh Francis writes books of a fantastical, adventurous, and often romantic nature. Her award-nominated books include The Path series, the Horngate Witches series, the Crosspointe Chronicles, the Diamond City Magic books, and the Mission: Magic series. She's owned by two corgis, spends much of her time herding children, and likes rocks, geocaching, knotting up yarn, and has a thing for 1800s England, especially Victorians. For more about her writing, visit Dianapfrancis.com and find her on Twitter as @Dianapfrancis.

LILITH SAINTCROW, The Jill Kismet Series

Lilith Saintcrow lives in Vancouver, Washington, with her two children and assorted other strays. She has been writing since she was nine years old. Find her on the Web at Lilithsaintcrow.com and @Lilithsaintcrow on Twitter.

STEVEN SAVILE, The Glass Town Series

Steven Savile has written for Doctor Who, Torchwood, Primeval, Stargate, Warhammer, Slaine, Fireborn, Pathfinder, Arkham Horror, Rogue Angel, and other popular game and comic worlds. He won the International Association of Media Tie-In Writers award for his novel, *Shadow of the Jaguar*, and the inaugural Lifeboat to the Stars award for *Tau Ceti* (co-authored with International Bestselling novelist Kevin J. Anderson). Writing as Matt Langley, his Young Adult novel *Black Flag* was a finalist for the People's Book Prize 2015. His latest books include *Sherlock Holmes and the Murder at Sorrows Crown* and *Parallel Lines*, a brand-new crime novel from Titan, as well as *Glass Town* and *Coldfall Wood*, forthcoming from St. Martin's Press in 2017. Find him at Stevensavile.com and @Stevensavile on Twitter.

CRAIG SCHAEFER, The Harmony Black Series and the Daniel Faust Series

Craig Schaefer's books have taken readers to the seamy edge of a criminal underworld drenched in shadow through the Daniel Faust series; to a world torn by war, poison, and witchcraft by way of the Revanche Cycle series; and across a modern America mired in occult mysteries and a conspiracy of lies in the new Harmony Black series. Despite this, people say he's strangely normal. He lives in Illinois with a small retinue of cats, all of whom try to interrupt his writing schedule and/ or kill him on a regular basis. He practices sleight of hand in his spare time, although he's not very good at it. Find him at Craigschaeferbooks.com and @Craig_schaefer on Twitter.

JEFF SOMERS, The Ustari Cycle

Jeff Somers was born in Jersey City, New Jersey. After graduating college he wandered aimlessly for a while, but the peculiar siren call of New Jersey brought him back to his homeland. Visit him at Jeffreysomers.com and on Twitter at @Jeffreysomers.

CARRIE VAUGHN, The Kitty Norville Series

Carrie Vaughn, the *New York Times* bestselling author of the Kitty Norville books, is also the author of the stand-alone novels *After the Golden Age* and *Discord's Apple,* and the Young Adult books *Voice of Dragons* and *Steel.* Find her at Carrievaughn.com.

SAM WITT, The Pitchfork County Series

Sam Witt writes dark thrillers infused with the supernatural. Informed by a rural midwestern childhood and big-city adulthood, he combines down-home folklore and legends with a hard-hitting, take-no-prisoners writing style. His Pitchfork County series follows the dark and twisting lives of a family intent on using their own cursed abilities to protect the place they call home from all manner of threats, from mad gods to meth cults. Find him at Samwitt.com and @Samwitt on Twitter.